SOME DISTANT VOICE

"Alex, don't look now, but there's a man over there watching us. I'm positive he's the same man that was at the table next to us tonight."

Alex reached inside the door and flicked off the porch light. "Throw your arms around me and kiss me—a long, passionate kiss."

"What for?"

"I want to get a good look at him when he doesn't know I'm looking."

He didn't give her a chance to respond, wrapping his arms around her waist, his lips slanted over hers first at one angle, then at another. She tried to ignore the heat of Alex's hand as it splayed across the small of her back. She tried to ignore the hard contour of his chest against the softness of her breasts. . . . Some distant voice warned, she'd regret returning a kiss like this, but right now she didn't care.

He nuzzled the tender skin below her ear, then skimmed the rim with the tip of his tongue, whispering, "I'm going to turn you around so I can get a look at that guy."

She almost asked, What guy?

PROMISE ME ANYTHING

MERYL SAWYER

A DELL BOOK

Published by
Dell Publishing
a division of
Bantam Doubleday Dell Publishing Group, Inc.
1540 Broadway
New York, New York 10036

The trademark Dell® is registered in the U.S. Patent and Trademark Office.

ISBN: 0-440-21464-5

Printed in the United States of America

Published simultaneously in Canada

January 1994

10 9 8 7 6 5 4 3 2 1

RAD

This book is dedicated to the memory of my grandfather George Sawyer and everyone else whose life has been altered dramatically by a moment in time—by historical events beyond their control.

Contents

I
TWO OF A KIND

The best way to love anything is as if it might be lost.
—G. K. Chesterton

1

St. Paul's Church, Knightsbridge, London: June 1990

"I see Brett is out of jail."

The woman's wrinkled lips tightened as she responded to her companion. "They should have kept her where she belonged."

Alex overheard the two elderly ladies sitting in the pew beside him and looked up. A tall blonde had taken the aisle seat directly in front of him while he'd been studying the dress shoes pinching his toes and waiting for the wedding to begin. He hadn't seen her enter the church, but as he gazed at her back, he found it difficult to imagine such an elegantly dressed woman in a prison cell.

He squinted, his eyes still not completely adjusted to the low light from the tiers of scented candles in sconces that filled the air with a hint of lavender and cast deep, dancing shadows across the vaulted ceiling's ancient beams. In the mellow glow of the candlelight, the guests chatted, a medley of muted voices accompanied by the lilting strains of violins being played in the choir stalls. Banks of white orchids with deep lavender throats cascaded from tall candelabra vases and sprouted from Grecian urns at the end of each pew. He smiled to himself.

Some clown had even taken orchids and woven them through the branches of the topiary trees flanking the altar.

"When Brett was in prison this time—" the woman beside Alex continued, gossiping in a loud voice about the blonde sitting in front of him. "Well, what *cahn* I say? She's *awb-noxshus.*"

This time? Alex gazed at Brett's earrings. Hold everything! From a starburst of exquisite diamonds hung a priceless teardrop stone. Siberian Ice. Unbelievable. The color and clarity were unmistakable—the frozen crystal color called River White.

Each teardrop was a hair over eleven carats. She turned her head slightly, revealing the soft curve of her cheek, and Alex had a better view of the gems. Cut by hand for an elite jeweler like Bulgari or Cartier. Why in hell would a woman with that kind of money be in jail?

"Brett is *exactly* like her mother," added the woman to Alex's right. "Exactly."

Like her mother? What was that supposed to mean? Alex studied Brett, hoping she would turn around. Her blond hair, a sunset of varying shades that reflected the candlelight, had been swept up—no doubt to show off the Siberian Ice—into one of the hairstyles that reminded Alex of sixties-style beehives. But last week in L.A. he'd noticed similar hairdos. Had to be the latest.

Brett must have heard the gossiping. "Old biddies," Alex muttered under his breath. Remembering too clearly his youth, he had no use for people who were deliberately cruel. Yeah, he'd overheard more than his share of cutting comments. And he'd endured them—just like Brett—giving no sign he'd heard.

Alex silently willed Brett to turn around, but she didn't. He was left studying her back. Her smooth bare shoulders had an underlying glow enhanced by the shifting candlelight. If her hair hadn't been up, it would have brushed her back with just a touch of natural curl. Soft. Sexy.

He straightened, momentarily forgetting he had rented

the largest tuxedo jacket the shop had, but like the shoes it was too small. He sucked in his breath and peered over her shoulder, taking advantage of his height. Her gown, the color of crème de menthe, suggestively skimmed her chest, but revealed only the rise of her breasts. Too bad. He preferred legs, but what the hell? He never held a dynamite pair of breasts against a woman.

Just then Brett raised her left hand and smoothed back the hair over her ear. No ring. No escort. Interesting. Either she wasn't married or she'd bagged the Siberian Ice in a divorce that had sent both attorneys into throes of financial ecstasy with the legal haggling. Better yet, she was someone's mistress.

Ellis Payne emerged from a side door, taking the groom's place at the altar. Dark hair, blue eyes; he was even more handsome than Alex remembered. He resented being forced into business with Ellis, but he'd had no choice. Uncle Vic had died leaving Alex "everything." What a joke! Everything Vic had was already half Alex's since they'd been partners for years. Now that Vic's funeral expenses were paid, "everything" Alex owned was the controlling interest in Ellis's company, Belage Diamonds.

Okay, so they were partners, but he'd be damned before he counted that snobby jerk among his friends. Alex supposed there were worse things than being Ellis Payne's partner. So why was he feeling so uneasy about this? Maybe he hadn't quite adjusted to losing Uncle Vic. Being jewelry manufacturers had been a dream they'd shared. Now he was on his own. And lonely as hell.

The organist played a Bach prelude, and the groom's parents came down the aisle. Eyes trained on Brett, expecting her to turn, Alex ignored the entrance of Ellis's parents, Ruth and Jock Payne, but Brett didn't turn.

"Oh, my." The woman beside Alex sighed. "Look at Ruth's dress. Isn't it *smah*-shing?"

"Truly *smah*-shing," her friend agreed. "An Ozbek."

Sounded like a Polish condom, but Alex looked anyway.

Ruth Payne wore a beaded gown that matched the lavender in the orchids. On the dark side of fifty, yet as slim as a
lollipop stick, Ellis's mother had a chest like the prow of a
battleship. Ruth smiled, emphasizing a generous mouth and
ice-blue eyes framed by black hair cropped short like a
China doll's. She had that overpreserved look as if she'd
been dipped in formaldehyde.

Alex smiled to himself. Ruth Payne of the "pushy-pretentious" Paynes. Uncle Vic had been dead-on when he'd come
up with that nickname. Ruth could tell you the price of
everything, but never knew the true value of anything.

"Look at Jock," gushed the woman next to Alex, drooling
over the groom's stepfather, Jock Payne. "So handsome."

Alex agreed. Jackson "Jock" Payne stood over six feet tall
with hair that gleamed like burnished pewter. He could
have been one of Britain's elder statesmen, but in fact was a
Scot who'd moved to the seamy side of the Thames as a boy.
Jock had started Payne Roofing at seventeen. He had expanded into construction and rode the early-eighties building boom to become one of the wealthiest men in the country. Today his blue trucks with the now-familiar motto
painted on the side, FOR A HOLE IN YOUR ROOF OR A WHOLE NEW
ROOF, could be found throughout England.

Alex had been watching out of the corner of his eye for
the blonde to turn, but she didn't. Ruth Payne beamed at
her friends until she spotted Brett. Her smile faltered and
her grip on Jock's arm tightened. Jock's gaze swung to
Brett, who still faced forward. Alex couldn't read Jock's
expression. Jock's mistress? No. Uncle Vic had insisted
Ruth kept Jock on a choke chain, and Vic had an uncannily
accurate way of assessing people.

"Look at Ellis," said the woman beside Alex as the groom
smiled at his parents. "Isn't he the image of Ruth?"

True. Jet-black hair, permafrost blue eyes, mental ban-
tamweights. Mother and son—the "pushy-pretentious"
Paynes—a perfect match. Alex wondered how Jock felt

about his stepson Ellis. Just then, Ellis's gaze fell on Brett and his smile vanished.

"What's going on here?" Alex muttered under his breath. "I'd rather be in L.A., but this may get interesting yet."

Seven bridesmaids sashayed down the aisle. What was this, a wedding or a coronation? Alex rose, and his gaze traveled the now-familiar path across the back of Brett's bare shoulders to the inviting curve of her neck where wisps of hair eluded the upsweep. A mole, small but distinct, crowned the top of her spine.

Was the blonde Ellis Payne's girlfriend? He wouldn't have dated a woman unless she was a knockout. No question about it. Ellis had the horsey, yachty—or whatever suited the occasion—British looks that gave women cardiac arrest. Ellis had his pick of beautiful women.

But why was Brett here if Ellis was marrying someone else? And what had she done to land herself in jail? Vic should be here. Honest to God, Uncle Vic had talked nonstop about the Paynes. But he'd never mentioned a blonde named Brett.

Strains of "Here Comes the Bride" urged the guests to watch as a young flower girl minced along dropping orchids the size of Alex's thumb. Brett faced forward, her head held at an angle that indicated her eyes were on Ellis. Alex looked down the aisle, anxious to see who it was Ellis was marrying.

"My, my, doesn't she look *smah*-shing?"

How could anyone tell? The bride wore a multilayered gown of white lace that enveloped her like a cumulus cloud and a veil a beekeeper would covet. She literally had to be steered down the aisle by her father, a tottering old man with oysterlike bags under his eyes who was having difficulty navigating the course.

"Friends, loved ones," the vicar began when the bride reached the altar.

Alex studied the stained-glass windows as the candles illuminated them, highlighting their sparkling jewel tones against the sky. Between the windows were angels carved out of stone blowing trumpets to the heavens. To Uncle Vic. Too bad he couldn't be here. Their invitations had arrived the morning Vic died. That afternoon he'd spoken his last words: *Alex, you're the best thing that ever happened to me. All I want is for you to be happy.*

Alex sucked in his breath, the too-familiar ache returning. Oh, God, he missed Vic. Late at night when it was dark and still, he could almost see Vic and hear his laugh. But morning always came and with it reality. It was hard to believe they'd never be together again. It was hard to believe he was just as alone now as he'd been as a boy before Vic had found him.

"Matrimony is the holiest and most blessed of all institutions," the vicar said, interrupting Alex's thoughts.

What a crock. No way would he put the matrimonial noose around his neck and let some woman hang him.

Alex blocked out the vicar's words, mentally picturing Brett holding back her tears as she watched the man she loved marry someone else. He was tempted to touch her sexy shoulder and say: *You can do better than Ellis Payne. The only thing he loves is his reflection in the mirror.*

After touting the delights of wedded bliss for a good ten minutes, the vicar said, "You may kiss the bride."

Ellis Payne lifted his bride's veil. Brett's shoulders trembled, gently rustling the soft silk of her gown. She'd need a lot of comforting at the reception.

"My, oh, my," murmured the woman next to Alex, her tears making tracks in her face powder. "So touching. So very touching."

Why do women cry at weddings? Okay, he could understand if Brett cried, but other women? A mystery to him.

"May I present Mr. and Mrs. Ellis Blyforth Payne," the vicar said as the newlyweds faced the congregation.

Brett's shoulders shook, but Alex gave her credit for

holding her head high. The couple approached and Alex looked closely at Ellis's bride. Peanut-butter-colored hair and eyes to match. Thin lips and a pug nose. She must have a trust fund that rivaled the Swiss accounts of Colombian pharmaceutical barons.

Alex trained his eyes on Brett. *Don't let him see you crying.* Expecting Brett to get up and leave soon, he waited, an opening comment on his lips.

The bride and groom were just two pews from them, the guests pivoting in their seats as the couple swept past, the bride's train gathering a harvest of miniature orchids. Alex stared at the back of Brett's head. Waiting. The candlelight caught the soft strands of hair bringing out the coppery-blond tones. Slowly, she turned. *I'll be damned.*

She was laughing, a low mellow sound that didn't carry above the music. Alex studied her remarkable face with its startling green eyes and a crown of amber-blond hair. Her small nose was overpowered by the rise of her cheekbones and by her dominant eyes with tiers of lashes a shade darker than her hair. Not beautiful, but she had a delightful animated quality about her.

Brett leveled a smile at the gossips beside Alex, the most arresting smile he'd ever seen. It was a fraction off kilter with the right curve of her lips slightly higher than the left, but this only added to its engaging appeal. It was the kind of smile you automatically expected to have dimples, but it didn't.

"Lady Bewley, how nice to see you," Brett said. "Lovely wedding, wasn't it?"

Lady Bewley patted her tightly permed gray hair into place. "At least Ellis had the good sense to marry the right woman."

The biting retort took Alex by surprise. Did the old lady have to be that cruel? He expected Brett to respond with a cutting remark, but she merely smiled. Uh-oh. He recognized the flash of anger in her green eyes, a deep-seated anger her smile disguised unless you knew what you were looking for. He'd used the same smile himself dozens of times when he'd been a kid and hadn't wanted people to know how much their words hurt.

2

Brett hurried down the steps of the church. No one greeted her, not even with a nod. What did she expect? They were all Ruth's friends or relatives. She wanted to hail a taxi and go home to her son, but Lady Bewley's parting words echoed in her ears, "Surely you're not attending the reception."

Brett had made her point, but she refused to let Ruth or her close friend, Lady Bewley, intimidate her. *She's exactly like her mother. Exactly.* Lady Bewley was determined to make trouble for her. Brett thought of her son, and Timmy's smile brought its usual charge of warmth. Nothing on earth made her happier than Timmy. No, she hadn't made a mistake. Ruth and her friends could be as mean as they wanted, passing judgment on her as if they had a direct line to God. She'd done the right thing, and Timmy was all the proof she needed.

A taxi pulled up and she climbed in, saying, "Spencer House."

"A party?" The driver was obviously impressed. Few people enjoyed the privilege of entering Spencer House in St. James.

"A wedding reception. Could you hurry? I need to get there quickly." *Before the receiving line forms.*

The driver rattled on about how Baron Rothschild's lease on Spencer House would be up in 120 years and Princess Diana's heirs would regain their ancestral home as he bullied his way into the traffic. "Bet Di's as pleased as punch."

Di. Brett could hear Ruth Payne's standard lecture on the lower classes, Ruth's own memory of her ancestors being highly selective. The aristocracy never called Princess Diana "Di." Only the tabloids and undesirables used it, and of course, Americans who had nicknames or initials for everything. Brett doubted there was a bigger snob on earth than Ruth.

"I 'ear it costs a bloody fortune to 'ave a party at Spencer 'Ouse." The driver shook his head. "I guess plenty of folks 'ave money to burn."

Like most people, he thought her earrings were rhinestones. She touched one, thinking of her mother and wondering which man had loved her so much he'd given her priceless diamonds. It was a mystery she doubted she would ever solve. Countless times she'd tried to find out who had purchased the gems. Everyone denied knowing anything about the diamonds.

"You'd be amazed how much people will pay to sip champagne and down caviar in the name of a worthy cause—one they won't remember the next morning—but won't give a tuppence to a homeless person," she told the driver.

When they arrived at the end of the street next to Green Park, she overtipped him; he probably had a large family to feed. She stepped from the cab, recalling her visit to Spencer House years ago with her mother when the *Economist* had its offices here.

Times had changed. The building had been steam cleaned, the soot that had stained the hand-hewn limestone over the decades had been removed, the steps repaired, and the broken Palladian windows replaced. Built two centuries earlier by the first Earl Spencer, the mansion had flourished during the glory days of the Spencer-Churchills. It had languished as the once powerful family's financial resources diminished. Finally, the blitz had reduced Spencer House to little more than a ghost of itself, a sad reminder of a nostalgic era when kings and ambassadors visited daily and the empire had been at its zenith.

Baron Rothschild had rescued the mansion, leasing it and painstakingly restoring it to its former glory. Brett thought the money could have been better spent on people, but didn't argue that Jacob Rothschild had saved an architectural legacy.

Upstairs in the Great Room she saw the rugs had been removed for dancing, revealing a highly buffed parquet floor inlaid with mahogany. A waiter in a uniform with enough gold buttons and epaulets to outfit several South American dictators handed her a glass of champagne. She immediately found the chocolate-dipped strawberries among the lavish display of food. The berries ringed the base of an ice sculpture of Venus that matched the fresco of Venus painted on the ceiling. Ruth Payne had outdone herself, making her son Ellis's wedding a tawdry display of Jock Payne's wealth.

"What did you expect?" Brett muttered under her breath. "Nothing but the best for Ellis." She struggled to quell her anger, knowing it was futile, but Ellis's marriage was difficult to accept. Impossible to understand. How could he marry a woman his mother had chosen for him, a woman he couldn't possibly love?

"More champagne?" The waiter refilled her glass.

Brett ate another strawberry, recalling the dark-haired man in the pew behind her during the wedding. He must be related to Lady Bewley. Well, he wasn't getting Ruth's stamp of approval—not in that rented dinner jacket. It puckered across his wide shoulders and his tie was one of the pretied varieties Americans favored. Not that she cared, but Ruth would notice—just as she would notice Brett's earrings.

"Am I sinking to her level?" Brett asked herself. After all, she had worn the earrings knowing Ruth would covet them. But that was only part of the reason. All she had to remind her of her mother were a few photos and the earrings. Wearing them gave her courage because her mother had always done what was right—no matter what anyone thought.

Lady Bewley had said Brett was *exactly* like her mother. *Exactly*. How she wished it were true, but she'd never be half the person her mother had been. Brett again pondered the four-year-old question of who had loved her mother so much that he'd given her diamonds worth a fortune. Jewels she'd never had the chance to wear.

Munching yet another berry, she reminded herself not to think of her mother. After all, she was already sad enough seeing Ellis marry. *I'll just stay long enough to let Lady Bewley see she can't intimidate me. And tell Ellis I'll have the last laugh.*

"Hello," came a low, vibrant voice behind her.

She turned, expecting a waiter with more champagne. Instead she found the man who'd been sitting behind her at the wedding. Tall with dark hair and a sportsman's tan, he had inquisitive blue eyes she'd thought brown in the muted candlelight of the church. She guessed he was about Ellis's age, late thirties.

"I'm Alex Savich." He extended his hand.

Alex Savich? Dear God! He wasn't supposed to be in London yet. Now what was she going to do? What if he questioned her about Belage Diamonds? She'd promised not to tell him anything about Ellis's company. *Keep your mouth shut.*

She'd imagined Alex to be a short, lithe man with red hair like his uncle, Vicktor Orlov. Not a tall, striking man with Gypsy eyes—expressionless, watchful. She offered him her hand, and his long fingers closed around hers in a cool, firm grip.

Managing a smile, she wondered if he had any inkling of the situation at Belage. Vic had been positive that his nephew would know what to do. They'd all humored Vic.

Who could argue with a dying man? But now, looking at Alex Savich's square chin and rough-cut features, she no longer harbored any illusions. Belage—and all her hopes—were history.

"You're Vicktor's nephew?" She remembered with horror that he must have heard everything Lady Bewley had said about her. Great! Now he'd think she was crackers. Brett wiggled her hand out of his, realizing he was holding her hand longer than necessary and masking her uneasiness with another smile.

"You knew Uncle Vic?"

"Oh, yes. He was quite a character. We're all going to miss him," she said, having difficulty understanding why Alex looked so puzzled. Surely, Vicktor had told Alex about her. Maybe not. Vic had been upset when Alex wanted to settle in Los Angeles, epicenter of sunshine and libido. Vic had rashly invested in Belage Diamonds without even consulting Alex, committing his nephew to a business in London.

"Vic must have mentioned you," Alex said. "You're . . ."

She hesitated, knowing if she told him the whole truth, he might ask questions about Belage she didn't want to answer. Why hadn't she stayed home? "I'm Brett—"

"Alex, frightfully good to see you," Ruth Payne cut in. Appearing suddenly with Jock at her side, she flashed her familiar drop-dead-you-bitch look at Brett. "Just last night I was telling Jock we hoped you'd attend, but with Vicktor having so recently passed on to his great reward, we hadn't dared hope."

Alex's eyes narrowed as he gazed at Ruth and Jock. "Dying of lung cancer isn't my idea of a reward for the best man I ever hope to know."

"Ruth and I are sincerely sorry about Vicktor," Jock said, turning toward Brett but not meeting her eyes. "I see you've met my daughter."

Brett didn't look directly at her father either. She

couldn't forgive him for what he'd done. His betrayal shouldn't still hurt, but it did. More than anyone else on earth, she'd wanted him to understand about Timmy. But no, he'd sided with Ruth. "Alex and I were just introducing ourselves."

"We're borrowing Alex," Ruth announced. "We want to introduce him to some of our oldest and dearest friends."

Brett tipped her glass toward Alex, the golden bubbles dancing against the rim. "You're in for a thrill."

Brett Payne, Alex thought, puzzled. Laughing at her own brother being married? Jail. What could she have done? Why hadn't Vic told Alex about her? Obviously Vic had met her while he'd been working with Ellis, but Vic had never mentioned Brett. What's going on here? He suddenly had the uneasy feeling Vic had been hiding something from him.

Hell, he didn't need any surprises right now. He had so little money it was frightening. And he was stuck with an albatross like Ellis in a business he'd never seen. How could Vic have invested their savings in Belage Diamonds? Didn't make sense.

"We're dreadfully sorry about your uncle," Ruth said. "We've taken a table at the Russian Ball in his honor. Count Ivanitsky was quite pleased, but he didn't seem to recall Vicktor Orlov."

Alex cursed Vic under his breath. "I'm positive Uncle Vic never met the count." Vic had been a notorious practical joker. He'd known Ruth never gave her unqualified approval to anyone without a title, so he'd pretended he was a noble. Great.

"Really?" Ruth sounded as if she'd just been told *she* had a terminal illness.

"Vic wasn't a Russian noble," Alex informed her. "His father backed the revolution."

"But"—Ruth looked at Jock—"Vicktor said Stalin expelled his father from Russia when he was just a boy."

"With Trotsky."

"Trotsky?" Clearly, Ruth was lost.

"Stalin's archrival," Jock prompted, surprising Alex. He knew Jock was an astute businessman, but understood he'd left school at an early age to start his business. "Many historians believe Stalin had him assassinated."

"An unfortunate misunderstanding, we're sure," Ruth said as Jock stepped away to greet someone.

Trotsky wouldn't have agreed.

"Well," Ruth said, steering Alex across the room, "we can't let this confusion over the Russian Ball upset us, can we?"

We? She kept saying *we* like Queen Elizabeth. The royal we—a royal pain in the ass.

"Evelyn," Ruth called, singling out a bridesmaid who could have haunted a house and charged by the room. "This is Alexander Savich."

Alexei Savich, not Alexander.

"This is Evelyn Rumsford-Chillingham. Now you two have a nice chat." Ruth scurried away.

Alex forced himself to smile. In truth Evelyn wasn't ugly, merely plain. She was the kind of girl who could be redeemed by a dynamite personality or, like Brett, with a winning smile. He felt sorry for her, sensing she had neither. And he knew Ruth had foisted him on her because she assumed he had money. Like her son, Ellis, Ruth Payne never wasted time thinking.

"Beautiful, isn't it?"

Alex realized Evelyn meant the ballroom. Poor thing didn't know what to say. For reasons he didn't comprehend, he intimidated women. He honestly liked women—in bed and out—but most seemed ill at ease with him. Even Brett had seemed flustered when she'd met him. He glanced around, attempting to look interested in what Evelyn was saying. Overhead hung a crystal chandelier with facets that sparkled as brightly as diamonds, and large enough to make him or anyone else raised in earthquake-prone Los Angeles nervous.

"Spencer House is the Princess of Wales's ancestral

home. She never lived here. Diana's family couldn't afford the upkeep."

Alex smiled weakly, his thoughts on Brett. Jail?

"Diana's father, Earl Spencer, took everything including all the priceless art to his country seat, Althorp. Then Raine . . ."

"Rain?" He gazed up at the Greek gods romping across the ceiling.

"*R-a-i-n-e,* now Lady Spencer, Princess Diana's step-mother. She did it," the plain bridesmaid said in a voice usually reserved for reporting a double homicide. "She sold all the paintings that rightfully belonged in Spencer House."

Alex looked across the room, but the dancers obstructed his view of Brett. The crowd shifted, allowing a brief glimpse. She moved and her green silk skirt parted like quicksilver, revealing exceptional legs. Then someone blocked his view, but he kept looking. Waiting. Brett appeared again, partially concealed by dancers, her blond hair gleaming in the soft light.

"You wouldn't expect such behavior from Barbara's daughter, would you?"

"Barbara who?" He'd lost track of the subject.

"Raine's mother, Barbara Cartland. You must have heard of her. She's the famous romance novelist. She's my favorite."

"Mine, too. Read 'em all the time."

"Really? I adore *Wings of Ecstasy.* Did you read it?"

"Yes. I remember one particular line." He gazed at Brett. "South of the duke's equator, his passion erupted like a geyser—a font of lust."

For a moment, Evelyn beamed at him, then turned the color of an eggplant. Finally she whispered, "Even though Raine had sold most of the art, Baron Rothschild restored Spencer House. Now Princess Diana's heirs will inherit something of value from her side of the family."

"Welcome news, I'm sure." He doubted either of Queen Elizabeth's grandsons would be strapped for cash, reduced to wearing rented tuxes. Not worth worrying about. Rothschild, though, was an interesting man. At Stanford, Alex had learned Jacob Rothschild was descended from one of the "five arrows" shot from Frankfurt centuries ago to establish the first multinational banking firm.

For generations, Rothschilds had dominated the financial world, bankrolling royal ventures when coffers were empty. Without Rothschild money, the British wouldn't have stopped Napoleon at Waterloo. If Rothschild wanted to restore decrepit buildings—the last echoes of the empire—and allow someone else's heirs to inherit them, who cared?

Alex would settle for having a jewelry manufacturing company with a reputation for premier designs. Yeah, and a house on Malibu's Carbon Beach with a Porsche would be nice too. He glanced around the room, looking for the bar. He wanted to get a double Stolichnaya and sit. Talking to Brett. But if he excused himself, poor Evelyn would be hurt, so he asked her to dance.

Dancing with a fence post. His toes were curled under, screaming: *You'll pay for this.* Through the mob of dancers, he spotted Brett. Still alone. He watched several guests move around her as if an invisible barrier of razor wire kept them away. An outcast. He remembered that feeling. He watched Brett smile, seemingly at ease. The way he had acted years earlier. Standing alone, pretending not to give a damn.

What had she done to make everyone snub her? Even her father? Certainly nothing serious or Uncle Vic would have reported it, delighting in the pushy-pretentious Paynes' escapades.

"Wasn't Brett arrested recently?" he asked Evelyn.

"Brett?"

"Yes. Ruth and Jock's daughter."

"Ruth isn't her mother. She's her step-mother."

Thank God for small favors. Uncle Vic never included Jock when he joked about the pushy-pretentious Paynes—just Ruth and Ellis.

"Was Brett arrested?"

"I—I really don't . . . know too much about it."

"What was the charge?" Alex noticed Jock dancing nearby and maneuvered Evelyn in his direction.

"Something about . . . destruction of government property."

3

From her post beside the rapidly melting ice sculpture of Venus, Brett watched Alex dancing with Evelyn, and wished she could leave. She'd received her yearly ration of snubbing by Ruth's friends and relatives. It couldn't possibly take much longer for the photographers to capture the newlyweds for posterity. Then she would tell Ellis—one last time—he would regret marrying a woman he didn't love.

Forcing a smile, she watched as the dance ended and Alex left Evelyn with Jock. Alex walked in her direction. *Don't even mention Belage. Let him find out for himself.*

Alex Savich was an attractive man. He had an overpowering presence that came partly from his straight-arrow gaze. His height accentuated his impressive shoulders and military posture, yet there was an effortlessness about the way he moved. Almost graceful, she realized, fascinated. He had the athletic agility of a speed skater or ice-hockey player that indicated years of rigorous training.

"Let's dance." He took the champagne glass out of her hand.

He didn't bother to ask; he just assumed. Brett could almost hear her mother saying: *Lovie, if a man gives you a problem tell him to N.O.D.—naff off and die.* Brett chose not to view Alex's lack of manners as a problem. Telling him to N.O.D. was not in her best interests. She needed to make a good impression on him, to reverse the damage done by those gossips, Lady Bewley and Ruth. Had Brett known Alex would attend the wedding, she never would have come and given Ruth and her friends a chance to poison his mind at the worst possible time. Everything she'd worked for all these years was riding on Alex. And so was Belage.

Alex drew Brett into his arms. "You don't like Ruth."

Brett gazed into his eyes, marine blue with hoops of black bordering the irises. Surely there must be something she could say to salvage his initial impression of her. Then she remembered Alex's uncle. Anyone who'd been in business with Vicktor Orlov had to have a terrific sense of humor. Vic loved to play tricks on everyone. "My problems with Ruth started when I was seven. That's when my father married Ruth and she came to live with us."

Alex felt a twinge of sympathy, having never known his own parents and having been raised by a grandmother who'd been Attila the Hun in drag. "Your mother died?"

Brett shook her head. The Siberian Ice dangling from her earlobes echoed the intensity he saw in her eyes. "Divorced."

Her mother hadn't been granted custody. Unusual.

"*Ruthless* and I never—"

Alex laughed, a deep masculine chuckle that took Brett by surprise. "Ruthless? Know what Vic called her? 'Pushy-pretentious' Payne in the ass."

Brett laughed, telling the chocolate-dipped strawberries and champagne threatening a revolution in her nervous stomach that Alex Savich did have a sense of humor. It had been impossible to judge what he'd been thinking. He had a diamond dealer's inscrutable expression—and incisive eyes that missed nothing. With luck, she could reverse the negative impression caused by Lady Bewley's comments.

"Ruth and I never got along from the moment she arrived

at our home, but the Hunt Ball incident totally finished us. She had the committee in the drawing room at Hayvenhurst —that's my father's country home—planning the seating for the annual ball. You see there's always a problem with undesirables."

"Undesirables?" he asked, his intriguing blue eyes never leaving her face. They didn't rove the room the way they had when he'd been dancing with Evelyn.

"Country life simply isn't what it used to be. Many of the old estates have been bought by American computer magnates turned country squires who trot around saying 'catch you later' when they mean 'good-bye.' "

She gauged his reaction to her criticism of Americans. Vic had told her Alex's parents had been Russians who emigrated to America. In many ways his uncle had been vague about Alex, but he had told her Alex was proud to be an American and even prouder to come from Los Angeles —proving it took all kinds.

"Sounds like a national disaster."

"True. Ruthless and her friends had to decide where to seat the number one undesirable: Spider Babcock. You remember him—the lead singer with Whips and Chains. After who knows how many platinum records, he retired and bought Wembly Hall next to Hayvenhurst. Spider was most generous. He donated his money to refurbish the Pildowne Hunt Club."

"So he had to be at one of the best tables."

"Exactly. But the previous year Spider and Camilla— that's his wife—had a snootful and mooned everyone as their chauffeur drove them past the clubhouse."

Alex chuckled and drew Brett just a little closer. She was a kick in the pants. "Spider sounds like my kind of guy."

"While Ruth and her cohorts were wrestling with this weighty problem of where to seat Spider, Ellis and I played one of our tricks on Ruth. That day, we were hiding behind a Chinese screen eavesdropping, when Camilla arrived."

"Spider's donation got his wife a seat on the committee."

"Exactly, but Ruth had called the meeting an hour early to give the committee an opportunity to discuss 'the unfortunate situation' of where to seat Spider. Finally, Camilla sailed in and asked Ruth what on earth was flying from the flagpole." Brett ran the tip of her tongue over her lower lip. He thought of more exciting places he'd like to see it.

"Ruth's uncle is a minor baronet. Every morning she has the butler run the standard up Hayvenhurst's flagpole. She thinks it makes the local gentry accept her even though my father's people were dirt poor and Scottish to boot."

Brett wondered why Alex was taking such small steps, barely moving. He was powerfully built with long legs that encouraged her to imagine him sweeping her around the room in a romantic waltz, but he didn't seem interested in dancing.

"Camilla listened to Ruth's family history, then said: 'Ducky, that isn't a standard flappin' in the breeze. It's yer bra.' "

Alex laughed so hard that heads swiveled in their direction. To hell with them.

The dance ended and Brett added, "Straightaway Ruth sent me off to a boarding school I hated."

Alex bet the bra was only the tip of the iceberg, but he didn't pry. He saw Lady Bewley dancing nearby and scowling at them. "What's the scoop on Lady Bewley?"

Relieved he hadn't escorted her off the dance floor, Brett wanted to keep him dancing, so Ruth or her friends wouldn't have a chance to talk to him. "You've heard of C.U.M.?"

"Come?" Encouraging news. If Brett was half as good in bed as she was at telling a story, leaving L.A. might not be as terrible as it seemed.

"That's short for the Committee to Uphold Morals."

Alex chuckled and Brett laughed along with him. The music began and Alex pulled her into his arms, again not bothering to ask. He brought her closer than before, didn't he? Maybe she was imagining things. Too much champagne.

His hand pressed against the small of her back, warm. No, hot. Instinctively, she arched her back, bringing her breasts flush up against his chest. She awkwardly edged back, avoiding his eyes, resisting the urge to remain where she was.

"Go on. I'm dying to hear more about C.U.M." Nice breasts. Not large, but soft and full.

"When the government decided to build a tunnel under the English Channel connecting England to the continent, there was a lot of controversy. For years Lady Bewley had been harping on the moral decline of the British, but no one paid any attention to her committee until she began to crusade against the tunnel. She provided a rallying point and her name has become synonymous with 'chunnel' politics."

"What the hell does the tunnel have to do with morals?" Thank God, L.A. was a moral no-man's-land. Live and let live.

Brett whispered, "You know the cheeky French."

Indeed he did. Next to California beach bunnies who were two steps away from needing the Surgeon General's warning label, Frenchwomen were his favorites.

"Lady Bewley insisted that if the tunnel were built, legions of French would race over here carrying satchels of pornography and brandishing dildos. I made the mistake of telling Lady Bewley that I'd be willing to take home the first Frenchman who came through the tunnel with a vibrator. Now she claims I have no morals." It wasn't the entire truth, but she didn't owe him her life history.

Hey, what about your mother? he wondered. Lady Bewley said Brett was exactly like her mother. Maybe Brett had reasons for not talking about her. Obviously something was wrong or Jock wouldn't have been granted custody. And let Ruthless pack her off to a school Brett hated.

"Lady Bewley has become quite a political force. Thousands of people joined C.U.M. to oppose the tunnel. She's been able to channel"—she paused and they both laughed at the pun—"them into trying to improve England's moral standards."

Alex doubted she'd told him the whole truth. He was tempted to ask more, but remembered the British were less likely than Americans to discuss their personal lives with strangers. He didn't blame them; he didn't want anyone questioning him either. He carefully phrased his next words, not questioning, but giving her an opening. "You know, I was sitting behind you at the wedding. I had the crazy idea that you were Ellis's girlfriend. I thought you were crying— not laughing."

Brett's expression became serious, dominated by dramatic eyes rimmed by tiers of dark blond lashes with tips so light that they couldn't be seen unless you were holding her. "I don't believe two people should marry unless they're over the edge."

"Over the edge?"

"When you find the person you love, you fall over the edge of life's cliff. Without that person you'll be out of bounds—that means nowhere—forever."

"I'd have to be over the edge to get married."

"Ellis was over the edge. He's in love with my best friend, Amy, but he married Lady Daphne instead."

"Why didn't he marry Amy?"

"Ruth thought he could do better. You see, Amy has a different religion from Ellis." Brett realized they were no longer moving. They were standing on the dance floor with their arms around each other. "Amy's so depressed that we're going away on a trip."

Before Alex could question her about her trip, the dance ended and Brett asked if he'd seen the Painted Room. He decided that he'd tortured his toes long enough. They left the dancers and went down the stairs.

"I didn't quite catch what Lady Bewley said in church," Alex fibbed, easing into his next question as they sat on a sofa in the Painted Room, which had enough gilt to blind him. "Were you visiting someone in jail?" Brett's eyes met his; he didn't like what he saw. Aw, hell, here it comes.

"I was arrested," Brett admitted. "Amy came to my rescue. She paid the fine and my attorney's fees."

Unusual. Brett had called her friend Amy, not her father.

"The government singled me out, charging me with destroying government property because of my mother . . . and father." No mistaking the defensive tone in her voice. "It's a long story."

Surprise. Surprise. "Go on."

"You've heard of bovine tuberculosis?"

He shook his head. Lately everything from sexual promiscuity to overeating had become a disease or an addiction.

"Tuberculosis has infected a lot of dairy cows. The government is concerned that the disease will be transmitted to the milk, then to people."

"That's difficult to prove. Next they'll be saying I got my cold from my dog."

"My point exactly: interspecies links between diseases are rare. But the badgers, who also have tuberculosis, share the same fields with the cows, and they're blamed for giving them tuberculosis." Her voice lost the edge of humor she'd had earlier. "The government's killing the badgers. Soon there won't be a single one left in England. The Badger Preservation Society warned them we wouldn't allow a badger annihilation to take place, but the killing continued. We took action."

Brett in action. The image of Ruth's bra, an architectural feat, flapping in the breeze, hit him. Don't tangle with Brett Payne. Unless you want to have the time of your life.

"The members of the society broke the locks on the holding pens and relocated the badgers in less populated areas."

"They put you in jail for that?" he asked, and she nodded. "Had you been in jail before?"

"Years ago," she said as if it wasn't worth discussing. "Mother and I were among a group arrested for protesting *your* government's nuclear weapons facility here."

Intriguing. How quickly she'd changed from the comedienne to an earnest woman. Beneath it all what was Brett really like?

A bell announced dinner. Brett rose, saying she had to dash. "I wasn't invited to the wedding. I warned Ruthless that if she forced Ellis to marry Daphne, I would stand up— you know, when the vicar asks if anyone in the church knows any reason—and tell everyone—his mommy made him do it."

Alex threw back his head and roared. How he missed Vic. He would have loved Brett. Two of a kind.

"Let's go somewhere and have a quiet dinner," Alex said.

"Let me fix you dinner." Brett prayed she could keep the conversation away from Belage Diamonds for the remainder of the evening. She doubted Alex would be interested in Belage, but her only chance was getting him to see the place for himself.

4

Alex followed Brett through the gate of her two-story brownstone in Chelsea. A yew hedge bordered the small square lawn and crimson impatiens bracketed the narrow walk. The night air was warm despite a misty fog edging in from the Thames, wreathing the branches of the plane tree and haloing the coach lantern on the porch.

Brett unlocked the door, calling softly, "Mrs. Pruitt, I'm home." She turned to Alex. "Mrs. Pruitt minds Timmy for me."

Timmy? A kid. Aw, hell. Divorced women with children were always on the hunt for a new daddy.

While Brett paid the elderly lady, Alex walked into the small living room. A preemptive strike on a toy store: Legos and blocks scattered about, an upside-down red wagon, a faded chintz sofa covered with more stuffed animals than Harrods stocked, and a coffee table with several partly finished puzzles.

"Make yourself comfortable while I run upstairs and change out of this dress." She headed up the narrow stairs.

Alex gazed around the room, his stomach rumbling, reminding him he hadn't eaten much all day. On the fireplace mantel stood two photographs in a large double frame. One was a photograph of a woman who had to be Brett's mother. Blond, green eyes, same killer smile. She wore her hair shorter, though, cut to midchin and revealing earrings like miniature chandeliers—made out of odd-shaped bones. Or maybe animal teeth. She was flanked by two moustached men who could have stepped out of the cast of *Viva Zapata.* Except the Uzis they carried were real.

The older man in the other photograph had sandy hair and nondescript brown eyes. Handsome in a washed-out, British sort of way. Probably Brett's stepfather.

He wandered down the hall and found a bathroom with a rubber duck in the toilet. He shuffled into the small kitchen at the rear of the town house and plopped down on one of two Bentwood chairs at an ice-cream table.

Brett sailed into the room. "There you are. Would you like a drink? All I have is gin."

"Great." Alex never drank gin, preferring vodka.

Brett had changed into taupe slacks that emphasized her streamlined legs and cute butt. A red vee-neck sweater almost, but not quite, hid the mole at the back of her neck. The diamonds still hung from her ears, jangling wildly now while she rummaged through a cabinet for the gin. She found a half-full bottle of Gunga Gin and put it on the table, then poured a generous amount into his glass.

He took a cautious sip. Wasn't Boodles or Bombay, but it wasn't *skivka,* rotgut, as Vic would have said in Russian. Brett opened the refrigerator where finger paintings hung among a cluster of magnetic alphabet letters. Someone had spelled out the name Timmy. She bent over to peer inside the small refrigerator, giving him a provocative view of her nicely rounded rear end.

"How about a cheese and mushroom omelette?"

On cue his stomach rumbled. "Sounds great." Brett didn't fit into any category he could identify. Who could anticipate what she would say or do next? He was ready.

Hell, he was more than ready for a woman like Brett. A challenge.

He scooted the other chair over. "Mind if I put up my feet?"

"Go ahead." Since Timmy had been born, she hadn't had a man in her home—unless you counted men like Ellis or Vic, which she didn't. Certainly not a sexy man like Alex who was now unhooking his bow tie.

Alex stuffed the damn tie into his pocket and unbuttoned his collar before it strangled him. His skin beneath it felt hot, chafed. He took off his jacket and slung it across the chair where his feet were now propped. Better. Much better. He knocked back a swig of gin.

So big, Brett thought; he dominated the entire kitchen. She fumbled in a drawer, finally locating the cheese grater, watching him out of the corner of her eye. He flexed his toes and the black ribbing on his socks stretched taut.

"I think I have a blister."

She set the grater down. "Let me see."

"Na-a-ah, it's no big deal."

No big deal—so American. "Come on now. Mommies know about these things." She tugged on one sock and it slid off revealing a bloody blister on his big toe. "I'll get some medicine."

Alex polished off the gin and poured himself another. Soon she rushed back in, then dropped to her knees to inspect his toe.

Brett folded back the cuffs of his trousers. Like his face, his legs were tanned, and he had muscular calves. She gently wiped the blood from his toe. Uncapping the iodine, she said, "This will only hurt a minute."

Alex studied her bent head, aware of the warmth of her hand as she gripped his foot and talked to him as if he were a young child. "Promise?"

Her wide green eyes met his; they exchanged smiles. "You're a big boy. You can take it."

No question he could take it, but the way she kept running her soft hand across the bottom of his foot was driving him crazy. "I cry easily." Just to keep her going.

She dabbed his toe with the iodine. He winced and sucked in his breath. His movement strained his shirt which gaped open to reveal a glimpse of chest hair and tanned skin. And a small gold cross on a filigree chain. Surprising, Brett thought. She didn't have the impression Alex was the religious type.

She clasped Alex's foot, her thumb firmly planted on the sensitive rise of his arch. Blowing on the aching blister, she massaged his foot, her thumb rotating against his bare skin. Round and round in lazy circles. The pain eased but she kept kneading his foot. A definite turn-on.

"All set except for the bandage," she said, releasing his foot. He still felt the imprint of her thumb on his sole. She secured the bandage and lightly patted his toe. "Done."

He wanted to tell her what was aching now, but smiled instead. She looked so damn pleased with her work. Then he saw the Ninja Turtle wielding a pizza-whacking samurai sword staring at him from the tape on his toe.

Brett started to turn away, but decided to tease him a bit more by giving him a kiss on the cheek as she would have Timmy. She pressed her lips to his cheek, then pulled back. "All better?"

Aw, hell. She was teasing him. Real funny. "No way."

She hesitated, her mind scrambling for some witty remark that would lighten the mood. The invitation in the depths of his eyes was unmistakable. For once she was speechless.

At the base of her throat, her pulse beat rapidly, and a shiver of desire, suppressed for years, surged through her, taking her by surprise. She meant to move away, she honestly did, but his nearness was so masculine, so compelling. Filled with a unique sense of anticipation, she touched her lips to his.

Her kiss was unexpectedly tender. Brett's lips didn't press, certainly they didn't part. They merely caressed. Now he wasn't one for kissing. Why waste time? But he waited, knowing she was full of surprises. What next?

The kiss sent the pit of her stomach into a wild tumble, the strawberries swirling through the chocolate, dancing on the champagne bubbles. She wanted, oh, how she wanted, to really kiss him, to let go. His tongue roved across her lips, and without realizing it, she parted them, allowing his tongue to seek hers. Already pounding furiously, her heart lurched, leaving her light-headed. His hand circled the back of her neck, gently squeezing and edging upward into her hair. She scrambled for all the reasons she should say no, but all the while her body ached for more.

"Mommy. Mommeeee."

Brett jerked away. "Timmy, what are you doing out of bed?"

Green eyes huge beneath blond bangs, the kid stared at Alex.

" 'Neeky By is 'fraid of the dark," the boy told Alex.

"Sneaky By is our cat." Brett's words come out in a breathless rush. "Timmy named him Sneaky By because he always manages to sneak by me and get out. I thought Mrs. Pruitt had put him in with Timmy." She patted her son's head. "I'll call Sneaky By."

Alex and Timmy stared at each other. A junior edition of Brett, the child appeared to be two or three years old. Dressed in a blue bunny suit with CRIB POTATO stitched on the chest, he clutched a stuffed giraffe. Hard to believe every stuffed animal the kid owned wasn't on the sofa in the next room.

"Dah-dee?"

Daddy? A word guaranteed to send a bachelor into rigor mortis. "No. I'm a friend of your mother's. I'm Alex."

Timmy looked at him as if he didn't quite believe him, but he repeated his name. "Al-wex." Then he smiled, Brett's smile. "I'm Timmy." Pointing to the bandaged toe, he said, "You have an oowie." Dragging the giraffe by a leg, he toddled up to Alex's feet, bent over, and kissed the Ninja

Turtle. "All betta." He smiled at Alex. "Mommy says a kiss makes it betta."

We were making it all better until you came along. Alex heard Brett calling "Kitty kitty." Timmy dropped the giraffe and took two uneven steps toward Alex, his small arms raised. A full second went by before Alex realized what the boy wanted.

An image flashed through Alex's mind, clear but painful even after all these years. He was hiding behind the door to his grandmother's small living room, listening to Vic Orlov doing the impossible—making her laugh. Now here was Brett's son, so young but afraid of no one. Alex lifted the boy onto his lap and gazed into his eyes, Brett's eyes.

" 'Neeky By hunts mouses in Mrs. Rwandall's garden. I—"

Brett reappeared, carrying a cat the color of English cheddar with a black sock—make that a knee-high. He spotted Alex and his hackles shot up.

"Come on, Timmy. Back to bed."

The child looked at Alex. "Tell me a story."

"Mr. Savich doesn't know any bedtime stories."

Not any fit for kids' ears, but I'm willing to tell you one.

"Night-night," Timmy said, then leaned closer to Alex, offering him his cheek.

What a kissy family. He pecked the boy's cheek. Timmy meandered off, glancing back at Alex. They disappeared and he poured himself another gin and waited. And waited. Hell of a long bedtime story. Never mind, the world was full of little people these days. You couldn't shunt them aside with part of a story. He rose and went to the counter, then picked up the cheese grater.

Brett paused coming down the stairs, wondering how to handle Alex. Why had she thrown herself at him? How could she have been so . . . so weak? She glanced at the photographs on the mantel and took courage. She'd fix Alex a nice dinner—as nice as it could be when all she had in the house was eggs—and send him on his way.

"I make a mean omelette," he said as she walked into the kitchen.

She saw it was almost done, fluffy and evenly browned, and hurried to set the table. "Sneaky By isn't afraid of the dark. Timmy is, although I have no idea why. He has a night-light. He's never been left alone."

"He'll grow out of it," Alex assured her.

"Just a little piece for me," she said as he started to serve the omelette. "I ate a lot at the reception."

Cute. She's flustered as hell. Not nearly as sophisticated as she'd like to appear. Gutsy, though, willing to torment that poor sap, Ellis, on his wedding day.

Nervously talking, Brett gave Alex a rundown of how steeplechase races worked. He ate without comment, his assessing eyes on her. Too often on her lips. She couldn't take it any longer. "I'd better wash that omelette pan before the cheese sticks."

She squeezed enough soap into the basin to wash a week's worth of dishes, then turned on the tap. A mountain of bubbles leaped off the water, and she covered them with the omelette pan. Behind her, she heard his chair move. She started scrubbing vigorously with the sponge.

Alex came up behind her, watching her earrings thump against her cheeks. "No dessert?"

"Sorry," she said, justifiably proud of how casual she sounded. "I wasn't expecting company."

"I have something in mind," he said, and she felt his breath fanning the back of her neck.

"Wait! How about a frozen Yorkie bar?" How could she have forgotten? She always kept a dozen of the chocolate candy bars in the freezer for emergencies.

"Forget it."

She started to turn, but his fingertips touched the sensitive curve of her neck where it met her shoulder; they lingered, barely making contact, but caressing just the same. Her pulse accelerated; she struggled to come up with a witty remark. She felt him edge closer, the full length of his body warm yet not quite touching hers. His lips coaxingly skimmed the side of her neck just behind her earlobe, his nose nudging her diamond earring aside, his eyelashes fluttering against her ear. The heady sensation of his lips on her skin made her grip the rim of the sink and inhale sharply.

He'd meant to kiss her once—behind the ear, anyway— but he'd spent so long gazing at the downy curls at the nape of her neck and wondering that he couldn't stop. Didn't even consider it. A trace of perfume lingered on her invitingly warm skin, a light fresh scent. Breathtaking. He eased the back of the sweater away and kissed the tiny mole. Once. Twice.

It was all Brett could do to hold herself in place and keep from turning and hurling herself into his arms. Dismayed at the magnitude of her own desire, she tried to summon all the reasons she should tell him to go. None came to her rescue. Instead, his demanding lips seared a path up her neck, again seeking the sensitive spot behind her ear.

"Sexy," he whispered, his lips still against her finely textured skin. Alex pulled one hairpin out of her hair and a cluster of curls fell into his hand and the soft strands flowed through his fingers. He freed still another, tossing the pin onto the floor. Half her hair was down now, longer than he'd anticipated and thicker. Silkier. It had a freshly shampooed smell with a hint of the same fragrance he'd noticed earlier.

"Nice," he said, secretly pleased that for all her bravado Brett was now at a loss for words. He couldn't resist kissing her neck again, parting his lips to taste the soft skin.

The edges of his teeth faintly scored the side of her neck, sending a shocking heat into her thighs, weakening her knees. Her brain sounded the alarm, but her body refused to listen. She wanted . . . she needed.

Suddenly the urge to see Brett's face, her hair down, overwhelmed him. He stopped kissing her and yanked out the remaining pins, releasing a torrent of dark blond hair, baby soft yet surprisingly thick. Glorious waves with high-

lights of platinum and amber tumbled over her shoulders.
Sexy as hell.

Brett allowed him to turn her, primed to say something.
Anything. She met his eyes, his gaze probing, mysterious. A
little dangerous. What was he thinking? She expected him
to kiss her, but he didn't. Taking both hands he furrowed his
fingers through her hair, routing a hidden hairpin that fell
into the dishwater. He stroked her hair in long slow movements. Over and over and over. Finally, he hooked one long
strand behind each ear, exposing her mother's diamonds.

He shook his head. "Breathtaking."

"They're almost flawless. Especially cut in Antwerp for
Garrard's on Bond Street. They—"

His lips cut off her words and her heart, already beating
with pounding thuds, drummed faster while her muscles
contracted with anticipation. It had been so long. Too long.
His demanding tongue traced the fullness of her bottom lip,
then nudged forward, impatiently seeking her tongue. With
an expert's touch, his tongue parried with hers while his
strong arms pulled her flush against his body.

For so long she'd felt no desire at all that her unexpected
response to his kisses amazed her. The past still claimed
part of her, but the crushing pressure of Alex Savich's arms,
his breathtaking kisses blocked her memories, unleashing
her passion with alarming force.

They continued to kiss, long exploratory kisses, his fingers
tracking through her hair. He pulled back, shifting his
stance. His legs now widespread, his hips pressed against
hers. Demanding. Aggressive. Sexy.

Her rapid breathing echoed his. The insistent pressure of
his arousal warned her that she had to stop now. Brett
pulled back, breathing heavily, rallying her courage, aware
she'd let this go too far. She knew better. "Please don't."

He didn't listen, lowering his lips toward her.

"I can't. Really, I can't."

He stepped back. "What's the matter?"

"You're very attractive, but . . ."

"But what?" Hostile tone; indicting eyes.

"I—I . . . Timmy's father may be home soon."

5

Still favoring his right foot, Alex walked down Hatton Garden, gazing at the buildings in the diamond center. How was it districts the world over looked alike? Displays filled the street-side windows: row after row of rings encrusted with diamonds, stacks of gold bracelets by the hundreds, gold necklaces so thick they could tow a Jaguar. Junk, most of it. The real quality was hidden from the public in offices above the street, open only to the trade.

The same people thrived in every diamond district, too. He could have been on Hill Street in L.A. or Forty-seventh Street in New York. Crybaby boomers roamed the area, living by the eleventh commandment: *Thou shalt not pay retail.* Packs of Japanese tourists with garlands of cameras and pockets stuffed with yen bought everything in sight. Lookie Lous, window-shopping, counted their hard-earned money. Occasionally he spotted professionals, dressed in suits, going about their business, bound for the offices above the streets.

The only truly British building on Hatton Garden housed the Diamond Club. Naturally, it wasn't open to the public. Diamond brokers knew one another, and they had a caste system. Belage Diamonds, a third-rate manufacturer, wasn't a pariah. But close.

Midway down Hatton Garden, Alex turned onto Greville and shifted the heavy package he carried to the other hip. He found Greville Court, a short cul-de-sac, and saw Belage Diamonds was in the same rundown brick building as Rubin and Son, well-known for making the tools of the trade. Not lasers, of course. Too sophisticated. Not one master jeweler in a thousand used lasers.

Upstairs, the elevator doors creaked open, and he stepped into a corridor with a permanent patina of dust and mildew. Down the hall, old-fashioned frosted-glass doors had a discreet plaque: BELAGE DIAMONDS—ESTABLISHED 1835.

He entered a marble-floored vestibule. Most manufacturers had similar security systems to qualify for Lloyds insurance. An outer door opened into a small waiting area. Beyond it was a bulletproof door. Unless the outer door had been closed, the inner door could not be opened; this prevented thieves from robbing jewelers and making quick getaways.

The receptionist, a gray-haired woman in her late fifties, glared at him from behind the inner door, but made no move to press the buzzer that would electronically release the lock on the second door.

Eula Mae Pruitt stared, disbelieving, at the tall, athletically built man in—heaven forbid—jeans and tennis shoes. Could this be Vic's nephew? My stars, Americans! Don't they know enough to wear respectable clothes? "Identification, please."

He showed her his card from the American Gem Society, holding it against the glass. She finally pressed the buzzer.

"I'm Miss Pruitt," she said, wondering why Vic hadn't better prepared her for his nephew.

"Alexei Savich. Call me Alex." He scanned the small area. Institutional green paint and a sagging sofa that was once gold but had faded to a dull butterscotch. Next to the window stood a card table with plants growing in jars of water. Hanging from the edge of the table were prize ribbons.

"Pits," Eula Mae tersely informed him, sensing his disapproval. "I'm president of the Rare Plant and Pit Council." She pointed to a garnet-leafed plant that trailed to the floor. "My beet took first prize in the pit division at the Chelsea Garden Show. Next year I intend to win with a kiwi."

Jee-sus, only Ellis would allow a fruitcake secretary to cultivate pits. Why hadn't Uncle Vic done something about her? "Shouldn't those plants be in your home?"

"They need to be rotated constantly to get proper light. I'm mating these kiwis to bear fruit. Telling the difference between a male and a female kiwi is a bit dicey—"

"I see." Sorry I asked. Brett, Lady Bewley, Ruth, now Miss Pruitt. Who said L.A. had a monopoly on flakes and nuts?

"Ellis said you'll be sharing his office down that hall."

"I'll need to see the company's current balance sheet, the profit and loss statement, as well as the sales analysis."

Alex set his package down and walked along the hall, curious about Belage. A room with the small torches the goldsmiths used was empty, the equipment antiquated. Next door he found a cutting room with no electronic gear in sight. The diamond-polishing platter had to date back to the twenties. He'd expected to see craftsmen in smocks sitting at long tables in the cutting room polishing facets, but they must be at lunch. He had intended to arrive earlier, but he'd spent the morning at customs getting his laser microprobe released.

The last room contained a drawing board; it must belong to the designer, Lamont. Mounted on the wall was the head of a very pissed-off panther, glossy black with daggerlike teeth. Alex scanned the walls. Where were the educational certificates and awards designers usually hung?

Remembering Vic's effusive description of Belage, Alex had envisioned a small, exclusive workroom that catered to jewelers like Garrard's, the Bond Street jeweler who'd made Brett's earrings. Expensive, one-of-a-kind pieces.

Brett, he thought, kicking himself yet again for being taken in by her winning smile. A royal tease. How was the kid that didn't know his own father? Don't ask. He certainly hadn't that night. At her words, he'd grabbed his things and marched—okay, hobbled—out of her place.

Hey, that's what happens to a guy who goes too long without sex. He hadn't slept with a woman since Vic had arrived in L.A. with cancer two months ago. No wonder Brett had gotten to him.

Inside Ellis's office was more green paint—the color common to government offices. And mental institutions. An antique safe stood in a corner. Look on the bright side: There isn't a safecracker still alive who'd know how to get into that contraption.

Miss Pruitt appeared with several file folders as he unpacked the laser microprobe he used for finding flaws in gems. Next to his master set of diamonds used to compare stones to check for color and clarity, the expensive laser microprobe was his most valuable possession.

"I'm expecting a package and Lev Rodynskov," he told her. "Lev will be doubling as a cutter and setter. When he arrives, we'll want to meet the staff. What time will they be back?"

"Ellis gave everyone a month's holiday. He thought you might need the time to acquaint yourself with Belage." This was a silly excuse, but everyone wanted to be far from the scene when Alex found out the situation at Belage. She'd stayed, convinced she owed it to Vic.

"A month? He thought I'd need an *entire* month?"

"Vic always said Ellis was a trifle of a nincompoop."

Sounded just like Vic. Alex grinned in spite of himself. "I take it you knew my uncle."

"Yes. I met him while he was working here." For a moment she looked down. "I'm terribly sorry he's gone. A great loss."

Tears collected in her eyes and it dawned on Alex who she was. *"You're* Eula Mae?" She nodded, blinking rapidly, fending back tears. *This* was Eula Mae, the paragon of efficiency? Vic had been death on the pushy-pretentious Paynes, but he'd raved about Eula Mae and the designer, Lamont. *Alex, with Eula Mae and Lamont to help you and Lev, Belage Diamonds will soon be selling to Cartier, Fred, Chaumet—the best in the business.*

"My uncle spoke very highly of you."

She beamed. "I came to Belage forty years ago when I was just seventeen. I know the business."

"Good." But the pits will have to go. "I'm going to need the combination to the safe and the master list of stones."

She brought him another folder, then rushed out of the room. Alex read the reports, the uneasy feeling he'd had since finding out he was now majority owner of Belage intensifying. Son of a bitch! Close to broke, the company was suspended in a financial twilight zone. Worse, sales were nonexistent.

How in hell was he going to become a premier jeweler saddled with this turkey? Vic had blown their savings on this joint. Unbelievable. All the years they'd worked, traveling Eastern Europe trading diamonds, saving money so they could open their own operation. For this?

Eula Mae appeared. "Mr. Rodynskov is here."

"Ma Neshma." Alex called to Lev, who was standing behind her.

Lev strode in, short but muscular with a corona of tight black curls that matched his troubled eyes. *"Ma Neshma,"* he responded in Hebrew. He bear-hugged Alex and kissed him on both cheeks, Russian style, like brothers. They hadn't seen each other in months, but it didn't matter. That night in the train station in Kiev had cemented their friendship forever. Now that Vic was gone, Lev was the only person Alex trusted.

"Vic invested all our money in this dump."

"Did Vic not ask you?"

"No. I was in Hong Kong, and he thought this was too good an investment to pass up. I wish he'd waited until I looked at the books. This place is worthless."

Lev didn't comment. He never questioned Vic or Alex.

"When Vic arrived in L.A. he was already half dead." Alex couldn't look at Lev. Instead he walked to the window overlooking the street. "I'm sorry I didn't send for you. Vic insisted . . . he wanted to die with dignity."

"I got your letter," Lev said quietly. "I understand."

"Vic wanted everyone to remember him the way he was."

"Happy. He love life." Lev's voice was more choked with emotion than Alex had heard since that night in Kiev almost fifteen years ago. "He love you, Alex."

"I know," Alex said, half under his breath. It was true. Vic loved him like a father, and Alex loved him just as much. Somehow it was impossible to believe he'd never see him again or hear his special laugh. How could he be gone? What was he going to do without him?

"I hardly had a chance to say good-bye," Alex told Lev.

Lev nodded; there might have been tears in his eyes. They sat in silence for a few moments until Lev said, "You tell me bring laser and get visa. I am here."

"Help me get this business rolling. We're going to make laser-set jewelry that will put Harry Winston on notice. You use the laser, Lamont designs, I handle the finances. There is some good news. Belage has a deal pending with Harvey Nichols—that's a local department store—to make custom pieces for their fall collection."

"This Lamont knows designs for laser setter?"

"Vic claimed he's the best. But remember, Lamont is French, which means he'll be prissy and independent as hell. We'll have to humor him; good laser designers are impossible to find."

"Pissy?"

"No. Prissy. Means he'll whine a lot and want things his own way." Alex reminded himself that although Lev's English was good and spoken only with a slight accent, he didn't understand slang or unusual words. "Let's open the safe and check his designs."

The ancient safe groaned open; inside were several *briefkes*. The pieces of paper were folded five times to make a diamond packet, and in the corner of each was a code in pencil that indicated the quality of the stone inside. He opened each, then handed them to Lev, who held the gems up to the light filtering in from the window. Natural light and the stark white of the paper made it easy to check the quality of the diamond without using a ten-power magnifying loupe.

Alex handed Lev the last *briefke*. M&M's. Not candy, but mistakes and *metsiehs*, Yiddish for bargains—the jargon of diamond dealers that dated back to the Middle Ages.

"Christ. No inventory. Ellis can't find his balls without a map. Sure as hell, he knows nothing about the business."

Alex reached for Lamont's portfolio. Inside were two dividers, one labeled HARVEY NICHOLS, the other LASER. "Promising." Alex was genuinely encouraged as he flipped through the designs Lamont had done for the department store proposal. Unique designs. Not allowing himself to become excited, he opened the laser section and studied the innovative laser designs set without prongs that detracted from the color of the stone and inhibited the dispersion of light.

"Lamont is very good," Lev said; *good* sounded like *gut*.

"Exceptional talent. Obviously, what Vic bought was a designer, not a company. That explains everything." Alex expelled a long sigh of relief, his faith in Vic restored.

Miss Pruitt brought in the package he'd been expecting. It was supposed to be an antique clock from Budapest but it contained a diamond shipment.

"Since everyone's gone," he told her, "call the painters. Repaint the place and get new furniture for the reception area. Now about those pits—" He hesitated.

Her expression remained the same, but her eyes shifted to the floor. Miss Pruitt. Preordained to be a spinster. A woman for whom life really was the pits. Forty years at Belage. Beyond depressing. "Get rid of the card table. Buy one of those multitiered greenhouse windows and put the pits in it. Find Lucite display frames for the ribbons and hang them on the wall."

She nodded, beaming, then trotted out the door. What the hell? He'd be the only manufacturer with prize-winning pits. It would give the guys at the Diamond Club something to bullshit about.

"This is the first of several shipments of diamonds from Eastern Europe that Vic arranged before he died. I'm to sell them for some owner who wants to be anonymous." Alex closed the door. "The commission I get from this I'll keep to run Belage. The rest goes to the seller's Swiss account. I'm going to need every cent to get this dog going."

They pried open the wood sides of the clock inside the box and emptied the contents onto the desk. Chunks of cloudy rough diamonds not yet cut or polished rolled out, stones of amber and pink and green. Some were shaped like peanuts, others like popcorn. Both men stared, disbelieving, at the rare stones.

"Fancies?" Lev used the industry term for colored diamonds.

"Hottest thing on the market, but I had no idea they'd found colored diamonds in Eastern Europe."

"Artisan miners?" Lev asked, referring to mine laborers who, despite rigid security, smuggled out rough stones.

In the diamond trade, taking rough stones wasn't considered stealing. It was part of doing business. No matter how tight the security, a few gems disappeared, especially in Africa. Zaire, in particular, was notorious for its artistic miners. A colony of Indian diamond traders had set up a permanent village outside Zaire's border, ready to offer cash for stones the miners pilfered. Such thievery was expected.

"Artisan miners sophisticated enough to have a Swiss account?" Alex shrugged. "It's possible, but it sounds too organized for artisan miners."

"Where do stones come from?"

"Good question. Someplace where their operation isn't ready to process colored diamonds. Albania. Possibly Russia."

"Then Gypsies smuggled them across borders."

"I suppose. Vic never said, but it's the only explanation. Remember, Uncle Vic's father was part Gypsy. Vic had contacts with Gypsies all across Europe." Along with the Jews, the Gypsies had always been persecuted. Several of the diamond mines used Gypsy laborers, paying them little more than slave wages, forcing them to live in rusty tin ghettos outside the mines.

"Gypsies with Swiss account?" Lev muttered.

"Hard to believe, isn't it? Gypsies rarely trust anyone except their own people, but in this case they'd have no choice. There's no way of sending millions back to them— especially when we don't even know where they are. Or who they are."

Alex picked up a piece of grayish-purple rough and cored a tiny hole in its shell with a special blade coated in diamond dust. He put the stone into the microprobe and focused the laser on the window into the heart of the gem that would tell him the details of the color and quality of the diamond.

Nothing, absolutely nothing—well, maybe a really dynamite woman—was as interesting as peering into the soul of a rough stone, looking for the first time at something nature had created eons ago. It reminded Alex of his first biology class when he'd looked into a microscope and discovered the world of microorganisms living in a drop of water. The laser microprobe magnified microscopic fissures and inclusions even a ten-power loupe would miss.

This stone, though riddled with thousands of fissures, would rate *vvsi*—very, very small imperfections—perfect by industry standards. The diamond wasn't the top-rated D color known as "gin and tonic" in the industry, but it was equally valuable. More so in this hot market for fancies.

"Flawless," he told Lev. "It'll polish out to a deep amethyst color."

Alex examined the diamonds, which varied in color from a rare pink to green and blue. "Loupe-clean. Flawless." He walked to the window and pointed to a tall, modern building on the next street, Charterhouse. "Intelco."

Lev nodded solemnly. The cartel monitored diamonds mined worldwide, tenaciously controlling sales. All diamonds first came to Intelco to be sorted and graded before being sent to dealers.

"I might be able to sell off contraband diamonds discreetly a few at a time, but not fancies. They're too rare. Intelco's computers would pick up any transaction immediately. I'll never become a first-rate manufacturer if the cartel finds out I'm selling fancies. They'll post a notice on the Diamond Club bulletin board saying I've violated club standards. I'll have to go to Bombay and sell diamond *melee* in a back alley."

How the hell did a group of tight-ass Brits maintain a stranglehold on the market? The cartel controlled prices, but unlike OPEC, they'd dominated the diamond trade for over a century, cowing governments. Several African countries had tried to break away only to have Intelco undermine them by severely discounting the same type of stones they were selling. Zaire, its economy on the verge of collapse, still hadn't recovered.

According to rumors that Alex firmly believed, when Intelco needed to take severe action, it used mobsters from Sicily, who literally eliminated the competition.

In this every-man-for-himself world, diamond dealers adhered to traditions that were centuries old. Stones were taken on approval with just a memo to confirm the transaction. Deals in the millions were sealed with a handshake and the Yiddish phrase *mazel und broche*—luck and blessing. Two rules applied to all dealers. First, no one reneged on his word. Second, and perhaps more important, no one crossed the cartel.

Not that operating outside Intelco's guidelines was illegal; it wasn't. The U.S. government refused to allow the cartel to open an office in America because Intelco's stranglehold on the market violated restraint of trade laws. Regardless, the cartel survived. And thrived.

It was a death sentence for a dealer's career to cross Intelco. Being blacklisted by the cartel would mean Alex would never get his hands on the gems he'd need to become a premier jeweler. Hell, he could even get himself killed.

"Make fancies into jewelry and sell them," Lev suggested.

"Where would I say I bought the fancies? I could claim I'd stumbled across Iran's crown jewels." The gems had disappeared during the revolution and still hadn't turned up —much to the displeasure of the cash-starved Iranian government. "Then I'll receive a death sentence like Rushdie."

"I am serious. Jewelers X-ray diamonds to make new colors."

Alex considered the idea. X-raying diamonds had been used for years to disguise flaws, although no one had yet perfected the method so the color could be predicted ahead of time. Often diamonds became murky colors that were worthless.

Again Alex stared at the building that housed the all-powerful cartel. Try to fool Intelco? A monumental risk. Still, did he have a choice? After Vic's debacle with Belage, Alex had so little money left it was frightening. He'd been counting on these diamonds to help him build Belage, never suspecting they were unusual colored gems. If he played it safe, not selling these stones, it would be years before he could build up Belage enough so he could sell it and return to L.A.

The thought of spending his life in London was as depressing as thinking of Eula Mae's forty years at Belage. Living in London had been Vic's dream, not his. The only serious disagreement they'd ever had centered on where to open their shop. No question about it, Vic had deliberately

maneuvered Alex into coming to London. And now he was
stuck, unless . . .

Again, he looked at Intelco. What the hell? *Maskirova*—
trickery—is in your blood. He could use the traditional Russian art of deception, a talent for bluffing that Europeans
didn't understand. *Go ahead, take the chance. You'll never get
back to L.A. if you don't.* The decision came surprisingly
easily considering the consequences, a decision he hoped he
wouldn't later regret.

"It's worth a shot, Lev. Can you rig up something that
would look as if it could be used to radiate stones?" Lev
nodded. "Great. When the time comes, I'll put out the word
at the Diamond Club that we're"—he mentally sifted
through a list of advertising bullshit—"artificially enhancing
our diamonds."

"Will Dash Boynton ask to see enhancer?"

"Probably," Alex grimly admitted.

Boynton was the cartel's enforcer. His real name was
Crawford Boynton III, but everyone called him Dash because he began every enforcement call by saying "Dash it
all." Then in discussing the situation, which was always
done in person, he frequently said, "I'll be dashed." Despite
all the dashes, everyone knew he meant "Get in line or else
you're finished."

Alex had O.D.'d on television during his formative years
and had conceived an image of a mob enforcer—a tough
guy with a silencer on his Magnum. Dash Boynton didn't fit
the profile, because Intelco's power was so great that it
rarely had to resort to violence.

The most violent incident during Dash's forty-four-year
tenure as the cartel's enforcer had happened when he and
an errant diamond broker had been walking on the eleventh
hole at Gleneagles, discussing the dealer's questionable
practices. The broker, no doubt nervous as hell, had tripped
in one of the Old Course's "pot bunkers" notorious for
swallowing golfers whole. He'd broken his knee. Not exactly

what the mob meant by breaking someone's knees, but then the British were so much more civilized than the Italians.

"Intelco isn't so smart, Lev. We can fool them."

Lev smiled, his eyes solemn, trusting. Too trusting. With Vic gone, the only person who meant anything to Alex was Lev. And Lev trusted Alex more than he should.

"Let's consider what might happen if you become involved, Lev. You've been safe in Israel."

Over centuries Jews had traded diamonds, always knowing that if they were forced to leave a country, they could take their assets with them because diamonds could easily be hidden. In most countries, not only were the Jews diamond brokers, but they were cutters and setters as well. With the settlement of Israel, an astronomical amount of talent had centered in one country. One more Ukrainian Jew in the Israeli diamond business wouldn't attract attention. No one would ask dangerous questions.

"If you work for me," Alex said, "setting fancies, we'll attract a lot of attention. Someone might pry into your background and discover who you really are. I don't want to put your life in danger."

"I know risk. I want to work with fancies . . . I want to work with you. I will take the chance."

"I'll protect you," Alex assured him, still not comfortable with the situation. Had he known Vic had made a deal for fancies, Alex would never have sent for Lev. But he understood Lev's willingness to take the risk. Working with fancies was a once-in-a-lifetime opportunity.

"No one must discover we aren't enhancing these diamonds," Alex said. "It'll be difficult to keep it a secret from the designer Lamont. Let's find out where he is and talk to him. Then I'll have a better idea how to handle him." Alex buzzed Eula Mae, thinking Vic probably loved those pits. "Where's Lamont?"

"On the way to Annapurna."

"Nepal? He's going trekking in Nepal?"

"She," Eula Mae corrected, looking puzzled over the confusion. "Brett loves to trek. She took Amy—"

"Brett?" Alex almost gagged on her name. Badgers, bras, Brett. "Not Brett Payne?"

"W-well," Eula Mae stammered, wondering what was wrong, "she is Jock's daughter, but she uses her mother's name. It's Lamont, an old Scottish name."

"Why the hell doesn't she use her real name?" Damn Brett. She'd tricked him, never once mentioning she was Belage's designer. Why not? What was going on here?

Eula Mae cast a nervous glance in Lev's direction, astounded Alex was so angry about Brett. Without her, Belage would have been forced to close months ago. "Brett doesn't speak to her father, and Brett's mother had a famous name so . . ."

"Who is her mother?" he asked, cursing himself for not asking Vic more questions about Belage.

"Constance Lamont died about four years ago. You must have heard of her. She raised funds for Greenpeace, CARE, Save the Children, and other organizations. You couldn't turn on the telly without seeing her asking for donations."

Now it made sense. Vic had always been a sucker for a pretty face. Brett with her sharp wit had captivated Uncle Vic. The entire evening Alex had spent with her, he'd known she wasn't being straight with him—about anything. He didn't give a rat's ass about her personal life. But she'd said she was going on a trip. The Himalayas—bullshit. No doubt she was in Paris or Antwerp or even New York. With her talent, she could get a job as a designer anywhere.

6

On the Trail to Annapurna I

The roof of the world, Amy Conrift mused, admiring the millions of crystal-white stars blazing in an ebony dome arcing from horizon to horizon. It was almost as if they were part of the sky themselves. They were awesomely high, but not as high as Annapurna, her snow-capped peak a glistening diadem against the heavens.

Amy found the towering peaks, the windswept heights, oddly comforting, heralding nature's majesty and reminding her that her troubles were minor. She'd loved—and lost—just as countless women had before her. She gazed up at Annapurna, realizing this trip marked a new beginning—without Ellis Payne.

"I think I'm getting crotch rot," Amy said, to get Brett's attention. During the long flight from London and the days on the trail, Brett had been unusually quiet.

"There's baby powder in my pack. Sprinkle it on your thighs and your—" Brett sat up and clamped her hand over her mouth. "Oh, my God, I almost said 'privates' the way Ruthless would."

Amy laughed. Now this was the old Brett.

"Seriously, I warned you not to wear your shorts too

tight. All that chafing and perspiring is nothing but trouble. Put extra powder on yourself tonight, and sleep without pajamas, just socks and a hat. You'll be warmer than you were last night and better by morning."

Inside their tent, Amy crawled into her sleeping bag and removed all her clothes except for her socks. She accepted the powder from Brett and rubbed a bit on her inner thighs. She didn't actually have crotch rot, just chafed thighs from her walking shorts. Yanking the hat, a knit version of something the Red Baron might have worn, over her long brown hair, she said, "I hope no one yells 'fire' and we have to run for it. Those Frenchmen will be hysterical when they see these outfits."

"Aren't you warmer?" Brett said from her sleeping bag nearby.

"Yes," Amy reluctantly admitted. "Your mother knew what she was talking about. Keep your head and feet warm and the down will take care of the rest."

"You bet she did. The year she spent in Nepal with the deforestation project taught her a lot."

The *chamri,* yak milk and whiskey they'd had after dinner and the altitude made Amy feel light-headed. Almost happy. "Do you know the first thing your mother said to me when I met her? 'There were no women at the Last Supper, but there will be at the next—and Jews, too.' "

Brett giggled. "Mother was never too good at details. It must have slipped her mind that they were all Jews, but she was dedicated. She leapt on the feminist bandwagon the minute it got rolling and never got off." She sighed. "And a lot of other bandwagons."

"She'd be proud to see the reforestation working. The natives are still burning firewood, but at least they're replanting."

Brett didn't answer, so Amy tried to sleep. She struggled not to think of Ellis honeymooning in a villa in Marbella. She heard Brett turning over, twisting in her sleeping bag. "Brett, what's bothering you?"

A moment of silence. "Oh, Amy, I did something incredibly foolish and I've been feeling guilty ever since. Remember, I told you about meeting Alex Savich at the wedding?"

"Yes." The description of the American who'd inherited controlling interest in Belage had glowed in the dark.

"I invited him home for dinner. The next thing I knew, I was kissing him. If Timmy hadn't interrupted us, I would have thrown Alex down on my kitchen table and—"

"Not on that tiny table."

"You know what I mean. I wanted—really wanted—to—to—" She took a deep breath. "Sheer willpower kept me from it. Even so, I let the situation go too far."

"He could have forced himself on you," Amy said grimly, stunned that Brett would be so foolish. "That's often how date rape—"

"I know. I know. I'm lucky he was a gentleman. He left in a huff, but he did leave." Brett let out a long sigh. "I don't know what happened to me. What would Owen say if he knew—"

"Don't feel guilty. You had a perfectly natural reaction to an attractive man. It's been, what?—almost four years—since Owen disappeared. How long are you going to wait?"

"Forever, if necessary," Brett said, and Amy heard the threat of tears in her voice. "Owen is Timmy's father. I can't give up on him until I'm certain he's not alive."

While Amy admired her friend's loyalty, she considered it unrealistic in light of the facts. Owen Northcote, an executive with Project Hunger, had disappeared in the Peruvian jungle while on his way to interview the *senderos,* Communist guerrillas. His body had never been found, but reports claimed he'd died in gun battle between the government and the guerrillas.

"Right now, Hugh MacLeod is in Lima checking into a rumor that the Dutch worker, Eekelen Willem, who was with Owen when he disappeared, is in a prison in the South."

Amy liked Hugh, an old friend of Brett's mother. He

worked for Amnesty International and his inquiries had kept Brett from mortgaging everything she owned to find Owen. If Amnesty's underground sources couldn't find Owen, no one could. Amy considered her next words carefully. "Don't get your hopes up."

"I'm trying not to—that's why I haven't mentioned it. I told Hugh to wire me as soon as he speaks with Willem. He knows I'm up here. If Hugh finds out anything, he'll send word."

Kathmandu, Nepal: American Express Office

By midnight, most runners went home. Few messages for tourists came in so late, but Terai sat on his haunches, Eastern style, smoking *bidi* with several old men who had no place to call home. Once he would have been on the trail, Mount Everest as his deity, but Terai was old, they said, too old to lead trekkers. Too old to be a *sherpa*. He was reduced to waiting, hoping for a job as a message runner that would earn him the few *mohor* it took to keep alive.

"*Daai,*" said the clerk behind the counter.

"*Baabu,*" Terai answered, meaning *father* although it was merely a term of respect. His father, a *sherpa* also, had died so many years ago that Terai had forgotten what he looked like.

"*Annapurna maa samaachaar pathaaunos,*" the clerk said. An urgent message for someone on the trail to Annapurna I. Terai tried not to look excited. This delivery could earn him enough money—after giving the clerk a generous bit of *baksheesh*—to tide him over if he didn't get another job for weeks. At his age, it became more and more difficult to find work.

Going top speed, his patched boots slogging in the mud of the waning monsoon season, Terai needed three days to catch up with the party. Once he could have done it in two. Easily.

Terai reached the encampment and approached the *sidar*,

the head *sherpa*. *"Sanchai,"* he said. *How are you?* Then
gave him the traditional greeting by holding his fingers at
chin height and touching his palm to the *sidar*'s. If he didn't
show proper respect, Terai would be reported to the clerk at
the American Express office and never work again. The
sidar, too, would expect a little *baksheesh.*

Terai showed him the message pouch, the writing in both
English and Nepali. The *sidar* jerked his head in the direction of the *charpi.* The small tent, set far away from the
main cluster of tents, had a trekker's hat on top of it, signaling someone was inside using the black pot the lowliest of
the porters carried. Only the foreigners, who crudely tried
to shake your hand with their right hand, used the tent.
Natives preferred the rocks.

Out of the tent came a woman with long curly hair, dark
like the earth, and eyes the color of the sky above the Himalayas. She took her hat off the top of the tent, showing the
facility was now free, and plopped it on her head.

"Hajur," he called and she turned. He handed her the
message.

Amy read Brett's name on the pouch, then raced through
the camp and found Brett on the far side of the encampment at the *mani* wall. It was one of several religious monu-
ments along the trail that had been constructed with rocks
inscribed by passing pilgrims, each adding a stone to form
the wall. Brett and Amy had used a Swiss Army knife to
carve their message, peace and love, into their stone. Then
Brett had stood on tiptoe and placed it on the top row.

The messenger dogging her every step, Amy handed
Brett the message. "It's from Hugh. Open it. Hurry." Amy
bounced up and down on the balls of her feet, almost stepping on the old man.

"Amy, he needs a tip. He's come all the way from Kathmandu," Brett said as she took the envelope, her hands
trembling. *"Tapaaiko naam ke ho?"* Brett asked his name.

"Terai," he answered, staring at the fair-haired woman,
wondering how the *sidar* had confused the two women.

True, all Westerners looked alike, but Terai had never made such a mistake. He'd memorized every trekker's name and face even though few had asked his name, calling him *sidar,* leader, instead.

Amy dashed to their tent, whipped back the flap, and found her money belt. She grabbed a one-hundred-rupee note. She mentally converted the bill; less than two pounds, a hefty tip for a London cab ride but nothing for a climb in these mountains. She pulled out several more bills, enough to tip a cabbie taking you to Heathrow in a downpour, and raced back to where Brett stood, the unread message still in her hand.

"Dhanyabhad, Terai," Brett said as Amy shoved the money into the old man's hands. "Thank you."

Counting his money, Terai walked to the *mani* wall. He touched a stone, one near the bottom. When he was a young man, full of hope and dreams long since abandoned, he'd carved it, gazing up at the snow-clad peaks he loved, and placing it there.

"Dhanyabhad," he said in thanks. Now he could make it through the winter—if no one found out about the money he had earned. And slit his throat for the fortune he had just hidden in his boot.

Amy saw the look of pain on Brett's face and quickly put her arm around her friend, fearing the worst. "Has Hugh MacLeod located that Dutch worker who'd been traveling with Owen?"

"No. He didn't find Eekelen Willem." Her voice was unsteady. "Hugh discovered a reporter who saw Owen and Eekelen killed during a shootout between government troops and the *senderos.*"

"Did he say when this happened?"

"About a week after Owen and Eekelen disappeared."

"Why did he wait all this time?" Amy couldn't keep the anger out of her voice. Brett had lived these past four years waiting, hoping. Praying.

"He was afraid someone would kill him or his family."

Brett moved away from Amy, her eyes on the ominous clouds swirling around Annapurna's peaks. "Maybe I should go there and speak with this reporter myself—to make sure."

"If he's afraid, he might not even see you or talk to you. Hugh MacLeod is convinced this man's telling the truth. That should be enough proof. Besides, this story confirms the rumors you'd heard when Owen disappeared."

"True, but I can't help feeling I should do something."

"You've done everything possible. Now you have to accept the truth."

"Why?" Brett gazed up at Annapurna, which was sheathed by clouds with leaden underbellies. "Why did two good people—people who were trying to make the world better—have to die in Peru?"

"A horrible coincidence. Your mother and Owen were both in the wrong place at the wrong time, that's all." Brett's mother had been killed in a traffic accident outside Lima the day after Owen disappeared.

Brett turned to Amy, tears welling up in her eyes. "Oh, Amy, what am I going to do?"

Amy put her hand on Brett's arm and said, "Think of Timmy."

Her son's smiling face, his wide green eyes duplicates of hers, came instantly to Brett's mind. But instead of cheering her as Amy intended, thinking of Timmy only saddened Brett more. "Now he'll never know his father."

"It'll be up to you to teach Timmy what his father stood for, the kind of man he was."

"You're right. Most men are only interested in money and power. Owen dedicated his life to helping others."

"At least the horrible uncertainty is gone," Amy said. "Now you know what happened to him."

Brett nodded, her future shimmering before her like a mirage, out of focus, out of reach—except for her son. Timmy, Owen Northcote's legacy, all that was left of a great man.

"Hajur." The *sidar* motioned for them to join the trekkers. While they'd been talking, the porters had readied the gear for the day's trek. Amy saw the old man still stood at the *mani* wall, his eyes, like Brett's, trained on Annapurna I.

"You go on," Brett said, looking around. "I'll catch up. I want to add a stone to the *mani* wall—for Owen."

"You're not staying here alone."

"I'm going to ask Terai to stay with me. He can guide me to the next camp. He's an experienced *sherpa,* you know."

So much like her mother, Amy thought. Brett could talk to a cigar-store Indian and get his life story in twenty seconds. Reluctantly, Amy hoisted her day pack and followed their party. Brett was stubborn; there was no point in arguing with her. She would be safe. The trail was easy to follow.

Terai still stared at the mountain peaks, but when Brett explained what she wanted, he agreed with a toothless smile.

"Now you know the truth," she said to herself, hunting for a stone to carve and add to the *mani* wall. "You won't feel so helpless because you can't find Owen."

The words brought a small measure of comfort. She located a stone with a flat surface and sat on a boulder. Using her Swiss Army knife, Brett began to engrave Owen's name in the rock.

Over the years, she'd prepared herself for the possibility that Owen might not return. His death wasn't the unexpected, mind-numbing shock her mother's had been. Still, his memory haunted her, the intense ache deep and overwhelming.

She forced herself to concentrate. She carved Owen's name into the rock, head bent, hunched over the stone, his dear face clearly etched in her mind. Silence. Comforting silence enveloped her, interrupted only by the sound of her knife on the stone and the occasional rush of the wind gusting through the mountain passes and whistling down the sheer ridges.

She worked for hours, Terai at a discreet distance, until

she'd scraped Owen's name into the rock. Then she rose, her legs stiff from sitting for so long, and walked to the *mani* wall. On tiptoe she placed the stone on the top row facing Annapurna I.

She dashed down the side trail she and Amy had taken the previous evening, stopping at the turnout where she knew the steep walls would echo her words to the heavens.

The rising wind lifted her hair from her shoulders and sent streamers flying back from her face. "OWEN," she called. A moment's pause, then Annapurna echoed back: Owen . . . Owen . . . Owen . . . wen . . . wen . . . en . . .

His name trailed off, bouncing back and forth between the sheer rocks. Finally she heard nothing but the lonely forsaken wail of the wind.

7

Brett rode the creaky old elevator to Belage's offices, filled with a sense of anticipation. Last night, after returning from Nepal, she'd called Eula Mae, expecting the secretary to tell her that Alex Savich had decided to close Belage Diamonds. Instead, Eula Mae told Brett about all the improvements Alex had made, including hiring a diamond cutter and setter who used a laser. A host of innovative designs—possible only with a laser setting—flipped through Brett's head.

With the proper direction, Belage would move to the forefront of jewelry design, and Brett's creations would be featured at exclusive stores. She'd been so elated at the prospect she'd been unable to sleep. But a dark cloud hovered over her thoughts, her hopes. Alex Savich.

Brett stepped from the elevator and entered the vestibule, smiling as Eula Mae pressed the buzzer. The office had been painted a soft gray that echoed the new charcoal carpeting. Botanical prints framed in gleaming chrome decorated the walls; Lucite frames with Eula Mae's prize ribbons flanked a multitiered greenhouse window. Everywhere there were ferns, some hanging from the ceiling, others in stands along the walls and in the corners where they concealed stereo speakers crooning soft music. A new sofa in a geometric print of black on gray had replaced the old one.

"Everything looks terrific," Brett said to the beaming Eula Mac, who was obviously in her element—a greenhouse. "I brought you something." Brett produced a plastic bag with a gnarled nutlike ball inside.

"A pit?" Eula Mae asked as if the present surprised her. Whenever Brett went anywhere, even if just for the weekend, she brought Eula Mae a pit. This one, of course, was special. It had come from halfway around the world. "What is it?"

"I'm not telling," Brett answered as she always did when she gave Eula Mae a pit. "You'll have to find out for yourself."

"It's like nothing I've ever seen," Eula Mae said, an unmistakable note of reverence in her voice. "I may have to consult the members of the Rare Plant and Pit Council to identify this one. It's from Nepal. That makes it easier."

Brett didn't answer. Technically the pit had been bought in Nepal's *bajaar,* but the plant was native to India's jungles and had been brought to the market by traders Terai knew. Brett calculated that it would take the council weeks to identify it, making Eula Mae the center of attention and envy.

"Alex asked to see you the moment you came in," Eula Mae said, tilting her head toward Ellis's office.

"Is Ellis here yet?" she asked, thinking the month was up and he must have returned too.

Eula Mae rolled her eyeballs toward the banjo fern hanging from the ceiling. Ellis rarely came in before noon, although Brett observed industry hours. No doubt, Alex had come in even earlier, contacting Antwerp to receive the daily quote on D-flawless one-carat diamonds, the industry standard. Since Belage used so much gold, he'd probably telephoned to get the price of gold, which was set each morning in London by Amy's father's company, Conrift Bullion.

She knocked on his door, and Alex called for her to come in. As casually as she could manage, she walked into the office, her winning smile on her face. "Hello."

No response. His dark head was bent over a stack of papers and he was writing quickly. He wore an expensive suit which, unlike the dinner jacket, fit perfectly, and a patterned tie that probably was considered conservative in Los Angeles but was racy by British standards.

Had she really been in this man's arms? Had she returned his kisses as passionately as she'd ever kissed anyone? Had she almost . . . "I'm back." She forced a teasing note into her voice.

He raised his head and studied her, the strong planes of his face tempered by the agate blue of his eyes. She kept smiling though she couldn't help noticing the relaxed attitude he'd had on the night of the reception had vanished, replaced by a diamond broker's noncommittal expression. His eyes were every bit as intense as they'd been on the night they met, but they seemed to flare with a hint of ruthlessness she hadn't noticed then.

"Is that supposed to make me happy?"

"Well, Elizabeth Gage was hoping I'd get lost in the Himalayas." She managed to keep smiling as she named London's premier jewelry designer. Of course, Elizabeth Gage hadn't a clue who Brett Lamont was, but one day that would change.

"You intend to continue working here?"

"Well," she hedged, "I was waiting to see what your plans for Belage were."

"Produce jewelry for first-class stores."

Brett continued to smile; this time the smile came from within. Being a world-renowned designer. Her dream. A dream that—until Alex Savich inherited Belage—had seemed like a distant star, faraway and untouchable. Here was her chance: laser-set jewels, the most innovative designs in the industry. With luck one day Brett Lamont's name would be mentioned right along with other female designers like Elizabeth Gage, Paloma Picasso, and Elsa Peretti. "Great. I'm ready to—"

"What I don't need is a flaky designer."

It took a full second for his words to register, and when they did, anger like invisible lightning arced through her. "Flaky?"

Alex waved a file folder at her, his expression still controlled, his voice level. "This is your personnel file. According to this, you took off"—he flipped it open—"six days for Horns of the Dilemma. Then four days for Save the Bison. A-maz-ing how much time— three hours here, a half day there—you spent on the Badger Preservation Society."

"Horns was a protest at the Japanese Embassy, calling for them to stop buying ivory, endangering elephants. The badgers—"

"I've heard about the badgers ad nauseam. The point is— you take too much time from work—"

"Ellis gave me permission."

"He would, not bothering to work more than a three-hour day himself, but I need a full-time designer, not some flake—"

"I'm not a flake." Really, she hated American slang. "There was nothing for me to do here. We didn't have any orders. The sales representative Ellis hired couldn't seem to sell our line."

Alex didn't respond, he just kept staring at her, his expression not revealing what he might be thinking.

"Not only do I design, I'm the goldsmith here as well. I've also done some selling. I found Purvis Keir, the buyer from Harvey Nichols who's interested in our line."

"I know all about your . . . talents. I—"

"Look, if this is about what happened after the wedding, I apologize. I—"

"Forget that night. I have. This company is facing bankruptcy. That's what concerns me. I can't afford a genetic do-gooder and a mama's boy who has no intention of doing an honest day's work. I'm firing Ellis."

"You can't do that! He owns twenty percent of this company."

"Yes. I can." He gestured toward several boxes in the corner of the redecorated office. "His things are packed. He can go home and live off—what's her name? Daphne. Lady Daphne."

"Daphne doesn't have pots of money—just a title."

"C'mon. The florist bill at their wedding surpassed the GNP of any banana republic. The food—"

"My father paid for the wedding. Jock did it to appease Ruth, to let her impress her relatives by marrying her son in style. If Ellis loses his job, he won't have any money—"

"Your father can—"

"He won't. Father warned Ellis that Belage was the last business he'd finance for Ellis. If it failed, Ellis would have to find another job himself."

Alex continued gazing at her, his expression remaining the same. "If Belage has any hope of surviving, it can't carry dead weight. Ellis goes. Once we're making money, he's entitled to twenty percent of the profits."

"You can't do that. He started this company." She spun around and rushed out the door. "If Ellis goes, I go."

"You blew it," Alex muttered to himself, staring at the door as it slammed behind Brett. Belage couldn't function without a designer, but it couldn't afford to carry dead weight like Ellis Payne either. What was he supposed to do now? Beg her to stay?

He rose and walked to the window. Outside, the carbon-colored sky promised more showers. Not again. The weather matched his mood, which had been increasingly despondent since Vic's death. Vic. That old coot had done it again, Alex thought, experiencing a surge of affection mixed with frustration. Vic had deliberately maneuvered him into leaving Los Angeles to live in London. Vic was too savvy by far to have been fooled into thinking all Belage needed was a little financial fine-tuning, which was Alex's forte. No, Vic had wanted Alex out of L.A.—permanently.

Vic had deliberately chosen Belage, and sunk their hard-earned money into a company that had but one asset, its designer. Okay, Vic had seen how valuable Eula Mae was, too, but Brett had been his primary target. Vic must have adored her, not just professionally but on a personal level. Definitely. They were two of a kind: storytellers, jokers.

And stubborn as hell. It was a dead heat to see who was more stubborn—Vic or Brett. Granted, he didn't know Brett well. His experiences with her so far had been a clash of hormones, and now a clash of egos. But he sensed her inflexibility.

"You'd think one wild card in a lifetime would be enough," Alex said to the rain that began to splatter the window. As much as he loved Vic—and he missed him more each day—he could be a pain in the butt sometimes. Letting pushy-pretentious Ruth think he was a Russian noble. Alex couldn't help grinning. What a character!

Brett Lamont, though, didn't make him smile. A month was a long time to wait, hoping she had been trotting around the Himalayas, not job hunting. Eula Mae assured him that Brett would return, but he hadn't expected her nonchalant attitude. *I'm back,* she'd joked as if she'd just returned from lunch. Then, when faced with the facts about her job performance, she'd gotten all huffy. True, he'd called her a flake—not the best choice of words, considering she was a talented goldsmith as well as a designer—but he did have a point about her work habits.

Aw, hell. If he had a prayer of resuscitating Belage, he needed Brett. Vic had spotted her talent immediately, but like many artists, Brett was unfocused. How was that for a better word than *flaky*? *Unfocused.* Yeah, sounded good. Now if only he could manage to persuade her to stay at Belage without Ellis.

Apparently she was as loyal as she was unfocused. She'd gone out of her way to harass Ellis on his wedding day, yet jumped to his defense the moment Alex threatened to fire him. She definitely heard the beat of a different drummer.

Alex reflected for a moment on what Eula Mae had told him about Timmy's father. Brett was loyally waiting for him, not seeing other men, even though most people were convinced the reporter was dead. Don't think about her personal life. It's none of your damn business—just persuade her to stay at Belage.

"This place looks *smah*-shing."

Alex turned and saw pushy-pretentious Ellis Payne walking into the office. Dressed as a counterspy, he wore a trench coat with the collar turned up and a hat with the brim pulled low concealing his dark hair and shadowing his blue eyes. Ellis extended his hand, and Alex shook it firmly as Ellis put his other hand over Alex's. Why did he always shake with both hands? Maybe he free-lanced as a born-again preacher.

"I have good news," Ellis said, shedding his undercover gear to reveal a typical British sports jacket that looked as if it had been loomed from straw. "I've always loved the weather, you know. I'm fascinated by cloud formations."

"I hope that isn't the good news."

Brett rushed into her office and stopped, seeing the panther mounted on the wall staring at her, his yellow-green eyes, frozen for eternity by a taxidermist in Nairobi, mocking her. What on earth had possessed her to quit the opportunity of a lifetime over that lughead, Ellis? Why, after the way he'd treated Amy, no one would blame Brett for tossing him to that shark, Alex Savich. But had she done it? No. Maybe Alex was right. She was a genetic do-gooder, inheriting a fondness for the underdog, the oppressed, from her mother.

She sank into the chair at her drawing board, automatically picking up her pencil. No, she reflected, sketching one of the designs she'd dreamed about last night, she'd defended Ellis because he deserved her loyalty. She might hate him for what he'd done to Amy, but Brett owed Ellis.

He'd persuaded Jock to lend him the money to buy Belage, not because Ellis had any interest in making jewelry, but because she did. Her pride had kept her from asking her father for the money—she knew she could get Ellis to do it.

Alex had called her a flake. What cheek. She put the finishing touches on the brooch she'd sketched, wondering where she'd find another job.

"Gut. Very gut."

Brett turned and found a man with somber brown eyes and thick curly hair looking over her shoulder at her sketch. From his accent, she assumed he was the new cutter. "I'm Brett Lamont."

"Lev Rodynskov," he said, with a slight accent. "I wait to meet you. We worried you had found other job."

"Really? Alex was worried?" Her spirits lifted. He hadn't intended to fire her, but, of course, she'd opened her mouth and quit. Was there any graceful way of changing her mind? She wanted this chance.

"Would you like to see enhancer?" Lev asked.

"Enhancer?" she asked, still struggling with the problem of how to handle Ellis.

"Did not Alex tell you?" he asked, his expression guarded.

"There's so much new here," she said with a smile, "I can't keep track of everything. Show me the enhancer."

"Let us wait for Al—"

"Nonsense. He's too busy. Show me."

Lev led her down the hall to the cutting room. He opened the door with a security card-key, the type hotels used. Lev stepped back for her to enter, then carefully closed the door. Inside on the table she saw what appeared to be a large box with an unusually thick blanket covering it.

"You must keep this secret," Lev cautioned her. "Somebody might steal our idea."

"Have you filed for a patent?"

Lev shrugged noncommittally as he dragged the blanket

off. "Lead," he explained, dropping it to the floor with a thunk.

"A lead blanket?" She stared at the contraption, a bulky box with a tiny window in the door.

"We use the blanket to"—Lev paused, searching for the right word—"protect against radiation."

"You're X-raying diamonds?" She'd heard of the technique, of course, but hadn't thought it was particularly successful.

Lev nodded and pulled open a drawer in the worktable, revealing a number of *briefkes*. "Look."

The first packet contained an oblong gem the color of the purple sage that grew at the base of Annapurna. It had the same grayish cast to it because the diamond had yet to be cut or polished, but she knew it would have the rich purple of an amethyst but with the sparkling intensity only a diamond possessed. "Magnificent. Truly magnificent."

The rest of the *briefkes* contained colored diamonds that were just as impressive. Fancies were the current rage in the diamond market. If her designs featured colored diamonds —*and* were laser-set—they'd be noticed immediately. She could easily become famous within a short time instead of the years it took most designers. Vic had been correct— Alex Savich was an innovator. With him in charge, Belage would vault to the forefront of the industry.

Why had she so impulsively quit? Why for once, just once, hadn't she controlled her temper and kept her mouth shut? Part of her wanted to scream *To hell with Ellis*. Another side of her couldn't quite bring herself to jettison the stepbrother who'd tagged along at her heels since the day Jock married Ruthless.

Ellis wasn't a bad person; he honestly wasn't. Ruth had coddled him, that was all. Thirty-five was a bit late to get the boot out of the nest. Jock probably wouldn't have kicked him out then, but Belage was Ellis's ninth failed venture in a decade. Surely there was a niche for Ellis somewhere.

"Brett," Eula Mae called, "Alex wants to see you."

"Ellis is with Alex," Eula Mae said when Brett stepped into the hall. "What goes on in that room?"

Eula Mae didn't know about the enhancer. She'd been the backbone of Belage for years. It was difficult to believe that they'd been able to keep this a secret from her. "Lev uses a laser to set the stones. He has his equipment in there."

"Would you like to have dinner with Timmy and me tonight?" Brett asked, deliberately changing the subject. She'd intended to tell Eula Mae about Owen when she'd spoken to her last evening, but she'd been too drained after explaining to Timmy that his father was in heaven along with his grandmother.

"Thanks awfully," Eula Mae said, squeezing her hand and nudging her toward Alex's door.

"Brett." Alex welcomed her with a shark's smile.

What cheek. First he's Mr. Iceberg. Now we're friends.

"Ellis has great news." Alex's tone was lighthearted as it had been on the night of the wedding, making her even more wary.

"Really?" she asked, noting her stepbrother's broad smile.

"I've been offered a position," Ellis said proudly.

Brett let out an inaudible sigh of relief, hoping Alex didn't notice. There was a God.

"Twickham Brashgood was staying at the villa next to ours in Marbella. He's offered me a ripping good position replacing Sonny Withers."

"Isn't he the weatherman on Channel eleven?"

"Righto. He's on at five, nine, and eleven."

"But you don't have any experience. You don't know—"

Alex cut in. "How many ways are there to say rain?"

Brett could have hit Alex, but Ellis looked puzzled. "Alex, there are many ways to tell the viewers to expect precipitation: drizzle, heavy mist, showers, thundershowers" —Ellis appeared baffled for a moment—"sprinkles, a downpour—"

"Brett, I've made your brother an offer, a cash settlement now and a percentage of the profits later. Isn't that fair?"

"Yes." She had no choice but to agree. Who knew? Television might be perfect for Ellis.

"I've got to dash," Ellis said, hopping up. "They're expecting me at the station. I'll send for my things."

"I'll walk you out." She'd wanted to talk to Ellis at the wedding reception, but Alex Savich had sidetracked her. When they were outside the office, she said, "I put the fear of God into you at the wedding, didn't I?"

"You gave me a start." Ellis waved good-bye to Eula Mae, who apparently already knew the "good news." He walked through the security door into the vestibule.

"Amy will get over you," Brett said, hoping she was right. Amy was far too intelligent, too ambitious for Ellis. His wife, Daphne, was pliant, even simpering, totally in awe of Ellis.

"You married a woman you didn't love," Brett said, her words echoing eerily in the domed marble vestibule reminding her of Annapurna repeating Owen's name. "You'll be sorry. I'll have the last laugh."

She pecked him on the cheek, then turned and signaled for Eula Mae to let her in again. She swept into the reception area and saw Alex with one wide shoulder wedged against the doorjamb of his office, filling the doorway, his presence pervading the room as he watched her.

"C'mere." He stepped aside. "We have something to settle."

8

Brett warily allowed Alex to usher her into his office and close the door, his stride precise, his bearing almost martial. He'd spent time in the military or had trained as a professional athlete, she thought, hoping he didn't expect her to apologize for siding with Ellis because she had no intention of doing so. Keep quiet until you hear what he has to say, she warned herself.

Their eyes met and held; she sensed a determination in him that left her off-balance. The diamond dealers she knew dropped that inscrutable expression when they weren't negotiating—but not Alex. Unlike his uncle, Vicktor Orlov, who'd been a diamond broker his entire life, Alex didn't joke or laugh, which would have effortlessly put people at ease.

"Brett, we need each other. I need a designer to work with Lev, and you won't find an opportunity like this anywhere."

She nodded her agreement, not anticipating his being so direct, but noting his tone was not conciliatory. Even so, she sensed the tension between them had altered subtly. She suspected he regretted their earlier confrontation as much as she did, and she sensed he'd be damned before he apologized, too.

"You can be a top-name designer in no time if we—that's all of us here at Belage—work damn hard. There's no room for someone who doesn't pull her weight. I can't have you dropping everything to go to some demonstration."

"I won't." She refused to let his curt tone upset her.

"I don't want to see your name in print except in Belage advertisements. I intend to build your reputation as a designer. It's important to keep focused on your profession. When people hear 'Brett Lamont,' I want them to think of jewelry, not badgers. I don't want you in jail. No matter how noble the cause, the public views breaking the law negatively."

She managed a smile, knowing this was the opportunity she'd been praying for since the day she'd walked out on her mother and enrolled in design school, but she resented his dictating how she should live her life. Somehow she managed to keep her mouth shut, resisting the urge to make a cheeky remark.

"A lot of exciting things are going on at Belage."

"Lev showed me the enhancer," she blurted out.

"Really?" A scowl marred his brow. Why hadn't she kept quiet? Obviously, the enhancer required strict security; even Eula Mae knew nothing about it.

She flashed him a smile but it made no impression. "I thought X-raying diamonds produced muddy brown or bilious yellow-green stones. How can you tell what trace elements are in the diamonds to select the ones that will be brilliant colors?"

He tilted back in his chair, folding his arms across his chest.

"I was really impressed with the stones Lev showed me—"

"He *showed* you?" For the first time, Alex raised his voice. "Give me your word you won't mention the enhancer to anyone. Pretend you know nothing about it. I don't want anyone stealing our idea. Your job is designing. Stick to it."

"I won't tell a soul."

Alex rose, walked to the window, and gazed out, although she couldn't imagine what he could see. Rain pummeled the window, falling from an ominous sky that promised a long storm.

"I should have told you at the reception that I was the designer here, but Vic insisted we all promise not to tell you anything about Belage. He wanted you to see for yourself how—"

"*Vic* made you promise?" His searing eyes scanned her face.

"He knew you'd see Belage's potential."

"I see it, all right." His tone sounded odd. She wasn't certain whether he'd agreed with Vic or was cursing him. "Brett, I'm going to level with you. I haven't any money left. We've got to make a profit—fast. So far sales are nonexistent."

"What about the Harvey Nichols account?"

"Purvis Keir is dragging his feet."

"Let me talk to Purvis. I'm certain I can convince him. He'd almost signed the contract for me just before the wedding."

"All right," he said, his tone anything but enthusiastic. "I have another appointment with Keir this Friday. Come with me."

As Brett left his office, Alex rocked back in his chair and let out a sigh of relief. For once things were going as planned. Sure, he was stuck with the wild card, Brett, but getting rid of pushy-pretentious Ellis . . . Trust me, somebody up there must be helping. Had to be Vic.

Alex sent for Lev and welcomed him with a grin. "We fooled Brett. She went for that bull about the enhancer."

They'd agreed to allow Brett to "discover" the enhancer on her own. Alex was to pretend to be upset that Lev had revealed their secret. With luck this ploy would convince Brett that the contraption Lev had rigged up was capable of radiating diamonds. Actually, the damn thing was a prototype for a microwave developed in the late fifties that Lev had found in a junkyard.

"Be certain to keep that security key with you," Alex cautioned Lev. "I don't want Brett checking out that enhancer, or—"

The office door swung open and Brett swept in, smiling, her eyes magnetic, brilliant. "I have a *fantastic* idea for the Harvey Nichols proposal."

"Have you ever heard of knocking?" Alex couldn't quite say it with anger, seeing how damned excited she looked.

"Sorry," she said, unfazed. "I didn't think."

Surprise, surprise.

"Let's make one piece using fancies. I think it'll convince Purvis Keir that he'll have to buy the entire line." She beamed at Lev. "That brooch I sketched this morning, wouldn't it be perfect?"

"Beautiful. Very beautiful." Lev nodded enthusiastically as she chatted on about her idea.

Great. Ten minutes with Lev and she's charmed him. "When did you create this little piece?"

"After I left your office. You inspired me," she said with an insolent smile.

Smartass. At least she's working. "Let me see it."

In a few minutes she returned with the sketch. Her smile had disappeared, replaced by an uncertain look of self-doubt that surprised him. The simple design she'd sketched featured shafts of wheat held together by a free-flowing ribbon.

"The ribbon is polished gold," Brett explained. "The wheat stalks are textured gold, but the kernels of wheat"—she pointed to the starburstlike cluster crowning the stalks—"will be canary-yellow diamonds mixed with clear diamonds."

"Has possibilities." Actually the design was unique and stunning, but he had no intention of admitting just how talented she was until she proved to him she could concentrate on designing. "Could you do a few other sketches using purple, blue, green and pink stones?"

"Not red?" she asked, clearly disappointed. "I know how rare they are, but surely if you can produce all the other colors, you can make red."

"Not for these samples. Maybe another time."

"All right. Do you think these—"

"I'm not promising anything—yet," he answered, again noting her insecurity. "Bring me a few more designs." That should keep her busy for a week at least. If his luck held, two weeks.

She whisked the sketch from his hand and hurried out without closing the door. Alex shut it, shaking his head. Besides the world-class legs and an uninhibited smile, Brett was sharp. Deceiving her about the enhancer wouldn't be easy. How could he explain being able to make every color but red?

"It is a tapestry to cut fancies so small," Lev said.

"It's a travesty, not a tapestry. That's a needlework piece that you hang on the wall. But you're right, it's a damn shame to cut those stones so small. Designs that use smaller stones are the answer to our problem. The cartel will think we bought the tailings from larger, imperfect diamonds. It'll buy us time—and make money, not as much as we'd make using larger stones, but we'll be able to hide what we're doing from Intelco."

"I see," Lev said, not without a trace of remorse. Every cutter longed for the rare stones that could be fired with unsurpassed brilliance by the perfect cut. "Brett wonders why we cannot make red diamonds."

"My answer—to Brett and Intelco, who's bound to ask— we'll make red if we get the right diamond to do it, the one with the exact combination of trace elements."

The next morning Alex arrived and found Eula Mae misting the ferns, raising the humidity inside Belage to the level of the air outside, where it had been raining for days. His mood still matched the weather—thanks to a lonely evening in his condo overlooking the Thames. Couldn't see a damn thing. He'd leased the place to be near the water. It was a piss-poor substitute for Malibu. When it wasn't raining, a Sherlock Holmes fog rolled in, making it impossible to see the water.

Could this really be August? No evenings sitting on the warm sand, watching the sun melting into the Pacific, its fiery splendor reflected in the shimmering waves. So, this is what hell is like. A guy from L.A. sentenced to eternity in the rain.

Last night he'd spent the evening reading industry literature in front of a faux fireplace that was supposed to look like a kiva. It was some harebrained decorator's idea of the Santa Fe look. Within sight of the Tower of London? The realtor even claimed the mural on the living room wall was a famous artist's version of the painted desert. What a crock! Looked like something that had come out of the bottom of a garbage disposal.

Alex had leased the condo because the price was unbelievably low for a unit furnished right down to plates with roadrunners painted on them. Now he knew why. No carpeting, just a few faux Navajo rugs thrown over tile. No curtains—how had the decorator put it?—to *inhibit* the view. Colder 'n hell—and this was supposed to be summer. He needed to find a hot blonde to snuggle with him and discuss the meaning of life.

For some reason he thought of Brett. Never mind, no sense thinking about hopping in the sack with her. She was determined to wait for some man who was probably dead. Forget her. He hadn't thought about her while she'd been gone—ooookay, a few times—except in terms of the business. But having the very lively Brett flitting through the office—talking nonstop—her finger in everything made it impossible to ignore her.

When she was around, he experienced an annoying sensation of excitement. He had to admit her enthusiasm for

Belage was catching. But she had a smart mouth. *You inspired me.* She'd hoot and tease him if she saw the Lucite cactus the decorator had planted in every corner of his condo. And the howling coyote painted on the shower door.

On his desk he found a letter from the mysterious person who owned the colored diamonds, informing him that a representative would be in London in two weeks with an exhibition of hand-painted Ukrainian eggs. He would want an explanation about why he'd yet to receive any money. According to information Alex had received earlier, the second shipment would be delivered with the eggs. Dammit, they'd better not be more colored diamonds. A nice shipment of regular stones would be great. He'd stand a better chance of hiding his activities from Intelco if the stones weren't attention-getting fancies.

As he talked on the telephone, checking Antwerp's fix on D-flawless stones, Eula Mae performed her morning ritual, polishing the fiddle-leaf philodendron that he'd placed in front of the antique safe in hopes of hiding it should any important clients—none on the horizon—decide to visit his office. He hung up and found Eula Mae standing beside his desk gazing intently at him.

Eula Mae wrung the soft cloth she used to polish the plants' leaves, twisting it with both hands. "Brett's received some terrible news. Owen Northcote, her husband, is dead."

"Jesus!" Maybe he'd been too hard on Brett yesterday. The pressure of inheriting a nearly bankrupt business added to the stress of trying to deceive Intelco made him edgy. All right, all right, more than edgy. But even if he'd been a bastard—he wasn't admitting anything—it was only because he'd been worried she'd found another job. It had absolutely nothing to do with the night of the wedding.

Dead.

Eula Mae kept talking, but he hardly heard her. Dead. The word thundered in his brain and with it came the image of Vic, his frail body struggling for each breath. Alex had prayed Vic would die; no one should suffer so much, especially a man who'd changed the course of his life to help a young boy.

Alex had taken off the gold cross Vic had given him on the night he'd found Alex hiding behind his grandmother's door. "Here," he told his dying uncle. "Wear this—for luck."

"Keep it. You're going to need it." Vic closed his eyes, but kept talking. "What am I going to do in heaven without you?"

"Heaven?" Alex forced a joke. "You're bound for hell."

Vic didn't answer. Alex stroked Vic's head; his hair was deceptively healthy, still thick and slightly wavy. They'd fought over where to open their business, but Alex had believed there would always be a chance to make things right. Until now. Was there any real way to take back his angry words? Soothe the hurt. "The question is—what I'm going to do without you? Thank you for . . . for everything."

Alex held Vic's limp hand, squeezing it tight.

Minutes went by, then Vic whispered, *"Alex, you're the best thing that ever happened to me. All I want is for you to be happy."*

An instant later, Alex knew he was gone. He cradled Vic's hand in both of his, saying a silent prayer, thankful his agony was over. But for hours he sat there, continuing to hold Vic's hand.

Vic—the only constant presence in his life—couldn't be gone. Forever.

But he was.

The finality of his death had registered only after Alex moved to London. Then the lonely days and even lonelier nights, when he couldn't call Vic or see him, brought home the reality of his death. And all he'd sacrificed over the years to make certain Alex had a happy life.

He understood how Brett must feel, facing the bleakness of death. She'd loved this man, stubbornly clinging to the hope he might one day return even though everyone else had given up. Now she was faced with the finality. The harsh realities. The loneliness.

And a son. Would having Timmy make it better or worse? Maybe a little of both: a comfort and a reminder.

"I said this job means a lot to Brett," Eula Mae interrupted his thoughts, her brown eyes full of concern.

"Sorry. My mind wandered."

"Vic," she said, her voice low, charged with sympathy.

How could she know? He hadn't mentioned Vic since the first day he came to Belage.

"He just wanted you to be happy."

Her words baffled him. How well had she known Vic? He'd talked about her, sure, but Alex believed their relationship had been strictly professional. "When did he tell you this?"

She deflected his question with a shrug and returned to polishing the plant.

Every time they talked, she mentioned Vic. Where did she get all this? Then it hit him: they'd been lovers. Vic had always kept his private life a closely guarded secret. Even when they'd traveled together, brokering diamonds in Eastern Europe, Vic never discussed his relationships with women other than to say he'd never found one he wanted to marry.

"Alex, look." Brett sailed into his office just as he was opening his mouth to question Eula Mae further. She mumbled "Good morning" to Brett and rushed out of the room.

Brett gave him a sheaf of designs, her expressive green eyes fired with excitement. It dawned on him that she was as adept at concealing her feelings as he was. If Eula Mae hadn't told him, he'd never have suspected Brett was mourning her husband's death.

Alex shuffled the papers, taking a speed of light inventory of Brett: blond hair swept up into a ponytail cocked to one side, the same side as her off-kilter smile. Oversize black sweater that hung almost to the hem of her black suede miniskirt. Long, long legs in black silk stockings.

"You don't like my designs."

Like many artists, she was insecure about her work, overly sensitive. She might show up uninvited at a wedding and brazen it out, but beneath it all her Achilles' heel was her designs. He kept his expression neutral, the way he always did when brokering diamonds. Letting anyone know your true feelings was an open invitation to be royally screwed.

"Give me a chance to look." He pretended to study each of the dozen designs, knowing full well every one was more creative than anything he'd seen in years. "When did you do these?"

"Last night."

One night? All this in one night? He looked up; his gaze met hers, noting that the special brand of turbulence that usually fired her eyes had disappeared. So she passed the lonely hours working, taking her mind off her troubles.

He opened his mouth to tell her how much he liked her designs, but stopped. Oddly enough, praising her might not be the best course. He deliberately took his time sifting through the designs, once, then twice, but never rendering an opinion or even an approving half smile. Let her think I'm very demanding. Let her try as hard as she can every time. Keep her focused.

"Where did you study?"

"At the institute in Milan. I graduated eight years ago. Later I took their correspondence course in laser designs."

"Where else have you worked?" Not that it mattered.

"Just at Belage."

"What were you doing all that time?" Part of him blessed her for waiting, but on another level this reaffirmed what he'd already sensed in her. She didn't have a clue about the magnitude of her own talent.

"After I finished at the institute, my mother needed me in Peru," she said tersely, not adding what he already knew about her mother's tragic death there. "When I returned, I was pregnant. No one would hire me. Then Ellis persuaded Jock to finance the purchase of Belage."

For you. Jock bought Belage for you, not for pushy-pretentious Ellis. Jock Payne hadn't made it up from the black hole of poverty without knowing how to invest his money. What had come between Brett and her father that she couldn't go to him for the money herself instead of manipulating Ellis into doing it?

"I've included the specifications for each piece," she said. "See, this one appears to be three carats when the stones are totaled, but it's less than one and a half."

"Uh-huh." He selected a sketch of a stylized flamingo pin that specified a pink diamond for the body. "Make this larger."

"I thought the diamonds might have a lot of inclusions that would show if I made it larger. Jewelers usually X-ray diamonds to hide their flaws."

"Lev will find something," he responded, reminding himself to watch what he did. Keeping the stones small insured their safety from Intelco. Still, her designs were so unique that he couldn't resist. "Increase the swipe."

She hesitated, then nodded. Broadening the top of a diamond while cutting down on the depth made it appear larger than the actual carat weight. First-class jewelers never cut corners, but then, they weren't faced with bankruptcy. And Intelco.

"Does this mean . . . ?"

He let her hang. Taking his time, he selected four designs and added them to the pile he'd begun with the flamingo. "You and Lev get to work on these."

She picked up the flamingo design. "Really?"

He watched her, fighting the urge to grin. The hand she put on his arm, though, and the knockout smile—disconcerting as hell. "You heard me. Get to work."

"Fantastic."

She looked into his eyes, and a vaguely sensual light passed between them. For a moment he thought she was going to throw her arms around him and hug him. Or kiss him.

9

The telephone on Brett's nightstand beside her bed rang, startling her. She'd fallen asleep with her sketch pad on her lap, her pencil still in her hand. She reached for the receiver.

"Brett?" Amy's voice came over the line. "Turn on the telly quick. Channel eleven."

Brett pressed the remote control. Ellis's face appeared on the screen, larger than life. And twice as handsome.

"Tonight was his first broadcast. I saw him at five and nine. Watch, this is a new format."

The camera pulled away, and Brett saw a map of Britain had been painted on the studio floor. Key cities like London were shown as round discs. Ellis was standing on London.

He popped open a red umbrella, saying, "Don't forget your brolly! Showers tomorrow." Like Mary Poppins, he hopped over to Liverpool, lowered the umbrella, and drew a smiling sun out of his pocket. "Lucky devils, sunny in Liverpool tomorrow with—"

"My God," Brett said. "They've made him a clown."

"But a handsome one." Amy's tone was definitely wistful, and Brett hoped Amy wouldn't spend each evening watching Ellis, wishing he loved her. "They let him do a little 'color.' At the end of the segment, he'll give tomorrow's 'Event of the Day.' In case you're interested, it's a grouse shoot in Scotland to benefit the Retired Fox Hound Kennel in Wyeburn-on-Hammet."

Brett thought Ellis appeared foolish, but she doubted many people would notice. With his looks, he'd have women across the country tuning in and fogging up their television sets. Maybe he'd found his niche at last.

"How are you getting on with Alex?"

"He's all business. That's okay. This is my chance, but I've had to leave Timmy with Mrs. Pruitt every night this week. I'm hoping to spend more time with him after we make our presentation tomorrow at Harvey Nichols."

"Call me and let me know what happens. Remember the showing Saturday night. I'm counting on you to help me hostess."

"I hate to leave Timmy again. I've been working late every night this week."

"Bring him, but be certain he knows not to touch anything."

Brett wondered if they made straitjackets for three-year-olds. It would be insanity to take Timmy to THE FIND. Amy's shop was one of the elegant boutiques off Sloane Square frequented by rich women who devoted their lives to discovering the newest restaurants, the hottest designers, the trendiest shops. The items at THE FIND were one-of-a-kind pieces priced outrageously because Amy had discovered her clientele never appreciated anything unless they overpaid for it.

In the past few years, Amy had gained a reputation for selecting "unique" merchandise from around the world—those special items "one simply must have" in a proper home. In truth, many of the items featured at THE FIND came from Campton Lock, where local artisans sold their goods on the sidewalk, their customers being punk rockers with skull-and-crossbone earrings.

It didn't matter where Amy bought the merchandise she

sold at her store. Anything she showed looked special, exclusive. Not only had Amy mastered the art of merchandising, she recognized the lure of "a happening." Several times a year she would have a showing and dole out invitations to her most select clientele.

Alex followed Brett into the Harvey Nichols store in Knightsbridge. On the ride over they hadn't exchanged more than a dozen words. All too aware of the undercurrent of strain between them, he hardly knew how to talk to her except defensively. In the office he'd often hear her happy chatter as she talked with Eula Mae or Lev, but she never spared him a smile.

Why the hell was he complaining? He wanted Brett to take her work seriously, didn't he? Still, it irritated him that she was the consummate professional with him.

"I'm glad you're not nervous," Brett said as they walked into the executive offices.

Says who? Last night he'd gone over the figures for the tenth time; he'd be out of money in a few months. Sure, he could unload a fancy—and risk a call from Dash Boynton.

Alex adjusted the portable display case he carried like an attaché and assessed Brett without moving his eyes. She'd furled her hair into a businesslike chignon that complemented her tailored navy suit and white blouse. It was a sharp contrast to the short skirts she wore around Belage.

"We have an appointment with Mr. Keir," Alex told the jewelry buyer's secretary, who then disappeared into the adjacent room.

"Don't forget to smile," Brett whispered to him.

You do the smiling, you're better at it, he thought, but he flashed her a grin for the hell of it.

"That's not a smile. All you did was show me your teeth."

"Purvis Keir. Who could name a baby Purvis?"

Brett elbowed him in the ribs as the door opened.

Keir greeted Brett with a smile that made his chin disappear into the folds of his neck. He nodded at Alex. "Mr. Savich."

Keir surveyed Brett with undisguised admiration while adjusting the knot on his silk tie and talking nonstop about the store. The man might have taken first, second, and third in a chin contest, but he fancied himself a ladies' man. Keir was in his early thirties; he kept his brown hair moussed and cut short like a porcupine.

"Let's see what you brought," Keir said, his eyes on Brett.

Alex opened the case. Years ago Vic had told him diamonds showed better against royal blue than black, so this case, unlike those of most jewelers, had been lined in deep blue velvet with a soft nap. The collection, a few pins, a necklace with matching earrings, and a ring, gleamed even under the fluorescent lights.

Purvis Keir stared at the jewelry, then slowly withdrew a loupe from his pocket and held it up to his eye, looking like an old-fashioned duke with a monocle. Brett opened her mouth to say something, but Alex silenced her with a wink. She responded with a disarming smile that left him wondering what she was thinking.

"Fancies. Astonishing designs." He examined the flamingo pin. "Astonishing."

"Look." Brett fastened it to the lapel of her suit.

"Mmm," Keir mumbled; he homed in on the pin with his loupe, concentrating on the pink diamond. "A bit more swipe than—"

"That's what keeps these pieces affordable," Alex cut him off.

"That's the beauty of this collection," Brett added. "It's unique but affordable. A woman wearing one of Belage's pieces will be the envy of her friends without breaking her husband."

"Hmm." Keir again peered at the pin through the loupe. "This stone seems virtually flawless."

"Microscopic flaws," Alex assured him.

"How much?"

Alex gave him the wholesale price while Brett removed the pin and put on a pair of earrings.

"It's a steal," Keir said.

Believe me, it is. "These diamonds are artificially enhanced."

"Enhanced? You mean X-rayed?"

"We want to keep our jewelry small, affordable," Alex said smoothly. "We'll reach a wider market that way."

"Look." Brett modeled the earrings they'd brought. The vibrant green stones caught the meager light and sparkled with an intensity even emeralds couldn't match.

Keir dutifully examined the earrings, letting his gaze meander down her neck to the deep vee of her blouse. Alex resisted the urge to grab his loupe.

Keir turned to Alex. "I'll give you a big order."

Brett beamed, but Alex wasn't celebrating—yet. After years of *hondling* with diamond traders, he knew that tone meant the negotiations were only beginning. Here it comes, the big IF.

"If we can agree to terms," Keir added.

Great, that means we'll finance you, letting you string out the payments over months. He'd expected terms like that, of course, a standard in the industry.

"And advertising budgets." Purvis Keir finished with an encouraging smile at Brett.

Brett, for once, kept her mouth shut, smiling and trying on the necklace for Keir's approval.

Alex had already anticipated this; advertising was usually shared by the store and the manufacturer. He expected a modest campaign, not a splash. "What do you suggest?"

"That depends upon how you plan to market this collection."

Tricky question. To call it the Belage collection would cut Brett out, but to put her name on it would risk letting another bigger manufacturer steal her. Aw, hell, it would be unfair not to give her credit. "We're calling it 'Brett Lamont for Belage' just like it's 'Paloma Picasso for Tiffany.'"

"That's wonderful news," Keir said to Brett.

She smiled at Keir, that totally uninhibited smile, as if *he'd* just uttered the words that would make her career. What could she possibly see in a man with three chins whose name sounded like a suppository?

"Advertisements in all the papers, four-color spots in the trades, radio commercials," Keir said with Brett grinning more—if possible—with every word. "And, of course, a champagne preview party next month when we show the winter collection."

Alex mentally computed the costs. Son of a bitch. He didn't have that much money. Not even close. Brett looked at Alex, her ambition outshining the diamonds dangling from her ears. And that damn smile with its slightly lopsided cant.

"Sure," he heard himself saying. "Sounds great."

"I'll have my solicitor write a contract."

They walked out, Brett matching his long stride. There was only one way of raising the money to fund Belage's half of the advertising campaign. He'd have to sell one of the colored diamonds. Jee-sus! Dash Boynton. Alex would come up against Intelco a hell of a lot sooner than he'd anticipated.

They stepped into the empty elevator and the door slid shut. For a moment they both stared at each other, not quite knowing what to say.

Brett spoke first. "I didn't think you'd promote my name like this. It's fantastic."

"I told you I wanted a top-notch designer."

"I know." She leveled another smile at him, her green eyes wide with disbelief.

He nearly smiled back.

"I just didn't expect it would happen so soon, or on such a large scale," she said.

That makes two of us.

"I'm speechless," she said.

"Thank God."

She kept smiling, her take-no-prisoners smile. He fought a losing battle with a grin and finally surrendered.

The door opened and a couple got in, saying, "Hussein's invasion of Kuwait will mean another rise in petrol prices."

The invasion had taken place yesterday; the morning papers had been full of the story. Alex had carefully read the articles, remembering Israeli diamond traders had warned him about Hussein years earlier. Back then, American diplomats were more concerned with Iran. Shortsighted, like most politicians.

"Do you think Hussein will invade Saudi Arabia too?" Brett asked Alex.

"He's a nut. Who can predict just what he'll do?"

"I don't think the Americans will let him get away with this," Brett said as the elevator reached the ground floor.

Well, maybe. Getting involved in the snakepit of Middle East politics was risky as hell. After Vietnam, who knew?

"I *know* the British won't allow Hussein to take over Kuwait," she added.

Outside it was raining hard, the wind whipping the rain against the buildings; there wasn't a taxi in sight.

Brett opened her umbrella. "Let's dash for the Underground."

Alex took the umbrella from her and held it over both of them. She moved a little closer. "Is something the matter?"

He shook his head. The rain pelted them harder now, buffeted by a frigid wind, so he put his arm around her.

"You're worried that we won't be able to make the pieces in time for the preview, aren't you?"

Believe me, the thought hadn't crossed my mind. "No. You work fast."

"Then, don't worry. Nothing can go wrong."

El Al was probably the only airline in the world where it was impossible to pick up a flight attendant. Security minded; every passenger was a potential terrorist. Oh, well, he was just horny. Concentrate on your problems; they're better than a cold shower. Alex checked his watch, estimating how long until they landed in Tel Aviv, bracing himself for his meeting.

What would Avram Ben-Itzik offer him for the blue fancy Alex wanted to sell? Half of its value—maybe less. Avram would know instantly that Alex was up to his eyeballs in alligators. If he weren't, Alex would be selling the flawless stone, the brilliant sapphire of the Mediterranean, in London or Antwerp.

What choice did he have? His only hope of avoiding the censuring eyes of the cartel was to raise the money he needed for the advertising campaign by unloading a fancy in Israel. The flood of immigrants, and their tendency to bring their life savings in jewelry, would give any broker an explanation for having a fancy.

He leafed through a newspaper, scanning the articles on Saddam's invasion until he saw a picture of Lady Bewley. He read the story and laughed out loud. Lady Bewley and the members of her Committee to Uphold Morals—C.U.M. —had picketed an exhibition of Rodin sculptures on loan from the Louvre. She'd denounced the nudes, claiming them sins of the flesh and "an insult to the moral fiber of the British people."

A lot of moral gibberish and latent fascism. Amazing, though, over five hundred members of C.U.M. had stood in a downpour outside the Tate to protest the exhibition. Maybe Vic had been right. Was the moral pendulum swinging back from an anything-goes attitude to a new level of conservatism?

On the elevator to the top floor of the building in the Ramat Gan, where Avram had his office, Alex rehearsed what he was going to tell the diamond broker. Brace yourself for a low-ball offer. Try to get more money by hinting you might be able to sell him a few more fancies in the future.

Two Hasidic dealers, the most orthodox of Jews, wearing full-length black coats, beards to their chests, and spiral

curled locks beneath black hats, were leaving as Alex passed
through the double set of security doors into the reception
area.

"Sorry to hear about Vic," Avram said, his high brow,
made higher by a receding hairline, furrowed into a frown.
"I'm going to miss him." Avram motioned to a chair. "You
said you had one of Vic's special diamonds for me to see."

Same old Avram; right down to business. Of all the Israeli
diamond brokers Alex knew, he liked Avram the best. He
had a blunt manner, but he could be trusted to keep quiet.
He knew all about Lev, but would never tell.

Alex pulled out the large *briefke* and Avram whistled as
Alex unfolded it and smoothed back the flaps so that the
summer-blue diamond lay in the bright sunlight against the
pure white. The facets Lev had so carefully cut and polished
shot sparks of light across the desk like a Fourth of July
sparkler.

"Mountain of Light," Avram almost whispered the term
experts used to refer to the Koh-i-noor diamond, one of the
British crown jewels guarded in the Tower of London. It was
the centerpiece of the Queen Mother's crown.

Alex had instructed Lev to cut the rough stone for maxi-
mum brilliance, using the connoisseurs' favorite shape, the
oval. Like the Mountain of Light, this extraordinary blue
diamond, the flawless blue of the English sky, gleamed with
an intensity unequaled by any other gem but a diamond. A
fine sapphire from Kashmir might come close, but even to
an untrained eye, the brilliance of a diamond was unmistakable.

"A fancy?" Avram picked up his loupe from its velvet-
lined holder and examined the stone. "Fifteen carats."
Avram looked at Alex, the loupe still held to one eye, magnifying his hazel iris. "Lev cut this. He's a master. He cuts
fast, no?"

It was a rhetorical question. Most diamond cutters "ro-
manced" a stone, checking it from all angles, studying it

sometimes for months before cutting it. Not Lev—he never wasted time with his life or cutting diamonds.

Avram took another look at the gem. "Where did Vic get it?"

"I don't recall him saying exactly."

Avram pulled the loupe from his eye and stared hard at Alex.

Hey, not recalling worked for Richard Nixon.

"It's stolen," Avram said.

There was no greater insult to a diamond broker than to offer him stolen goods, making him part of a dishonest deal in a profession that prized honesty. Sure, dealers haggled, and they took advantage of one another whenever they could, but they didn't lie. A dealer's word had to be unimpeachable.

"To be honest, I don't know where this came from," Alex hedged. "Before Vic died, he told me to expect several shipments. I assumed they'd be regular stones, but they were fancies."

Avram's eyes met Alex's; the Israeli stared intently.

"I know it sounds strange, but Vic wasn't himself in those last months before he died. He never told me who he'd traded with. My guess is that he cut a deal with the Gypsies for the stones."

"Or the Russians. I heard a rumor that they've discovered fancies at their mine near Rostov-on-the-Don."

"Vic would never have traded with the Russians," Alex assured him. "They have an exclusive marketing agreement with Intelco."

"You're right." Avram nodded. "Never mind Dash Boynton. They would call in their Sicilian connection."

Just the thought of what Intelco would do to anyone cutting into their lucrative deal with the Soviets raised the fine hairs across the back of Alex's neck. He didn't mention the Swiss bank account. Somehow Swiss accounts and sending representatives didn't sound like Gypsies, but Alex didn't have a better explanation.

"How much do you want for this stone?"

Alex quoted the current market value, not jacking up the price just to hondle or cutting it, fearing the cartel. "I'm selling it here so you can say you bought it from some desperate immigrant and recut it. That way, Intelco won't question it."

He saw no reason not to be honest. After all, Avram had taken in Lev, then trained him. Since Alex's father had died, Avram was Vic's closest friend. "I need the money."

Avram gazed at the stone, his usual look of detachment replaced by excitement. "I don't have that much cash. How about trading for a few clear diamonds plus cash?"

Alex nodded, already having anticipated getting stuck with a handful of inferior gems. But the stones Avram took from his safe weren't M&Ms; they were top-quality diamonds, a fair exchange when added to the cash Avram had offered. "What's the catch?" Hell, diamond brokers bargained like any rug merchant down at King David's Gate.

"Actually, I'm going to ask you for a favor."

There you go. "Shoot."

"This thing with Hussein could blow up at any minute," Avram said, his eyes earnest, concern in his voice. "I have children and grandchildren here. A wife. A yenta for a mother-in-law. My business has to go on, war or no war."

Interesting problem. One that hadn't occurred to him. Overseas trading would certainly be curtailed by a war.

"As a precaution, I'd like you to store part of my supply. If there's trouble, I'll either come to London and trade out of your facility, or have you do it for me."

"Sure," Alex said, wondering how many Israeli diamond brokers would be this farsighted. Not many. He'd bet most would wait to see how the situation developed before moving the diamonds. One thing was certain, if they did transfer their inventories out of Israel, they wouldn't use banks. Through the centuries, diamond dealers relied on their own contacts, not trusting banks who might suddenly confiscate their diamonds.

They exchanged diamonds and Alex left. How lucky can one guy get? A fair trade, hell, more than fair.

He'd be tight timewise if he stayed to sell the stones, but he didn't have a choice. He'd have to send Lev to meet the envoy with the shipment of diamonds on Saturday night. The exchange was set to take place at some posh West End shop that specialized in collectibles—expensive junk. It shouldn't be a problem for Lev.

10

"I have a loveseat just your size in my office," Amy said to Timmy as she stood with Brett in THE FIND. "You can rest there while your mother and I work."

"I don't wanna sleep." He thrust out his lower lip.

"Maybe I should just take him home," Brett said.

"Let me talk to him." Amy took Timmy's hand, thinking Brett needed to start dating. Amy had specifically invited Kent Rushmore to the opening so Brett could meet him. "Timmy will be safe in my office. I can see the door from the reception desk where I'll be. Grab a glass of champagne and relax." Amy sank to her knees, her face now level with Timmy's. "Would you try something for your aunt Amy?"

Timmy eyed her balefully, sucking his thumb. "What?"

"Snuggle up on my sofa with your book. If you don't fall asleep, I'll come back for you." She settled him in her office and almost had the door shut when she heard Timmy's voice.

"Auntie Amy, don't turn off the light." He pointed to the zebra. "Muffie's 'fraid of the dark."

"I won't," she promised, then closed the door. As much as she loved Timmy—and longed to have her own child—Amy had to admit he was a handful. How Brett did it all alone, she'd never know.

Brett rushed up and gave Amy a hug. "Thanks, awfully. Today was one of those days. I had to promise Timmy I'd take him to the zoo tomorrow before I could even get him to eat a bite of his supper. I'm not spending enough time with him."

"Mmm." Amy looked toward the entrance, hoping Kent would arrive so she could introduce him to Brett before she was too busy with her guests. Boris Tenklov ambled in, gazing around the room as if looking for someone. "See the man who just came in? Who would wear a coat in this weather?" After the wettest, coldest August in a century, summer had arrived. The balmy air had forced Amy to open every door and window. "He's Boris Tenklov. He escorted the eggs from the Ukraine here."

"Why? Are they that valuable?"

"Yes, not because they're gold or anything, but each *pyanky* takes weeks to paint. Still, I think it's strange the Russians would send a trade representative with such a small shipment."

"Maybe they want to see how the *pyanky* sell. If they go quickly, perhaps the government will increase production." Brett touched a fragile goose egg with the tip of her finger. It had been hand painted in an intricate design that combined hundreds of fine lines in a mosaic pattern. "Real works of art."

"Boris guards the *pyanky* as if they were the crown jewels, but I'd rather have Timmy helping me unpack them. Do you know what *Comrade* Tenklov did? Of the three dozen I'd ordered—and waited two years to get—only one was damaged en route. But the minute I left the room, good old Boris thought he'd help me unpack, so he took out several and managed to break three of them. I had the oddest feeling he'd broken them deliberately."

"Why would he do that?"

"I don't know, maybe he's part of the KGB. He lurks around even though he doesn't speak much English."

"I doubt he's a KGB agent. This is the era of *perestroika,* remember? I—" Brett paused as another man came in the door. "That's Lev Rodynskov, the new laser setter at Belage." Brett tugged on Amy's arm. "Come on. You'll like him."

Amy saw Kent Rushmore's Bentley limousine pull to the curb. "Brett, I—" She stopped, seeing Lev approach Boris Tenklov. "Your friend knows the Russian. That's strange."

"No, it's not. He's lived in Tel Aviv for years, but he's originally from Kiev. That's probably why he came tonight."

"Boris must have invited him. I certainly didn't." Amy watched Lev. Short, and in his mid-thirties, Lev had a muscular build and a craggy nose that emphasized his serious brown eyes.

"Lev," Brett called as they approached. He turned, obviously surprised to see her. "What are you doing here?"

"Vell, I . . . ah . . . I wanted to see the eggs. My people's art."

While Brett discussed the unique creations, each brightly painted with lustrous colors that gleamed in the gallery's lights, Boris listened, his eyes flitting from one speaker to the other. He understands more English than he lets on, Amy decided, wondering why he didn't at least unbutton his trench coat.

"Oh—" Brett turned to Amy—"I almost forgot. This is Amy Conrift, Lev. She owns this shop. Amy, this is Lev Rodynskov."

For the first time, Lev looked directly at Amy, which wasn't unusual. Men noticed Brett first. Lev's eyes swept over Amy at the speed of light, mumbling something that might have been hello before he turned back to Brett.

Amy watched Brett lavish one of her high-voltage smiles on the Russian as they were introduced. There seemed to be a subtle tension in the air. What was wrong? Amy asked herself. Maybe she'd read too many spy novels, but Boris

Tenklov made her uneasy. "Brett, there's one of my best customers." She waved at Kent Rushmore. "Go introduce yourself. I'll be right there."

Brett left and Amy turned to walk away. Out of the corner of her eye, she saw Ellis stepping out of a taxi. What's he doing here? She hadn't invited him, she thought, watching him help a woman out of the cab. Not Daphne. Amy really couldn't face Daphne. Amy stared, silently cursing Ellis as Ruth Payne emerged from the car and took her son's arm.

"Is something wrong?"

Amy turned to answer Lev and manufactured a smile. "I'm just hoping people buy the *pyanky*."

Why on earth had Ellis come—with Ruthless of all people? The woman had single-handedly ruined their relationship. She'd be damned before she had anything to do with either of the Paynes. Ignore them. How long could they stay? Surely Ellis would have to leave soon to make it to the studio for the eleven o'clock newscast.

Amy grabbed Lev's arm. "Take a close look at these eggs." She guided him toward the back of the shop away from the Russian and Ellis. "Wouldn't your mother *love* one of these eggs?"

Lev checked the price tag, then looked at her as if she'd just emerged from the Black Lagoon. What did he expect? This was THE FIND. Her clients expected exorbitant prices.

"In Ukraine women paint the eggs and give them as gifts at Easter. My family is Jewish," Lev informed her.

"So's mine," she said, realizing her fine features and dark hair and blue eyes were quintessentially English, and Lev hadn't guessed their common religion. "*Pyanky* are works of art. Anyone would appreciate their beauty."

"Not my mother. She could live five months on what this cost. She would rather have warm coat."

Amy realized she'd sounded callous. She wasn't, of course. She prided herself on helping Third World artists.

Any artist. But Lev had a brusque manner. She was more comfortable with gentlemanly men—like Ellis.

Lev started to move away, but Amy touched his arm, managed a warm smile, and batted her eyelashes. It always worked for Brett. She wasn't letting this man go; she didn't want to face Ellis alone. "Your mother wants a coat. I have the very thing."

She steered him past her office, noting the door was still closed and hoping Timmy had fallen asleep. Ellis would never find her inside the storeroom. "What size is your mother?"

Lev shrugged, studying her, his eyes filled with a special intensity she couldn't decipher. She resisted the impulse to take a step back. She removed the protective bag from the shipment that had arrived only yesterday.

"It doesn't matter. One size fits all," she said, uncomfortably aware that he was still staring at her. She shook out one coat, a soft camel-colored creation with deep pockets and a fringed hood and a matching scarf.

"Put it on." His words came out like an order. What on earth was she doing in the storeroom with this man when she should be up front selling *pyanky*? But the thought of having to face Ellis forced her to remain where she was.

Amy shrugged into the coat, then quickly buttoned it. Lev lifted the hood with hands like ham hocks. How did he cut a diamond, something Brett assured her was akin to brain surgery—and was often more expensive? He tucked in her stray curls, wasting the time Mr. Guy at MoHair had spent to make her beautiful for tonight, but she didn't protest. Something about Lev Rodynskov intimidated her. He stepped back, his appraising gaze taking in every detail of the coat.

Say something! Amy tried another smile, which she hoped appeared heartfelt. "Feel how soft it is."

He ran his huge hand up her arm, the heat from his warm palm penetrating the fabric. He rested his hand on top of her shoulder. His compelling eyes drilled into her.

"This material is . . . thin. No good for cold winter."

"It's a spring coat. It's supposed to be lightweight."

He frowned, making her again feel shallow for living in a society where coats changed with the seasons. She never minded the hardships of living in poor countries while she sought "the new and the unusual" for THE FIND. She went out of her way to disguise her wealth, not wanting those less fortunate to feel uncomfortable. But those people never came into her shop, into her world—and judged her.

As she hung the coat up, Lev picked up the tag dangling from the sleeve. Mercifully, the shipment had just arrived so she hadn't priced it yet.

"What?" He pointed to the logo on the tag, a ginger-colored Afghan. Above the dog was stylized script: HAIR OF THE DOG.

"Hair of dog," Lev muttered. "Alex say it is a drink, no?"

Lordy, how could she explain? "This material is specially woven in Wales." She touched the coat that was every bit as soft as cashmere. "It's collected from salons that groom dogs."

"Dog fur?" His loud words came out from between clenched teeth. "You want my mother to wear dog?"

"Amy, is that you back there?" Ellis called.

She put a finger to her lips, signaling Lev to keep quiet.

He leaned close and whispered in her ear, ruffling her already mussed hair. "What is wrong?"

"I don't want to see that man," she whispered back.

Lev whirled around and before Amy could stop him, he was at the door saying, "Leave. Amy does not want you here."

Amy shrank back against the Hair of the Dog collection. What else could go wrong tonight?

"Amy," she heard Ellis call to her. Lev had the door blocked with his body. "I need to talk to you for a minute."

Amy opened her mouth to tell him to go to hell, but before she could she heard a body slam against the wall with a piteous moan. Amy dashed out of the storeroom and found Lev with his fist in Ellis's gut and one enormous hand clamped around his throat.

"You have five hours to get out of here."

Even Ellis realized Lev meant five seconds. Without a backward glance, Ellis sprinted toward the front of the shop.

Ahead Alex saw a crowd milling about on the sidewalk sipping champagne and enjoying the warm evening. Summer had finally arrived. About time. He scanned the group of people for Lev but didn't see him. Perhaps Lev had spoken with the man representing the seller of the diamonds and left. He turned, angling his shoulders so he could move through the clusters of people while looking through the window into the shop. More people staring at hand-painted eggs as if they were precious gems. A sucker is born every minute. Maybe more often.

Boy, was he tired. It had been a breakneck journey from Tel Aviv, where he'd managed to sell the diamonds Avram had traded him for the blue diamond. Yeah, he'd gotten lucky—twice. He'd sold the diamonds for top dollar. And he'd called a woman he'd met on a previous trip. Two problems solved. Now, if his luck held, he'd find that the representative hadn't left.

"Wel-l-l, hello," said a breathy voice beside him.

Alex turned and saw a woman at his elbow. A conflagration of shoulder-length curls framed a heart-shaped face and emphasized dark brown eyes fringed with false lashes that reminded him of daddy longlegs. While the other women were dressed for a funeral in fashionable black, the redhead wore a crotch-skimming dress in a bright tangerine shade that didn't come close to covering her breasts. Get the idea: it would be a capital offense not to share her body with the world.

"Hello." Alex kept moving, anxious to find the envoy with the diamond shipment.

"I'm Latrice Laveaux," she said in the same breathless

voice, her hand on his arm. The way she said it, Alex felt he should know her name. "I'd love a glass of champagne." She put one hand on her hip and cocked it to the side, wagging her spidery lashes.

He pulled away, saying: "I'm meeting someone."

He moved through the crowd, then paused outside the shop door, looking over the crowd for Lev. Nothing. He turned to go inside but felt something grasping his knees.

"Al-wex."

He looked down at the child hugging his knees. "Timmy?"

The boy gasped for air. Obviously, he'd been crying for a long time. Alex picked him up, cuddling him.

"It's all right," he said. "Where's your mother?"

Timmy shook his head, the tears still running down his cheeks, his breath coming in uneven gasps. Alex found his handkerchief and wiped Timmy's nose. "What's the matter?"

"Th-they l-locked me in closet." Fresh tears spilled out of his innocent green eyes.

A flare went off inside Alex's head. He heard his grandmother turning the key, locking him into a hot dark closet. What the hell was wrong with Brett? "Your mother locked you in a closet?"

Timmy bobbed his head, his thumb now in his mouth, tears still beaded on his wet lashes. Alex looked around for Brett but didn't see her. He spotted Latrice moving through the crowd like a glowworm. She smiled, a come-hither smile, and winked at him.

Alex balanced Timmy on his hip, set to confront Brett. Instead of spending so much money on stuffed animals and toys, she could damn well hire a baby-sitter rather than locking the kid in a closet. Jee-sus, he'd never have figured Brett would be so negligent, but Timmy wouldn't lie.

"Alex," Lev called from the sidewalk just beyond the shop. Next to him stood a tall man in a trench coat. In this weather? Holding Timmy, Alex made his way to the shadowy area.

"*Gospodin* Tenklov," the diamond envoy said to introduce himself, with a heavy accent common to the valley around the Don River where Uncle Vic's family had originated. Alex noted Tenklov had dropped the usual *comrade* and now used the Russian term *Gospodin,* meaning Mr. "Your son?" Tenklov asked in excellent English.

"A friend's. Brett's," he added for Lev's benefit.

"Put him away," Tenklov said.

Alex instantly distrusted Tenklov. He carried himself with an air of authority Alex associated with high-ranking Soviet officials. Having Tenklov talking to Lev made Alex nervous. "Speak Russian. Timmy won't understand."

"What won't I unnerstand?" The tears had subsided to an occasional hiccup, his eyelids at half-mast.

Alex guided Timmy's head to his shoulder, saying, "Rest for a few minutes, and I'll teach you a new word in Russian."

Timmy snuggled closer, his head nestled against Alex's neck, bringing the scent of talc and baby lotion. Alex walked down the street away from the well-lit shop, the two men at his side.

"Have you sold the diamonds?" Tenklov asked in Russian, his voice low although there wasn't anyone nearby.

"Those diamonds can't easily be marketed. You know that." Now this was a wild guess, but Alex had a feeling, from the way Tenklov acted, that he was no underling. "I don't want Intelco to become suspicious. I think the best way to sell off the first shipment is to cut the stones into small gems, then set them."

"That won't make as much money as—"

"Then I'll return the diamonds and let your employer find someone else to sell them who's willing to risk his neck."

"The cartel has"—Lev slashed across his throat with his finger—"killed for less."

"Da," Tenklov agreed. *Yes.* "We know the risk."

We? Alex wondered. Was this like Ruth with the royal *we,* or did Tenklov go beyond that? Was he part of this scheme? Could he even be the seller?

"Who's selling these diamonds?" Alex asked, stopping in a shadowy corner where they could talk. Timmy had fallen into a sound sleep, his thumb still in his mouth. Alex eased it out, waiting for Tenklov's reply.

"I don't know. *Samizdat.*"

The underground. Well, maybe, but Alex suspected Tenklov knew more than he was saying. Things were loosening up in Russia, getting out of hand, some said. It was possible an enterprising bunch of Gypsy miners had teamed up with a bureaucrat or two and masterminded this scheme.

"They paid me to bring you the next shipment," Tenklov continued. "I don't know anything."

"More colored diamonds," Lev added quietly.

"How the hell"—Alex began, but quickly lowered his voice, afraid of waking Timmy—"do they expect me to sell them? Who knows how long it'll take? Don't expect a lot of money to appear overnight in that Swiss account."

"We are patient men."

We again. Interesting. "It'll take time."

"Boris has another shipment with him," Lev said.

Tenklov opened his trench coat, revealing two gold Mont Blanc pens in his shirt pocket, and handed Alex a package the size of a paperback book. "These were hidden in the shipment of eggs. We'll let you know when to expect the next shipment." Tenklov walked away without saying goodbye.

"Two gold pens," Lev said, disgusted. *"Shishki."* A bigwig.

Alex recalled his first visit to Russia years ago with Vic. He'd pointed out that every society had its status symbols. Back then, Russian men wore regulation suits that looked exactly alike, but you could always tell the high-ranking officials by the number of pens in their pockets. In those days the pens, mostly cheap ballpoints, were lined up like cigars in a box, filling shirt pockets. The more you had, the more important you were. Times had changed; now they flaunted expensive gold pens.

"The diamonds are from Russia. I think the Rostov mine."

"I agree." Alex stroked Timmy's fine hair, thinking out loud. "Maybe the Gypsies have cut a deal with the bigwigs."

"Working together?" Lev's expression said he had his doubts.

"You know Uncle Vic hated the *shishki*. I can't imagine him dealing with the bigwigs."

"*Apparatchiks,*" Lev said, old-line bureaucrats who'd spawned a system of corruption and nepotism unrivaled in the West. "Vic never deal with them. *Kooperativnos,* yes."

Alex nodded—*kooperativnos,* entrepreneurs working for themselves. Yeah, Tenklov had the balls it took to go into business for himself. Despite the status-symbol pens, he might not be a party member. On the other hand, if Tenklov were a party man, he could ask dangerous questions about Lev. "This is a big risk. Bigger than I'd thought."

The crowd had thinned; the caterers were picking up champagne glasses and napkins as Brett said good night to Kent Rushmore, accepting his invitation to the theater next week. She could see Amy's matchmaking at work. Amy wouldn't rest until she found Timmy a father.

Brett glanced at her watch, thinking it had been almost an hour since she last checked on Timmy. He'd been asleep for almost three hours. Thank heaven. Now pray he slept through the night. She hurried to the office and eased the door open. The blanket and book were on the sofa, but Timmy and the zebra were missing.

She stood, frozen in limbo, shattered—the way she'd felt when she learned her mother had been killed, the way she'd felt when she was forced to accept Owen's death. Now Timmy was missing. A jolt of near-hysteria hit her.

She rushed out to the center of the gallery, half expecting to find him playing with the pricey eggs. Her eyes swept the room, skipping across the clusters of people still chatting. She spotted his zebra on the floor beside a display case and let out a sigh of relief, expecting to find him playing on the far side of the case. She dashed over.

"Timmy, sweetie—" Her body stiffened with shock. Timmy wasn't there. He'd never leave his beloved Muffie. Why, he slept with him every night.

It was impossible to steady her erratic pulse as a tidal wave of panic engulfed her. Timmy: blond, cute, so outgoing. She sprinted to the door, panting, telling herself to remain calm. Outside. He could be playing outside.

Nothing.

She grabbed an elderly lady's arm. "Have you seen a little boy wearing a red sweater?"

"Yes. The poor child was crying and his father took him that way." She pointed toward the dark area beyond THE FIND.

Brett whipped around searching the dark succession of closed shops, the streetlights blocked by leafy plane trees. She was unable to control the spasmodic trembling within her. Kidnapped. Every mother's nightmare. "Timmy! Timmy!"

Out of the shadows strode two men; one held a small child, the dim light catching his blond hair.

Brett charged toward them, her fists clenched. "Timmy." She slammed to a stop. Alex? Lev? Thank God. Relief surged through her, leaving her weak. For a fleeting moment, she wondered what Alex was doing here, but decided it didn't matter. She reached for the still-sleeping boy, his tow head nestled against the curve of Alex's neck. "Timmy, darling."

He lifted his head, his eyelashes fluttering sleepily. "Mommy." He turned his head away, clinging to Alex.

"What's the matter? Tell Mommy." Timmy wouldn't look at her.

"Why'd you lock him in a closet?" Alex demanded.

"I didn't."

"You did so."

She heard the threat of tears in her son's voice. She wanted to hold him, to tell Timmy that he was the most important thing in the world to her. But now he was too upset—too stubborn—to listen. Guilt silenced her; she didn't deserve Alex's criticism, but she knew she wasn't spending enough time with her son.

The last guests were leaving and Amy stood with her clerk tabulating the night's sales. All *pyanky* had sold and she had taken orders for another three dozen—if she could get them. She spotted Lev bounding through the door but ignored him. After he'd punched Ellis, Amy had joined her guests, dismayed at Lev's actions. The man was barbaric.

"Trouble," Lev told her. "Come."

Omigod, what now? With this man, no telling. Amy followed him and saw Brett arguing with a tall, dark-haired man holding Timmy.

"Who's he?"

"Alex Savich."

Really? Brett hadn't exaggerated about how attractive he was, Amy thought, walking toward them. Compelling blue eyes, strong features, a confident set to his shoulders. And right now, he was angry with Brett. Oh, no, not more trouble between them. Brett had indicated things were going better—and now this.

"Hello." Amy extended her hand. "I'm Amy Conrift."

He nodded curtly, his eyes on Brett. Amy dropped her hand.

"Amy, tell Alex that I did *not* lock Timmy in a closet." Her words were evenly spaced, low, but edged with anger. Amy knew Brett could go off any second like a Roman candle—and regret it later. Her job meant so much to her. Next to Timmy, it was the most important thing in Brett's life.

"Actually, I put Timmy down for a nap on the loveseat in my office. It's quite small, but it's not a closet."

"He wasn't locked in," Brett explained, her tone strained.

"Of course not," Amy assured Brett, feeling guilty for not having watched him more carefully, "He must have had trouble opening the door. It sticks sometimes."

Brett was still glaring at Alex, who showed no signs of backing down or handing Timmy over to his mother. *Two of a kind,* Amy thought. Neither would apologize easily.

"I have an idea," Amy said to Lev because he was the only one who looked approachable. "Let's go somewhere and have a cup of coffee and talk. I think we're all a little tired."

"Gut," Lev said. "Where?"

"I have to put Timmy to bed," Brett informed them.

"I'll make the coffee at your place while you tuck in Timmy," Amy said, thinking this might be the perfect opportunity to throw Alex and Brett together and smooth things over. She could see why her friend was attracted to the American. Who wouldn't be?

Alex and Brett took the backseat of the taxi, so Amy was forced to share the small jumpseat with Lev, his arm circling her shoulders. She remembered the way he'd attacked Ellis. What had Ellis wanted? she asked herself for the hundredth time. She turned to say something to Lev. They couldn't all spend the rest of the night in silence. Someone had to start a conversation.

"Al-wex," Timmy said. "Teach me a new word. You promised."

"Da. Can you say *da*?" He waited while Timmy repeated the word several times. "It means *yes* in Russian."

Amy leaned closer to Lev, whose gaze was on the man standing in the shadows as the taxi pulled away. "Isn't that your friend, Boris Tenklov?"

11

Brett left Amy and Lev in her kitchen. Lev was refreshing, she thought—intelligent—practical to a fault—and easy to be with as well as inordinately talented. Lev was secretive, though, never discussing his past. An insular man, he evaded questions about his family. Brett had no idea if any of them was alive.

She reached the top of the stairs and heard Alex's husky voice as he said something about an evil man everyone hated. This had better not be a story that was going to give Timmy nightmares the way *The Hobbit* had. Inside the room she found Timmy's clothes in a tangled heap at the foot of his bed. She put the Sneaky By in his usual spot on Timmy's right side, but he hardly noticed.

"I'll come kiss you good night later," she promised, retreating, but Timmy didn't answer. His eyes were on Alex; even Muffie, his beloved zebra, had been shunted aside.

Brett trudged down the stairs, thinking how wonderful it would have been had Owen lived. Timmy would have a father, not just to tell him bedtime stories, but to be a role model. And to share the awesome responsibility of raising a son. She missed Owen more than she could have imagined; knowing he was gone forever saddened her, made her feel more lonely than usual. She tried to envision Owen upstairs reading to his son, but she couldn't. For one frightening moment, she couldn't even remember Owen's face.

She dashed into the parlor and saw Owen's photograph beside her mother's. He was smiling the same comforting smile that had won her heart. She touched the silver frame, thinking of her own father and how close they'd been when she was Timmy's age. Before the divorce. Before Ruthless. And now they were little more than strangers. For Timmy's sake she ought to rectify the situation; it was obvious he needed a man in his life. And who better than his own grandfather?

She pulled herself up short. Even if she could forgive her father, she didn't want Ruthless around Timmy. Just seeing her stepmother across the room tonight, basking in Ellis's reflected glory, brought back painful childhood memories. No, she wasn't ready to forgive her father.

"Where's Alex?" Amy brought in coffee mugs.

"He's reading Timmy a story. He'll be right down."

Brett poured Lev coffee as he sat beside Amy. "I was surprised to see you and Alex at the showing. How did you know about it?"

Lev stared into the depths of his cup as if reading tea leaves. "Alex told me," he finally said, still gazing into his cup.

"Is Boris Tenklov a friend of Alex's?" Amy asked.

Lev looked up, his serious eyes meeting Brett's. "They have a . . . a . . . mu-mu . . . a friend they both know."

"A mutual friend?" Amy offered.

"Yes. That is the word."

"Just what is Tenklov's job?" Amy asked.

Lev shrugged. "I do not know. Alex and I just say hello and how is his family, then we look at eggs."

Brett sipped her coffee, stunned that Lev would lie. She'd been in the shop all night. Alex hadn't set foot inside until he'd come in with Timmy.

Brett opened her mouth to ask Lev just when Alex had looked at the eggs, but spotted Sneaky By slinking down the stairs, attempting to sneak past her. She pounced on him just as he cleared the last stair. "I'll be right back."

She reached the landing and noticed only the night light was shining from Timmy's room. On tiptoes she went in and saw him fast asleep, his arm curled around Muffie. For once his thumb wasn't in his mouth. She set Sneaky By on the bed, then bent down and gently kissed her son's head.

Out in the hall again, she stopped and stared at the light coming from her room. What was Alex doing in her bedroom? She slowly walked down the hall, wondering how to handle the situation. She stepped inside, not knowing what to expect, but angry he'd had the nerve to go into her room. Stretched across the bed, his legs hanging over the edge, Alex smiled at her, a teasing smile.

"What are you doing?"

"Does having me on your bed make you nervous?"

"Of course not," she shot back. Too quickly.

This time he smirked.

She turned to leave. "There's coffee downstairs."

"Come back here," he said, his voice low.

She faced him, but held her ground and stood in the doorway.

"I'm not after your body. Women are easy to find, but it's damn hard to find good designers."

She smiled, embarrassed to admit she had thought he had sex in mind. It was hard to look at Alex and not think about sex. Since she'd first met him, she'd been aware he had an arrestingly virile manner that translated into undeniable sex appeal.

He patted a spot beside him on the bed. "Talk to me. Give Lev some time alone with Amy."

"Lev and Amy?" She giggled. "He's not her type. He—"

He motioned for her to come sit beside him. "She's Gordon Conrift's daughter, isn't she?"

Brett nodded, walking self-consciously toward the bed.

What good reason could she have for not sitting beside him? She sat, taking care not to get too near Alex, which was difficult since he was sprawled across most of the bed. Out of the blue, it occurred to her that there wasn't room for two people in this bed unless they were snuggled together like bedbugs.

"Amy's perfect for Lev. It's easier to marry it than make it."

"What's that supposed to mean?" she asked although she had a good idea what he was implying. Conrift Bullion was one of the three London gold exchanges that set the world's price of gold each morning. The British aristocracy were content to be born with silver spoons in their mouths; the Conrifts had gold.

"It's easier to fall in love with a rich girl than a poor one."

"You rat—" She stopped short, recognizing the faintest flicker of amusement in his eyes. "You're teasing me."

"Think so?" he answered with a subtle note of humor.

She nodded emphatically. Alex Savich was hard to read, but she was beginning to understand him.

"You're right. Some men might look at Amy and see an open cash register drawer, but not Lev."

Owen hadn't cared about money either, she suddenly thought. He'd never mentioned money; it would never have been important in their relationship.

"I think Lev would be good for Amy." He propped himself up on his elbows. "Because he isn't like any of the men she knows. Besides, they're both Jewish. What more could her family want?"

"Her mother's dead. Only Amy's father is alive. Gordon Conrift wouldn't be satisfied with a extraordinarily talented Jewish son-in-law. He'd want him to be rich, too. And British. But don't worry, Lev isn't Amy's type."

Alex shrugged, then pushed back his cuff and glanced at his watch. "Just in time for the weather report."

Before she could tell him where it was, he'd found the

remote control on the nightstand. The television clicked on and Ellis's handsome face filled the screen.

"Tomorrow," Ellis said as if on cue, "will be a topping day. Take your picnic hamper and go down to Brighton where the sand crab race to benefit the Faux Pas Society"— he looked to the side—"will be." Evidently someone off camera had said something. "I mean the Four Paws Society. You know, folks, cats and dogs—horses too, I guess. Trot down to Brighton and see the Ascot of crab racing."

Alex shook his head. "He's got shit for brains."

"But he's doing the best with what he's got."

His eyes met hers and they stared at each other for a moment, the silence uncomfortable. Then they began to laugh, his laughter masculine, rich, deep. The way it had been the night of the wedding. Their laughter mingled in the space between them, but it stopped abruptly when their eyes met. She giggled self-consciously and she gazed down at the comforter, smoothing it with the palm of her hand.

Alex turned off the TV. "Brett."

The timbre of his voice had shifted, taking on a more personal tone that unsettled her. She tried to read him the way she had earlier, but couldn't. He brought himself to a sitting position and moved so near her that she could feel the heat of his body. She held herself rigid, her pulse hammering in her ears.

He cupped her chin with his palm, his fingers resting on her cheek. His eyes were deep blue, almost black. Intense, powerful eyes. She held her breath, waiting.

"Sorry about Timmy's father. That's a tough break, kid."

Brett nodded, releasing a relieved sigh. For a moment there, she'd been afraid he was going to kiss her.

Amy glanced at her watch. What was keeping Brett? She'd disappeared upstairs over half an hour ago, leaving her to make meaningless talk with Lev. He knew nothing—and couldn't care less—about the latest trends, but he was interested in politics. The years he'd spent in Israel had made

him an armchair expert in the current showdown with Saddam Hussein. In many ways, Lev was more interesting than
most of the men she knew. Certainly he was more intelligent than Ellis, but he lacked . . . lacked what? Sophistication, she decided.

"Time to wash dishes," Lev announced.

"Alex hasn't had his coffee."

He peered at her intently, his brown eyes echoing his
smile. "If Alex wanted coffee, he would come for it. No?"

Amy understood what he meant; Brett and Alex were
attracted to each other. Maybe something was going on
between them. A man would be good for Timmy, she
thought, and even better for Brett.

She followed Lev into the kitchen, where he immediately
took charge as he had earlier when they'd made the coffee.
When everything was in order, they returned to the parlor.
There was still no sign of Alex and Brett, so they quietly left
the house.

"An Underground station's a block from here," Amy
said.

"Too far for you to walk. We go to corner and find taxi."

They'd play hell trying to find a taxi at this hour, but Amy
didn't challenge him. Lev expected her to follow his lead; he
had a forcefulness about him that almost dared her to question him. Ellis had been exactly the opposite, only too willing to let her make his decisions for him. And she liked that,
liked the feeling of power it gave her.

Luck was with her. A taxi left off an elderly couple just as
they walked up to the corner. They climbed into the backseat and Amy slid across to the far side of the taxi.

"Shepherd's Place," she said when the driver asked for
the address. The exclusive address earned a respectful look
from the driver, but if Lev had heard of the street adjacent
to the American Embassy in Mayfair, he didn't show it.

The driver sped away from Chelsea and Amy settled
back, wondering once again why Ellis had come to the

showing. What had he wanted? Did he regret marrying Daphne?

"Why do you laugh at people?" Lev asked, breaking into her thoughts. "You sell them what they do not need for much, much money and make a joke of them."

"No, I don't." She let out an audible sigh, checking the shops along Brompton to see where they were. They'd just passed Harrods; soon she'd be home and rid of Lev.

"You do. Coats from fur of dogs. Alex say one time you sell cow . . . ah . . . cow—"

"Cow paddies. They were a joke to make people laugh. They came in a fancy gold box that said 'Texas Chocolates' in script."

"How much did these 'chocolates' cost?"

"I don't remember," she fibbed. She'd put an outrageous price tag on them—it had been Christmas—and sold every one.

"Why do people buy such things?" *Things* came out as *zings*.

"Because," she replied, unable to keep the exasperation out of her tone. She resented his holier-than-thou attitude; obviously he didn't understand life in the West. "Some people have more money than they know how to spend. So they want something different, something novel."

"They want a book?"

"No. Novel also means unique." He looked at her blankly. "Different. And they feel better if it costs a lot."

"Why?"

Why? How could she explain, she wondered, as they turned onto Park Lane. Not long now she would be home— thank heavens.

"Why they want to throw money away?" he persisted.

She imagined his past life. The Ukraine. What did she know about it? Beyond *Fiddler on the Roof*—nothing. The attitudes of her clientele were strictly limited to an affluent society, a world beyond Lev's comprehension.

She finally said, "It makes them feel superior—that

means better—than everyone else because they have money
to spend on"—she stopped herself before she said "useless"
—"things others can't afford."

Mercifully, the taxi halted at the entrance to Shepherd's
Place. "Good night," she said. "It was nice meeting you."
She didn't attempt to pay the driver, certain Lev would be
profoundly insulted. Obviously women's liberation hadn't
penetrated the borders of the Ukraine.

"Wait." His words a command. "I walk you to your
house."

"That's not necessary. I live only two doors away. It's a
pedestrian street. No one comes down here unless they live
here." She didn't add that one of her neighbors was an Arab
sheikh who had an armed guard posted at his door.

"No. I see you safe inside."

She allowed Lev to march her down the narrow lane
cobbled in flagstone and lit by flickering gas lamps that
dated back to Queen Victoria's reign. She nodded to the
sheikh's guard as Lev took her key and opened her town
house door.

"Good night." She stepped into the dark foyer, then realized she'd been too curt. Lev couldn't help who he was,
what he was. "Thank you for walking me home," she added
in a softer tone.

"Do not laugh at me."

She opened her mouth to respond, but he grabbed her in
one swift motion, holding her immobile. His lips molded
themselves over hers, his arms pulling her into the powerful
curve of his body. He applied a touch of pressure, his firm
lips warm on hers; instinctively she parted her lips and his
tongue eased into her mouth. He applied a little more pressure and just the right amount of suction.

Dear Lord, she thought, surely she couldn't be enjoying
this. The hot gliding of his tongue over hers brought a shiver
of excitement. Heat radiated from his body, sending an unexpected rush of warmth through hers, pooling between her

thighs. Before she could think, she returned his kiss, her arms around him, her breasts flush against his sturdy chest.

One strong hand caressed the nape of her neck, stroking slowly, then edging downward and finding the zipper of her dress halfway down her back. She felt the cool rush of the night air on her back as he eased the zipper down. Omigod, she thought, wanting to protest, but before she could he'd unhooked her bra. He drew back, breaking the kiss. She stood gazing at him, his face shadowed, the light coming from behind him, shining down on her.

He pulled down the top of her black silk dress, the rustling of the soft fabric sounding loud in the quiet foyer. Gooseflesh blossomed across her breasts, the nipples going rigid beneath the sheer, lacy cups of her strapless bra. He yanked it off and flung the bra aside. Dimly, she heard the clink as it hit the Sèvres vase on the entry chest.

"Milochka," he whispered.

Something about his husky voice and the foreign word struck her as erotic, as seductive as his kiss. Before she could come to her senses, he touched her breasts, caressing the nipples with the ball of his thumb, tantalizing the sensitive skin. Her knees began to tremble, and she felt lightheaded the way she had when she'd reached Annapurna. He palmed the stiff peaks of her breasts, then lifted them, molding them to fit his huge hands, squeezing gently, rhythmically.

In the silence magnified by the marble foyer, she heard the echo of her rapid breathing and felt the heavy thud of her pulse hammering in her throat like a voodoo drum as his large hands coasted over her breasts. She heard Lev's breathing, too, his breath coming as quickly as her own. In the balmy summer air she smelled a trace of Molinard, her own perfume, on his lips.

He gathered her in his arms, her bare breasts molded against his lightweight shirt. With a soft, exultant sigh she clung to him. This time he kissed her slowly, gently, and she realized that somehow, in his own way, he'd made his point.

Lev backed up. "Tomorrow, *milochka*," he said, his voice husky but with its usual authority. "I come for you at noon. You help me buy my mother a warm coat."

Before she could answer, he was out the door and down the steps. She looked up and saw the guard across the way had stopped pacing, his observant eyes trained on her bare breasts.

Alex cracked open one eye, groggily aware that something had awakened him from the best dream he'd had in months. He'd been with Vic in their favorite café in Budapest, talking and watching the girls walk by. What the hell?

He found a buff-colored cat sitting on his chest picking its teeth with its hind paw thrust out and purring like an out-of-tune motor. Sneaky By? Right. He was still in Brett's bed. Jee-sus. What time was it? He lifted the cat off his chest and checked his watch. Almost dawn. The last thing he remembered was Brett going to check on Timmy. He must have fallen asleep.

What had happened to Lev? Why hadn't someone awakened him? He swung his legs to the floor, surprised that someone had covered him and taken off his shoes. Had to be Brett.

He walked into Timmy's room, expecting to find Brett sleeping there, but Timmy was alone. The light of the full moon guided him down the narrow stairs, and in the parlor he saw Brett curled up on the sofa, a blanket half covering her shapely legs. He walked closer, wondering if he should wake her and tell her he was leaving, or let her sleep.

Her face, in the satin sheen of moonlight, appeared fragile, her honey-colored lashes casting shadows across the rise of her cheeks. He squinted, reading the nightshirt's neon-pink script in the dim light: HOT TO TROT.

Yeah, right. If there was one woman on this earth who wasn't hot to trot, it was Brett. He'd lay odds that she hadn't been with anyone since Timmy was born.

She'd slept restlessly. The soft fabric of her gown clung to the curves of her breasts, stretched across the taut line of her stomach, and pooled at the top of her long, bare legs. Her hair tumbled, wave over wave, caressing her cheek and flowing over one shoulder, shimmering like platinum in the crystalline moonlight.

She arched her back, shifting her position, her nipples jutting the gauzy fabric outward as she parted her legs. The blanket, already half off, slid down and fell onto the rug. Her lips parted and she sighed or perhaps moaned. What was she dreaming? He was tempted to shake her, but she sighed again and seemed content. He picked up the lightweight blanket, inhaling an elusive hint of the floral scent she used.

He intended to cover her. He honestly did, but the moonlight caught her long legs and forced him to recall the texture of her skin beneath his lips. So smooth, so invitingly warm. A gnawing ache twisted inside him.

He touched her thigh just above her knee and watched for her reaction. Nothing, only the rhythmic rise and fall of her breasts. His fingertips skimmed along her leg, barely maintaining contact, inching up under her gown to the delicate skin of her inner thigh. He closed his eyes, savoring the moment. Even without moving his hand more, he knew she wasn't wearing panties.

Stop. He imagined Brett waking, angry sparks firing her green eyes. Who would blame her? But when he looked at her, she was smiling, not her twenty-four-carat smile, but a sensuous smile he'd never seen before now.

Christ. She was getting to him. So what else was new?

He slowly withdrew his hand and covered her with the blanket, taking care not to disturb her. Then he made himself a promise.

12

Amy suppressed a weary sigh. She'd lost count of the coats she'd modeled for Lev; they'd been at Harrods for hours. As he fastened the buttons, she couldn't keep her eyes off his hands. What did they say about men with large hands? In school she and Brett used to joke about it, speculating about their dates.

"You like?" Lev asked, adjusting the oversize collar, then straightening the lapel. His knuckles trailed over the fabric, brushing across her chest; a ripple of excitement surged through her. All she could think about was the way he'd kissed her, the insistent stroking of his tongue, his hands on her bare breasts.

"It's nice," she said, all too aware of his brown eyes gazing into hers. She suspected he knew what she was thinking. She'd pegged him for an unsophisticated man, intelligent, artistically gifted, but a man unaware of the subtleties of sexual seduction. Perhaps she'd been wrong.

Amy carefully assessed his body: dark eyes, slim hips, burly chest, head of thick black curls. Ordinarily she liked taller men, ordinarily she preferred handsome men, ordinarily—she stopped herself. Lev was attractive in his own way, she admitted, watching the supple muscles of his forearm flex as he took out his worn wallet and paid cash for the expensive coat.

He wore a blue polo shirt unbuttoned at the neck to reveal a whisk of dark brown hair, and corduroy trousers that had seen better days. Lev certainly hadn't taken any pains with the way he'd dressed, she realized, looking over her shoulder at her reflection in a mirror. The strapless yellow sundress she'd finally selected complemented her long dark hair and blue eyes.

"You hungry?" Lev asked after the clerk had wrapped the coat and they were at last leaving the department.

"Sure." The lie came easily. She hadn't eaten a thing and now it was almost past teatime, but she wasn't hungry. They could grab a quick bite, then back to her place. This time she'd get him upstairs and between those silk sheets.

He hailed a taxi and settled her inside, placing his shopping bag between them, directing the driver to take them to Wok on the Wild Side in Soho. Wok? She fought down a moan.

They rode in silence as the taxi slugged its way east through the heavy Sunday afternoon traffic. Amy gazed out the window, thinking Brett wouldn't believe this. She'd tried to call her this morning to tell her about what happened last night, but didn't get any answer. Then she'd remembered that Brett had promised to take Timmy to the zoo.

The taxi drove through showbiz Soho into the seamier side—the Chinese fringe—and halted in front of one of those trendy little upstart cafés that had sprung up across London in the last few years. The restaurant had a faux-marble exterior that looked strangely out of place considering Le Sex Shoppe, featuring female wrestlers, was next door. She waited on the walk, looking into the restaurant. Inside a chalkboard announced the special of the day: Nouvelle Cajun Tofu. Definitely an upstart café, but hardly one she would have expected Lev to pick.

His hand latched on her arm. "This way."

He guided her down the street beyond Le Sex Shoppe,

which would open in two hours with whipped cream wrestling. They went by a health food store whose sign proclaimed: LESS LUST FROM LESS PROTEIN. Perhaps she should cut back on the prime rib she loved so much. Beef might be at the root of her hormonal upswing. Nothing else she'd thought of so far could explain her reaction to Lev. "Where are we going?"

"My home."

Really? Her pulse accelerated. So he'd decided he wasn't hungry either. He smiled at her, and again she had the uncomfortable feeling he knew what she was thinking.

He led her down a dark narrow passageway between two buildings. A battle-scarred alley cat peered at them from inside a large bag where he was gnawing on something putrid. The hot air trapped in the passageway ripened the smell of the garbage. He hurried her around to the back alley.

"Up." He nodded toward an outside staircase that wasn't wide enough for more than one person.

She mounted it slowly, thankful she wasn't in high heels that would have caught in the wide cracks between the boards. His place was probably a windowless room with a bed and a loo.

Her father would disown her if he saw her here, she thought, remembering the mansion in Belgravia where she'd grown up. And this was a world away from their country home, Fallhaven, with its stream that glimmered through the stately oaks and wound through the meadows of wildflowers. She imagined herself on the terrace of their villa in Marbella facing the azure Mediterranean, watching the daily parade of ships passing Gibraltar. No. Her father wouldn't disown her. He'd kill her.

She stopped on the landing and waited for Lev. Turn around, she told herself, go home. Eat less beef and forget this man. He gave her a sly smile as he unlocked the three locks, then nudged her inside.

"My goodness." She looked around at the enormous

room with its vaulted skylight. The peg-and-groove floors had been bleached to a soft rose-oak hue that glowed in the amber light of late afternoon. In one corner stood a four-poster bed and a small chest of drawers while in the other corner was an exercise mat and a set of barbells. At the far end of the room was an old refrigerator, an Aga stove, a legacy of the thirties, and a redwood picnic table with two benches.

"Come." He took her hand, lacing his large fingers through hers. "You will like this."

You bet I will, she thought, the heat of his hand shooting up her arm, warming her entire body. He took her across the large room, their footsteps echoing in the nearly empty room, toward the bed, its polished posters and carved headboard gleaming in the mellow light, beckoning her. She hoped she hadn't built this up too much. Maybe last night had been her imagination running wild, having been without a man for the longest period since she began dating. She almost veered right when they came to the bed, but Lev steered her to the door beyond.

"You will like this," he assured her.

She stepped out onto a small rooftop garden with a white wrought-iron table and chairs. Potted Italian cypress screened the area from the building next door. White wicker baskets of moss-green asparagus ferns had been mounted on the brick walls.

"Eula Mae and her friends did this," Lev informed her with pride. "A *dacha* garden. Sit. I will bring the food."

A minute later, Lev appeared with a long tray that he set in the center of the table. Amy didn't recognize anything. Lev dashed back inside, then reappeared a moment later with plates and napkins in one hand, two glasses in the other, and a bottle of vodka under his arm.

"*Zakuski*," he explained, setting the table. "How do you say it in English? Appetites?"

"Appetizers? These are just the appetizers? There's more?"

He sat across from her, his forearms resting on the table. "Yes." He pointed to some rolls smothered in tomato sauce. "*Golubtsi.* Cabbage rolls with chicken and—and"—he searched for the correct word—"spice in the middle." With a wave of his fork, he named the other appetizers. "*Khachapuri.* Cheese pie."

How could she eat all this? She'd been slightly overweight her entire life. Everything that went into her mouth went directly to her hips and thighs. "Excellent," she said with total honesty.

"*Kharcho* is next. Soup from beef with sour and sweet taste."

Beef? Uh-oh.

"After soup," he continued, "we have *kotletki.* Then for dessert—" He smiled again.

She knew what she wanted for dessert, but if she ate a quarter of this, he'd have to roll her into that four-poster bed.

"Dessert is special. *Bulochki.* Cheese and raisins in bun."

She sipped the vodka he'd poured her; she'd never drunk straight vodka before, and it was smoother than she'd expected. "I didn't think Russians ate like this. Last year when I was in Leningrad, our hotel hardly had any of the items listed on the menu. The shops were empty."

Lev's eyes became serious again, the way they'd been the night she'd met him in the gallery. "My family never eat like this. But they told me how it had been when they were children before Communists. I came to the West and learned how to cook."

"Cook? You *made* this yourself?"

"Yes. Of course."

She sipped the vodka, surprised and delighted. Lev must have gotten up before dawn to have made an entire meal. No man had ever cooked for her before—unless she counted Trevor Horvath, who'd invited her for dinner, then had the chef from Le Gavroche on hand to prepare the

meal. But the show hadn't been for her; like most men she'd
dated, he had wanted to impress her father.

"I like to make my own food. I like to go to market and
see all the things I did not have in the Ukraine."

"You have relatives still there?"

He studied the tines of his empty fork, then shook his
head.

"But your mother is there."

He shrugged, his eyes still lowered.

"Don't you know where your mother is?" He must; he'd
parted with a lot of moncy to buy the coat. "Surely you hear
from her? Hasn't *perestroika* made communication a lot easier? Couldn't you go back and visit her if you wanted?"

His eyes met hers, angry and troubled. "I live in the West
now. I will never return to the Ukraine."

There was something guarded about his expression, suggesting the dark undercurrent in his personality that she'd
sensed at the showing when he threatened Ellis. What had
happened to make him come to the West, make him so
bitter? Don't ask, her inner voice warned. He isn't going to
tell you. He doesn't trust you yet.

When they'd finished the dessert, Lev cleared the table,
adamantly refusing to let her help. She relaxed in the garden, sipping her second vodka, the cool evening air a welcome relief after the heat of the day. The potent liquor had
gone to her knees, leaving her feeling weak and incredibly
full. She couldn't remember the last time she'd eaten this
much. She'd be on that icky liquid diet for two weeks. But it
would be worth it, she thought, recalling the pleased expression on Lev's face as she enjoyed the meal he'd prepared.

Lev came out again. "Come. I will take you home."

Home? Her brain must be muzzy from the vodka. He
couldn't be taking her home without even *trying* to make
love to her. This could not be happening to her.

But it was. The next thing she knew, they were standing in
front of Wok on the Wild Side, hailing a taxi. Lev chatted
amiably about his experiences in Israel, amazed that she'd

never been there, while they rode home. She listened attentively, having decided all was not lost. Evidently he planned on her inviting him in for coffee—after all, he hadn't offered her any—then adjourning to her bedroom.

"Would you like to come in for some coffee?" she asked after unlocking her door, ignoring the sheikh's guard, who was leering at her.

Lev patted his tummy. "No room. I eat much, much."

He didn't want to come in. What did she do now—just say good night? Unbelievable. She'd wasted an entire day and put on ten pounds and for what? Nothing.

"Thank you for dinner," she said, stalling for time, trying to decide if there was a polite way of luring him inside without embarrassing herself if he should refuse.

Men. A flare of rage shot through her. Ellis. Lev. Did she need them? Of course not. She'd be damned if she'd beg Lev to come inside. If he wanted her, let him make the first move the way he had last night. She waited a moment until it lengthened, becoming embarrassing.

"Good-bye." She stepped inside, slamming the door, cutting off his good-bye. She stomped into the parlor and flung her purse on the brocade loveseat. What had gone wrong, she asked herself. No man spends hours in the kitchen unless he cares about a woman. So why hadn't he even kissed her? Then she remembered his warning about laughing at him. She understood now; he'd been laughing at her all day, knowing how much she wanted him. And he'd expected her to make the first move.

To hell with him. We'll see who has the last laugh. I don't care if I ever see him again or not.

Not true, she admitted; the heady feeling she'd experienced last night when he kissed her returned with startling clarity as she thought of making love to him. Even her body began to respond. All that beef. She closed her eyes, telling herself that this couldn't be happening to her—not with this man.

Go after him. Bring him back.

She wanted him to make love to her, needed it badly. Why deny it? Aggravating as it was, embarrassing as it was, she was in lust, so just accept it. No one had to find out, not even Brett.

She knew she'd have to race to catch him before he reached the corner and found a taxi. Barefoot, she slid across the cool marble of the entry, yanked open the door, and charged through.

Lev caught her, although she almost bowled him over, hugging her. He wasn't laughing. He was grinning like the Big Bad Wolf.

"You bastard." She shoved him inside and slammed the door, catching a glimpse of the guard standing slack-jawed like a Neanderthal who'd awakened to find himself in Piccadilly Circus.

"You've been playing a game with me," she said, but didn't give him a chance to answer.

She kissed him, plowing her fingers through his curly hair, her hips pressed against his. His lips opened, his tongue darted into her mouth as his arms crushed her against him, roughly, almost violently. She relaxed against him, giving in to his superior strength, thrilled that his embrace was even more exciting than she'd anticipated. Through her lightweight sundress and his cotton shirt, she felt the heat of his body.

His hand skimmed across her bare back, sending a chill of anticipation as she remembered his unzipping her dress last night. This time, she'd fool him. She hadn't worn a bra nor did she have on any underwear except for a pair of panties, a wisp of lacy silk as thin as a bubble and just as transparent.

But he didn't touch the zipper—he was content to let his hands rove across her back while he kissed the sensitive curve of her neck. He trailed moist kisses across her shoulders, edging lower to the top of her sundress, his emerging beard leaving whisker tracks on her tender skin. Not that she cared; she hardly noticed except that the prickly sensation combined with the searing kisses hit with the force of a tsunami, heating her thighs.

She knew what she wanted. And she wanted it now. She couldn't last much longer. "Lev," she whispered, nibbling—she hoped seductively—on his earlobe, "let's go upstairs."

His tongue delved into the heated hollow of her cleavage. He eased his tongue up and down, long, slow strokes that she felt in the pit of her stomach, imagining what he'd be like inside her.

"Oh my," she managed to whisper, her thighs parting as he pressed against her. "You're just too good at this."

His head came up and he moved back, one hand resting on her shoulder, the other hanging at his side. What was wrong now?

His free hand swept between her thighs, cupping her with his large hand, then squeezing, gently but with enough pressure to illicit a low gasp of pleasure. A raw act of possession even though he'd never been inside her.

She sucked in her breath, dead certain he could feel the moisture through the lightweight dress. He eased his hand up and down, his middle finger pressing slightly more than the others.

"*Milochka*, you like?"

13

"What's that?" Timmy asked as they came up the walk to their house and saw the boxes on the steps.

"Work for Mommy." She'd forgotten she'd promised the Badger Society she'd stuff envelopes for their upcoming fund-raiser. It was the least she could do now that she wasn't actively protesting with them, Brett thought wearily, but not tonight. A day at the zoo with a three-year-old could exhaust an army.

"You listen to the answering machine while I bring these inside, but *don't* touch the erase button." She had the boxes halfway up the stairs when she heard Timmy yelling at her.

"Auntie Amy is saying somethin' funny."

"I'll be right there." She hurried downstairs to the hall telephone. "Run up and wash your hands and face." She pressed replay. "Then I'll fix you some Beanie Weanies for dinner."

Amy said, "I guess I didn't catch you before you left for the zoo. I want you to do me a favor. Alex speaks Russian, doesn't he? Ask him what *mee-looch-ka* means." A long pause. "I *have* to talk to you. Call me."

Brett listened to the next message: "Brett. It's Hugh Mac-Leod. I'll call you later. I want to see you and Timmy."

The next message was from Eula Mae. "My stars, you tricked me. The pit isn't from Nepal. The council has been forced to consult an expert from Belgium. See you tomorrow."

She erased the messages, laughing at Eula Mae's and thinking she'd spoken to Hugh only once since he sent word confirming Owen was dead. No doubt he was worried about her. Hugh had been such a close friend of her mother's—he'd been devastated by her death—that Brett had come to think of him as an uncle. It would be wonderful for Timmy if Hugh spent more time in London, but his position with Amnesty International required him to travel.

Timmy bounced down the stairs, his red shirt damp from washing his hands. She decided to wait until Timmy was in bed; from Amy's tone this promised to be a long conversation. She was probably mooning over Ellis again.

Brett settled Timmy at the kitchen table and poured him a glass of milk. "After you eat, I'll give you a bath and tell you the story of—" she paused, trying to think of a short story.

"Tell me Al-wex's story 'bout Gee."

"Gee Who?" All day it had been Al-wex this and Al-wex that. She was sick of Alex Savich's name. But she had to admit he'd been a positive influence. Timmy had awakened, last night's trauma apparently forgotten—and Brett forgiven. To his credit, Alex had told Timmy big boys don't suck their thumbs, and Timmy informed her he was too old to suck his thumb. Never mind that she'd begged him to stop a thousand times.

"The letter g. A-B-C-D-E-F-G," he said, proud he knew the alphabet by heart. "An evil man stole the g."

"You must have misunderstood. He couldn't—"

"He did. He did."

Brett knew that stubborn, overtired tone only too well.

"He stole the g. The people were very, very, very mad 'cause the g belonged to them."

"Okay, why did he take it?"

"They didn't have that letter where he came from. It dinna matter. The evil man couldn't really steal the g." He pointed to his head. "It's here." He thumped his chest. "And here." He grabbed for his glass of milk, and she held up two fingers, signaling him to use both hands.

Why would Alex make up a tale about someone stealing a letter? True, Timmy was much brighter than most children his age, but Alex's story had confused Timmy. Brett swung open the pantry door for a tin of Beanie Weanies, not the healthiest choice, but they were Timmy's favorite. When he was overtired, it simply wasn't worth arguing with him to get him to eat what he should.

The doorbell chimed. "It's probably Auntie Amy."

Timmy scampered off; a minute later she heard, "Al-wex."

Brett groaned out loud. What was he doing here? She looked as if she'd been mauled by one of the gorillas. Adjusting the belt on her periwinkle-blue shirtwaist, she saw the chocolate spot from Timmy's ice-cream cone on the pleated bodice. She walked into the parlor where Timmy was jabbering about the zoo.

"I thought you two might like to go out for pizza," he said, looking casual in khaki trousers and a navy shirt rolled back at the cuffs and open at the neck to reveal his gold cross.

A pizza. Junk food. Really, so American.

"What's a pissa?"

"Pete-za," Alex told Timmy. "You've never had a pizza? You don't know what you're missing. It's better than . . . than—"

"Betta than Beanie Weanies?" Timmy asked, awed.

"Much better. You'll love pizza." His gaze shifted to her, and she found herself wishing she'd taken time to comb her hair. "How about it, Mom? Feel like a pizza?"

"Do I look like pizza?"

"A frozen one."

"What's a pitsa look like?" demanded Timmy.

"Run upstairs and get a sweater, and I'll show you a pizza."

Irritated at Alex's assuming attitude, Brett started to tell him to naff off and die, but stopped herself, anticipating Timmy's disappointment if he came downstairs and found Alex gone. She couldn't face tears two nights in a row. And she wondered why Alex had come, then quickly deciding last night had put them on a different footing. They were allies now, not adversaries.

Suddenly she remembered Amy's question and asked, "Do you know what the word *mee-lutch-ka* means?"

"Did someone call you *milochka*?"

"No. A friend used the word, and I want to know if it's Russian and what it means."

"*Dushinka* would be the Russian equivalent of *milochka*, which is a Ukrainian word. It means darling."

Really? Where would Amy have heard that word? Surely, Boris Tenklov hadn't used it. "Just a minute. I'm going to run up and get a sweater too." She raced upstairs and quickly dialed Amy's number. It rang so long that Brett almost hung up.

"H-h-hello," came a strangled voice, panting for breath as Brett identified herself. "Oh, Brett. Oh. I—ah—"

"Are you all right?" The response was a grunt or maybe a moan. "Are you back to riding your exercycle?" Another grunt. "I just called to tell you *milochka* means *darling*."

"Th-thanks." The line went dead.

Surprised at Amy's reaction, Brett put on a cotton sweater that would hide the stain and went downstairs. Timmy was sitting on Alex's lap, telling him all about the zoo.

On the way to the pizza parlor Brett asked, "Did you tell Timmy a story about someone stealing a *g*?"

"Yes." Alex turned to Timmy. "Do you remember his name?"

Timmy shook his head, adoring eyes on Alex.

"His name was Stalin," he said, and Timmy nodded, repeating the name several times. "He took the *g* out of the Ukrainian alphabet back in the thirties, claiming it wasn't the same as the Russian *g*. He considered Russian a superior language."

"That doesn't make any sense."

"Stalin didn't have to make sense; he was a dictator. He felt threatened by the Ukrainians. It's always been the richest part of the Soviet Union—raw materials and food. It's also Russia's intellectual heart with a huge number of Ukrainians opposing Communism. Forbidding the use of their *g* meant it was impossible to speak Ukrainian. The *g* in Russian carries the *h* sound the way it does in English. The Ukrainian *g* is a pure *g* spoken without the *h* overtone."

Alex turned to Timmy. "What lesson does this teach us?"

"No one can steal what's in your head or—or—"

"Your heart," Alex finished for him. "Last year the law was overturned and Ukrainian is again the official language."

"They got their *g* back," Timmy added.

"That's your idea of a bedtime story?"

"Hey, it's a story with a moral. The kind of story Uncle Vic always told me."

"When you weren't quite four?"

"I didn't meet him until I was eight."

The taxi pulled up in front of a brownstone with a huge sign that forced you to look directly into the barrel of a gun. The lettering above it proclaimed GODFATHER'S PIZZA. Alex held the door for them as another car pulled up and dropped off a man who followed them into the restaurant, giving Brett a curious look.

The interior was as black as a bat's cave, illuminated by four enormous video screens showing a boxing match. They were led to a small table in the far corner by a cute waitress

on skates. Fascinated, Timmy sat in a booster seat while
Alex quickly explained the men on the big screen were fighting, and he should watch to see who won.

Alex scooted his chair close to Brett. "Like Chianti?"

"Yes." Chianti always reminded her of the two years
she'd spent in Milan at design school. She let him order the
wine and a giant deluxe pizza—hold the anchovies—before
putting her hand on his arm, leaning closer so he could hear
her over the din of the people cheering on the beefy man on
the screen who now had his opponent pinned against the
ropes.

His eyes dilated in the darkness, leaving only a border of
cobalt blue. "Did you read today's papers?"

"No. We left for the zoo early," she said, looking over
Alex's shoulder at a man who seemed more interested in
watching them than the action on the television. He was the
same man who'd come in with them and given her an odd
look.

Alex pulled a piece of paper out of his pocket. "Read
this."

He brought the small candle closer so she could see, and
she checked on Timmy. He was clapping and laughing as
the winner, a hulk of sweat, received a medal for his efforts.

She quickly scanned the short article, swallowing hard,
trying to control her anger. That bitch, Lady Bewley, was
rallying C.U.M. for a boycott of her jewelry at Harvey Nichols, saying Brett was a degenerate who designed "lewd"
jewelry.

She didn't look up, pretending to reread the article, feeling Alex studying her. She should have known becoming an
important designer wasn't within her grasp. Normally she
didn't feel sorry for herself, but it seemed the moment
something important was within her reach, it was snatched
away. From her sixth birthday, when her mother delivered
her to her father, then disappeared from her life, things
she'd wanted had eluded her.

She prided herself on making the best of setbacks, staying

upbeat, being happy, thankful for life's blessings. Like Timmy. She heard her son laugh, a rich yet childlike sound, so young, so full of innocence.

"Why don't we take my name off the collection?" she asked, bridling her anger, sounding calm despite the heavy weight she felt inside. "I won't go to the opening—"

"Too late. The ads are set. Even if it were possible, I'd be damned before I let that old bat dictate how I run my business." Alex paused as the waitress delivered the Chianti. "Don't worry about it. The article was buried in one of the Sunday supplements. I doubt if many people read it. I'll call C.U.M. headquarters tomorrow and tell her I'll sue her if—"

"For telling the truth? She says I have an illegitimate child and spent time in jail. It's the truth. I'm not sure there are grounds for a suit. Calling my designs 'lewd' is a matter of interpretation, isn't it? This is a woman who picketed the Rodin exhibition. If she convinced her followers to boycott him, she'll have no trouble persuading them my designs are lewd."

"I'm still going to warn that bitch."

Their pizza arrived and Brett sipped her wine while Alex helped Timmy, who immediately declared pizza better than Beanie Weanies. She sat silently through dinner, eating only one piece of pizza, angrily thinking about how Lady Bewley could ruin her career.

And Alex. He didn't deserve all these problems with Belage, which only promised to get worse.

They returned home and Timmy insisted Alex tell him a bedtime story; Brett put on coffee, then followed them upstairs with Sneaky By in her arms. Alex was just finishing the story of the g; Brett wasn't surprised. When Timmy liked a story, he asked for it night after night. She smiled to herself, noticing Timmy's little hand was balled into a tight fist. He was determined to stop sucking his thumb.

"He's a good kid," Alex said as they went down the stairs.

"He's the most important person in the world to me."

"He seems much smarter than most children his age."

"He is. That's why I'm enrolling him in school early."

Alex was silent for a moment, then said, "Has he asked why his name isn't the same as his father's?"

"No. After all, he's only three going on four."

"Then you haven't told him you didn't marry his father."

He followed her into the kitchen and sat sprawled in the exact chair he'd used the night of the wedding, his long legs extended and casually crossed at the ankles. That was then and this is now, she reminded herself while pouring the coffee. Now they were in business together. Now they had a future together.

"Is there anything about your past I should know before I call Lady Bewley? Anything damaging?"

"Nothing I haven't already told you." She held the cup between her hands, thinking. "That article stopped just short of saying I was promiscuous. That's not true."

"I didn't think for a minute you were." He almost smiled and she wondered what he was thinking. "You were engaged to Owen when he disappeared?"

"No." She sipped her coffee, stalling. This was getting a little too personal, but she felt she owed Alex an explanation. He was giving her a chance to become a top designer. He had the right to know everything. Who knew what that old biddy might dig up?

"I'd only known Owen a little over three months when he disappeared." Alex's expression remained neutral, his eyes on her. "When I said good-bye to him that last morning, I barely mustered the courage to tell him I was pregnant. I thought he'd be angry, but he wasn't. He said we'd work it out as soon as he returned."

"So Timmy was an accident?"

"Yes. I'd come to Peru just after I finished design school to patch things up with my mother. You see, she'd wanted me to work with her and the World Relief Committee. I tried it but I didn't have my mother's strength. Every time I saw a hungry child I wanted to take him home. Do you know what I mean?"

Alex nodded. "Yeah."

"I don't think anyone really understands unless they've walked through a camp of starving children and known there weren't enough supplies to save even half of them. I made it through a year in Bangladesh and almost two years in rural China, then Mother moved to a project in Somalia. They'd been having a terrible problem with rebels shooting at the relief trucks, so there were no supplies on hand except for some powdered milk. I found a group of toddlers sitting around an anthill eating the ants. They looked at me with those expectant eyes relief workers always see, eyes that pray you have food. Of course, I didn't. We were down to one meal every other day ourselves.

"Something inside me snapped. I sat down beside them and began eating ants too. Mother found me sitting there. I didn't talk for two days. When I did, I told her I didn't have it in me to spend my life going from camp to camp seeing the suffering. I told her my dream was to be a jewelry designer."

"She accused you of being selfish."

"Yes. I told her that I would do what I could. Donate money or raise money—anything but work in the camps. She didn't understand. I didn't see her for almost three years. I went to Peru after I finished design school.

"I'd only planned on being in Peru a few days before returning to London to get a job when I met Owen. He and my mother were having dinner when I arrived. Mother was stunned to see me because I hadn't told her I was coming. But Owen smoothed things over. He has"—she took a deep breath—"had a wonderful personality with a terrific laugh. We spent most of the next weeks together—the three of us."

"You must have found some time alone."

She ignored the sarcasm in his voice. "Of course. We fell in love and—"

"Didn't he use protection?"

She never blushed, but she felt the heat shoot up her neck. Honestly, Americans. No topic was too personal. "Of course. Owen purchased condoms in Lima, but one of them broke."

"One? He was wearing only one?" Alex frowned.

This really wasn't any of his business. He didn't need the intimate details. Couldn't he just listen?

"I thought Northcote was a relief specialist who'd spent years in the field. Didn't he know enough to wear two?"

"Two at once?"

Alex pushed his cup aside. "Look. Any man that's spent time in Third World countries knows they make lousy condoms. They break. They leak. Hell, everyone knows you have to use two at once. We joke and call it 'double bagging.'"

"I didn't know."

"Doesn't matter. What's important is that you had Timmy." He gave her a strange look, a look she couldn't decipher. "You loved Owen . . . a lot."

"I fell in love with him that first night, listening to him telling my mother about the *sendero* guerrillas in Peru. He was a fascinating man, a compassionate man. He wasn't interested in fame and fortune—just in getting food and health care to people who needed it."

"But you knew him only three months."

"That was long enough," she responded, her tone defensive. "Haven't you ever been in love?"

"No. Heavy-duty lust, sure, but love, no way."

"Haven't you had a long-term relationship with a woman?" She couldn't believe she'd asked him this. It was none of her business. Still, she had to admit she was curious. Eula Mae told her lots of different women left messages for Alex at work.

He rocked back in his chair, balancing on the back two legs and studied the ceiling. "The longest relationship I ever had lasted a week. I was snowed in at a ski chalet in the

Alps. I spent most of the time in the sack with a psychiatrist. I gave her what she wanted, and she analyzed me."

"Really?" She couldn't keep the curiosity out of her voice. Had the psychiatrist penetrated Alex's facade? Brett had caught brief glimpses of his thoughts, his feelings, but only fleeting impressions. Other than the fact that he'd loved his uncle and was close friends with Lev, she couldn't have told anyone much else about Alex. "What did the psychiatrist say?"

He studied her a moment; she had the definite impression she'd crossed some invisible line.

"She had an interesting theory. She claimed I used sex to humiliate women and insisted I hated women. That's not true. But she believed men who don't have a mother's love, don't—how did she put it?—learn to love."

"But your mother loved you, didn't she?"

"I'm sure she did, but both my parents were killed in an automobile accident shortly after I was born. I was sent to live with my grandmother."

"Then she became your mother. And you learned love from her."

"Something like that." He stood, saying, "I've got to run."

She walked him to the door, wondering about his grandmother. Something wasn't quite right here. But she knew better than to ask another question. He didn't know her well enough to talk about his past. Not unlike Lev, she thought. "I'll see you tomorrow," she said as she opened the door.

He stepped onto the porch, then turned to her. "Don't worry about Lady Bewley. This will work out."

Over his shoulder, she saw a man standing across the narrow street. "Alex, don't look now but there's a man over there watching us. I'm positive he's the same man that was at the table next to us tonight."

Alex reached inside the door and flicked off the porch

light. "Throw your arms around me and kiss me—a long, passionate kiss."

"What for?"

"Do you have to question everything? I want to get a good look at him when he doesn't know I'm looking. If he's really following us, he'll duck into the shadows the moment he thinks we've spotted him."

He didn't give her a chance to respond, but wrapped his arms around her waist, his lips slanted over hers first at one angle, then at another. *One kiss,* she thought, her eyes open, letting her arms circle Alex's neck and watching the man across the street. She was dead certain he was the same man.

Before she could ask herself what possible reason he'd have for following them, Alex's tongue flicked softly between her lips, leisurely gliding forward, seeking hers. *Just one kiss,* she reminded herself. What did the Americans say? No big deal. The big deal was he was an expert at kissing. It was a long, seeking kiss that promised much, much more. Nobody, but nobody had ever kissed her the way he did with such sinful skill.

She steeled herself against feeling anything. After all, moments ago she'd been telling him how much she loved Owen, which was true. She was letting him kiss her only to distract the man who'd followed them.

She tried to ignore the heat of Alex's hand as it splayed across the small of her back. She tried to ignore the masculine firmness of his body, the hard contour of his chest against the softness of her breasts. She tried to ignore the satin heat of his tongue as it matcd with hers.

But she couldn't.

The kiss seared through her as he cradled her body to his, pushing against her. Her head felt light, her arms heavy, her thighs hot. Her arms circled his neck, her fingers tunneling into his thick hair as her tongue parried with his. Some distant voice warned that she'd regret returning his kiss like this, but right now she didn't care.

He nuzzled the tender skin below her ear, then skimmed the rim with the tip of his tongue, whispering, "I'm going to turn you around so I can get a look at that guy."

She almost asked, "What guy?"

He turned her in a slow circle, his lips on the sensitive curve of her neck. His warm breath drifted over her face, bringing the enticing aroma of coffee. Coffee enticing? She'd better get a grip on herself.

He kissed her again, his tongue arrowing into her mouth and evoking a fresh stab of desire deep within her. She had no choice but to return his kiss, did she? Standing up on tiptoe, she laced her fingers through his hair, tugging a little, rotating her hips—just slightly—against his, letting her suddenly bold tongue make love to his. She didn't protest when his hand wandered lower to gently fondle her bottom.

Gradually Alex ended the kiss, slowly easing away, his hands resting on her waist. Her arms slid down his shoulders, her breathing quick, shallow and far too loud.

He had the audacity to smirk. "Hot to trot, huh?"

Heat flared to her cheeks, but thankfully it was too dark for him to see. "I was merely trying to be helpful."

"Yeah, right. Why can't you admit it? There's something physical going on between us. Don't fight it."

"You think you're irresistible," she countered, opting to go on the offensive, knowing all the while he had a point.

"You just proved it. Let's go upstairs."

"Not on your life. I don't believe in casual sex. When I make love to a man, it's because I love him."

"Make an exception. You know you want to."

"Naff off and die!" She opened the door and stomped inside, intending to slam it on the jerk, but he was too quick for her. One muscular shoulder wedged against the door was all it took to keep it open.

He laughed, a low husky sound, very masculine. Too sexy for words. "Is that Brit for fuck off?"

"You bet."

He trapped her head between his hands, and gave her a

kiss, a quick peck like a good night kiss for Timmy. "No hard feelings?"

Naff off was on the tip of her tongue, but she bit it back, cautioning herself that this man held the key to her future. She orchestrated a smile as phony as a two-pence rhinestone. "None."

"When you change your mind, let me know."

"I hate him," she told herself as she climbed the stairs. It wasn't until she reached her room that she realized she'd been too distracted by his kiss to ask him about the man. Had Alex recognized him?

14

The following morning Alex heard Brett arrive, her voice animated as she talked with Eula Mae. Something about pits. He fiddled with papers on his desk, bracing himself. Sure enough, seconds later Brett sailed into the office. Without knocking. He kept his head down, the picture of concentration.

"Alex, did you recognize that man last night?"

He didn't look up, but glimpsed her short skirt. "What man?"

"Don't play games. You know what man."

He slowly raised his head, taking in her gauzy blouse with the outline of a lacy slip or bra beneath, the gold filigree chain around her throat that dipped into the vee of the blouse, her jaw set but her lips tipped upward—even now when she was thoroughly pissed—promising her usual smile. She wore her hair in what he'd come to think of as her work style, drawn high on her head and cocked to one side in a ponytail. She had to keep it off her face to use the goldsmith's torch, but he still preferred it down. The way it had been last night.

"Alex, did you recognize him or not?" Alex shook his head. "He was the same man who was in Godfather's."

"A coincidence."

"No. I've been thinking about it." She ran the tips of her fingers—the same fingers that had twined through his hair —across the surface of the desk. "He's following you to get the plans to the enhancer."

Plans? He almost laughed. That contraption was only taking up space in Lev's workroom. If he didn't need the damn thing for a cover story, he'd pitch it today. Brett, though, was worried, which made sense. Any woman who'd spent years in relief camps, then risked jail to rescue badgers, worried about others.

"No. Anyone would realize I've filed for a patent."

"Why else—"

"Coincidence," he assured her, knowing why they'd been followed but not willing to discuss it with her.

Her eyes narrowed, a veil of thick lashes, their tips the color of white gold, shadowing her green eyes. He kept looking at her with that unflinching gaze Uncle Vic had taught him to use on other diamond brokers. Her lips moved, and he glimpsed the pink tip of her tongue; she was set to argue. But she didn't, crimping her mouth into a taut bow, ruining the fullness of her lower lip. She opened the straw bag hanging from her shoulder. "I was wondering if you could enhance this stone."

Aw, hell.

She showed him a wedding ring that had to be over thirty years old. Even without a loupe, he saw it was an inferior stone cut in the old mine style, the bottom coming to a deep point.

"It was my mother's," she said, an emotional note in her voice. "It's not worth much, but I thought I might wear it if you could make it another color so it won't look like a wedding ring."

"Let me check it with the laser microprobe." He took it from her and walked the short distance to where he'd installed his equipment, then mounted it and looked through the viewer. Ugh! When had he last seen a stone with this many flaws?

"Could I look?"

"Have you ever used a microprobe?" She shook her head. "Look through this, then adjust the field focus here."

She gazed into the double-barreled microprobe, then quickly looked up, leveling those big green eyes on him. "I've used a loupe on it, but this is much, much more powerful. I've never seen so many inclusions."

"You don't want to try to enhance it. It'll turn"—what would be most disgusting?—"a brackish green."

She went for it. "Oh, I see." Disappointment etched her face; she caught her sexy lower lip between her teeth.

"Would you like to use the microprobe on a really fine stone?"

She nodded, her expression eager, her lips tilting upward into that off-kilter smile. It tipped slightly to one side while her ponytail was cocked to the other, her trademark smile that revealed a row of white teeth as striking as a matched set of pearls.

Telling himself that he was crazy to show her this stone and risk her asking questions, he took out one of the colored diamonds Boris Tenklov had given him at THE FIND.

"That's a new safe," Brett commented as he swung the large door shut, the stone in the palm of his hand. "It's really big."

"We needed it." Actually, he hadn't needed it yet; Avram hadn't moved any of his diamonds to London, but if Bush kept rattling sabers with Saddam, who knew when there might be war in the Middle East?

He placed the uncut popcorn-shaped stone in the microprobe. He calibrated the machine to duplicate northern light, the industry standard, pure light. He moved aside and let Brett look, but stayed very close. "What is it?"

"Hmmm," Brett muttered, he reached around her, touching her shoulders, adjusting the machine, magnifying the stone even more.

He felt her body tense and casually moved his arm. *Naff*

off and die. He chuckled to himself, his eyes on the back of her head. The stream of honey-gold hair dangled over one ear, falling down her cheek, releasing a soft hint of floral each time she moved. Loose tendrils coiled across the nape of her neck, one almost hiding the small mole on the back of her neck. Almost.

Naff off? As much as she hated to admit it, she wanted him. Badly. Believe me, one day she'll give in. "Well?" he asked.

"The Romans dedicated the emerald to Venus," she said. "And in the Middle Ages it was a symbol of faith and immortality."

Quit stalling. "You're saying it's an emerald."

She raised her head and shook it, slapping him once across the nose with her ponytail. "It's green, but—" She faced him. Those eyes. "I should see feathery inclusions, shouldn't I?"

Pretty good. He almost smiled; trained as a designer, she didn't have much experience in grading and selecting stones. And Ellis, who needed to send out an all-points bulletin to find his brain, couldn't have taught her.

"And it has a sparklike trace of amber," she added, her eyes on his. She paused, but he didn't comment. "How am I doing?"

"I'm listening."

"It has bubbly inclusions like champagne."

Okay, she'd done better than he'd anticipated, knowing the difference between bubbles and striations. But had she been deceived by the color?

"It's the most beautiful shade of kelly . . ." She paused, her voice low, the light from the nearby window playing across her face, highlighting her eyes, "like premier Colombian emeralds."

Actually, the diamond was the exact shade of her eyes, a clear green spiked by minute stitches of gold that gave it more intensity than an emerald. It was a diamond, but she'd missed that—just as he'd bet she would—swayed by the color of the stone.

She ran the tip of her tongue over her lower lip; he recalled what she'd done with her tongue last night. Just a matter of time. All things considered, the hunt was usually more fun than the catch. He liked trying to outmaneuver her because she was a challenge. Most women chased too much.

"It's a diamond," she blurted out. "A green diamond."

Jee-sus. He'd underestimated her, but maybe he could bluff her out of her decision. He laughed, convincingly, he thought, but she merely stared him down. "You sure?"

"Positive." Her lower lip moved forward just a fraction, reminding him of Timmy's pout. "Like the Dresden Green."

That got him. She'd named the most famous green diamond in the world. He conceded, "You're right."

"Really?" Her face broke into her megawatt smile. She bounced on the balls of her feet, her arms coming up and stopping just before touching his shoulders. In spite of herself, she'd almost hugged him. "When you cut it, that diamond will be worth a fortune—even more than the Dresden Green."

And risk Intelco's finding out? No way. He turned his back on her and took the stone out of the machine. "It was a good-luck piece that belonged to Vic. I can't sell it." Hearing a knock, Alex turned and saw Lev. "Come in. Brett was just leaving."

His tone sounded curt, but she didn't seem to notice, smiling another of her high-voltage smiles and thanking him. She walked out and he stole one—okay, two—looks at her great legs. He motioned for Lev to close the door.

"There was a man following me last night."

"The cartel?" Lev's forehead furrowed into a frown.

"No. They don't know anything about the enhanced diamonds—yet. Even if they did, they're pros. I'd never have seen their man. I'm sure Tenklov had me followed. He's putting me on notice. They don't have any choice but to let me market their diamonds, but they don't trust me. They deliberately let me know they're watching me. They may be following you, too."

"I am careful always. No man followed me."

"Good." He studied Lev, regretting, not for the first time, he'd brought Lev here, exposing him to danger. But he knew Lev well enough to realize he wouldn't return to Israel now, not with those colored diamonds begging to be cut and set. "I want you to be very careful. I don't want Tenklov checking into your past."

Lev nodded, his eyes intense, grave. A moment later, he smiled then asked, "What is whip-cream wrestling?"

"It's female wrestling. They used to wrestle in mud but now whipped cream has become popular. Why?"

"I have tickets for us this Thursday night."

Alex chuckled; good old Lev. He was fascinated by the oddball culture of the West. If they hadn't had it in the Ukraine, Lev wanted to see what he'd been missing. Alex and Lev spent two nights a week together. Usually they had dinner and talked while playing chess, but occasionally they went to a movie or a concert. Last week Lev insisted they go to the Skinflint concert. The heavy-metal band performed in their frayed underwear, driving a crowd of teenagers to the brink of hysteria with obscene gestures and four-letter words that would have turned construction workers blue.

"Whipped-cream wrestling, huh?" Alex preferred one-on-one and skip the whipped cream. Too messy. "How was your weekend?"

"Amy liked my cooking." Alex would have bet his life on that. "I'm giving her lessons."

"Sounds like fun." Over the years, Lev had given several women cooking lessons, but none of them had managed to get a ring on her finger, which was odd because Lev missed his family. He recalled family life with a fondness Alex had never experienced.

Lev's reluctance to marry might be psychological. Not

that he went for psychoanalytical bullshit. But Lev had a
dark undertow to his personality no one—now that Vic was
gone—understood but Alex. It stemmed from that night in
Kiev. Everything had changed for Lev that night. Everything.

Lev left and Alex walked over to the window. The summer sunshine penetrated the spaces between the closely
built structures, giving the diamond district a brightness he
hadn't noticed before now. The area seemed less depressing. The turn in the weather had lifted his spirits, he realized; he hadn't thought about Vic quite as much these last
few weeks.

But now as he let his gaze drift across the rooftops to the
crucible of power in the diamond market—the six-story Intelco headquarters on Charterhouse Street—he wished Vic
had told him more about this diamond deal. Even to help
some Gypsy friends, Alex couldn't imagine Vic cooperating
with the Communists, particularly when the deal would
cause trouble with the cartel.

Son of a bitch—the cartel. Bad enough being dogged by
Tenklov's man; soon the cartel would be taking a closer
look. This week advertisements would appear touting Belage's "enhanced" diamonds and the showing at Harvey
Nichols. Right now, the cartel didn't give a rat's ass about
him, but too soon that would change.

Hey, remember, maskirova *is in your blood. What's the
cartel anyway? Nothing but a bunch of tightass Brits intent on
controlling diamond prices. Should be easy enough to fool
them because no one ever tried—at least not on this scale. All
right, all right, if they found out, he was a dead man.*

In her office, Brett tried reaching Amy at THE FIND, but
the clerk told her Amy hadn't come in yet. Was something
wrong? Amy had been so odd last evening when Brett returned her call.

Eula Mae walked in saying, "You're a clever boots. You
said that pit was from Nepal and it isn't."

"I *never* said so. You *assumed* it was because I'd been there."

"It's from India. We've established that now."

"A big place." It should take them quite a while longer to identify the pit Terai had helped her purchase, keeping Eula Mae in the Rare Plant and Pit limelight.

Eula Mae touched the ring Brett had placed on her work-table, and Brett told her it had been her mother's.

"An old mine cut. I have one, too, except it's a River White."

Those crystal-white diamonds were not mined but were exposed by nature, usually being found in rivers; those sources had disappeared around the turn of the century. "Really? Your mother's wedding ring?"

Sadness veiled Eula Mae's face. "No. My engagement ring."

"I see," Brett said, although she didn't. She and Eula Mae were close, yet the older woman had never mentioned having been engaged. Whatever had happened caused Eula Mae to turn inward, giving her love to plants instead of to a man.

"I brought the ring today," Brett continued, striving to smooth over the awkward moment, "hoping Alex would—" She caught herself. How could she have been so careless?

"Enhance your stone."

"Alex told you?"

"No, but I see and hear things."

Brett got up and closed the door, laughing. "Do you know how Mother raised all that money? Everyone thought she had a special way with men, but she didn't. She was convinced God was a woman, so she relied on women for help. She always said a secretary knew more about a company than the director did. She'd get their advice on how to wrangle money out of the boss."

Brett put the ring in her desk drawer. "I'd like to try enhancing this, but Alex refuses. Is that door ever un-locked?"

"Never. Lev cleans up himself. He and Alex have the only keys, those newfangled card keys."

Brett reminded herself that curiosity killed the cat, but she still wanted to get into that room and see the enhancer at work—just once.

II
MOONLIGHT
AND DIAMONDS

15

"It's Purvis Keir on the line again," Eula Mae told Alex.

He shook his head; Keir had been waffling all week, terrified about what a boycott by C.U.M. members would do to the store.

"We're really nervous," Keir said immediately. "Is it possible to postpone this exhibit until next spring or maybe summer?"

The gutless jeweler of the West End. Uncle Vic always said: The best defense is a good offense. "According to the contract you insisted upon, postponing is out of the question. If I back out on you, it would cost me thousands in damages. My solicitor tells me you're liable if you—"

"Now, now. I wasn't suggesting we terminate our agreement, but I think the political climate might be more conducive to showing this collection in the spring."

"The contract specifies the exact date of the exhibition —next Saturday. I've spent a fortune on advertising."

"The directors thought—" Alex could almost hear him sweating.

"Look," Alex said, knowing Keir's career was at stake. "Tell them this publicity will bring everyone to the store to see what the fuss is about. You'll sell more goods, not less."

"Maybe," Keir conceded, then hung up.

Eula Mae appeared at the door to his office, her face almost as gray as her hair. "Where's Brett?"

"She went downstairs to the findings broker, who's making her a clasp."

"Timmy's school just called. He's been in a fight."

"I'll get her."

Brett smiled when he found her, but her happy expression quickly faded. He must look as pissed as he felt.

"There's been a problem at Timmy's school."

"Is he hurt?"

"No." He ushered her to a waiting taxi.

"A fight?" Brett asked when he told her. "Timmy adores other children. This is his first term at preschool. How could he have made an enemy so quickly?"

Now Brett was a whole lot smarter than this, so he kept his mouth shut and let her think about it.

Half a block later, she said, "I could kill Lady Bewley."

"Kids are cruel." Believe me, I know.

"He's three going on four. I never thought parents would tell children so young that one of their classmates is illegitimate."

"Kids are all ears. One of them might have overheard a parent or something." The cab inched passed the Ritz, then stopped for the usual snarl at Green Park. "You told Timmy, didn't you?"

"Sort of. I mean, he knows his daddy died before we'd had a chance to marry, but I didn't present it as a bad thing because I don't think it's anything to be ashamed of."

"All this publicity and you didn't even—" He shut his mouth, seeing she was on the verge of tears. He slid across the worn leather seat and put his arm around her. "If he sees you're upset, he'll be even more upset."

She gazed up at him, her eyes misty. "You're right. I

should have warned him, prepared him. What am I going to tell him now?"

"I'm coming in with you. I can help with this."

The Ridgemont Preparatory School was wreathed in enough ivy to have given ten American universities instant respectability. Alex could tell by the Rollses and Jags picking up children and the prissy uniforms with shorts the boys wore—you'd never get a kid in L.A. to wear them—that this school was costing Brett more than she could afford. They found the headmistress's office down a long polished corridor that smelled of chalk dust.

Brett had Alex wait in the reception room while she went in alone to see Miss Prudence Throckmorton. Entering the office, she felt like an errant child again, remembering the numerous trips to the headmistress's office. She'd been an excellent student, but "high-strung," they said, prone to pranks. In truth, she'd merely wanted to get her mother's attention.

"Miss Lamont." The headmistress greeted her with a frown that emphasized her too-high forehead and hair that surely would have been gray or white had it not been dyed blue-black.

"Is Timmy all right? May I see him?"

"He's in the nurse's office. I want to talk to you alone first." She leaned forward, her crossed arms resting on the desk. "Timmy was accepted here on a provisional basis; he's one of our youngest students. A few years ago, we didn't have a preschool program, but with changing times and mothers who think they must have careers—"

"My career isn't a luxury. I have to support us."

Miss Throckmorton rose, walked around the desk, and sat in the high-back chair beside Brett, facing her. "When younger children are mixed in with older children, the older students sometimes pick on them. Today, several of the older boys began calling Timmy names. He punched one of them in the nose, bloodying it, I'm afraid."

She shuddered inwardly, imagining sweet Timmy, who

liked everyone, so angry that he'd struck another child. *Why couldn't Lady Bewley leave him out of this? He's never hurt anyone.* Suddenly, Ruthless's words came to her: *If you don't have an abortion, your child will live with your sin the rest of his life.* Sin? Since when was loving someone a sin? It wasn't, but she couldn't help accusing herself of failing Timmy for not—somehow—sparing him this.

"Timmy's one of our most intelligent students," Miss Throckmorton continued. "I understand during his story time, he told the class how Stalin stole the *g.* Fascinating. I hadn't heard that tale myself, but Mr. Walen-Roberts, the senior history professor, tells me it's true. Timmy's teachers also tell me he's exceptionally bright. He'll be reading before the end of this school year. So, the question becomes how to handle this."

Brett opened her mouth to suggest killing Lady Bewley, but Miss Throckmorton cut her off.

"I have absolutely no use for that Lady Bewley and her committee," the headmistress said. "Timmy must understand, however, that we can't have fighting here."

Numerous parents recommended Ridgemont, and Brett had visited many schools before settling on this one. A school was more than bricks and ivy; the attitude of the staff meant everything.

Brett left and found Timmy sitting on Alex's lap in the reception area. He had a small cut on his lip and a bruised cheek; his expensive new blazer was dusty and torn at the elbow.

"Are you hurt?" Her voice cracked.

He shook his head. "Are you gonna spank me?"

Where would he get that idea? She'd never spanked him. "Of course not." She patted his head, running her hand over his thick blond hair. "But you have to promise me you won't fight."

Timmy's lower lip shot out; she knew this wasn't going to be easy. "If anyone calls me a bassard, I'm hittin' him."

Brett started to protest, but Alex winked at her, then stood, holding Timmy's hand. "Let's go."

In silence they walked outside, each holding Timmy's hand, and hailed a passing taxi. Did Timmy know what bastard meant, she asked herself, thinking he'd mispronounced it. Probably. Children grew up too fast these days.

Inside the taxi, Timmy crawled onto Alex's lap. Alex tugged on her arm, and she scooted across the seat until her thigh was flush against Alex's. Cradling Timmy with one arm, he put the other around her, almost forming a circle.

"When I was your age"—Alex's voice was more serious than Brett had ever heard it—"children teased me every day . . . for years."

Wide-eyed, Timmy asked, "Are you a bassard?"

"No. They teased me because after school my grandmother made me go to another school, a ballet school."

"Ballet?"

"The Nutcracker," Brett reminded him. "Ballet dancers."

"Dance school? Is that bad like bassards are bad?"

"The other children thought ballerinas were fairies." His voice was steady, yet it held an undertone of humiliation.

"Fairies? Like the Fairy Godmother, like the Tooth Fairy"—Timmy paused, clearly confused—"like Tinkerbell?"

Brett forced herself to remain silent. She knew what Alex was saying, but Timmy didn't. Her heart went out to Alex, imagining a lonely boy, orphaned, living with a cruel grandmother.

"Are fairies boys or girls?" Alex asked.

Timmy answered without hesitation. "Girls."

"When someone says you're a fairy, what are they calling you?"

"A girl," Timmy said, disgusted, "wiff wings."

Men, Brett thought, recognizing the universal voice of the male. At three? How could anyone so young have already relegated women to a second-class status? Her mother would have set the two of them straight, but she knew Alex was only trying to be helpful. She suspected he'd under-stated the situation, not wanting Timmy—or her—to know how devastating this had been.

"Did you cry?" Timmy asked, his tone sympathetic.

"Sometimes when I was alone where no one could see me."

"Did you fight like the boxer in the pissa parlor?"

"At first. Then I got smart."

"What did you do?" Real respect here.

"I ignored them." He brushed Timmy's swollen lip with his finger. "I knew they'd get me in trouble—if I let them."

Tears sprang into Timmy's eyes. "Al-wex, I'm sorry they were mean to you." He nudged forward and kissed Alex on the cheek.

Alex's eyes narrowed with a fleeting look of heartrending emotion that Timmy had unintentionally exposed, revealing a chink in his psychological armor. Brett looked away, thankful the taxi had pulled up in front of her Chelsea home. Timmy with his child's insight sensed the deep hurt in Alex Savich.

They climbed out of the taxi, and Alex said, "I want you to take a nap."

"Don't leave," Timmy said, near tears.

"Take a nap. I'll be back in an hour or so."

His word was law; Timmy marched toward the house.

"I want to talk to you when I come back," Alex told Brett.

16

After putting Timmy down for a nap, Brett went into the kitchen and began preparing dinner for Hugh MacLeod, her mother's old friend, but Brett's thoughts were on Alex. She tried to remember what Vicktor Orlov had told her about him. Surprisingly little. He'd never mentioned how attractive Alex was; nor his education; nor his troubled youth. Was any of Alex's family still alive?

She had the roast in the oven when she heard a knock and found Alex holding a huge box wrapped in paper from Hamleys, the exclusive toy shop on Regent Street. "You didn't."

"He's had a rough time. This'll take his mind off—"

Timmy thundered down the stairs. "Al-wex."

Alex told him that he'd brought him something special; Timmy ripped off the paper. "Look, Mommy, a fire engine."

"It has miles of hose and it sprays water," Alex said.

Inwardly Brett groaned, envisioning damp drapes, damp beds, a damp Sneaky By. Alex lifted it from the box, the bright red and chrome delighting Timmy. She followed them out to the back garden where Alex demonstrated how to operate the toy. Timmy filled its water tanks and busied himself putting out an inferno in the impatiens.

Alex put his hand on her shoulder. "I think Timmy's seen the worst, at least for a while. Here's what we need to do. We have to make certain the showing is a success so that old bag doesn't get the best of us. Have Amy contact those high rollers she had for her opening."

"An old friend is coming for dinner tonight. I could ask him to speak to some reporters he knows to see if they could give us more favorable coverage."

"Can you get Jock to come?"

His question took her by surprise; the door to the past had slammed shut the day of her mother's funeral. The only time she'd seen her father since then had been at Ellis's wedding. And they hadn't spoken.

"Why do I need him?" Annoyance punctuated every syllable.

"Lady Bewley insists you're such a degenerate that your family won't speak to you." He studied her a moment. "What is the problem with Jock? Vic and I liked him."

Brett gazed lovingly at her son; he was on his muddy knees adjusting the fire engine's ladder so he could get to the wisteria vine climbing the garden wall. "If I'd listened to my father, I would have had an abortion."

Alex looked at Timmy, who chose that second to glance up and flash them his cutest smile. "Brett," Alex said, his voice low, gentler than she'd ever heard it, "it's easy to discuss abortion in the abstract. But Timmy's here now. Don't you think it's time to give Jock a second chance?"

He'd voiced thoughts she'd had before, but had stubbornly rejected. "Maybe," she admitted, then amended it to, "All right. I'll call him."

Alex smiled; immediately she felt she'd made the right choice. She shouldn't be selfish or stubborn when Alex's investment as well as Lev's and Eula Mae's jobs were at stake.

Alex checked his watch. "I have to go. I'm due at the Diamond Club for the monthly dinner."

He said good-bye to Timmy, telling him to ignore the teasing, and Brett walked him to the door, uncomfortably aware she needed to say something. She'd done a great deal of soul-searching since the night he kissed her, and had diagnosed her response to him as the inevitable result of spending too many years alone. But now, she'd weighed the afternoon's events, admitting she and Alex had shared an intensely personal experience. Her feelings for him were becoming alarmingly confused.

He opened the door and she said, "Thank you for everything." Her words sounded hollow, trite. She studied the apron she wore, then raised her head to meet his eyes. "Honest to God, I don't know how I would have handled Timmy without you. Timmy identifies with you; now he knows he isn't alone."

He studied her, but didn't say anything.

"How long did your grandmother make you take ballet lessons?" The question came unexpectedly, maybe because she'd been wondering since she heard him talking to Timmy.

"From the time I was three until I was fourteen. She wouldn't have let me quit then except Uncle Vic convinced her—" he stopped abruptly.

"Convinced her what?"

"I was too big to be a ballet star."

An image of Alexander Gudonov flashed through her mind; he was at least as big as Alex. Nureyev was tall, too. There was more to this than Alex wanted to discuss, but her sixth sense cautioned her not to ask.

He bent down and kissed her cheek, sending a quivery heat through her body. "Remember, we're in this together."

She stood in the doorway and watched him walk down the street until he turned the corner and disappeared from sight. With heart-knocking alarm she longed for a real kiss like the one they'd shared last time they stood here.

*   *   *

Brett had dressed for dinner and was basting the roast when the doorbell rang. Timmy had brought his fire engine inside and was too preoccupied with putting out a fire under the kitchen table to answer it, so Brett went, wondering who it was since it was too early for Hugh.

"Eula Mae called me," Amy said when Brett opened the door. "Is Timmy all right?"

Brett led Amy to the parlor sofa. "He's in the kitchen playing. I think he's fine—for now. But we could use your help to outmaneuver Lady Bewley."

"Anything. You know that."

Brett explained how crucial it was for the exhibition to be a success, and Amy volunteered to personally telephone her clients and encourage them to attend.

"Thanks. I really appreciate it." She studied Amy, deciding something was different about her today. "Is everything okay with you? You look . . . happier."

"Things couldn't be better."

Brett thought Amy sounded sincere and was grateful she seemed to be getting over Ellis. "What happened to you the other night? Why did you leave without saying good-bye?"

"Lev thought you and Alex wanted to be alone."

"That's ridiculous. Alex persuaded me to leave you and Lev alone. I think Alex was up to something. Well, it didn't work, did it?"

From the kitchen Brett heard Timmy playing, mumbling *brrrm brrrm brrrm* as he wheeled the fire engine across the floor.

"Did you ever find out why Ellis came to THE FIND?"

"Yes. He called and said he was worried about me. He came with Ruthless so I wouldn't get the wrong impression."

"Really? Why didn't you call and tell me? I've been trying to reach you for days."

"I've been taking cooking lessons."

Brett couldn't help laughing. "The take-away counters at

Fortnum and Mason's food halls will close without your business, not to mention Partridge's delivery service." She laughed again, but Amy didn't even smile. "You *are* serious. Well, tell all. Where are you taking the lessons?"

"They're . . . ah . . . private lessons."

Something was strange here, but she wasn't sure what it was. There was more to Amy's sudden domestic bent than she was telling, which was odd because they usually shared everything. "Who's teaching the class?"

"An instructor in Soho."

"What's her name?"

Amy shifted her head, her brown hair fluttering across her shoulders. Finally she said, "Lev's giving me lessons."

It took a full second for the implication of those words to register, then Brett felt foolish for assuming he wasn't her type. "I see," she responded although she was still having difficulty imagining Amy and Lev as a couple.

"No. You don't. I don't even understand it myself."

"Lev's inordinately talented, creative." Then Brett remembered what Alex had said. "It's time you dated a different type of man. Maybe you'll love him more—"

"This isn't love. It's—it's . . . sex. He's terrific in bed." Amy stopped and shook her head. "Don't look so shocked. You don't have to love a man to sleep with him."

"I do. I can't imagine—" She cut herself off, knowing she was being too judgmental.

"That's your problem, Brett. You're waiting for Mr. Perfect to appear. Can't you be with a man the way I am with Lev—for a little fun?"

"That's a dangerous attitude these days."

"I'm not advocating promiscuity," Amy retorted with a flare of hostility. "I practice safe sex." She threw up her hands, shaking her head. "I knew you wouldn't understand. That's why I haven't called you."

The harshness of her friend's words affected her deeply. This was Amy, the friend who'd stood by her when she'd been most alone in those weeks after Owen's disappearance and her mother's untimely death. The friend who'd insisted she have Timmy. The friend who'd kept her financially secure during those difficult months.

"Oh, Amy, I'm sorry if I've upset you." Brett hugged her, her throat constricting. "If you were my sister, I couldn't love you more. I want to understand. I honestly do."

"Right now," Amy said, her voice upbeat, "I need someone to help me forget Ellis. Lev isn't the love of my life, but I like being with him. Haven't you ever felt like that?"

Hearing the excitement in Amy's voice, Brett was suddenly lonely. She'd always expected to be sharing her life with Owen, but now she truly realized she was alone. The gnawing ache deep down where she kept Owen's memory resurfaced.

"Come on, Brett, admit you have similar feelings for Alex."

"He's a friend. That's all."

Brett persuaded Timmy to park the fire engine beside his bed and go to sleep before she served Hugh MacLeod coffee after dinner.

"He's very bright," Hugh commented, his hazel eyes seeming larger because his hairline had receded since Brett had last seen him. "How's he taking the fuss in the papers?"

"That's why I wanted him to go to bed. I need to talk to you." She explained what had happened today and how she and Alex intended to fight Lady Bewley and her friends at C.U.M. "Do you think I'm doing the right thing?"

"Absolutely. I've devoted my life to fighting people like her. Do you think there's a fundamental difference between a dictator who tortures political prisoners and that woman? Of course not. If she had total power, no telling what she'd do. Like a dictator, she has a flagrant disregard for the truth, for justice." He leaned forward, his voice registering anger although remaining controlled. "I'm going to contact some reporters I know. I think both sides of this story deserve attention. So far, this has been discussed only in the tabloids. Let's see how responsible journalists deal with it."

"That's what Alex said."

"Alex?"

"Alex Savich, the owner of Belage."

Hugh's observant eyes, honed by years of questioning people on behalf of Amnesty International, assessed her carefully. "A close friend, I take it?"

"He's been great. He believes in my talent. He's put a lot of money into promoting my designs. I don't want Lady Bewley to cause trouble for Alex."

Hugh hesitated, measuring her. She wondered if he suspected what she couldn't even admit to Amy: Alex was more than a friend. Undoubtedly, he did. Hugh could read people better than anyone she knew. He'd spent his life investigating allegations registered with Amnesty International. Each charge had to be investigated and documented before the committee would launch a campaign. He could judge with astonishing accuracy what people didn't say as well as what they did.

Hugh MacLeod, heir to the MacLeod Scotch fortune, had been her mother's closest friend ever since Brett could remember. While her father, Jock, had been more like Alex, focusing on making money with his business, Hugh reminded Brett of Owen Northcote. Owen had had little use for material comforts; he'd ceaselessly tried to help suffering people.

She was on the verge of telling Hugh more about Alex, but stopped herself. How could she when she hadn't analyzed her own feelings enough to express them truthfully to her best friend? Instead, she changed the subject.

"I've never really understood why Lady Bewley has this vendetta against me. I know she's a close friend of Ruth's, but Ruthless got rid of me years ago."

"It's not personal—exactly. Lady Bewley hated your mother. She can't hurt her, so she's going after you."

"But why? What did my mother do to her?"

"Nothing. But years ago when she started C.U.M. no one would listen to her, but your mother—you're so much like her it's astonishing—would whiz into London from some relief camp and grab the spotlight, raise millions, and leave. Lady Bewley worked day after day for a crumb of media attention. She once accused your mother of being a publicity-seeking opportunist who'd deserted her child."

Deserted. In her heart of hearts, Brett admitted she had felt deserted as a child, left to fend off Ruth Payne. "Mother wasn't an opportunist. She went to parties when she returned to London because she needed to forget the horrors of the camps. Believe me, I know. The only horror Lady Bewley has seen is the construction site of the 'chunnel.'"

Hugh chuckled. "True, but it doesn't make her any less dangerous. It's about time England really saw C.U.M. is forcing a minority viewpoint on the majority." He shook his head, and the worry lines across his brow appeared deeper. "Trouble is, this showdown with Saddam Hussein in Kuwait has everyone's attention right now."

"Saddam will back down and—"

"I've investigated many charges of torture in Iraq; Hussein's deranged. Mark my words, this will come to war."

A soft knock at the door interrupted them. Brett answered it and found Lev and Amy at the door. She invited them in for coffee and introduced them to Hugh.

Amy said, "We have a great idea. Let's contact some of your mother's supporters and make them aware of the situation."

"I don't know," Brett hedged. She hated the thought of riding on her mother's coattails, not making her own name.

"I'll handle it," Hugh said with a smile.

"Gut," Lev said, "so no problem." *So* came out *tzo* with the Eastern European overtone.

Lev beamed at Amy, who smiled back, happier than Brett could ever remember seeing her. Just sex, Brett thought. As Alex would have said: No way.

"You're from . . . ?" Hugh asked Lev, letting the question hang.

"Israel." Lev seemed offended by the question.

"Hugh's with Amnesty International," Brett said, assuming this would explain his interest.

Hugh smiled, his benevolent smile that Brett imagined him using to put dictators at ease, or to calm anxious witnesses terrified of government reprisals. "You were born in Russia."

"Ukraine." Lev's tone was positively forbidding now, and Amy shot Brett an anxious look.

But Hugh didn't seem to notice. "How long did it take you to get an immigration permit?"

"Too long." Lev glared at Hugh as if he were being interrogated by the Gestapo.

Time to change the subject, Brett told herself. "I see that Alberto Fujimori has been elected president in Peru." She turned to Lev, certain he was confused about what type of organization Amnesty International was. "Hugh represents a human rights group called Amnesty International. He wages campaigns to see political prisoners are released." Lev didn't look one bit mollified. "Peru has just elected someone we hope will change the country for the better."

"From Japan?"

Hugh took over. "Fujimori's ancestors came from Japan. They were expelled as undesirables because they were nothing but poor farmers. In Peru they've banded together and become wealthy and very successful. They're quite a political force."

Brett saw that Lev seemed to be relaxing; evidently he'd needed an explanation about Amnesty International. "Is there any hope of getting Fujimori to look for Owen's body?"

"I'll see what I can do," Hugh assured her. "I'll be spending the next few months in Peru reviewing documents that Fujimori has promised to release."

"Come." Lev pulled Amy to her feet. "Good night."

They were gone almost before Brett could thank them for coming. She couldn't help asking Hugh, "Was there something odd about Lev's behavior?"

"Experience tells me that your friend Lev is a man with a past, a man with something to hide."

17

Alex greeted the few men he knew while waiting in line to pass through the metal detector at the Diamond Club. He checked the bulletin board where typed notices alerted members to infractions of club rules. The club in Bombay finally caught that jerk, Jamal Tabori, for reneging on a deal. These men were pariahs now, ostracized and forced to deal with back-alley brokers.

Aw, hell. He was damn close to being an outcast himself. One word from Intelco and his name would be on Diamond Club bulletin boards worldwide. The only thing that could save him was if—and this was a really big if—somehow the colored diamonds weren't from a cartel-controlled mine.

"Savich," called a friend, motioning for Alex to join their group as they went into the dining room.

"Do you know Stan Doppelt?"

Alex extended his hand, interested to meet the man who'd created the Star-Burst, a new cut that added extra facets on the bottom of an emerald-cut diamond, giving it unusual brilliance. Doppelt was one of the true talents in the industry.

They talked together passing through the buffet line where a chef carved prime rib, and the Indian members could help themselves to *samosas* and *ras gulabs*. More than half of the members of the London club called Bombay home. India had been the earliest source of diamonds, and their brokers still exerted extraordinary influence, particularly the five Mehta families rumored to be the largest-volume diamond wholesalers worldwide. On the far side of the room was the kosher line.

Alex followed the group to one of the larger tables, and sat, listening, feeling like an interloper. He didn't have Uncle Vic's—or Brett's—knack for easy conversation with strangers. He should come to lunch at the club to get to know people, but working shorthanded at Belage, allowing Brett to double as a designer and a goldsmith while Lev cut and laser-set, how could he take three hours off to sit around the club bullshitting?

He spotted Dash Boynton in the buffet line; the prime rib Alex swallowed stalled halfway to his stomach. It was the first time he'd seen the cartel's enforcer since arriving in London. Actually, he'd met him only once—briefly—in Antwerp. Boynton heaped his plate full, then lumbered in their direction. Alex almost moaned aloud; the only empty chair at their table was next to him.

Closer Dash came, his eyes trained on Alex. His sixth sense kicked in. Showdown. Thanks, Grandmother, for all those years of ballet lessons with your rigid standards, your rules, your cruelty. He'd learned to dance, his mind a thousand miles away with Vic, never even breaking a sweat when his grandmother lit into him. He wasn't going to give himself away by sweating now.

Sixtyish, body like a flabby tombstone, Dash had glossy black hair with a pronounced widow's peak that reminded Alex of Dracula. Vampire-white skin, too. True, all Brits were a bit pasty-faced—what did you expect in this climate? —but Dash's skin seemed paler against his dyed hair. Alex chuckled to himself, amazed he could actually find any humor in this situation. He must be losing it.

"Mr. Savich, dash it all if I haven't been looking for you."

At those feared words "dash it all," conversation at the table stopped as surely as if they'd been watching a master cutter cleave a huge diamond and accidentally shatter it in a thousand worthless pieces. Everyone knew "dash it all" meant Intelco suspected Alex of some infraction. They waited for Boynton to request a private conversation that would confirm this. Alex couldn't allow Dash to ask him to sit at another table for "a chat." He'd be finished.

Alex looked up, pretending to see the enforcer for the first time. "Boynton, I've been hoping to see you. I want to talk to you." He swung out the chair, knowing Boynton, the original tight-ass Brit—all right, chubby-cheeked Brit— would be unfailingly polite and take a seat.

Maskirova is in your blood, Alex reminded himself as he casually cut a piece of prime rib and chewed it while Dash settled into the chair next to him. Alex admitted he had a streak of perversity that could get him killed. He refused to join the ranks of other dealers who kiss-assed Intelco so much their lips had calluses. Not Alex Savich.

"I've got this terrific designer, Brett Lamont." He waved his fork, including the rest of the table in what normally would have been considered a private conversation. "Constance Lamont's daughter. Remember her?" A few solemn nods; no one spoke. "I'm having an exhibition of enhanced diamonds next week at Harvey Nichols. Everyone in the Diamond Club will be getting invitations in the mail, but I'd like to invite you all personally." He nudged Dash's arm. "Think you can make it?"

Caught with his mouth full, Boynton grunted. Alex congratulated himself on his move. Who would suspect him of trying to trick Intelco while inviting the elite of the diamond trade? It would take *cojones*—big balls—as the Chicanos in L.A. would say—to even *think* of pulling such a stunt.

"Exactly what are enhanced diamonds?" Dash's words were measured the way Alex remembered Brits speaking in 1930s movies—as if they had a pencil balanced on their upper lips.

"I'm glad you asked that question." Trust me, you were planning on getting me alone and finding out. Alex knew someone had leaked word of the advertisements set to appear tomorrow, or else Boynton wouldn't have had any reason to single him out tonight. So far, their ads hadn't once used the word *enhanced*.

"Enhanced"—Alex included everyone at the table—"is some advertising genius's way of saying I'm producing colored diamonds by X-raying them."

Somebody say something—please. All eyes were on him, but no one spoke. At a time like this he could really use Brett. Like Vic, she would have told some joke. Or even just smiled.

"I've refined the process to the point where I get stones with fair color." Wait until they saw what he meant by fair color.

"You've registered a patent," Boynton demanded.

"Absolutely, registered in Washington—pending, of course. You know bureaucracy."

"Good idea," Doppelt said. "I trademarked the Star-Burst to keep the competition at bay."

"My thinking exactly." Well, not *exactly*. He'd made drawings, hired a patent attorney, and filed papers knowing it would take years—God bless the red tape choking the patent office—before anyone even reviewed the patent. When they did, they'd have an obsolete microwave on their hands, but until then he'd look legit to the cartel.

"What about security?" Boynton wanted to know. Belage was in a building that dated back to the turn of the century.

"The Mossad."

Awestruck silence. Everyone at the table stopped chewing. The Mossad, the Israeli security force, were world experts. It was rumored they'd designed the state-of-the-art security system at 550 Hill Street, L.A.'s most prestigious diamond center. If you'd consulted the Mossad, you must have something invaluable to protect. In fact, the only time

Alex had encountered the Mossad was when they debriefed Lev.

"Did I mention I'm laser-setting these stones?" he asked Dash, who'd somehow managed to down most of his meal while Alex had been talking. Someone ought to tell the guy to slow down or he'd eat himself to death.

Now he'd gotten them with the hat trick: X-rayed diamonds, Mossad security, laser settings. Whoa! A rising star. He took another bit of stone-cold prime rib, chewing and smiling. And thinking to himself that he was so full of bullshit his blue eyes must have turned brown.

"No. You never mentioned lasers." Dash trapped him with a vampire's unwavering stare. "How big are these diamonds?"

I knew you'd ask that question. "One's about a carat, but soon I'll be able to buy bigger, better stones to enhance. Just because they're not large doesn't mean these designs aren't impressive. You're going to have to see Lamont's designs for yourself."

"I'll be there," Boynton assured him.

I would have bet my life.

18

"Show me the lewd stuff." The reporter from the *Evening Outlook*—most called it the *Evening Outrage*—gawked at Brett as she stood behind the jewelry display in the Harvey Nichols department store.

Brett waved her hand at the cases filled with glistening black sand Alex had flown in from Hawaii. Artfully arranged on the Kona sand was the *Lamont Collection for Belage: Gifts from the Sea*. Resting on the bed of sand were leather bound copies of Anne Morrow Lindbergh's book, *Gift from the Sea*, opened to the passage that described the gift from the sea Brett had created. Each piece of jewelry represented something found in the ocean, from conch earrings set with hundreds of pale blue diamonds to the exquisite pelican whose body was the largest stone in the collection, a shell-pink diamond.

"Isn't there a penis or somethin' that looks like one?"

"Perhaps the pelican's beak."

"Yeah, right." The reporter leered at her. "You're Lamont." He made it sound as if she were a serial killer. "So you don't know who the father of your kid is."

Even though she'd been warned to expect inflammatory questions from reporters who were only interested in a risqué story, a white-hot explosion of rage hit her. She reminded herself not to let him bait her, not to be drawn into an argument about something that wasn't any of his damn business.

"Okay, buddy. You're just leaving, right?" The look on Alex Savich's face left no room for debate. With a sullen shrug the reporter walked away, and Alex turned to Brett. "Don't let him bother you. We've already sold more than half the collection and taken lots of orders."

"That's fantastic." She glanced at the crowd, looking for her father. Nothing. "Are the C.U.M. pickets still out there?"

"There are more of them than when we arrived, but do you think it's hurting sales?"

"No." The store was crammed with people and was doing more business than Harrods after-Christmas sale. Amy had mustered her clients, and Brett had contacted old friends of her mother's. Hugh had persuaded responsible reporters from *The Times* and the *Observer* to cover the story, and they'd successfully defused the charges Lady Bewley had made. Even Ellis had helped by featuring her exhibition during the color segment of his broadcast, proudly telling the world she was his talented stepsister.

But where was her father? Calling him had been one of the hardest things she'd ever done. She'd swallowed her pride and asked him to attend for Timmy's sake. He'd promised to come. She scanned the crowd again, but Jock Payne wasn't anywhere. Lev stood off to the side talking with Amy, whose gaze sung anthems of adoration. Earlier, Eula Mae had trooped through with members of the Rare Plant and Pit Council.

"Looking for someone?" Alex's eyes were on one of the models who was parading by, showing a shimmering silver cocktail dress.

"Just looking." She glanced down at her own dress, a demure black gown that wouldn't add fuel to Lady Bewley's charges that she was a loose woman. At Alex's suggestion, she'd worn her hair up and from her ears dangled her mother's diamonds. They made her feel glamorous despite the frumpy dress.

She glanced at the striking model with ice-blond hair whose eyes were on Alex. Brett couldn't blame her. Alex definitely stood out in a crowd, his athletic build and height complementing his angular features.

"I'm taking everyone to Annabel's to celebrate afterward."

Brett couldn't help smiling, and Alex responded with a slow suggestive smile that filled her with anticipation. She looked forward to relaxing with him, toasting Belage's success. It had been an unbelievable grind, but it had been more rewarding than she could ever have imagined when she saw her very own jewelry on display. It was fun working with Alex, who understood her ambition, who didn't let obstacles like Lady Bewley upset him.

Alex winked at her. "Catch you later."

Really, so American, she thought, watching him walk away. And so very sexy. Too bad he knew it. Not that he flaunted his effect on women; he took it for granted. She was looking forward to celebrating with him; since Timmy was spending the night with a friend, she did not have to rush home.

Alex roamed the crowded jewelry salon, looking to see if Dash Boynton had arrived. So far an amazing number of Diamond Club members had visited the collection, but no sign of Boynton.

Alex stationed himself at the far end of the marble-floored gallery, pleased with himself. Even more pleased with Brett. Not only was she a talented designer but she was a helluva salesperson. Look at her. Smiling—naturally—at a white-robed Arab who lived in the world's largest ashtray floating on a sea of black gold. The denizen of the dunes whipped out a credit card. Yup, she'd sold him the most expensive earrings.

The model in the silver dress that reminded him of tinfoil

sashayed by, distracting him with a flirtatious bob of her head and a slinky pirouette worthy of a stripper. He glanced back to Brett, but she was busy with the ruler of the shifting sands.

Was he getting anywhere with her? Alex doubted it. He didn't expect Brett to come around until she admitted she wanted to sleep with him—if he lived that long. Forget it. But how could he? He was horny as hell. Again.

For some reason he thought of Timmy, probably because Brett must have looked just like him when she'd been young. A charmer. Timmy had knocked him for a loop the other day by kissing him, comforting him when Alex had been trying to make the kid feel better. Kids were like that, he reasoned. They cut through to the heart of the problem without the usual adult bullshit.

Brett, of course, had picked up on exactly what he was saying. Like all women she'd die trying to pry the details out of him. Forget it. He intended to keep his past private.

"Hello, again," said a busty redhead in—of all things—a strapless green dress of dyed snakeskin or maybe lizard. Ugh. She wore huge silver earrings shaped like lightning bolts. He caught his reflection in one and adjusted the knot in his tie.

She looked familiar, her smile as suggestive as her exposed cleavage, but he couldn't place her. So what else was new? The world was full of beautiful women that came on to you. The hell of it was, when he really wanted one, she had scruples.

"Have you been here long?" the redhead asked, her long, spiked lashes dipping low, then fluttering.

"Since dawn." Something familiar about those phony lashes.

"You don't remember me?" Her lips drew into a carmine pout.

"How could I forget you?" Good question.

"I'm Latrice Laveaux. We met at THE FIND."

"Yeah." The orange glowworm dress on the bombshell figure like an old-time movie star.

"Sex," the woman said, opening her eyes wide.

Behind Alex a flash went off, then he heard the *zzzt zzzt* of an autowind camera. "I beg your pardon?" He must have misunderstood. He'd met some ballsy chicks, but this—

"You're supposed to say sex instead of cheese. Whenever a photo opportunity occurs, part your lips just enough to—"

Alex stopped listening to her breathy explanation. Dash Boynton had walked into the jewelry salon, frowning. What else. He left the woman, heading toward Dash with a smile.

"Hey." He slapped Dash on the back. "Great seein' you."

Dash nodded, full of humor as usual. Last time the guy had cracked a smile was when the Nazis surrendered.

"That's your designer." Dash's eyes were on Brett.

"Let me introduce you." He guided Dash over to the counter and made the introductions, wishing he'd been able to take Brett into his confidence about the "enhanced" stones and tell her how important it was for Dash Boynton to believe they were producing the colored diamonds themselves.

"Nice earrings," Dash said, looking at the Siberian Ice dangling from Brett's ears.

Treating Dash to one of her smiles, she leaned forward, inviting him to take a closer look at her earrings. There you go. Alex gave himself a mental pat on the back for thinking to ask Brett to wear the earrings to distract him.

"Aaaahh, modern versions of Marie Antoinette's earrings, aren't they?" Dash said with a sigh, surprising Alex. Usually Dash was as animated as a corpse, but precise, anal. The kind of guy who ironed his jockstrap.

Brett's eyes widened. "I don't know, are they?"

"Yes. Louis XVI had them especially made for her. They were almost flawless stones—"

"From India," Alex cut in. "Back then, all diamonds came from the Godavari and Krishna rivers. It was another century before diamonds were discovered in Africa."

"Yes. The rajas believed diamonds brought victory and they were an emblem of fearlessness." Dash spoke as if in a trance, his eyes never leaving the diamonds.

"What happened to Marie Antoinette's earrings?" Brett asked.

"During the Reign of Terror, she tried to escape and the earrings were taken from her." Dash's voice was low, reverent. "They disappeared without a trace. Then in the 1920s Pierre Cartier here in London sold them to some American."

"Marjorie Merriweather Post," Alex explained. "They're in the Smithsonian now."

"Where had they been?" Brett asked. "Don't all major diamonds have a provenance, a history?"

Dash shrugged; he'd yet to take his eyes off the Siberian Ice. "Cartier claimed they'd belonged to some Russian grand duchess, but no one ever recalled seeing her wear them."

Brett touched an earring and it shot sparks of light. "Would you know anything about the provenance of these diamonds?"

Now this was crediting Dash with more knowledge than he might have. He worked in the security division and wouldn't be expected to know this.

"Two matched stones, flawless," Dash said. "They came from a Siberian mine about five years ago. They were in the box assigned to Rutherford Ames-Sloheath, right here in London."

"But they were cut in Antwerp." Alex was nervous; Dash knew much more about diamonds than he'd expected.

Dash took his eyes off the gems and looked directly at him. "True, but they were set by Garrard's on Bond Street."

"They were given to my mother, but Garrard's wouldn't tell me who'd bought them."

Dash's face remained impassive. Alex's sixth sense told him Boynton knew exactly who'd purchased the earrings.

The lull in the conversation became too long, so Alex

said, "From now on, they'll be known as the Lamont Earrings. That's how rare diamonds get their names—from their first owners." Too damn bad none of the colored diamonds would remain large enough to merit a name.

"Did you know my mother?" Brett asked Dash.

A slight hesitation, then, "Yes. She convinced me to contribute to several of her causes."

Naaah. Everyone knew it was easier to pick fly shit out of pepper than to get Dash Boynton to open his wallet. Just goes to show—a winning personality is priceless.

"Mother loved earrings—the bigger the better. But she gave everything she had to famine relief. She intended to return these earrings. I'd return them myself if I knew who—"

There was no mistaking the plea in Brett's voice, but Dash ignored it. Might as well try to put out a four-alarm fire with spit than to get Dash to reveal who'd bought those diamonds.

Dash thumped his plump fingers on the display case, his eyes now trained on the display. "Let me see that necklace."

Bull's-eye. Dash had picked the necklace, a daisy chain of starfish, because it had the big stones, kelly-green diamonds. The largest stone was actually in the pelican, but one of the clerks was showing it to a customer, and Dash hadn't spotted it. As planned, he'd been too distracted by Brett's earrings to look around at the other pieces the clerks were selling, but Alex had to be careful not to underestimate Boynton.

"Laser-set," Dash said. "Who's doing your work?"

Alex silenced Brett with a wink. "An Israeli."

"Mmm." Dash fondled the necklace, then took out a loupe. He propped it under his eyebrow, looking like Dracula with a monocle, and examined the necklace. Stone by stone. "Hardly any inclusions to speak of."

No kidding.

"Alex is very talented," Brett commented. "He knows just what trace elements will produce given colors."

Lord have mercy.

Dash dropped the necklace onto the counter and zeroed in on him with the loupe. "How is that possible?"

"Hey, Dash. Do I ask you for trade secrets? I've got a patent to protect." Alex grinned.

Dash removed the loupe, and Alex winked at Brett, hoping she'd understand it as a signal for her to talk.

She took the cue. "There's a wonderful piece right over there. You have to see it."

Jee-sus—not the pelican.

Dash eyed Alex suspiciously as Brett handed him the pin. Alex forced himself to smile, leaning casually against the case.

"Loupe-clean," Dash exclaimed.

Really?

"Nice pink color."

If you say so.

"We're having trouble producing red," Brett announced.

Dash gazed at her without removing the loupe, his pale blue eye magnified to twice its normal size. "Why's that?"

Uh-oh, a trick question; Alex knew he'd primed Brett with an answer that would satisfy Dash.

"The trace elements that produce red are nearly impossible to find. Remember Christies' auction last year? That red diamond went for just under a million. How big was it, Alex?"

Exactly .95-carat. "About a carat, I guess."

She turned to Dash. "We can make pink, but red is hopeless."

A tragedy, sure, but one the Intelco loved. The last thing they needed was someone who could throw the whole market off by producing red diamonds. Obtaining pink wasn't a problem; Australia mined pinks, although the quality was suspect. But red diamonds were the most valuable gems in the world. And the rarest.

"Think of the De Young diamond," Brett added.

No. Don't think of it. Alex groaned inwardly. The dia-

mond, a startling shade of pink, was almost three carats, the
largest and most perfect stone around. But not as big as the
one he had in the safe.

"Or consider the Hope diamond," Brett went on. "Such a
beautiful shade of blue. Isn't it about fifty carats, Alex?"

Aw, hell. Could he shut Brett up? Dash Boynton didn't
need to be reminded the most famous diamonds in the
world were colored stones. He didn't need encouragement
to think of Belage as a threat. "Of course, I can't afford to
fool around with large stones like that."

"You plan to keep your diamonds small," Dash said. It
wasn't a question; it was an order.

"Who's that man with Alex and Brett?" Amy asked Lev.

"He is from the diamond-trading cartel."

"He doesn't look too happy, does he?"

"Mr. Boynton never is. Perhaps he invites Alex to be a
sight holder."

"What's that?" She smiled at Lev, thinking how easy it
was to be with him.

"Ten times a year Intelco sight holders come to London.
They get—what you put shoes in—full of diamonds."

"A shoebox full of diamonds?" She asked and he nodded.
She'd heard of the cartel, of course. Several of the execu-
tives did business with her father, but she never knew they
doled out diamonds in a shoebox. It didn't make sense.
"Surely, the sight holders select diamonds and then pack
them in a box the size of a shoebox."

Lev laughed. "No choosing. They take what Intelco give
them. Some good, some bad. They trade stones they do not
want."

"So the best diamonds go to the sight holders. If Alex
became one of them, he'd have access to the best diamonds
in the world, wouldn't he?" At Lev's nod, she added, "Can
he afford it?"

"Perhaps one day."

"The enhanced diamonds are such a success that—" She

stopped, fully intending to try to extract more information about the process from Lev, who'd been evasive, but she saw her father coming toward her. "I'll be right back," she told Lev.

"I came to see your friend's designs," Gordon Conrift said without preamble. "You can't go anywhere on the street without hearing about these enhanced diamonds."

The street referred to the diamond district. Conrift Bullion supplied most of the gold used to make jewelry in Europe. She should have guessed her father would be curious.

"Brett's talented, don't you think?" she asked as she followed her father to the display case. Over her shoulder she noticed Lev had disappeared. Thank heaven—she didn't want her father to be rude to him.

Her father's frown rippled upward, emphasizing his bald head and Friar Tuck fringe of dead-white hair. "Yes. She's creative. But who's doing the laser-setting? He's just as talented."

"An Israeli, I believe."

Her father leveled his gaze at her. "What about you? Have you found someone to give me a grandson?"

"All you ever think about is an heir. It's positively old-fashioned. One of your cousin's sons is perfectly capable of running Conrift Bullion if you'll just train him."

He dismissed a gaggle of cousins with a wave of his hand. "I want a Conrift. It's up to you. Marry and give me a grandson."

"Sorry to disappoint you but—"

"What about that man you're seeing?"

How on earth could he know about Lev? "What man?"

"The clerk at your shop said you've been seeing someone."

"You won't like him any more than you did Ellis. Lev—"

"Lev? He's Jewish then." Her father smiled at her for the first time in years. "Wonderful."

"He's poor," she warned, knowing no one outside the Cousinhood, London's elite circle of wealthy Jews, would satisfy her father. "And we're not serious. We're just friends. That's all."

"Lev." Gordon Conrift was still smiling. "I want to meet him. This Tuesday. Dinner at your home. Have him there."

Without another word, her father marched out the door, and Amy stood gazing into the display case, seeing every grain of sand as another reason why her father would never approve of Lev. Did she care? No. But she didn't want to expose Lev to her father's arrogance, his ambition, his greed.

"Milochka," Lev whispered as he came up to her.

"Lev, my father is Lord Conrift, director of—"

"Conrift Bullion. They get up each morning and tell world what to charge for gold."

"It's a family company. We've been in London since the Middle Ages, and there's always been a male to head the company—until now. My father never forgave me for being a girl."

She shook her head, noticing his expression had softened. "What about you? Do you have brothers or sisters?"

For a moment, she didn't think he was going to answer. "Only child," he said. "Alex is like a brother."

Were they that close? Probably. They spent two nights a week together. But brothers? Why not? She and Brett were as close as sisters, closer than some sisters, actually.

"What about your father, Lev? Is he alive?"

Again, he seemed reluctant to answer, almost resenting her asking. "No, but I love him very much. If we live in same place I would talk to him each day."

"Do you talk to your mother often?" she asked, but he gave her a strange look. "I thought with *perestroika* it was easier to call the Ukraine."

This time, he didn't answer, the chatter of shoppers around them filling the void. He's a troubled man, she recognized, but why? She almost questioned him further, but didn't, deciding to leave their relationship as it was—physical. Maybe there were things about Lev Rodynskov she'd rather not know.

"Lev, my father would like to meet you. Are you free for dinner this Tuesday evening?"

What was that all about? Brett wondered as Alex guided Dash Boynton away from the counter. She knew he was head of Intelco's security service, but why was he so interested in Belage's collection? Intelco must feel threatened by Alex's ability to produce colored diamonds. If the advanced technology Alex had developed became widespread, it would throw the colored diamond market into a tailspin.

Before she had time to consider just what Intelco might do to keep enhanced diamonds off the market, she saw Jock Payne's silver-gray head above the crowd. Beside him walked Ruth—what had Alex said?—pushy-pretentious Ruth, looking as if she had a hot poker in her back. Ruthless said something, her lips barely moving, then she stalked off in the direction of the fur salon. Brett looked down, pretending not to notice her father approaching, marshaling her thoughts. After all this time, what would he say?

She sensed him standing in front of her and knew she had to look up. She met his eyes, the color of the single malt scotch he loved to sip on cold winter evenings, eyes that had lovingly watched her as he read her fairy tales, eyes that never missed any of her school plays. What had gone wrong? The answer remained the same as it had for the last twenty-two years: He'd driven her mother out of the house, then married Ruthless.

"Hello, Father." She couldn't quite thank him for coming.

His eyes traveled across her face, taking in her hair, her eyes—the earrings. "You look exactly like your mother."

There was more than a trace of sadness in his voice. His silver hair was now brushed with white at the temples. He'd aged. Had it been that long? Too long.

"Those earrings are astounding on you."

She didn't add that they'd been a gift to her mother. And she was relieved that he didn't comment further, evidently assuming the earrings belonged to Belage.

"You've created some very special pieces here," Jock said, his eyes on the jewelry in the case, the tension between them thicker than London's fog.

"I had plenty of help." She went on to explain Lev and Alex's contributions.

"I've met Alex Savich several times," he said, looking her directly in the eye, "with Vicktor Orlov. They sold Ellis some diamonds. Savich had a good head for business, if he could keep away from the ladies."

Out of the corner of her eye, Brett saw Alex talking with the model who'd changed out of the silver gown into a black lace dress that fit her like shrink-wrap. Her father was right; men like Alex Savich had too much temptation come their way to resist.

"I'd buy something for Ruth but—"

"I don't expect you to." She imagined what it had taken for her father to persuade Ruthless to defy her close friend, Lady Bewley, and attend the exhibition. "Everything's sold. We're just taking orders."

"Wonderful." Her father smiled. There was no mistaking the pride in his eyes. "I never doubted your talent."

She didn't remind him that he'd pressed her to go to Oxford and had thought design school was only a glorified trade school. She understood; he'd worked his way up in life without an education. Even though he'd gone to great pains to educate himself, he'd regretted not having a degree. He'd wanted for her what he'd never been able to achieve himself.

"Thank you for coming. I really appreciate it."

"You didn't need me. I see several of your mother's old friends here." His gaze swept across the room to where Hugh MacLeod stood. "The press reported the situation fairly, once the major papers began covering the story."

She didn't give Hugh the credit he deserved. Her father

had never liked Hugh, although she could never understand why. It had to be that her father associated Hugh with Constance Lamont's insistence upon a career.

"The news coverage helped this exhibition," she admitted.

"But it hurt my grandson."

The simple statement, the honesty in her father's eyes, that sympathy she remembered from her own youth, took her by surprise.

"Does Timmy know he has a grandfather?"

"No." She felt ashamed of herself for not having told Timmy the truth, but at the time it seemed best.

"I'd like to see my grandson."

She wanted to refuse, to remind him that if he'd had his way, Timmy wouldn't be here. But she thought of Alex's comment about its being easier to deal with abortion in the abstract. The reality was quite different.

"I can come around tomorrow morning."

"Timmy's at a friend's." She saw the disappointment in her father's eyes. He thought she was lying to him the way she'd lied to Timmy about having a grandfather. "Could you come later for Sunday tea?"

Her father smiled, a heartfelt smile that colored all her childhood memories of him. How her mother must have loved him, and how it must have hurt to have Jock divorce her.

19

"Alex will be here soon," Lev assured Brett and Amy.

Brett was anxious to see him. Her sense of elation had heightened all evening, becoming giddy euphoria at Belage's astounding success. Their success. Brett glanced at the bottle of Cristal champagne chilling in the silver urn beside their table at Annabel's. "I wish Alex would hurry."

"Lev thought Alex is going to become a sight holder," Amy said. "That's why that man from Intelco came tonight."

Lev sheepishly took a swig of his vodka. Brett suspected Lev knew Intelco was interested in Alex's enhancer. They'd all but threatened him to keep his colored diamonds small. But how could they justify doing that? If Alex bought larger stones—would she ever love it—there was no reason he couldn't enhance them. The cartel controlled the sale of diamonds, but they had no right to dictate what you did with them.

But they could get rough. Was Alex worried? she wondered. There had been something strange about the way he'd handled Dash Boynton. Alex had been too casual. She'd seen him concerned about other things; he became less talkative and very controlled. Tonight Alex had been putting on an act. She was learning to read him and spot the hairline cracks in his composure.

Wait until she got him alone. She'd find out. Where was he, anyway? She had so many things to tell him—to share with him. She wanted to toast their success. And talk. And dance. Maybe . . . she let herself consider—just consider —the possibility he'd take her home. If she did, she'd have a hard time resisting him, she admitted. Did she really want to?

Why was she fighting it? They were attracted to each other just as Alex had insisted. Guilt made her deny it. Owen should be here; he should be the one she longed to have hold her. But he was gone. She'd waited faithfully, praying every night, putting her life on hold until she knew he'd died. Owen was a cherished memory, and she'd never forget him. Part of her would always love him. But reality hit her. Reality was Alex Savich.

Again she scanned the crowd, searching for Alex. It was well after one o'clock, and the club was so full she could hardly see the entrance. Suddenly Alex's dark head appeared at the back of a group walking into the club. She scooted her chair a little closer to the empty chair they'd been saving for him.

Alex emerged from the crowd, his arm around a striking blonde's waist, drawing her close as he guided her toward their table. The model from the exhibition. Now she wore an eye-catching electric-blue dress that fit her like wet silk.

For a moment Brett was too stunned to even realize he'd reached the table and was introducing the model. The coiling tightness in her chest took her breath away. She'd thought . . . she'd assumed . . . she'd been counting on . . . She realized Alex had introduced her to Sylvia.

"Hello." The word wedged in her throat.

"Brett," Alex said, his arm still draped around Sylvia, "move over toward Lev." He settled Sylvia in the empty chair beside Brett and signaled the waiter to bring another chair. Amy shot an anxious smile at Brett. "Sorry we're late," Alex said. "We swung by Sylvia's place so she could change."

"What happened to Eula Mae?" Amy asked Alex.

"She had a migraine."

There was a flurry of activity as one waiter brought Alex a chair and another opened the champagne, deftly popping the cork with one hand and catching it with the other.

"*Really,*" Sylvia exclaimed. "So clever."

"We have a lot to celebrate," Alex said, his tone intimate, his eyes on Sylvia.

"*Really.* Such fun." The model giggled, a low throaty laugh that even Brett had to admit was sexy.

"The Lamont Collection was a smash," Amy said, filling the pause Brett couldn't.

Alex raised his glass and the others lifted theirs. "To Belage."

He clinked his glass against Sylvia's first, then Lev's, then Amy's, finally reaching over Sylvia's arm to touch the rim of his glass to Brett's.

"To Belage." Brett managed a smile, but her voice sounded flat, void of its earlier happiness. The muscles in her throat were so achingly tight she could barely swallow the champagne.

"I understand everything sold and there were lots of orders," Amy said, continuing to talk when normally Brett would have.

"*Really,*" squealed Sylvia. "*Really?*"

"Philippe Deauville's even talking about putting a Belage section in his jewelry salon in the Place Vendôme in Paris."

Her smile paralyzed in place, Brett listened, not daring to say a word, overwhelmed by what she was feeling. She hadn't fallen for him, had she? Of course not. She knew better. Victor Orlov had warned her that Alex was a playboy. Even her father mentioned it. What she was feeling *was not* jealousy. She'd been alone too long, and seeing Lev and Amy together had heightened this empty feeling.

She was better off, much better, having Alex as a friend.

He was her employer, after all. Women came and went with Alex. But a friend was forever. Like Amy, who was now flashing her another encouraging smile as Alex explained his plans for Belage.

A terrible sense of being an interloper assailed Brett. Amy and Lev were so—so right together, his hand on her arm. Alex had both hands on the table, but Sylvia snuggled against him, the same look of adoration in her eyes that Timmy had when he was with Alex. She was a single woman —an outsider. A throbbing loneliness assailed her, an ache so deep she'd gladly trade it for physical pain. How soon could she gracefully leave?

"I'm going to the loo," Amy announced. "Coming, Brett?"

She almost said no, but the telepathic bond between them took over. Amy wanted to get her alone.

"I'm sorry, Brett," she said when they were inside the loo. "This isn't much of a celebration with Sylvia."

"It's all right. I just wasn't expecting her."

"Come on, Brett. You can't fool me."

Brett looked into the gilt mirror and smoothed her hair with her fingers. The soft upsweep was slowly giving way; a few tendrils had curled against her cheek. "I'm more attracted to Alex than I realized. We've been working too closely."

"He can't be serious about Sylvia," Amy said, reapplying her lipstick. "Has she said one word to you?"

"Of course not. She thinks cellulite is contagious."

Amy laughed, but it didn't make Brett feel any better.

"Sylvia has a one-word vocabulary," Brett consoled herself. "Teasing, she says, *reeeally,* then giggles at Alex's story of the mixup at the dry cleaners when someone got his loud L.A. tie by mistake. Or, a horrified *real-leee,* when he told her Harrods closed their fur department." She grimaced at her reflection in the mirror, knowing she sounded bitchy but unable to stop. "I love her breathy *really*—just to keep him talking. At one point he even managed to bring Sylvia to the verge of hysteria with three *reallys* when he mentioned a diamond trader from Antwerp faxing him erotic love letters instead of a diamond quote."

"You need to start dating, Brett. A healthy relationship with a little sex would be good for you. You've been alone too long."

Back at the table, they found Alex alone; Lev was waltzing with Sylvia. Before Brett could make an excuse to leave, Alex insisted she dance with him.

Alex pulled her closer than she expected, his arms holding her firmly, his palm resting on the small of her back, its warmth surprising her. Reminding her of other times he'd held her. And kissed her. She caught a whiff of the very masculine men's cologne he wore, and it almost brought tears to her eyes. *What on earth is wrong with you? Rampaging hormones, what else? Say something witty, for God's sake. Impossible. Then say something—anything.* But she couldn't.

"You were terrific tonight," Alex told her.

The intimate tone of his voice brought her up short. There were a dozen incidents she'd planned to share with him, but all she could say was, "It went better than I expected."

Despite the milling dancers, some doing little more than moving in place, Alex guided her through a succession of deft turns worthy of Fred Astaire. Had he taken ballroom dancing, too?

She tried to ignore the pressure of his leg against hers as he led her, distracted her. Conscious he was looking at her, she inched forward, not caring that she was moving closer to him, only interested in getting out of his line of vision. She gazed over the curve of his shoulder, watching the other dancers.

His arm tightened around her, conforming her body to his, but she pretended not to notice. Still, she couldn't ignore the heat she felt as her breasts pillowed against his chest, the way their hips met, their stomachs pressed against each other, or the insistent pressure of his thighs against hers.

It was the longest dance in recorded history, but finally it ended. Lev and Really-Really were nearby.

"I'm tired." Brett tried to smile. "I'll see you all later."

"Timmy looks exactly like you when you were his age," her father told her as they sat in her back garden having tea.

"He takes after Mother. We both do."

Jock Payne nodded, his expression sad, his eyes on his grandson, who was playing with his fire engine. Their meeting had gone much better than Brett had anticipated. When Timmy had returned home, Brett explained his grandfather was coming for tea. Timmy accepted it with the ease of a child who doesn't yet know the rules of the social game. And he'd greeted Jock with the same affection he had for everyone.

Her father had been thrilled to meet Timmy; she'd resisted the temptation to remind him that if Jock had had his way, Timmy wouldn't be here. Jock and Timmy had spent time playing with the fire engine, getting to know each other while Brett made her father's favorite Scottish biscuits, Kirriemuir Heckles, for tea.

"I know the last weeks have been hard on him," Jock said.

"Hugh says"—she stopped, noting the angry glint in her father's eye—"Lady Bewley was jealous of Mother and only attacks me because she can't hurt her."

"I think she'll leave you alone. Everyone praised your work. She lost credibility, condemning your jewelry as lewd."

"The damage was done, though," Brett responded, watching her father sprinkle pepper over his strawberries, a Scottish custom he'd taught her.

In spite of herself, she thought of Alex. His childhood had been troubled, so deeply troubled that he couldn't talk about it, so troubled that he didn't communicate very well on a personal level. Except sexually. She'd spent the better part of the night—a lonely night with Timmy away—assuring herself that she was better off not having an affair with him.

"Do you still hate me for marrying Ruth?" His question was startlingly direct, his tone wounded.

"I don't hate you. I never did." She glanced at her son, sad he'd never know Owen's love the way she'd known Jock's. She had to be honest with her father; their feud had gone on long enough. "I idolized you. I loved Mother, but you were the center of my world. Mother was always too busy for me. You were the one who read me stories and took me to the zoo, but I never understood the divorce. Why didn't you want Mother to have a career?"

"It wasn't that simple," he said, his voice world-weary. "Divorce rarely boils down to one thing. If I had it to do over again, I'd have compromised."

Jock was as stubborn as her mother had been; neither was willing to admit fault in any situation. It was a trait she'd inherited. Already she saw signs of stubbornness in Timmy.

"I want to be part of your life," Jock said, "and Timmy's. I love you too much to let the past come between us."

She realized how much she'd missed him, the Scottish burr he'd never quite lost, the habits he'd brought from his homeland. His loving ways. Timmy needed him even more now with Owen gone. She needed her father, too, more than she'd allowed herself to admit. "Papa, I love you. I've missed you."

Tears limned Jock's eyes. The only other times she could recall her father crying was the day her mother had left, divorcing him. And the day of her funeral.

Alex rocked back in his office chair. An offer he couldn't refuse. Why me? Dash had just called with Intelco's offer to buy his enhancer patent. Same crap Detroit pulled on rival auto-parts inventors. Buy the patent, then sit on it. If the technology didn't suit your purposes, keep it off the market.

Trouble was, there was no technology for the cartel to keep off the market. In two seconds any third-rate engineer would know the plans they'd filed with the patent office were worthless.

Jee-sus! He was up to his eyeballs in alligators. He'd hedged, lying through his damn teeth. Dash had been pissed, assuming he wanted to up the ante from what was already a fair—hell, a more than fair—offer. Nothing to do now but stall.

A knock at the door startled him. He knew it wasn't Brett. She'd been cool, a consummate professional, but cold since the night of the exhibition. Anyway, she rarely knocked. "Come in."

Eula Mae entered, a plant mister in hand. Next to those in Kew Gardens, his plants were the most pampered in London. He liked her, though; she reminded him of his mother. Well, what he imagined his mother would have been like. Intelligent. Caring.

"Vic would be proud," she said, releasing a vaporous mist over the fern by the window. "Belage is making a tidy profit."

True, but Vic was responsible for this mess with the cartel. He must have known this deal was dangerous.

"Uncle Vic was one in a million," Alex said. The diamond deal aside, there had never been anyone in his life like Vicktor Orlov. And there never would be again.

"He only wanted for you to be happy."

Alex stared. Those were Vic's dying words. *Alex, you're the best thing that ever happened to me. All I want is for you to be happy.*

He wondered if Vic, after years of roaming, had found the right woman only to discover he had terminal cancer. Had their relationship been that serious? He couldn't bring himself to ask, not wanting to think Vic had found happiness when it had been too late. "Well, Vic should be pleased. I'm happy now."

"Are you? Then what's wrong between you and Brett?"

"Nothing, why?"

"Vic thought . . ." She approached him.

For a moment he imagined her aiming the spray bottle at him and blasting him between the eyes. Criminy. Then it hit him. He saw Vic's master plan. "Vic was playing Cupid, wasn't he, trying to get me together with Brett?"

Eula Mae sprayed the philodendron, which she always polished rather than misted, ignoring Alex. Brett had the talent, the eye for design Vic admired. And she was attractive—okay, not gorgeous, but pretty. Even prettier when you'd worked with her. When you'd kissed her.

Uncle Vic had tried to manipulate him into falling for Brett. Grudgingly he admitted Vic had almost succeeded. Almost. But he was years past letting anyone manipulate him.

Having discovered Vic's trick with Brett, he wondered if there was something Vic deliberately hadn't told him about this diamond deal. And the mysterious seller.

"Alex." Naturally, Brett hadn't knocked. "Here are the designs for the Deauville proposal." Once the proposal was on his desk, she turned, giving him a provocative view of her cute butt, then left. Things had been touchy since the night of the exhibition.

She was pissed. Big-time.

Admit it or not, the lady had been angry that he'd brought that numbnuts Sylvia to Annabel's. He'd meant to shake Brett, to force her to admit to herself that she wanted him. He'd expected a veiled reaction, a subtle awakening. What he got was The Big Chill. His male ego reveled in it, of course. It meant she cared more for him than he'd suspected.

And he liked her too. Would he let Vic manipulate him from the grave? Forget it. This was his life, and while Brett fascinated him, if he slept with her, she'd start plaguing him to marry her. Worse, there was Timmy to consider, a one-in-a-million kid. No way would he hurt him.

Thinking of Brett, he let his anger with Vic subside. Sure,

she was talented, an asset to Belage, but he wasn't letting
Vic trick him into a serious relationship. But he did have to
do business with her. And, he freely admitted, she had
strengths he didn't. Talking—especially salesman's chitchat
—wasn't his long suit, but Brett could handle it. Easily. One
day soon, he'd hire a competent sales rep to sell Belage's
line and he'd stay in the office doing what he did best,
trading diamonds and keeping an eye on finances. Bullshitting the cartel.

He picked up the telephone and pressed the button for
Brett's extension. She answered immediately. "Brett, next
week I have to meet with Philippe Deauville in Paris."

Dead silence. They were back to ground zero.

"Do you want to come to Paris with me?"

20

Brett stood beside Alex in Philippe Deauville's workshop on the rue Gambon across the street from Chanel. Pinch yourself, Brett thought, this has to be a dream. The triumphant exhibition had been nothing compared to this —if Philippe liked her designs. Deauville jewelers had made jewelry for centuries; some of Marie Antoinette's favorite pieces had been created especially for her by Henri Deauville, founder of the dynasty. Even being considered for a small display area in Deauville's was an honor.

"We're combining these finest Burmese sapphires with pearls in a custom necklace for Elizabeth Taylor," Philippe said with more than a trace of pride.

Brett checked her impulse to sigh. The sapphires were alive, vibrating with fire and color, and the pearls were an astonishing set of triple-A quality with a luster rating that might very well exceed five—the top of the scale. The craftsman setting them used a small jeweler's hammer to shape the still-warm gold.

"Nice ruby," Alex commented, and Brett turned to another table where a polisher held a dark red ruby at the end of a dop stick. "Pigeon's blood. The darker the ruby, the more valuable it is."

Was Alex nervous? she wondered. Impossible to tell. But she was, feeling like Sneaky By with his tail on fire.

"Let's go into my office and look at your portfolio." Philippe held the door open to what could easily have been mistaken for Marie Antoinette's boudoir. Yards and yards of pale blue damask with frilly tassels and gilt furniture that could have belonged to the Sun King himself filled the room.

Brett opened her portfolio. Like a mantra, she thought, *Please let him like these. Please let him like these. Please . . .*

Philippe bent over her designs. "Your style is much different from what our clients are accustomed to purchasing."

Deauville Joaillier sold high-quality gems set traditionally or in the Art Deco style that had been revived several years earlier. Brett had immediately seen her designs were much more modern, not using straight edges, but relying on free-flowing lines that made the gold look molten. Lev's laser setting created the illusion of the jewels resting in gold rather than being set. They were different. Unique, Alex had once said. She looked at him over Philippe's bent back, and he winked.

Philippe inspected the last design. "Most impressive."

Brett inhaled sharply, not daring to look at Alex, holding her breath. Praying.

"Let's start with a small order, enough for a case in our Place Vendôme shop, *oui?*"

Oui! Oui! Oui! Brett smiled, beaming first at Philippe, then at Alex. *Move over, Elizabeth Gage. Step aside, Paloma Picasso. Look over your shoulder, Elsa Peretti.*

"Let's go to the shop. I'd like you to meet Claude de Verre, manager of the salon where we'll display your jewelry."

Claude was not—to use one of Alex's favorite sayings—a happy camper. His brow grooved the moment he looked at the first design. "*Merde,* my clients . . . I don't know."

"It won't hurt to try them," Alex said, his hand on the

very small case that Philippe had suggested for Belage's Lamont Collection. "This is a consignment arrangement. If they don't sell, we'll take them back."

Oh, no, Brett seethed, not consignment goods. Belage would be at risk again, putting out a lot of cash to produce a collection that would have to sell itself. It certainly wouldn't get a boost from Claude de Verre.

Philippe intervened. "I was most impressed with what I saw at Harvey Nichols. Those jewels sold amazingly quickly."

Claude sniffed. Clearly, he didn't consider his clientele on a par with the riffraff that frequented Harvey Nichols.

"People are worried about Hussein's invasion of Kuwait," Alex reminded them. "They're reluctant to spend huge sums of money in case there's a war."

"But they'll still want to give presents." Brett directed her comment to Philippe. "My designs feature fancies—the hottest gems on the market."

"Because they're small, they're affordable," Alex added.

It was the same pitch they'd used on Purvis Keir, Brett remembered. She and Alex worked well together—just the right blend of creative talent and business acumen.

"Settled." Philippe waved his hand at the small display case. "This is Belage's. Let's celebrate—lunch at Le Jockey Club."

Brett tried to be positive, but couldn't. She realized Claude de Verre deeply resented his opinion's not being valued more highly. He'd do everything he could to sabotage the collection.

Claude graced her with a smile, and she almost let out an audible sigh of relief. Then she saw he wasn't smiling at her. His eyes were on a man who'd entered the shop. "Monsieur Dunay."

"Etienne." Philippe extended his hand to an imposing man with hazel eyes and chestnut hair.

"I hope I'm not interrupting," Etienne said, his eyes on Brett.

Handsome in an immaculately tailored suit, Etienne had that look of questionable sexual allegiance Brett often associated with Frenchmen. Even so, there was something arrogant about the look he epitomized—something sexy.

"You're not interrupting, Etienne. Let Claude show you our latest pieces," Philippe said.

"Anything special?" Claude asked almost too helpfully.

Etienne shrugged, his eyes still on Brett. She tried to ignore him, to appear casual while waiting for Philippe.

"We have a rare black-pearl necklace," Philippe said.

Philippe's tone conveyed the kind of obsequiousness only money could buy. But why did Etienne keep staring at her?

"I need something . . . like a bracelet. Something not too personal." He finally tore his gaze away from Brett and looked at Philippe. "There's a woman I don't intend to see again."

His words were so offhand, so dismissive, that Brett instantly imagined a woman crying herself to sleep loving this man. Not unlike the way she'd felt the other night at Annabel's. She hadn't cried, but she'd been unable to sleep. Men. Her mother was right: they were insensitive jerks.

He turned to Brett. "What would you suggest, mademoiselle?"

"I suggest you not try to buy your way out of a relationship. Go to her. Tell her as gently as possible that it's over."

A silence fell over the shop, even the clerks who'd been polishing the glass cases stopped. *Omigod, what have I done?*

Etienne chuckled, an ominous sound; she couldn't decide if he was amused or just too polite to reveal his anger. "Your name?"

"This is Brett Lamont," Philippe hastened to answer. "She's a jewelry designer. She's doing a few pieces for us."

Brett wished she'd kept her mouth shut. Alex hadn't invited her along to antagonize people.

"This is Etienne Dunay," Philippe rushed on. "He's the head of the Dunay Vineyards in Epernay." He turned to

Alex, saying, "This is Alex Savich from Belage Diamonds in London."

Etienne's eyes never left her face, leveling at her what other women might have considered to be a meltdown stare. Brett, though, didn't give a damn. All she could think was she'd ruined their chances with Deauville. "Which are your designs?"

Claude said, "We're just studying her portfolio."

Etienne extended his hand. "May I?"

Alex unzipped the leather case. She couldn't read his expression, but she knew he was angry and couldn't blame him. On her tombstone belonged: she could never keep her mouth shut.

Etienne examined her sketches, his mouth crimped into a taut line. Not quite as tight as Alex's, though.

Etienne looked up. "Not bad for such a *salope*."

She managed a smile as if she didn't know he'd used French slang to call her a bitch.

Philippe chuckled, a low, forced sound.

"Let me know when these are delivered. I want first choice."

"Of course," Philippe said, his relief obvious, and even Claude smiled. "We're going to lunch at Le Jockey Club. Join us?"

Unfortunately, Etienne said, "Yes."

The austere nineteenth-century town house on rue Rabelais, a short street just off the Champs-Elysées, had nothing more than the number 2 to identify it as one of the world's most exclusive gentlemen's clubs.

It had been established after the Napoleonic wars, Philippe told them, when horse breeders were reeling from the toll the prolonged war had taken on their stock. Their best stallions had been requisitioned, most dying in battle, and the club was organized to rectify the situation. Today Le Jockey had evolved into a club where members' interests focused on business.

Brett knew a lot more about the club than Philippe realized. Its members—all male—adhered to a caste system. Money alone could not breach its protective social barriers. You had to trace your lineage back to the "real" French aristocracy, those lucky souls who'd somehow eluded the guillotine.

Then there was the marriage factor. Members must demonstrate their devotion to maintaining the aristocracy by marrying within its ranks. She recalled her mother telling her about the son of a family who'd been in the club for seven generations but who was blackballed—reportedly the term originated at this club—because he married an actress.

A footman in navy livery with gold buttons opened the door and they walked into a vestibule. Ahead was a massive staircase—*the* staircase—that led to the second floor, which was restricted to male members. She knew there was a library on that level as well as a billiards room, card rooms, and suites where members stayed, and, of course, the male-only dining room and bar.

"I'll check my messages," Etienne said.

She should have known. Etienne Dunay was among the elite of France, a man whose wealth and influence they should be courting. She caught Alex's eye and knew he was thinking the same thing.

As Philippe and Etienne greeted a mutual friend, Brett ignored Alex's censuring gaze and looked at the staircase. *Where did Mother get the courage to challenge the men of Le Jockey?*

She turned and found Etienne studying her with the speculative gaze she'd noted earlier. "You're Constance Lamont's daughter."

Better get used to this, she thought, resenting that people always associated her with her mother. Comparing them. Why had she been so spiteful all those years ago, hurting her father by legally changing her surname? If she hadn't, she'd be more secure, her name unknown until she made her mark as a designer. "Yes. She was my mother."

Etienne chuckled, sounding genuinely amused this time. "That explains it."

"Explains what?" She didn't like the grimace on Alex's face.

"I was having dinner with my father and his friends that night," Etienne said, but she didn't ask what night—she knew. "Your mother came in and charged right up the men-only stairs to the dining room. She lambasted us for fifteen minutes, saying we should be ashamed of our gluttonous selves for eating so well when everyone in Bangladesh was starving."

"They threw her out?" Alex asked.

"No, actually she raised millions that night."

Brett couldn't resist. "And she left by the men-only stair-case."

Alex grabbed one arm and Philippe took the other; they quickly steered Brett toward the elevator that would take them to the third-floor guest dining room, bypassing the tempting stairs.

Brett nosed in and out of dozens of Left Bank shops, some tatty, some chic, and savored her first free afternoon in months. After a lunch that had truly been relaxed and festive, the men had excused themselves to attend to business and Brett had been left alone. Now the sun had dropped behind the buildings and a fall breeze kicked red-gold leaves across the cobblestones. Her feet ached—obviously, a man had invented high heels—so she went back to her hotel.

Near the Seine and St.-Germain-des-Prés, Relais Christine was an elegantly remodeled sixteenth-century abbey. Brett had come often to Paris, usually with Amy, who had an aunt here. They'd spent hours roaming the raffish Left Bank, meeting students and artists, enjoying its unique charm, but they'd never stumbled upon this particular hotel. How had Alex found it? she wondered as she passed through its ancient gate trellised with vines into the cobble-stone courtyard.

The Deauvilles had become very wealthy, she thought. In Marie Antoinette's time, Henri Deauville had merely been a court jeweler. Now his descendants belonged to the Jockey Club and had a chateau in the Loire Valley. They were members of France's elite, not just craftsmen. Philippe Deauville had invited Alex and Brett to his chateau for a small party he was giving that weekend. Alex and Etienne had accepted, but Brett had declined. Her father had taken Timmy during her two-day trip, and she felt it would be an imposition to stay.

Her key clutched in her palm, Brett mounted the narrow flagstone stairs that led to her room, an elegant chamber with massive beams and a unique loft bed. It was under-stated with simple furnishings and classic fabrics befitting what had once been an abbey. She planned to soak in the tub, gazing out at the heart-catching view of Paris at dusk.

She opened the heavy plank door. Then stopped. Dear Lord! The room was filled with baskets of flowers. Every type of blossom imaginable. Every color combination possi-ble. They were arranged artfully but in a casual design like the baskets of flowers sold in the corner stalls.

Tiptoeing across the wooden floor, she told herself Alex couldn't possibly have sent these. He'd excused himself af-ter lunch for another meeting, surprising her because he hadn't mentioned it. Alex hadn't said anything about dinner either.

She opened the card propped up in the basket of flowers on her night stand. It read: *The Loire Valley—the garden of France.*

"What kind of a message is that?" She searched the other baskets for another card. Nothing.

She called the desk, but they didn't know who'd sent the flowers. Could it have been Alex? Did he want her to come with him to Philippe's chateau in the Loire Valley? Still puzzled, she called Hayvenhurst and asked for her father.

"How's Timmy?"

"He's right here. Let me put him on."

"Mommy? Guess what Grampa got me?" He didn't even pause to let her guess. "A pony. We named him Fe-wix."

Felix? It rhymed with Alex, she thought with a sigh. "Let me speak to Grampa." She waited until her father came on. "A pony? He'll never want to go home."

"I want him to visit as often as possible. You, too."

The thought of being in the same house with Ruthless made her head swim. "Are you sure Timmy's not a problem? How's Sneaky By adjusting?"

"He bagged two mice. How's it going there?"

She took a few minutes to describe the day's events right down to the lunch and the soufflé Jockey Club with its bittersweet chocolate and stripes of orange. But she didn't mention anything about her mother's exploit there. Her father had never forgiven her mother, blaming her for the divorce.

"I'm proud of you, Brett," he said, unmistakable sincerity in his voice. "You're remarkably talented."

"Thank you." An awkward silence followed. "Would it be a problem if I stayed here? I've been invited to a special party at the Deauville chateau in the Loire Valley."

21

Checking his watch and seeing they'd have to hurry to make his dinner reservation, Alex rushed through the Relais Christine courtyard, anxious to talk to Brett. Tonight he planned to surprise her by taking her to Le Coup Choux, a restaurant in an old priory near the Sorbonne. The restaurant was off the beaten path, and like the Relais Christine, their hotel, it had an interesting history. Best of all, it was a quiet, romantic spot.

He picked up his key at the desk, then took the stairs two at a time. He knocked at Brett's room, but there wasn't any answer. Not even eight. She couldn't have gone out to dinner yet. No one in Paris dined this early. He telephoned the front desk to leave her a message and was told a gentleman had called for madame and she was out for the evening. Son of a bitch!

He flopped down on his bed and studied the ceiling's rough-hewn beams, silently cursing Brett. Trying not to think of his meeting earlier with Dash Boynton.

Alex had left Le Jockey that afternoon satisfied he'd cinched the deal with Deauville. For good measure, he planned to attend the party at his chateau over the weekend. With luck he could interest some of Philippe's wealthy friends in Brett's jewelry.

He'd met Dash across from the Luxembourg Gardens at Dalloyau's pâtisserie shop. Dash had been seated at one of the peach-and-gray banquettes overlooking the lush greenery when Alex had arrived—ten minutes late.

"Sorry I'm late. I was just wrapping up a deal with Philippe Deauville to handle Lamont's designs."

Dash eyed him speculatively over a forkful of flaky *chausson de pomme.* Deauville was one of the premier jewelers in the world and one of Intelco's handful of sight holders, the elite men who had first crack at buying the cartel's best diamonds.

"I recommend the *quelle finesse*—chocolate mousse, crème Chantilly covered with caramelized sabayon." Dash closed his eyes with reverence. Sweets and diamonds—Dash's passions.

"Just tea," Alex told the waiter. All morning it had been in the back of his mind that Dash had deliberately tracked him down. What was so important that it couldn't wait until Alex returned to London? Brace yourself: the shit's about to hit the fan.

"We're prepared to increase our offer—"

Alex held up his hand; this was exactly what he'd expected. He tried to look sincere. "Look, the original price was very fair, but"—he lowered his voice as if there might be a hidden microphone in the *Negresco* the two old ladies at the next table were devouring—"I'm still in the testing stage."

Dash's bushy eyebrows canopied sunken eyes that were devoid of emotion. Honest to God, he really did resemble Dracula. Okay, an overweight Dracula. A vampire with a sweet tooth instead of a blood lust.

"Here." Alex pulled some papers from his attaché. "Look at my experiments. You'll see for yourself that I need to verify my results and do a little fine-tuning. I don't want to cheat you by selling you something that doesn't work."

Dash glanced at the sheaf of papers, then put them into his briefcase. Of course, Alex knew Dash couldn't decipher all the geological bullshit Alex had thrown into the phony experiments. The results would baffle an expert who'd undoubtedly say Alex knew a lot about trace elements. But could he really use that information to predict what colors he'd get when he X-rayed them?

All he was doing with this little maneuver was buying time. As soon as he'd disposed of the last shipment of fancies, he'd tell Intelco: *Sorry, boys, but the results aren't good enough to make this machine worth selling*. This scheme topped all the half-assed ideas Alex had ever had, but for the life of him, he couldn't come up with anything better. "Naturally, I'll expect a few concessions from Intelco."

"Naturally." Dash's tone could have vaporized a diamond.

"I'll want to become a sight holder. In addition to the agreed-upon price for selling you the enhancer patent, I'll want a ten percent share of the sales of colored diamonds to Japan."

"What?" Dash's eyes were trained on him like a revolver.

This really was a kick. Alex privately chuckled. He had to be nuts; he was loving this game. If only Vic could see him now. Mentioning the Japanese had been nothing short of genius. Years ago, diamond sales leveled off and Intelco was desperate for a market. An American ad firm persuaded Intelco to wean the Japanese away from pearls, which they'd preferred for centuries.

At the beginning of the advertising blitz fewer than 5 percent of Japanese women wore diamond rings, but by the time millions had been poured into slick advertisements 75 percent of Japanese women wore diamonds—about as many as wore them in America. No wonder a museum-quality statue of a samurai warrior dominated Intelco's boardroom.

"Enhanced fancies will tap a new market—worldwide," Alex said. "But Westerners are strapped for cash right now. I'm suggesting Intelco launch a campaign in Japan if my enhancer is proven."

What a pain in the butt. Why didn't Dash say something?

"Fancies will create a new craze in Japan," Alex continued. "They will offset the pearl stampede Princess Kikoman caused."

"Princess Kiko-san," Dash corrected him, but his eyes became sharper. Alex could almost hear the click-click-click of his mental calculator.

He'd deliberately muffed her name to get a rise out of Dash. The princess, a commoner, had married the emperor's second son. Like Princess Diana, she'd charmed the nation. Wearing a pearl choker. Reviving an interest in the diamond's archrival. "You see how fickle the Japanese are. They'll go for fancies."

"I don't know about their trade barrier," Dash hedged.

"Come on. Intelco managed to get the Japanese to allow the sale of regular diamonds. This won't be any problem for you guys." American businesses played hell getting their products into Japan, but the cartel had its ways. It wasn't fair. That was why it felt so great to screw Intelco for a change.

"Do you visit Paris often?" Etienne Dunay asked Brett.

"No. I used to come here a lot with my friend Amy." She smiled at him over the rim of her champagne glass. After she'd finished speaking with her father, Etienne had called to ask if she'd liked the flowers and to invite her to dinner. She'd been tempted to say no, but considering his request to see her jewelry, she decided it would be better to go. "We stayed with Amy's aunt in the rue de Grenelle."

"Aaah," Etienne said with appreciation as she'd suspected he would. Known as seventh heaven for the seventh *arrondissement,* the Faubourg St.-Germain was home to the oldest families in France, their magnificent eighteenth-century *hôtel particuliers,* private mansions with lush gardens, hidden behind high walls and heavy doors. Like Le Jockey, the area had a cloak of privilege that kept it the last bastion of French nobility.

"I took your advice," Etienne said quietly. "I spoke with the lady in question."

His girlfriend, she realized. The one he wanted—how would Alex say it?—to dump. "Was she upset?"

Etienne shrugged, looking off across the red and silver *belle époque* dining room of the Castel-Princesse nightclub. Three weeks ago exactly she'd been in Annabel's, London's equivalent of the legendary Castel-Princesse. And she'd gone home miserable, but tonight was going to be different because she didn't care about Etienne the way she did Alex.

"Would it have been easier to send the bracelet?" she asked and he nodded. "Why don't men want to discuss their feelings?" Even now she vividly remembered the withdrawn expression on Owen's face when she'd told him she was pregnant. She'd assured him it was her problem, not his, but she felt he deserved to know he was going to be a father. He'd been reluctant to discuss it. Finally, he reassured her by saying he'd take care of everything as soon as he returned.

"Men don't talk about their feelings because women become emotional. They cry and plead."

Even though her hackles went up just hearing his words, she felt sorry for him. Ending a relationship was painful; he had no idea how to handle his feelings. Not unlike Alex, she thought, wondering where he was tonight, who he was with. "Women don't mean to make men uncomfortable. They're just being honest."

Etienne touched her hand. "Were you honest with your husband when your marriage broke up?"

"I've never been married."

Etienne looked confused. "At lunch you spoke of a son."

She gave him a brief summary of Owen's death.

"I'm surprised you haven't married," Etienne remarked.

"No one's ever going to measure up to Owen Northcote." It was true; Owen had been different. And if she was lonely at times, it didn't mean she intended to marry. She'd raise Timmy alone—many single mothers did.

Her statement made Etienne smile, and she suddenly saw
through the polished veneer of sophistication. He was
bored. All she represented to him was a diversion. He'd
found her mother to be unique. She was nothing more than
a pale copy of an interesting woman. On some level she
resented this, wanting to be appreciated for herself, but on
another level this realization relaxed her. She couldn't
imagine crying over Etienne Dunay.

But he was fun. They finished dinner and danced in the
club's *cave*. She found herself telling him about the time
she'd spent in the relief camps, and her work now with the
Badger Preservation Society. She'd recently taken on the
job of writing their newsletter. She felt guilty because she
couldn't do more.

"When did you realize you wanted to become a jewelry
designer?" asked Etienne.

"I made jewelry first for my doll, then for my friends. I'd
buy old costume jewelry at jumble sales and redo the
pieces."

"I remember your mother's earrings the night she
charged into Le Jockey. They were large fangs balanced like
a chandelier."

"I made them. They were her favorites, but they weren't
fangs. They were tusks from very young elephants. They're
constantly slaughtered so the East can have their ivory fix.
Mother deliberately wore those earrings so people would
ask her, then she could tell them how the elephants suffered. She said every time she looked in the mirror she
knew why God had put her on earth." She sighed. Sometimes she was ashamed of herself for letting her mother
down, for choosing an easier life.

They were dancing, swaying to a waltz; Etienne hugged
her and whispered something in French.

"Don't worry. I'm not going to cry. I miss her, that's all."

"My father sent an enormous floral tribute to her funeral.
He was quite taken with her. Her death was senseless.

Didn't she know the way they'd loaded the rice was dangerous?"

"I guess not." Bags of rice for the relief camp had been
piled high in the truck that had no protective headrests on
top of the passenger seats. The driver had swerved to avoid
one of Lima's potholes and bags of rice had shot forward,
hitting her mother in the back of the head, breaking her
neck. She died instantly.

"I lost them both the same week, you know, Owen and
my mother."

"You're very brave."

"Not really. You do what you have to do. I have my son to
remind me of Owen. And I keep the head of a panther over
my desk. Mother and I found him when the Kenyan police
raided a big-game poacher's trophy shop. He reminds me of
all the animals who die needlessly. Someone has to speak
for them. Now I do what I can, but when I'm rich I'll do
more. Much more."

III
OVER THE EDGE

22

"The rich are different," Alex said to himself as he sat on a stone bench in the Deauville's topiary garden. "They can afford the upkeep on a joint like this." He looked back at the chateau, its golden walls sheathed in plum-hued shadows from the setting sun, which had transformed the pristine blue sky to a rare shade of violet like a flawless amethyst.

He'd driven down from Paris in the late afternoon with Philippe and found most of the other guests had already arrived. He'd been assigned a choice suite, a small turret overlooking a pond full of throaty bullfrogs and an informal garden that brought a heady floral scent up to his room in the tower.

He'd gone on a long walk, hoping a little exercise would clear his head. But he couldn't stop thinking about Brett. He was dead certain she'd gone out with Etienne Dunay last night. "What the hell could she see in that wimp?"

"Okay, so, he oozes Gallic charm. Proof positive that bullshit can be delivered with a French accent. Brett's too smart to fall for a creep like that."

"Are you sure?" his inner voice asked.

"Hell, no. Women are suckers for candlelight and roses. So what else is new?"

What did he want from Brett, anyway? Back in London, he'd been pissed as hell to learn Vic had set him up in Belage to get him together with Brett. That alone was a good reason to keep his distance. Why get railroaded into a relationship?

"Christ! You've never had a relationship." It would be too simplistic to blame it on his grandmother, although he didn't doubt his problems relating to women started with her. The trouble was, women always wanted more than he could give. Brett would be looking for a daddy. As much as he liked Timmy—and identified with him—he wasn't ready for that responsibility.

"So why are you out here in the garden talking to yourself?" Damned if he knew.

Alex walked toward the chateau, whose leaded glass windows shone like jewels. He had about an hour to dress and meet Philippe and the other guests on the terrace for drinks. He stepped inside and heard a familiar voice.

"Alex," Brett said, "I've been looking for you."

Her smile was so welcoming that he forced himself to look happy to see her. That jackass, Dunay, must have changed her mind about coming. "What are you doing here?"

"Etienne is going to introduce me to his wealthy friends."

Yeah, right. Then what? Can't you guess?

"You're not still angry, are you? I opened my big mouth to Etienne, but he's very enthusiastic about the Belage Collection."

Trust me, that's not what he's interested in. "Great."

"I have something for you in my room."

He followed her up the slate stairs into her room. Under normal circumstances, he'd be glad to have Brett help him promote Belage. But that jerkoff, Dunay, wasn't interested in her career.

Brett smiled, not her usual smile, but a mischievous grin

and handed him a small brown bag tied at the top. "Open it in your room. I'm positive it's just your size."

"Thanks." He was touched she'd thought to get him something.

She nudged him toward the door. "I've got to get dressed."

Alex hustled up the stairs, the bag clenched in his hand. A pen? Naw. Too light. A tie? No way. Too small. A tie clip? Well, maybe. She said "your size," remember? Not socks.

Inside his room, he untied the bag. Inside he found a foil wrapper the size of his thumb. What in hell? He had to move to a lamp to read the near-microscopic writing on the foil.

THE WORLD'S SMALLEST CONDOM: FOR THE LITTLE PRICK IN YOUR LIFE.

He laughed. The more he thought about Brett, the harder he roared. Honest to God, there wasn't anyone like her.

For the third time, Brett checked her reflection. Wow! The dress flattered her figure, sculpting every line without being too tight. She'd purchased the strapless lavender gown in a Left Bank shop because it allowed her to show off one of Belage's sample necklaces and matching earrings. The diamonds, one of her more unique designs, were a shade darker than the dress.

She walked over to the marble nightstand where she'd put the box from Erotica Exotica on the rue Camille. "Be brave," she told herself. "You can't be celibate for the rest of your life. Start tonight with Etienne. Then you won't lie awake at night mooning over Alex Savich."

She pulled one condom from the box and shook her head. Would one be enough? Take two—just in case. But where could she put them? She didn't have an evening bag. She tried stuffing them in her bra, but the demicups pushed her

breasts higher, making her look cheap. One in each shoe—
that was the ticket.

Her toes a little pinched, she went down the stairs one
step at a time, listening to the lilting music coming from the
terrace and the sound of voices. There's nothing to be nervous about; she tried without success to reassure herself.
Women face this problem every day, recovering from di-
vorces or deaths and dating new men. If it happens, it happens. If not, who cares?

Out on the terrace, she looked for Etienne among the
throng sipping drinks. She didn't see him, but she did see
Alex.

"Brett, I've been looking for you." She turned and found
Philippe saying, "Etienne wanted me to give you a message.
There's a terrible problem at the vineyards. He asked me to
tell you how sorry he was that he had to leave."

Etienne couldn't take time to tell me himself, she thought
glumly. Surely he could have spared a moment to say good-
bye. Her mother had been right: men were insensitive slobs.

"New dress?" Alex stood beside her, scanning her from
toe to head, not looking one bit too pleased.

"Yes. I'm supposed to be attracting buyers, remember?"

He nodded, but she couldn't tell if he approved or disap-
proved. "Thanks for the present. It's a perfect fit."

"I knew it. The minute I saw it, I thought of Vic. He
would have hooted." Now Alex looked less happy. "What's
the matter?"

"You and Vic—two of a kind."

"Someone has to have a sense of humor. Lord knows you
don't."

He took her arm. "Okay, Sunshine. Let's sell a few
gems."

After dinner in the great hall, the guests moved back to the
wide stone terrace. Brett didn't feel like dancing; the useless
condoms in her shoes made her toes ache, but she was too
elated to say no when Alex asked.

"We're a good team. I think everyone here tonight will at least come to Deauville's to see Belage's jewelry, don't you?"

"Perfect partners." He pulled her close. "Everything's as good as sold. Philippe will reorder in no time."

She recalled the last time she'd danced with him at Annabel's and how miserable she'd been, so miserable she was ready to jump into bed with a man she didn't know, a man who didn't have the courtesy to personally say good-bye. She'd been wrong to think one night with a stranger would cure her unhappiness. She needed someone special. She wanted more than just a night.

"Relax," Alex whispered, his breath fanning her ear.

Relax? In his arms? She'd been holding herself away from his solid chest, but her nipples kept brushing against him, stiffening at the recollection of the times he'd kissed her. She took a deep breath and told herself any normal woman would be susceptible to Alex's masculine vitality. But she worked for him and had *no* business harboring any romantic fantasies.

He pulled her flush against him. "That's more like it." He whirled her around the dance floor, his hand caressing her back.

She almost forgot just why it was such a bad idea to get involved with him. Desire ribboned through her veins as potent as any narcotic. Obviously she'd been alone too long.

"I've been wanting to dance with you since that night at the reception." He maneuvered her around the corner of the terrace into the shadowy area where no one else was dancing. Against her face she felt his cheek, recently shaved, with a hint of a woodsy after-shave, an aroma she found extremely erotic. The enticing movement of her silk skirt against his thighs as they glided in a slow circle almost made her forget her throbbing toes.

"Just a minute." She pulled away. "I'll be right back."

She dashed down the walkway to the dimly lit fountain area, then removed her shoes. The cool stone welcomed her bare feet and she stretched her aching toes. Once she removed the foil wrappers from her shoes, she hesitated, wondering what to do with them. She certainly couldn't toss the condoms into the bushes.

"Two?" Alex said with a chuckle, suddenly appearing beside her. "You actually thought that wimp could get it up twice?"

Although he'd laughed, there was a strident edge to his voice she'd never heard before. She was a bit ashamed of herself for even *considering* sleeping with Etienne. But it wasn't any of Alex's damn business. "Be prepared, I always say."

Alex pocketed the condoms, scowling. "I thought you had higher standards than to hop in the sack with a man you hardly know."

"Naff off and die! You men all have double standards. It's all right for you to sleep with that bimbo, Really-Really—Sylvia. But it's wrong for me to be with a man."

He moved closer to her, glaring down at her, his blue eyes almost black in the waning moonlight. "Why him? Why not me?"

"I . . ." the word trailed off, eclipsed by the burble of the fountain. "We should maintain a professional relationship."

Hands on her waist, he pulled her to him, holding her so close she could feel each breath he took. "Bullshit. You're pissed about Sylvia. That's why you went for that wimp frog, Etienne."

She opened her mouth to deny it, but his lips captured hers, his tongue mating with hers before she could utter a sound. The kiss was so hot, so aggressive, that she wanted to move away, but his hands roved down her back to cup her derriere, cradling her against the heat of his lower body.

He pulled back, suddenly, his gaze intent. "I never slept with Sylvia. I just wanted to make you realize you felt something for me. Guess I proved my point, didn't I?"

"You were *trying* to make me jealous?" The thought

hadn't occurred to her because it seemed so unlike something Alex would do. But knowing he had done it filled her with a heady sense of her own femininity and kicked her sex drive into high gear.

"It backfired. So I had to get rid of Dunay."

"What?" The word came out in a rush; it was hard to concentrate, feeling the mounting pressure of his arousal. Blood thrummed through her veins with the hypnotic rhythm of a tom-tom.

"I faked a call from his vineyard, saying the new cooling system he told us about at lunch went haywire. It was freezing his wine. The guy couldn't get back to Epernay fast enough."

"Oh, Alex," she said, amazed he'd do something like this, but thrilled that he had. "What am I going to do with you?"

"I have a great idea." His hips rotated against hers.

The night drew its seductive cloak around them: the gentle splash of the fountain, the glow of the fairy-tale chateau, the soft music floating on the breeze that ruffled the majestic oaks. And the deep shadows where they stood concealed by darkness.

He kissed the sensitive curve of her neck, then traced the moist tip of his tongue across the rise of her breasts, his warm palm cradling a full breast, the ball of his finger teasing the nipple beneath the sheer silk. Heat pooled between her thighs as she furrowed her fingers through his thick hair.

"Oh, Alex." She clung to him, experiencing something intangible, frighteningly elusive, verging on mystical, yet as timeless as the stars courting the moon above. Had she fallen in love with him? No, surely not.

He coaxed one nipple free and with possessive lips drew the taut nub into his mouth. He applied suction and darting strokes of his tongue that sent another surge of heat through her thighs. He drew back and blew softly, stiffening the peak, raising goose bumps across her breasts despite the warm summer air.

His head dipped down again, recapturing the beaded tip,

and she caught her lower lip between her teeth to keep from crying out. She let her hand drift down the solid length of his torso to the curve of his hip, then to his firm thigh. Her fingers slid across his trousers, seeking the rigid bulge beneath. Her hand locked over him, then released, then squeezed harder.

He stopped and she heard his breath catch in his throat. Emboldened, she thrust her hand under the waistband of his trousers. And found what she wanted. What she needed. What she'd needed for so long. She wanted him inside her. Now.

He dipped down, his hand coming up under her skirt and coasting up her bare leg, then cradling her mound. His expression was a gambler's with a handful of aces. "Hot to trot, huh?"

"Two can play this game." She ran her thumb over the smooth tip of his sex. Smiling right back at him.

Alex yanked the lacy panties; the fabric ripped and he pulled them free. He dangled the bikinis in front of her, then stuffed the moist swatch of lace into his pocket. "Don't ever tell me you don't want me again."

She started to jerk her hand away from him, but he held it in place. He lowered his lips to hers, his tongue parting her lips, seeking hers. He was right, she silently conceded. Why fight it? She wanted him in a way that she'd never wanted another man.

Suddenly his hands were under her skirt again, stroking her bare bottom. She parted her legs, adjusting her stance, silently inviting him to touch her. Alex got the message. His fingers gently sifted through the damp whisk of hair between her thighs, parting the sensitive folds. He stroked, slowly, deliberately teasing her, matching the seductive movements of his tongue.

"Alex, please. Let's go upstairs."

"You're so damn wet." His finger now inside her, stroking the satin heat, the pad of his thumb still caressing her, making her gasp with pleasure. He slowly withdrew his finger as he lifted his lips from hers and gazed down at her. She waited, her breath stalled in her throat, longing for him to touch her again. His tongue again invaded her mouth with an enticing thrust and his finger returned, gliding even more deeply inside her this time.

"Upstairs," she managed to whisper, but his response was to deftly move his hand until her body pulsed with a need so overwhelming it surpassed mere desire.

He stopped short of bringing her to a fulfilling climax. "Don't ever tell me no again."

"Naff off and die," she mumbled as he led her up the stone path to the chateau, his strong arm supporting her.

Inside her room, Alex slid the deadbolt into place. He'd promised himself that one day he'd make love to her, but, hell, he hadn't counted on this desperate yearning to possess her that went beyond passion. Knowing she was with Dunay had made him madder than hell. Angry enough to fake a phone call to get rid of the bastard. Something he'd never imagined himself doing.

Jealous? Damn straight, and she'd been jealous too. And he loved it. She'd shocked him with the uninhibited way she responded to him. Maybe what he felt—what they felt—went beyond mere desire, but he couldn't deal with that right now.

Brett looked at him expectantly, her eyes overly bright. She's unsure of herself, he realized, touched.

"Has there been anyone since Owen?"

"No," she said, her voice a shade shy of a whisper, almost lost in the soft music coming through the open window.

He couldn't keep from smiling, but he didn't know what to say, how to express how pleased he felt. "Know what I want?" he asked, the timbre of his voice pitched low as he slid his hands over her bare shoulders and found her zipper, releasing it with one swift motion. "To see you in nothing but"—he touched her earrings and the necklace she'd designed for Belage—"these."

He slid her dress down her breasts, the silk so sheer, so

delicate it seemed to disintegrate beneath his hands. The fabric bunched at her waist, and he paused. Her breasts weren't large, but they were lush, crowned by jewel-hard buds. He eased the dress over the gentle flare of her hips, caressing her delicate skin as he went, inhaling the floral traces of her perfume. Breathtaking.

The silk dress pooled at her bare feet, and he stepped back, taking in everything about her. Blond hair piled high. Sensual lips, slightly parted. Long, show-girl legs bridged by a cloud of dark blond curls. The diamonds glittered deep lavender in the moonlight. She touched the necklace and he saw her lower lip tremble, her eyes uncertain.

"Undress me." He refused to allow her to have second thoughts. He let her fumble with his belt while he kissed her breasts, drawing one hard bead between his lips, sculpting its firmness with sensual strokes of his tongue, gently tugging on it.

Finally she had him undressed. Well, almost. He still had on his socks, and his shirt was unbuttoned but not off. Close enough for government work. He'd waited for this moment for months; he couldn't wait another second.

"Alex, don't we need protection?"

Aw, hell, how could he have forgotten? He always practiced safe sex. Looking into those adorable green eyes, he knew exactly how. "Good thing you brought two."

"There's a full box on the vanity."

He stomped over, the heft of his rigid cock painful. A box. She'd bought a whole damn box. For that wimp, Dunay. He ripped open a foil wrapper and sheathed himself. "What in hell is this?"

Brett laughed. "They glow in the dark. They're supposed to be easier to find, to put on."

He bounded across the room, his Day-Glo orange erection throbbing with each step. "If you laugh, you'll be sorry."

Reaching for him as he lowered himself to the bed, she giggled. He nestled his hand between her thighs, nudging them apart. She stopped laughing and he furrowed through the wet curls with insistent fingers. She was ready; hell, more than ready. With a powerful thrust, he planted himself inside her.

Her hips rose to meet his. "Go ahead. Make me sorry."

"Smartass," he managed between powerful strokes.

He plunged deep, slowly withdrew, almost completely leaving her, then delved deep again. Over and over, he thrust, barely maintaining control, gaining momentum. Brett moved with him, arching her hips to meet him, moaning her pleasure.

"Alex." His name came through her lips. Sexy. Erotic. He wanted her to say it, over and over and over.

When her nails scored his back, her breathing as labored as his own, Alex knew she was as close to a climax. Sucking in his breath, he felt the shuddering of her body. He let himself go, the ultimate—totally satisfying—surrender to the desire that had kindled the first night they met.

She smiled up at him, brushing a damp curl off his brow. "Alex. I'm not one bit sorry I laughed."

Then she smiled, a special smile he'd never seen. A sensual, intimate smile. A smile that knifed through to his soul.

23

"Alex warned me that he's never had a long-term romantic relationship, and he wasn't interested in—how did he put it?—getting tied down. So, I'm taking this one day at a time."

Amy was convinced Brett had no idea of what she was getting into. Heavens, she hadn't had a clue herself when she thought she could keep her affair with Lev on a purely physical level. It had backfired the second week—not that she'd admitted it until last night when Lev again mentioned returning to Israel if they went to war with Hussein.

"What about Timmy?" Amy asked.

"Except the nights Alex is with Lev, he's with us. Naturally, Timmy is getting attached to him."

"Then there'll be a problem if you break up." Amy decided Brett's situation was more complicated than hers. At least when her affair ended, there'd be only one broken heart.

"I know Timmy will be upset," Brett conceded. "Millions of single mothers must have the same problem. I guess there's no easy answer, is there? I'm trying my best." Brett shrugged apologetically. "How's it going with Lev?"

"Great"—she paused—"except I'm going to have to introduce him to my father. I was supposed to have Father for dinner weeks ago, but got out of it. It's set for tomorrow night. Father has some misguided notion Lev will marry me and give Father what he longs for—an heir to Conrift Bullion."

"Has Lev asked you to marry him?"

"No, and even if he did, Father wouldn't approve of him."

"What about Lev's family? Do they want him to marry?"

"I don't know. He refuses to discuss them. Has Alex told you anything about Lev's family?"

"Nothing. Alex never talks about his family either."

"Great. We're both involved with secretive men. What next?" Amy walked over to her Louis XIV secretary. "I won't see Lev tonight because he and Alex are going to a concert. Could you give this to him?" She handed Brett a plastic card that looked like a credit card.

"Omigod. Where did you get this?"

"It must have fallen out of his pocket when we were—" She stopped, unwilling to tell Brett she'd found it on the pantry floor after they'd made love. "What is it?"

"It's a security key to the enhancer room. Alex would go into orbit if he knew Lev had lost it."

"Don't get him in trouble; slip it to him in the morning." She gazed at Brett. "I don't like that look. What are you up to?"

Brett arrived earlier than usual at Belage and found Eula Mae misting the ferns in the reception area.

"We've identified the pit," Eula Mae said with unmistakable pride. "It's from the Gir forest in India. It's quite rare. If I'm able to get it to grow and flower, I'll take the silver trophy at the Chelsea Garden Show."

"You'll get it to grow. You have the magic touch."

"How'd you get an Indian pit? That's what threw us. We would have identified it earlier, if we'd known it wasn't from Nepal."

"I arranged for a delightful old *sherpa* named Terai to get a job with the reforestation project, and he was so grateful that he bartered with Indian traders to get the pit for me."

"I can't understand why the traders would bring the pit to Nepal. It could never grow at that elevation."

"They grind them up to sell as an aphrodisiac."

"My stars, you can't mean it."

"It's true." Brett searched in her purse. "Guess what I have?" She waved the security card. "What would you say about taking a peek at the enhancer?" Eula Mae looked shocked, but nodded eagerly. "My mother's ring is still in my desk. If I can figure out how to operate the enhancer, I'm going to put it in."

A few minutes later Brett said, "It doesn't appear to be too complicated," when she looked at the enhancer with a dial resembling a clock. "This looks old. I wonder how long Alex has been developing it."

"You'd better hurry. He'll be here soon."

"I should take the diamond out of the setting, but I don't have time." Brett put the ring inside the compartment and closed the glass-windowed door; then she studied the dial that had numbers from one to thirty on it. "I'm going to try fifteen."

"I think that means minutes. Alex will be here in ten."

"Okay. I'll do it for five minutes, but it might not be enough time to change the color." She closed the door. "Get that lead blanket ready to throw over this the second I press the start button. We don't want to be unnecessarily exposed to radiation."

She touched the start button and a loud ticking noise began. Eula Mae heaved the cumbersome blanket over the boxy enhancer. But not before Brett saw a flash of blue-white light. *Bamb-zzzit!* The ticking stopped.

"Omigod! What happened?" Brett peeked under the corner of the blanket. The glass window was opaque with black soot. She gingerly opened the door and found the inside of the compartment, which had been pristine white, was charred. The platinum band on her mother's ring was covered with soot as well, but the diamond appeared untouched. "I've broken the enhancer. Get out of here before Alex comes. Don't say a word. Let me handle this."

Brett went back to her office and put the ring away. Alex had kept the door locked so no one would touch the machine. And what had she done—the first chance she got? She heard Alex saying good morning to Eula Mae. She walked down the short hall and softly knocked on his open office door.

"Good morning," he said, all business. They'd made a pact to keep their affair private. In the office they were to behave professionally. "What's up? You never knock."

She handed him Lev's security card.

"How the hell did you get this?"

"It fell out of Lev's pocket."

"It's not like him to be so careless."

"It was an accident." She shifted from one foot to the other, not quite able to bring herself to tell him the rest.

"Is there something else you wanted to discuss?"

"I've done something very foolish."

"I'm to blame, too." Eula Mae's voice came from behind her.

"No. You had nothing to do with it. It was my idea."

"I helped. I'm responsible—"

"For Christ's sake, tell me what you're talking about."

"I was curious about the enhancer," Brett began, her voice low, "so I used Lev's card to open the door." Alex looked as if he wanted to strangle her. She continued in a breathless rush, anxious to get it over with. "I put my mother's ring in the enhancer. It blew up or something."

"Of all the stupid—"

"I helped her," Eula Mae cut in.

Alex threw them a disgusted look and charged out of his office, the security card in his hand. They followed slowly, Brett hoping the damage to the enhancer was minor. They were standing in the doorway watching Alex as he inspected the charred interior of the enhancer when Lev came into his office.

"Is there a problem?" Lev asked, moving past them.

"Those smartasses put a ring in here and it arced. I'm sure it blew the transformer."

Filled with remorse, Brett listened to them discussing the necessity of replacing the transformer immediately. "Arced?" she asked. "The metal on the setting transmitted so much electrical current that it caused a small explosion. How's that possible? X rays don't use electricity." Then another thought occurred to her. "It reminds me of the time I put a metal pan in my microwave."

Brett had been with Alex long enough, trying to sell their jewelry, to know the speed-of-light look he threw Lev meant he had something to hide. Then she recalled the astounding green diamond Alex had let her see through his laser microprobe.

"You're not X-raying diamonds, are you?" Alex and Lev remained expressionless, but she wasn't deceived. "Now it makes sense. You keep this door locked so we won't know Lev is cutting and polishing fancies, not enhancing diamonds. He's working on natural stones." Alex's expression was inscrutable, but Lev was frowning and looking at his polishing disk as if it were a crystal ball. "Where are you getting the fancies, Alex?"

He met Brett's expectant gaze, a trusting look, really. She'd been honest with him, telling him about her personal life, her problems. And how had he responded? He'd kept her at arm's length, never confiding anything more than was strictly necessary—even about Belage. Certainly he never told her anything about himself.

He shifted his gaze to Eula Mae, feeling the silence in the office becoming awkward. Eula Mae. Vic had loved her, trusted her. Alex couldn't help feeling he owed her something. Hell, he owed them both an explanation. Where on earth could anyone find a better team, a group that worked such long hours doing jobs most manufacturers used two or three people to do?

"You're smart, Brett. This enhancer is really an old microwave; that's why it arced when you put metal in it. We're not X-raying stones at all. But I don't know where the fancies are coming from." He could see Brett wasn't buying this. "Do I, Lev?"

"No. Vic make a deal with someone, but we do not know who."

Alex told them about Boris Tenklov and the mystery surrounding the fancies, not omitting his problems with Intelco. He finished saying, "You're all sworn to secrecy. No one—and I mean *no one*—should ever suspect we're not enhancing the diamonds. One slip could get me killed."

"I'll never say a thing," Eula Mae assured him. "Vic hated Intelco. He claimed if they released all the diamonds they have, prices would fall. They keep a stranglehold on the market so prices remain artificially high. Free trade in diamonds is impossible. It's not fair."

Brett looked as serious as he'd ever seen her. "I know you think I'll blurt this out at some inopportune moment, but I promise I won't."

The one thing Alex didn't mention was how Lev would be at risk if the Russians knew where he was. "Actually, having all of you know the truth will be helpful. Belage needs to expand. I plan to hire people to reduce your workloads and fill orders faster. We need to work together to make certain none of the new employees discovers the truth."

"Let us put the enhancer in a closet," Lev suggested. "I do not like working in a room with the door closed all the time. I am having closet phobia."

"Claustrophobia," Alex automatically corrected him. "But that's a good idea. Then we can put a polisher and a goldsmith in with you." He looked at Brett. "I'm moving into your office unless you think I'll bother your designing."

"Why would you want to move into my small office?"

"Avram Ben-Itzik, a dealer from Tel Aviv, is going to be

using my office. I'm going to partition it so half will be his office, and the other side will be set up for a clerk who'll help Eula Mae."

"Why is an Israeli dealer coming here?" Brett asked.

"He's afraid Israel might go to war with Iraq. Avram has a courier delivering his diamonds next week. I'm going to trade for him until he sees what's going to happen."

"Do you think it'll come to war?" Eula Mae asked.

"I hope not." He sincerely meant it. If it did, there wouldn't be a force on earth that could keep Lev from fighting for Israel. When he'd needed a country, they'd come through for him. As a laser expert, his talent would be invaluable.

"In 1700 King William III knighted Solomon de Medina, the man who founded our dynasty," Amy's father told Lev as they sat at the dinner table in her town house. "That's how long the Conrifts have been part of English aristocracy."

Lev seemed interested, but Amy wanted to throttle her father for immediately launching into the family history, an obvious ploy to let Lev know how important he was.

"Your people, I take it, are from the Ukraine. What does your father do?" Trust her father to immediately assess Lev's social status—not that any Ukrainian Jew could equal a Conrift.

"My father worked in a shoe factory. He died years back. My mother lives outside Kiev."

Gordon Conrift, who preferred to be called Lord Conrift, flushed. Clearly, his daughter had invited him to meet a totally ineligible suitor. But Amy met his censuring eyes dead-on. She didn't care what he thought. But she did care what Lev thought. Evidently he missed his tightly knit family. Would he understand about her father's snobbishness?

"We're related to the Montagues, the Samuelses, the Rothschilds," her father said between bites of salmon *encroûte* that Lev had slaved over; he'd insisted on helping her prepare tonight's meal, "and the Montefiores. Hugh Montefiore recently retired as a bishop of the Anglican Church. We're related to everybody."

You forgot to say "that's anybody," Amy mentally added. Her father had just ticked off the names of the Cousinhood, England's elite community of wealthy Jews whose fortunes had been made the previous century in banking.

"Anglican bishop?" Lev was puzzled. "Is he not a Jew?"

"Englishmen are Englishmen regardless of religion." There was more than a touch of hostility in her father's voice.

"Interfaith marriage," Amy explained. "Some people are born Jewish and later baptized, like Benjamin Disraeli, who was one of our best prime ministers. But no one in our family has ever married outside the faith." When she'd considered marrying Ellis, she'd never seen her religion as a problem, but of course, Ruth Payne had.

"Amy and I go to the Hambro Synagogue," Lev told her father with pride. "Which synagogue do you attend?"

Gordon Conrift laid down his fork, obviously speechless for a moment. "Conrifts don't attend synagogue except for weddings, bar mitzvahs, and high holy days. I don't have time to do a lot of praying."

"You are armchair Jews," Lev said, openly critical.

Of all the scenarios she'd envisioned for this evening— none of them good—she hadn't considered Lev would be the one to become angry. Lev expected her to go to synagogue with him; she hadn't mentioned she rarely went.

Lev pointed at her father with his fork. "When I grow up anyone who is caught praying goes to *gulag.* It was worst for Jews. We never light candles or have bar mitzvah. First time I am in synagogue is when I come to Israel. There I find faith. There I am free to speak to God."

At the word *Israel* Gordon Conrift frowned, a deep vee that rippled upward emphasizing his bald head. To him, Israel was a four-letter word. "Zionists."

"When Israel became a nation," Amy explained, "many

British Jews like our family opposed it. They felt that a Zionist state would stamp them as outcasts in their own countries. People would say we belonged in Israel with the rest of the Jews."

"Everything we've earned over the centuries would be lost." Her father shoved his plate aside. "It hasn't happened, but too often we hear: 'If you don't like the way you're treated, go to Israel.' "

"What would happen to Jews in bad countries if there was no Israel?" Lev asked, his voice ominously low.

"A charitable country would take them in."

"Like England took in Jews during the Second World War?"

The color leached from Gordon Conrift's face. "My father was among those who opposed taking in European Jews." Amy gave him credit for being honest. "At the time the world was in a depression. Englishmen didn't have work. We couldn't support hordes of immigrants. If we'd known about the death camps, we would have taken them in, but we didn't know."

"The government knew," Lev insisted.

"But the people didn't—until it was too late." Amy hated taking her father's side, but she had no choice. Her grandfather had been against accepting poor Jews. "Many British people were terrific. Harold Macmillan—you've heard of him?—let a group from Czechoslovakia live on his Sussex estate."

"Did your family take in anyone?" Lev's tone was icy.

"We gave money to relief efforts," Amy said, "but no one actually lived with us."

"Those Jews who were smart enough to leave Germany had nowhere to go. Times have not change. Where do Jews who want to leave Russia go? A lucky few to America, but the rest go to Israel."

Her father tossed his napkin aside. "Just my point. If there had been no Israel, some other country would have taken you in."

Lev vaulted to his feet, almost knocking his chair over. "You are wrong. If not for Israel, I would be dead." He pivoted on his heel, then stormed toward the door.

"Lev, wait." Amy rushed after him. He already had the front door open before she caught up to him.

He studied her. "I do not know you. I do not want to know this kind of family." He slammed the door shut.

Amy fought the hot sting of tears. If she'd had any idea of what to say to Lev, she'd have gone after him.

Her father put down his coffee cup, totally unperturbed by the situation. "I hope you weren't serious about that man. He's all wrong for you. Not only is he a religious fanatic, he has the map of Israel plastered across his face."

She sank into her chair, telling herself this was worse than she'd imagined. Besides being a total snob, her father was the worst kind of anti-Semite—a Jewish one.

24

"This bed is just the right size." Alex snuggled closer to Brett, nuzzling the nape of her neck where her long hair concealed the tiny mole he always kissed. Actually, her bed was too small; his feet hung over the edge, but he didn't mind. Hell, he hated getting up and sneaking out of Brett's house each night so Timmy wouldn't discover he was sleeping with Brett. He wondered if he had time to make love to her again before he had to rush to catch the last Underground to his place.

"Alex," Brett whispered, her breath falling softly across his cheek, "I've been thinking."

God forbid. He knew that tone of voice too well. When women started "thinking," and saying it in that tone of voice, it meant they were getting serious about you. He'd believed he could work Brett out of his system just by sleeping with her once or twice. So far, it had been almost three weeks and he wasn't ready to give her up. But he didn't want to make a commitment either.

She leaned on one arm, her hair falling over her bare breasts. Sexy as hell. Look at the intensity in those green eyes. Serious as hell. She stroked his chest, twining her fingertips through the curly hair, generating an immediate physical reaction in his groin. So what else was new?

"I'm worried about you, Alex. Your life is in danger. Can you get out of this deal of selling fancies?"

"Probably, but Intelco already thinks I have an enhancer—"

"Stop now and let someone else take the risk selling those fancies, then tell Dash Boynton the enhancer doesn't work."

"Belage needs the money I earn selling those fancies. We can't expand without capital."

"Couldn't Belage grow more slowly?"

"We wouldn't be able to go ahead with the Deauville deal. Would you be willing to give up that opportunity?"

"Yes, if it meant you'd be out of danger."

All right, here it comes. He braced himself to hear her tell him how much she loved him. Then she'd say something like: If you really love me, you'll quit.

She ran her hand up his chest, and he had to steel himself not to kiss her. With the soft tips of her fingers, she traced the line of his cheek. "It's not worth the risk to go on. We have a good team at Belage. We'll make it—perhaps not as quickly as we would with an infusion of cash—but we'll be successful."

Be grateful, he told himself, she's kept this discussion less personal than he'd expected. "I never wanted to move to London. I'm here because Vic's deal with Ellis left me no other choice, but I want to return to L.A. as soon as possible. Without the capital from the fancies, it'll take years to build Belage to the point where I can sell it. I'm not willing to wait. There's one more shipment coming, and I intend to accept it."

She sighed, her lashes lowered. He waited for another plea, but it didn't come. Perhaps telling her the truth stopped her. He liked her—okay, more than liked her—but she might as well know right now that he was moving back to L.A.

"I want to be known as a master jeweler, not just another diamond trader. I also want a car and a condo that's bigger than Sneaky By's litter box. Belage is the ticket, but not without substantial sales. It's your big chance, too, isn't it?"

Brett looked at him, her eyes solemn. "I'd never risk anyone's life—particularly yours—to further my career."

"Risking my life may be a little strong. I may have overstated the danger," he said, determined not to upset her. He worried more about Lev, but so far, they had no indication the Russians even remembered him.

"We don't know who's sending me those fancies. Perhaps the mine doesn't have an agreement with Intelco. The worst that can happen if they do is the cartel will blackball me through the Diamond Clubs, and I won't be allowed to trade for top-quality gems."

He sat up, swinging his legs to the floor and looking around for his trousers. "To be honest, it's a challenge. I hope the fancies come from a cartel mine. I'd love to screw them. They've stuck it to everybody. They deserve it."

Brett didn't respond, but he could feel her watching him as he dressed. He expected her to say something more about how much he meant to her, to beg him to give up this scheme. She didn't.

The telephone rang and she quickly answered it. Brett listened then said, "I'm sure if you talk to him, Lev will understand." Brett paused. "Do you love him? . . . Then tell him. People need to be honest with each other. If that's how you feel, say it. I'll bet when he thinks about it, he'll admit you aren't responsible for the way your father has behaved . . . Good idea. Call me as soon as you've talked to him."

"What's wrong?" Alex asked, taking care to keep his voice low.

"Lev got into a tiff with Amy's father over Zionism."

Alex sat on the edge of the bed. Brett looked adorable with her concerned frown. She'd be up all night worrying about Amy.

"I told Amy to go to him and tell him she loves him. I told Owen as soon as I realized how I felt."

"What did Owen say?" Why was he asking?

"He said he loved me, of course."

You had to ask. "Of course. Well, don't count on it working with Lev. He may not forgive her."

"Why not? Lev seems troubled. Does this have something to do with his life in the Ukraine?"

"That's his business." He stood, saying, "I'll let myself out."

He expected her to respond, but she didn't. Outside, the night air was brisk with a hint of fall in a breeze that kicked along the deserted street, scattering new-fallen leaves. He automatically checked the shadows, but didn't see anyone. Evidently Tenklov thought Alex had gotten the message. If the cartel was tailing him, they'd have pros he would never spot.

He hurried up the street, his mind on Brett. She worried about him, but she didn't love him—or she would have told him the way she'd told Owen. Yeah, she liked him enough to have an affair with him. That was all. A relief, for sure. Or was it?

Trust me, it's better this way. She's still in love with Owen. Alex had studied his photograph on the mantel. Owen was at least fifteen years older than Brett and not particularly handsome. Alex took for granted that women found him good-looking, but he knew that wasn't his appeal.

The ditzy shrink he'd spent the week with during that blizzard had explained what attracted women to him. "Color in the blanks," she'd said. He never told anyone too much about himself, so they imagined him to be exactly what fit their fantasy. He left long before a woman discovered anything to tarnish that image.

So, how did Brett see him? Obviously not as husband material. Thank you, God. She probably thought of him as a friend, a mentor. A business partner. Okay, maybe a cut above that.

For all Vic's scheming to get him together with Brett— and for all his worrying about it—he wasn't risking anything by sleeping with her. She'd taken him at his word, satisfied to maintain their working relationship and not let their private lives interfere. Amazing. He wouldn't have thought it possible. Most women couldn't keep sex and love separate the way men could.

Admit it. You're just a little bit pissed that she hasn't flipped over you. What the hell did Owen have that you don't?

Brett rolled onto her back, unable to sleep, and bumped into Sneaky By. He'd joined her in bed after Alex left over an hour ago. Alex planned to leave, to sell Belage. What a bombshell. Somehow, she'd seen them as a team, working together for years. And years. But Alex had a different agenda entirely.

What did she expect? He was a much more complex man than she'd thought. He could say what he liked, but he was gambling—with his life—by selling those fancies. For what? So he could return to L.A., or to get a thrill out of tricking Intelco?

"Not very admirable goals," she informed Sneaky By, who responded by making dough on her tummy, "but there are reckless men like that, men who love danger."

Not Owen, she thought. He'd lived with danger because it came with his job. Relief workers often risked their lives to get food into war zones. But for Alex to take foolish chances was ridiculous. Still, she doubted anything she said would stop him.

"What will it be like when Alex leaves?"

Tonight's revelation had stunned her. How could she prepare herself? Remember, sex is safer than love, and she had to admit sex had become more important to her than she'd ever imagined possible. But love? Riskier yet.

"He doesn't want a commitment," she warned herself. "Enjoy this while it lasts, and concentrate on your designing." The telephone rang and she grabbed it, expecting Amy.

"Brett?" It was Alex; she sat up, clutching the sheet. Something had to be wrong for him to call this late. "I'm in bed thinking." She wished he was still beside her. Just hearing his voice triggered an ache of desire. "A man I knew from L.A. contacted me. If I put up half the money, he'll invest the rest and back *us*"—she noticed the way he emphasized *us* "—in a Belage boutique on Rodeo Drive."

Don't do it, Alex. She almost screamed the words into the receiver. This was happening too fast. Too much money was flying around, money Belage didn't have, money they wouldn't get without Alex's risking everything.

"It's the chance of a lifetime, Brett. For both of us."

"We should wait and consolidate our position here."

"No guts, no glory." He chuckled, then there was silence; Brett had no idea what to say. "Listen, I should have leveled with you a long time ago, darling."

Darling? Not even in the throes of passion had Alex ever called her darling. She wanted him to say it again, and again.

"There's not a designer in the world with your talent." Tears sprang into Brett's eyes. She knew him well enough to know he'd never say something like this unless he meant it. "You deserve this chance. In two weeks, I'll be flying to Los Angeles. I want you to come with me. Let's work on this deal together."

25

Amy followed Lev as he stalked across his flat to the picnic table that served as a dining table. She took a seat opposite him and shrugged out of her jacket, too aware that he wore nothing but shorts. She longed to hug him, to find comfort against his burly chest, but if he didn't listen to what she had to say, she'd never feel his arms around her again.

"You said you don't know me, but you do know a little about me from the time we've spent together. Wouldn't you agree that I'm basically a good person? I help artists by displaying their work, giving them more than fair prices." A curt nod. "I'm self-sufficient. I built THE FIND with no help from my father."

"Really?" Lev commented, his tone guarded.

"My father paid for my education, but we've never been close. From the moment I met her, Brett's been like a sister to me. Father despised her because Jock Payne started as a roofer, but it never mattered to me. I've been a good friend. I lent her money when she had Timmy and her family wouldn't help her."

"You care for nothing beyond your small world."

"I can't deny it. Until you came along, I never thought much about politics"—she took a quick breath, knowing

she was touching upon a sore point—"or religion. You've
made me look at myself, and I've been changing without
even realizing it."

He studied her intently but said nothing.

"Lev." She reached across the table and curled her fingers
into his warm palm. "I love you. If you care for me at
all"—she didn't dare say *love*—"please give me a chance."

He gazed down at their hands. "We are much much different."

"We were getting along fine until you met my father.
You're blaming me for what he is, even though I'm nothing
like him."

"Perhaps," he conceded. He was silent for a moment, his
eyes weary pools of experience—most of it depressing.
There was an underlying sadness to Lev that even in their
happiest moments never completely lifted. "You say you
love me, *milochka*."

At the endearment, her heart tripped over itself. "I didn't
know what love meant until I met you." Several weeks ago,
she'd told him about Ellis; she now realized Ellis's attraction
was her ability to manipulate him. Lev was his own
person, so convinced of his opinions that he challenged her
own. "I do love you."

"But you do not know me." He hesitated, gazing down at
her small hand clasped in his. Then he looked up, his sad
eyes meeting hers. "You do not know that I have done an
evil thing."

The tone of his voice and the forbidding look in his eyes
alerted her. There'd always been something about him, a
secret inner self she'd never known. In truth, she'd ignored
the dark side of his personality, afraid to confront it. "Tell
me. I'll stand by you—no matter what."

He swallowed hard; for a man who was usually direct,
even blunt, she could tell this was difficult. A ribbon of fear
flowed through her, pooling in the pit of her stomach.

"I will start back at the time when I was not yet a man. I
was much trouble to my family. I stay out late and smoke

cigarettes my friends smuggle into Ukraine from Turkey. I fight always with my father and my mother, too."

"Did you have any brothers or sisters?"

"No. I go to university in Kiev and I am happy to live away from my family." He paused, and Amy considered how surprising this revelation was. She'd been under the impression Lev was very attached to his family. "I graduate as electrical engineer with specialty in lasers. So I get a good job in Odessa at military plant, but it is away from my family who still tells me what to do."

"What did they want you to do?"

"To be engineer at Kiev power plant and live at home. My father dies. My mother cry and cry. I give up job as laser engineer in Odessa and work in Kiev."

The bitterness in his voice ricocheted off the walls. Amy hadn't expected anything like this, recalling the hours he'd taken to select a coat for his mother and the fondness in his voice when he'd spoken of her.

"In Russia every man must go into army for two years. A laser engineer goes into the special intelligence unit. I know Soviet laser system but I am no longer laser engineer so I must go as lowest soldier. In army the officers are very cruel to new soldiers. It is expected."

"Hazing. We call it hazing. They used to do it a lot in the boys' schools here."

Lev waved his hand dismissively. "Not the same. *Dedovshchina* means torture. Each year more new soldiers die this way than die in Afghanistan. Sometimes they have been shot, or beaten to death. Sometimes worse happens. It is expected. Army claims soldiers kill themselves, but body comes home shot hundreds of times. Or worse."

"How awful. I am surprised that Hugh MacLeod at Amnesty International—"

"Red Army have silence code. If soldier tells, his family is in danger. Red Army is hardest on Jews. Russia has no religion under Communists, but they always know who are the Jews."

Amy grimaced; in England Jews were respected. There was some subtle bigotry; Ruth Payne was evidence of that, but Jews were accepted, even welcomed into society.

"The officers are very cruel to me. One more than the rest. Kirkalev would not leave me alone. He assign me to forty-eight hours marching around a box of rifles. Guarding them, he said. I never get chance to eat or—" He waved his hand. "I say nothing. I do not wish trouble. He have me do pushups in hot sun until I cannot get up. Then he has men beat me and put me in cell for one week without food for not obeying orders."

Amy couldn't imagine such cruelty without recourse. Lev must have felt trapped, helpless. How had he stood it? It was a miracle he survived. Her throat tightened, suppressing a sob. All her heartaches with her father seemed silly in comparison to what he'd suffered.

"I am assigned to take boxes of submachine guns on the train to Leningrad with Kirkalev and his men. It is night when we come into station. The only peoples around are waiting for overdone train from Moscow at the front of station. Kirkalev tells men to go to *traktir*—a pub—and I will unload the cases from boxcar at the back of the big station."

"Alone? Could you lift them?"

"Yes. But I know this is not what will happen."

There was an edge to his voice that went beyond bitterness, beyond pain. She anticipated Lev telling her he'd killed Kirkalev in self-defense.

"Kirkalev gives me order."

She waited, squeezing his hand, which she still clutched tightly, but he didn't finish. "He ordered you to kill yourself, so he could claim it was a suicide."

"No, *milochka*."

"He told you to draw your gun. That way he can shoot you and say you had tried to kill him."

He shook his head, and she understood. Lev had seized

the opportunity and killed this man before he could torture him again. "Kirkalev say drop my pants."

Her stomach heaved. "Dear Lord."

"It happens all the time. Usually a group of them corner a new recruit. I am lucky. There is only one man with a gun. New recruits never have ammunition—or they would kill the officers." Lev's mouth crimped into an angry line. "I unhook my belt and slip it off while Kirkalev watches. He thinks I am obeying order and puts down his gun. I hit him in the eye with my belt and knock him to the ground. Then I hear a noise, and a man asks what is happening. It is Alex."

"Alex Savich?"

"Yes. He came on train from Moscow."

"He saved you. Thank God."

"No. Alex hit me on head and I go down. When I open eyes Kirkalev laughs with Alex, drinking a bottle of vodka. They have my wrists tied with my belt."

This time Amy didn't hazard another guess about what happened next. Clearly, this was a situation beyond her comprehension.

"Kirkalev comes for me. He tells Alex his turn is next. Kirkalev speaks Russian with a Kazakhstan accent, so at first Alex does not understand. He thinks I am bad, but now he knows what is happening. Alex hits Kirkalev. He falls to ground and I jump on him like this." He held out his two arms, his wrists together the way they'd been bound that night. "I slug him with both hands. He hits side of the building with his head. He is dead."

Silence filled the room; she hadn't a clue how to comfort him. He was right, she thought, her heart going out to him. They had little in common. She'd suffered psychological abuse from a disapproving father, but nothing like this. "It was self-defense. No one can blame you."

"If Soviets find me, they will court-martial me. Even *perestroika* cannot save me from the Red Army."

"How did you get away, Lev?"

"Alex and Uncle Vic hide me. They bribed the border guards."

"With diamonds?"

For the first time that evening, a suggestion of a smile crossed his lips. "They have something better than diamonds. They have suitcases of Levi's and rock-and-roll tapes. No trouble. I go to Romania, but I have no country to live in."

"Israel took you in."

"It was not easy. Alex and Vic had nothing left when we get to Romania. The Romanians were going to send me back, but Alex went to Israelis. He persuaded them to buy me."

"Buy you?"

"Yes. Sometimes Israel trades money or arms for people. It is very quiet-quiet, but it happens. They paid Ceauşescu a million dollars to give me a Romanian passport and exit permit. To pay them, I work with Mossad on laser security. They use lasers to guide missiles. Also I studied Russian lasers used on jets. They blind—how do you say it?—for a little bit?"

"Temporarily?"

"Yes. Lasers temporarily blind pilots. They wear special laser-protection goggles, but"—he shrugged—"they not always work. Several times lasers from Soviet planes have temporarily blinded pilots. The Mossad wanted me to help them. If there is war. They will need me. I know how the Soviet laser systems work, and the Iraqis have Soviet equipment."

She could very well lose Lev to Israel, to something more powerful than another lover. She understood much more about him now—and his fondness for Alex—but how could she win a place in his heart? Family. Obviously that was the key, but his relationship with his parents had been entirely different from what she'd expected.

"Lev, there's something I don't understand. I thought you

missed your family. Wasn't that the reason you insisted we entertain my father?"

"Yes. I wish many times I spent more time with my family. No family is perfect, but I love them, and they love me. Now, I cannot even visit my father's grave. I would like to put yellow daffodils on his grave. He liked them very much. In the spring they grew wild along the Don and he pick them for Mother. I wish I could put some on grave and tell him I love him. And I miss him. I never knew what I had until I lost it."

26

"Great view, huh?" Alex asked as he sat with Brett in Geoffrey's looking at Malibu beach. Below the cantilevered deck the surf crested, pummeling the rocks and shooting spume into the air. Farther out, sailboats heeled over, their white sails a brilliant contrast to the blue of the water.

"Beautiful," Brett agreed, forcing enthusiasm into her voice. From the moment their jet had descended through a gray meringue of smog, Brett hadn't liked L.A., but she'd kept her opinion to herself. Alex had been boyishly eager to show her the city.

"You can't beat this weather."

"You're right," Brett had to admit. For late October it was as warm as London during the summer, and not a sticky, humid heat, either, but the balminess she associated with the south of France. "You don't have to spend all your time showing me around. After the meeting this afternoon, drop me off at the hotel and go visit your friends."

"What friends? I've been away twenty years. The only people I see here are diamond traders, and that's strictly business."

She was going to mention his grandmother, but decided against it. Keep this impersonal—as impersonal as it could get when you had sex on a daily basis with a man—she reminded herself. Alex had never volunteered anything about himself; she wasn't going to pry. "Maybe we should order. It's a long drive back to Beverly Hills. We don't want to keep Mr. Creeley waiting."

After they ordered, Brett and Alex sat quietly, enjoying the open-air restaurant and the view of the sea. Brett was accustomed to Alex's silences. In the beginning they'd made her nervous, prompting her to talk, but now she understood Alex spent more time thinking than most men.

"My grandmother's dead," he told her, taking her by surprise. He leaned toward her, his blue eyes earnest. "I don't have any old school friends here I want to see. I could call up my elementary school buddies and say, 'This is Twinkletoes, remember me?' Or I could phone junior high or high school pals and say, 'This is the fairy. How about getting together?' "

His words coupled with the bitterness in his voice almost brought tears to her eyes. In spite of her promise to herself, she asked, "Why did she make you study ballet?"

"Irina, that's my grandmother, had been part of the Kirov troupe, not a lead dancer, but a very competent one. Then my mother, Katya, was born. From the time she walked Irina groomed her to become a prima ballerina. Irina was deliriously happy to discover her own daughter had extraordinary talent.

"At eighteen my mother had been dancing professionally for six years and was touted as the next star. Irina accompanied her troupe to Vienna. There they defected and went on to New York." Alex twiddled his fork. "My grandmother never told my grandfather good-bye. She just went off as she always did in her job as wardrobe manager, but this time she didn't return."

"He must have been devastated to lose them both."

"He's dead now. I visited him once. All he could talk about was Mother. He never mentioned my grandmother."

Alex waited while the waiter served them. "In New York, Balanchine catapulted Mother to stardom. Irina was in seventh heaven."

Brett noted the sardonic smile that replaced his serious look. "What happened?"

"Mikhail Savich—Mischa to his friends. My father came from Minsk. He was driving a taxi in New York and picked up my mother one day. She moved into his cold-water flat in Hell's Kitchen."

Brett had no difficulty imagining a young girl who'd lived a straitjacket life of ballet falling for Alex's father. And if he'd been half the lover Alex was, she'd never have left him.

"Grandmother had a conniption. You see, not only was my father penniless, his father had been part Gypsy. They're as discriminated against in Russia as the Jews. She threatened to disown my mother if she married my father. She married him anyway and immediately became pregnant, which meant she had to quit the ballet. Irina didn't attend the wedding. She moved to Los Angeles and taught ballet."

"Your parents died in an automobile accident shortly after you were born, right?" she asked and Alex nodded. "There was no one to take you except your grandmother."

"She hated me; I look exactly like my father. But she was determined to make me the next Baryshnikov."

Brett couldn't imagine living with hate during those tender years when a child needs love. Her earliest memories were filled with images of loving parents. Even when Jock married Ruthless, Brett never questioned his love. Now, as an adult, she still felt the power of his love; she sensed her own vulnerability and needed his love more now than she had as a child. But Alex had never experienced these emotions. His only connection seemed to be to Lev. And his dead uncle, Vicktor Orlov.

"Vic rescued you, didn't he?"

Brett waited for him to explain, but Alex just nodded and signaled for the check. She almost asked, but didn't. When he was ready, Alex would tell her the rest of the story. She had the distinct impression he hadn't told her the worst.

By the time they reached the Rodeo Collection on Rodeo Drive, her hair was a bramblebush of wind-whipped curls. When they stopped, she applied lipstick and tugged a comb through her hair. Alex hustled her into the complex of exclusive shops that opened onto a central courtyard. Enough Carrara marble had gone into the Rodeo Collection to have rebuilt the Roman Colosseum. She knew the rents had to be astronomical.

Not only would the rent be high, but the competition stiff. Across the street was Cartier and next door was Fred. Ordinarily she would have been thrilled at the stellar company. Not now. Not if it meant Alex would be taking foolish risks.

"Brett Lamont," Alex said when they arrived outside a shop on the third level, "this is Bunster Creeley."

She extended her hand to a tall, rawboned man in his late thirties with woolly hair that had obviously been permed to disguise a receding hairline. "Howdy, ma'am."

"You're from Texas."

"Dallas," he answered with unmistakable pride and an inflection that told her Dallas was the Paris of America. "G'ahead." He nudged her into the small shop.

While the men discussed square footage and comparable properties in Beverly Hills, Brett looked around, her misgivings diminishing. The shop was very small; it wouldn't take much jewelry to fill it. Maybe this wasn't such a bad idea after all.

She wondered why Alex was determined to return to L.A. Then the answer dawned on her. He'd been the class scapegoat, humiliated daily. If he returned to live on Malibu's Carbon Beach—a stretch of sand no wider than a beach towel—in a house where you could hear your neighbors flush the toilet, he'd be on millionaire's row. He'd be a success. He'd prove to himself that he was better than all those kids who'd teased him.

Was that much different from her own goal of becoming a

renowned designer, proving to Jock and Ruthless—especially Ruthless—that she was a success? She considered this for a moment and decided she'd even be showing her mother that she could accomplish something in her own right, moving out of Constance Lamont's shadow.

"The shop's not too small, is it, Brett?" Alex asked.

"T'aint big enough to fart in." Bunster laughed. "Tellya what. Let's start here, then move to somethin' bigger."

"Good idea," Brett said, hoping she wouldn't have much to do with Bunster. She'd agreed with the Texan, convinced that Alex was determined to open in Beverly Hills. If she could minimize the capital he committed to the project, she'd do it. God knew, she'd tried to talk him out of this with no success.

The men discussed the details, and Brett listened, astounded at how expensive the rent was despite the size of the shop. What was more, it would require an enormous investment on Alex's part to cover the expenses of custom display cases, a special safe, and a top-flight security system.

"We'll sign the papers tomorrow," Alex told her. "We'll be set to open late next spring."

"Let's celebrate," Bunster said. "I'm havin' a few friends over tonight. Ya'all come."

Brett would have refused, preferring to spend the evening alone with Alex, but he accepted. They said good-bye to Bunster and waited outside the complex for the valet to bring their car.

"You're quiet. Something bothering you?" Alex asked.

"We'll have to sell a lot of jewelry to make any money. I'm wondering how much of my success has been the result of the Harvey Nichols exhibition when my mother's old friends and an avalanche of publicity created a sellout. I'm concerned that my designs without a boost from my mother's name may not fare so well in France. And here in Los Angeles, where everything is so trendy, I might not have my finger on the pulse of the market."

He put his arm around her, something Alex never did in

public, a spark of some indefinable emotion in his eyes. "Didn't I tell you that you have exceptional talent? I was going to save this news for a special bottle of champagne tonight, but I guess you need to hear it now. Philippe Deauville called and reordered for all his shops. The Lamont Collection sold out the first week."

"You're kidding." She threw both arms around him, hugging him tight, amazed. He pulled her close, his lips meeting hers. The first night they'd made love had released a dam of pent-up desire. But what she felt now went beyond passion. Not only did she and Alex have common goals, he had the faith in her that she needed to find in herself.

One hand on the steering wheel, guiding the convertible along the winding road that led to Bunster Creeley's home, Alex glanced over at Brett. She wore a jade-green sheath that deepened the color of her eyes and brought out the platinum tones in her dark blond hair. Sexy as hell. What's the matter, buddy? You just made love to her. Sure, but he was ready to turn around and head back to their bungalow at the Beverly Hills Hotel and forget Bunster's party.

"Where are we?" Brett interrupted his thoughts.

"We're on Coldwater Canyon. He lives just off this street."

"I meant what city. So far I've been in Malibu, Pacific Palisades, Brentwood, Westwood, Beverly Hills—"

"This is B.H.P.O., which stands for Beverly Hills post office. It isn't really Beverly Hills because the kids can't use the B.H. schools, but the area has a B.H. zip code so their parents can say they live in Beverly Hills." She looked at him as if he were making this up. "Hey, that little zip translates to megabucks for these homes."

"I guess they want to be associated with movie stars."

"Not many stars live in B.H. anymore. Most of them are in Malibu. Beverly Hills schools are loaded with English-as-a-second-language students. Most of them speak Farsi."

"Iranians?"

"Sure. When the Shah bagged it, the smart money moved to B.H. Look for the Mercedes with blue-and-white bumper stickers in Farsi script. Translated, it's *Ayatollah—Asshola.*"

"Really? I don't understand California. You're sure we should be investing here . . . with Bunster?"

He put his hand on her thigh and gave it a playful squeeze. "I'm positive. Bunster sounds like a hick—a crude hick—but it's just an act. He plays the Texas bit to the hilt. Trust me, he's an astute businessman. He owns the jewelry shop in the Mansion at Turtle Creek in Dallas. Every year he brings in Elizabeth Gage's collection and has an exhibition that draws people from across the entire country."

"Really?" Brett smiled. Elizabeth Gage's name rang her bell, all right. The premier designer in London, Gage's name meant more to Brett than Paloma Picasso or Elsa Peretti.

"Stop worrying," he said, although he knew she wouldn't. From the moment she'd found out about the enhancer, she'd been concerned. He turned off Coldwater Canyon onto a narrow side street. "See that house on the left?" She looked and he added, "That's where Charlie Manson's gang murdered Sharon Tate and her friends. Bunster lives just up the street."

That got her, taking her mind off Belage. He parked outside the house that was some harebrained architect's idea of Japanese modern. Judging from the throng of cars parked around, Bunster's "few" friends translated to fifty.

They were greeted at the door by a silicone-boobed blonde who wasn't sure who Bunster was but thought he must be around somewhere. Alex guided Brett through the crowded living room out onto the patio. The view from the hilltop was impressive with the city lights sparkling in the distance.

"I'll bring you a gin and tonic," Alex told Brett.

He fought his way through the mob—L.A.-style highfliers and women who'd had plastic surgery so many times nothing about them was original equipment—toward the bar.

"Alex." Bunster stepped out of the crowd, a willowy blonde and a redhead dogging his every step. "Where's Brett?"

"On the patio. I'm getting her a drink."

"Later," Bunster said to the girls, motioning for them to leave. He pointed to the redhead. "That one nekkid." He rolled his eyeballs. "I tellya. You'll have the same problem. Enough bucks and women are all over ya like stink on shit."

Jesus, I hope not. But he knew it was true. Money was a powerful lure. Is that what he had to look forward to, Alex wondered, a lot of phony women interested only in his money?

"Anythin' between you and Brett?"

Every protective instinct Alex had fired at once. "Stay away from her." The anger in his voice took him by surprise.

Bunster held up his hands like an old-time rustler surrendering. "Hey, jest askin'."

When Alex returned to the patio, two men were talking with Brett. Typical L.A. The older one had his shirt unbuttoned to the waist displaying a poodle chest with a twenty-dollar gold piece hanging on a chain as thick as Alex's finger. The second guy was dressed like a drug dealer—probably the real thing—in a black shirt buttoned all the way up to the throat and baggy-black pants nipped in at the cuffs.

Brett was listening attentively, smiling. Naturally. Alex handed her the drink, then slipped his arm around her waist. That did it. The wolves retreated.

Bunster joined them, two blondes in tow as well as four guys who introduced themselves as producers. Great. In L.A. all it took to make you a producer was a business card. Bunster explained he was opening Belage in the Rodeo Collection. Properly awed at the prestigious address, the group began discussing diamonds. Clearly, they believed bigger was better.

"Actually," Brett said in her well-modulated British accent, "smaller stones that have fewer flaws are more valuable."

"Really?" commented one producer, his eyes skimming over Brett. In about one second he'd be stepping on his tongue.

Alex drew Brett closer, and she gave him an odd look. "We're specializing in colored diamonds."

"Oh? Well." The producer looked disappointed. Everyone did.

Brett moved away from Alex. "It's the latest rage in Paris."

"Aaaah," approved the producer who'd asked the question. Alex couldn't tell if he really cared or was just trying to impress Brett, but the word *Paris* convinced everyone else.

Bunster said, "We're going to make money up the ole wazoo."

The group effused their approval. Alex doubted any of them, except Bunster, could even afford one of Belage's baubles. This was a groupie crowd unlike the people they'd met at Philippe's chateau who'd actually come through and bought their jewelry. But Brett hadn't picked up on the flash-and-trash act yet. She went on smiling and flirting. Selling, he told himself.

"Whyncha get some grub?" Bunster suggested and the group schooled together, heading into the house.

Alex walked beside Brett, slipping his arm around her. She stepped to the side, away from him.

"Alex," she whispered, "didn't we agree to behave professionally? I don't want anyone to think I'm designing for Belage because of our relationship."

Alex slowed his pace, letting Brett move ahead and follow Bunster into the dining room. His pride bruised, Alex walked to the bar, kicking himself for what he'd said that night at Philippe's. But how the hell was he to know he'd feel this way?

What way?

Goddammit, how did he feel? He ordered another Stolichnaya, considering. He'd been dead certain he didn't want a romantic relationship that lasted more than just a few nights. But this was the best time he could remember—and he didn't want to end it. What did he want then?

A relationship.

For crissake. He'd never had a real relationship before. And he'd sworn he wouldn't let Vic maneuver him into this. Yeah, well, he'd vacilated for months now, unable to make up his mind just what he did want. How was it he could roll the dice with Intelco, making a decision that could cost him his life so easily, yet he couldn't decide what to do about Brett?

He knocked back the icy vodka in one gulp, his eyes skimming across the crowd for Brett. There she was, a pack of wolves bird-dogging her. Something tightened in his chest, but he refused to acknowledge what he felt as jealousy.

A smart man would marry her. Jee-sus! Was he actually entertaining the idea of marriage? Why not? As a kid he'd spent hours locked in that dark closet, pretending his grandmother didn't exist, pretending he had loving parents, pretending he was only playing hide-and-seek with his brothers. When had he stopped wanting to be part of a family?

A shrink would say he was driven to prove himself over and over. He'd spent twenty years proving he was someone worthy of respect. Did that matter anymore?

"Hello." A woman with butter-blond hair sidled up to him, wearing a chain-mail dress. With nothing underneath. "Hi, there. I'm Devon La Roche."

Trust me, that isn't your real name. "Alex Savich."

"Where do you live?"

Now this was L.A.'s social barometer. A car was half your identity, your address the other. Neither was paid for. Why the hell did he want to move back, anyway? Brett tried to hide it, but he knew she hated L.A. "I live in London."

"I aaa-dore London. What do you do there?" She ran her hand up his arm, her nails teasing the muscles beneath his sport coat.

"I've just started a business."

"Oh, you're a consultant, too."

Half the men in L.A. were producers, the other half were consultants, which was just a glorified way of saying they were unemployed. His eyes drifted across the room to Brett. She wasn't as beautiful as most of the women in the room, but she had a natural, unaffected warmth. And that damn smile.

"Where are you staying?" Devon asked.

"The Beverly Hills Hotel." The words were out before he could stop them. He hadn't meant to encourage this woman, although he wished Brett would look his way and notice he had a knockout with her hand practically in his pants. No such luck.

"Is it true they're closing the Beverly Hills Hotel for two years to give it a face-lift?"

"Yes. The Sultan of Brunei owns the joint, but it needs work. It's the only thing in L.A. that hasn't had a face-lift."

He'd stayed there although he couldn't really afford it because Brett would like it. The movie stars didn't impress her. She did like the privacy of their bungalow, and she enjoyed the pool, where she could sun herself even though it was almost November.

"Would you like to go back to my place and relax?"

"I'm with someone." He stepped away from the bar and went out onto the patio. Mercifully, it was deserted.

Okay, buddy, what's your next move? Damned if he knew. Would Brett *even consider* marrying him? No way. She was still in love with Saint Owen.

And then there was Timmy. A one-in-a-million kid. If he married Brett and it didn't work out, Timmy would pay the price. The kid idolized him, and Alex had to admit he loved it.

So what are you going to do? God Almighty, it was easier dealing with the cartel.

27

Back in their bungalow, Brett watched Alex open a bottle of Cristal champagne, positive he was angry with her. As Alex would have said, she'd blown it. The instant she'd reminded him they should behave professionally, he'd deserted her. It had been Alex's idea to keep their relationship professional, but she had to admit he'd become less professional on this trip. And he had opened up a little, telling her about his family.

"Instead of leaving tomorrow afternoon, why don't you stay through the weekend?" Alex handed her a glass of champagne. "We'll drive up the coast to Big Sur. You'll love it."

He'd cold-shouldered her all evening and hardly said a word on the drive back to the hotel, but now he was suggesting she stay with him. What an enigma. He was an insular man, not given to sharing his feelings. She had to be satisfied with what Alex offered—total support for her designing. And sex.

What she felt for Alex wasn't the deep abiding love she'd had for Owen. This was more passionate simply because she and Owen had been forced to rush their lovemaking in Owen's hotel room. They were always hurrying, usually to meet her mother. Their bond had been more intellectual and less physical.

"I'd like to stay, Alex, but I promised Timmy—"

"Wouldn't he be happy to stay in the country a few extra days and ride his pony? I'm sure your father wouldn't mind."

Brett was tempted. "My mother would promise me she'd come for me, but more often than not I'd be left waiting. I want Timmy to know he can count on me."

"I understand," he answered, but she wondered if he did as he sat beside her and touched the rim of his champagne flute to hers. "To us." He measured her, his look so galvanizing that it sent a tremor through her. "We're terrific partners."

"Then what was going on tonight? You hardly spoke to me."

"You didn't have time for me."

"I was trying to promote Belage. Anyway, you were too busy with that blonde in the chain-mail sheath." She could have bitten her tongue off. She didn't want him to think she was jealous, because she wasn't. But she was angry at being left to hype Belage while he flirted.

Smiling, he put his glass on the small coffee table. She didn't like his grin. Not one bit. He took her champagne and set it beside his. Still grinning.

"What's so funny? You know, you really upset me, Alex. You never say what's on your mind."

He pulled her roughly, forcefully, against him. The pressure of his arms was so masculine, so tantalizing, that she almost lost her train of thought.

"You want to know what I'm thinking?" he said, his voice pitched low. "I'm crazy about you and I don't know what in hell to do about it."

Shock siphoned the lecture on communicating from her mind. What was Alex saying? Was this the man who didn't want a commitment? Before she had time to respond, he kissed her, his lips unexpectedly tender, restrained. Her tongue had to coax his into a lazy duel, and she realized what he was trying to tell her had nothing to do with sex.

He was telling her that he cared about her, stopping just short of using the word *love*. How did she feel? Should she encourage him by saying—saying what? She honestly didn't know how she felt. But she did know she wanted to understand Alex.

"Tell me what happened with your grandmother," she said, fully aware the question caught him off guard. He was expecting her to say how she felt about him. "Please."

That one word, spoken so softly prompted an immediate reaction. His face, usually so difficult to read, contorted as if he were in pain. "I was eight when Vicktor Orlov visited us. He was here trading diamonds and decided to check on me. Normally, Grandmother would have slammed the door on *anyone* associated with my father, but you knew Vic. He could sweet-talk anyone, even my grandmother. But he couldn't persuade her to stop my ballet lessons."

"You were happier after he came, weren't you?"

"Yes. He visited once a month, trading diamonds, and he took me places and did things with me. Those times were the high points of my childhood. I can still remember every place we went and what we did. I had nothing else to look forward to, you see. Everyone at school called me 'Twinkletoes' or 'Commie.' Back then they thought anyone Russian was a spy."

His arm was around her, but she felt she was holding him.

"My grandmother locked me in my room each night. If I disobeyed her—in any little way—she'd lock me in my closet for hours on end. She never spoke to me unless she had to."

Ruth Payne had been upsetting with her subtle digs and open favoritism of Ellis, but nothing like this. Brett felt childish for holding a grudge against the woman for so long.

"By the time I was fifteen, the kids had been calling me a fairy for years. I had no friends, and to make things worse, the teachers liked me because I was quiet and got good grades. Well, that's the kiss of death when you're that age."

Brett nodded, guiltily recalling how she and Amy had ignored the girl at their school who'd been the teachers' favorite.

"One girl was nice to me, which means she said hello when we met in the hall and kept walking, but she did say hello. She was my lab partner in chemistry."

The timbre of his voice had altered slightly, and Brett realized that she'd meant more to a lonely fifteen-year-old than most puppy loves did.

"She wasn't too bright, but I loaned her my notes and did all her chemistry experiments for her. I saved all the spending money Vic gave me for months so I could take her out. It took me weeks to get up my courage to ask her."

Brett shifted in his arms, tensing.

"I stopped by her locker after class. I'll never forget the look on her face. She literally went white and shrieked: 'I'd never go anywhere with a fag.' There wasn't a kid up and down the entire hall that didn't hear her. They laughed, hooting and slapping each other on the back. I walked out of there and never went back."

Brett opened her mouth to say something—anything—but couldn't. How well she remembered her first boyfriend, Digby Finch-Baker. She would have died on the spot if he'd said anything so cruel. Is your ego ever as fragile as it is during that time in your life, the age when you first discover the attraction of the opposite sex?

"I promised myself it would be the last time anyone teased me. Or laughed. I ran away to Hollywood Boulevard. Even then, it was a mecca for runaways. It was pure hell: drugs, gangs, fights, prostitution. But I loved being on my own—until my money ran out."

"Why didn't you contact Vic?"

"He was traveling and I couldn't find him. A man offered me money to let him take some pictures, so I went with him."

"You didn't." How many times had her father made her swear never to get into the car with a stranger?

"He took me to a mansion in Beverly Hills, and he did take some pictures. Then I found out what gay really meant. I beat the shit out of him."

"A few weeks later a private detective Vic had hired found me. I moved in with Vic and finished high school at another school."

"Didn't you see your grandmother?"

"No, she didn't want me unless I would become a ballet dancer. She's been dead for years now."

Brett thought about what he'd shared with her. She didn't completely understand him, but what she'd learned helped her unravel some of the mystery about Alex Savich.

"Are you happy now? I want you to be. You deserve it."

He cupped her chin with his warm hand, tipping her head back so he looked directly into her eyes. "I'm happier now than I've ever been. You make me happy. I love you."

She merely stared, stunned by this unpredictable man. She wanted to tell him she loved him, but she couldn't quite get the words out. Somehow it seemed impossible that she could have mourned Owen so intensely only to have fallen in love with Alex. Her feelings couldn't change this quickly. Could they?

The silence that engulfed them unnerved her. She had to say something, to let him know she cared without going too far. Yet.

"I've never felt quite like this about a man. I'm crazy about you, too."

"It's not too late to change your flight and stay," Alex told Brett the next morning as they sunned themselves beside the pool.

He hated himself for asking. After last night, he expected her to change her mind. Forget it. Timmy meant a lot to Brett. He wasn't exactly jealous of the kid, but he had to admit he would have felt more secure about their relationship if Brett agreed to stay. Hell, what was he worried about? Okay, she hadn't said she loved him. But he knew Brett too well not to know she cared a lot. So, how much was a lot? As much as he felt?

"Look," Brett said, "isn't that your friend from Bunster's?"

Alex saw Devon La Roche sashaying very slowly around the pool so everyone noticed her. Her bikini, three triangles of silver lamé held together by a snare of razor-thin straps, accentuated showgirl legs. And Dolly Partons.

"Don't ever let me catch you in a suit like that."

"Why not? All the men seem to be enjoying it."

"That's just why." He lowered his sunglasses and winked at her. "I'd rather keep my pleasures private."

He leaned back, soaking in the warm rays of the sun, his eyes closed, wishing Brett would change her mind about leaving.

"Alex," a sultry voice said, and he realized Devon had stopped in front of his chaise. "It's been aaa-ges."

Hell, it was only last night. "Did you meet Brett?"

Devon shook her head, her butter-blond curls bounced across bare shoulders. "I'm here with my uncle." She turned and waved at a man who was definitely old enough to be her uncle, but bore no family resemblance.

Brett stood. "I've got a flight to catch."

Alex vaulted to his feet, muttering good-bye, and followed Brett to their bungalow, secretly pleased at Brett's tight voice. Hell, she might not have told him she loved him, but she sure got pissy in a hurry whenever a woman took an interest in him.

He couldn't actually believe he'd said those three little— usually fateful—words. He could practically hear Vic saying: *All I want is for you to be happy.* As usual Vic had been right. Brett was the woman for him. If only she'd admit she loved him.

"I'm going to miss you these next two weeks."

"Oh, Alex, I don't want to nag but—"

"Then don't. We've been all through this. After I go to Hong Kong and interview a few craftsmen for Belage, I'm flying on to Bucharest. I'm picking up the last shipment of diamonds. You know we need them to fund the shop here." Brett nodded, but Alex could tell she didn't agree. "I'd walk you to the taxi, but I'm expecting a call from Choy Tsung in Hong Kong any minute," Alex told Brett as the bellman took away her suitcases.

Brett slid her arms around his neck and looked up at him with those radiant green eyes. Jeez, he missed her already. "Darling, promise you'll be careful."

He held her snugly, not wanting to let her go, loving the feel of her body against his despite her layers of clothes. She ran her fingertips down his bare spine to the waistband of his swimming trunks. Then she gave them a playful snap.

"Hey. What's that for?"

"You didn't promise." She said it in a teasing voice, but her expression told him she was dead serious.

"I promise to be careful. Don't worry. I'll see you in two weeks." He pressed his mouth to hers, caressing her lips more than kissing them. Why start something he couldn't finish? He drew back, his lips just inches from hers; gazing into her eyes, he willed her to appreciate how deeply he meant what he was going to say. "Always remember I love you."

"Oh, Alex." She clung to him, a smile trembling on her lips. "I'm so crazy about you."

Okay, then spend the weekend with me.

Brett pecked his cheek, then pulled away. "I'd better hurry. The taxi meter is probably already running."

He stood in the doorway, his eyes following her until she disappeared from sight. A tight ache gripped him, the same feeling he'd had when Vic died. He hadn't expected love to be quite this painful. They'd be apart only two weeks, for God's sake. Closing the door, he spotted Devon still strutting around the pool. She waved, but he pretended he hadn't seen her.

Alex flopped down on the couch and used the remote control to find the Raiders game on TV. The bright light from the window dimmed the screen, so he closed the curtains and tried to concentrate on the game while he waited for Tsung to call.

He and Vic had met Choy Tsung years ago in Hong Kong. Tsung had bought many of their diamonds. Now Tsung—and half of Hong Kong—wanted out before the Communists took over the island from the British. Alex was more than willing to help. It was the only way he knew to pick up talented craftsmen without spending megabucks to lure them away from their current employers.

He heard a knock on the door and rose to answer it, flicking off the television. He swung open the door, the sunlight blinding him after sitting in the nearly dark room.

"Howdy," Devon said, smoothing back butter-blond curls. "There's a party tonight. I thought you—"

"I'm busy." Alex blinked, trying to get rid of the spots before his eyes. Behind him the telephone rang; it was probably Tsung. "Gotta go." He pushed the door shut.

"Hello." He waited, hearing the slight bleep from the satellite relaying the overseas call. Out of the corner of his eye, he saw Devon had followed him inside. Talk about nerve.

"Alex." Tsung's distinctive voice came over the line. "I am waiting for you to meet my people. I have several who will be perfect for Belage. When will you arrive?"

Alex felt the heat of Devon's body standing directly behind him. He covered the receiver with his palm, turning to her. "This is a private conversation. I'll catch you later." He spun around, checking the desk for his ticket with his flight number.

Tsung said something about how talented his niece was, but Alex hardly heard him. Devon's breasts brushed his back, barely touching but grazing his bare skin with erect nipples. He didn't need to turn around to know she'd taken off her bikini top. He elbowed her away, trying to concentrate on what Tsung was saying about his niece.

"I'm on fl-flight"—his voice stumbled—"six fifteen." Like a laser, her hand flashed beneath the waistband of his trunks and homed in on his cock. Son of a bitch. "Arrives at noon."

"So big." Devon pumped him a few times, and Alex tried to twist away, but his resistance was crumbling. Fast. "Mmmm," she moaned, massaging him with skilled fingers. "The big Kahuna."

Tsung said something about sending the limo; Devon whispered something about the blow job of the century.

"G'bye." Alex slammed the receiver into the cradle; it was hard to breathe now. Devon was so professional, she might as well give up her amateur status—if she claimed one. She had his trunks down, now pooled around his ankles.

She stepped back, her full breasts swaying. With a flick of her wrist, she snapped the tie on the bottom of her bikini. The triangle of silver lamé fluttered down between her sleek thighs and landed on her silver sandal, revealing a smooth crotch shaved bare. And soft looking—like baby skin.

She touched his balls, lightly, gently with the pads of her fingers, slowly running them over the surface. Then she traced the seam of his cock with the edge of her fingernail. He inhaled sharply. She edged forward, her hand gloving his shaft, and touched the sensitive tip to her velvet-smooth mound. Circling, slowly circling.

He fought the urge to shove her onto the settee and ram into her ripe body, thinking of Brett. He loved *her*. He didn't want—to make love to anyone else. Certainly not a woman he hardly knew who had brazened her way into his room.

She dipped his shaft between her thighs into the soft folds. Hot. Wet. Slick.

He jerked back. He'd have blue balls for a week, but he'd be damned before he lowered himself to touch this woman.

"Get out." He drew in a deep, steadying breath.

"C'mon, hon." Her hand clamped over his hardness. "You want it bad. You know you do. Let Devon take care of you."

He grabbed her wrist and twisted it hard. "Get out of here."

"What's the matter? I'm not good enough for you because I don't have a British accent?"

"That's not all you're missing." He put his hand on his throbbing cock, asking himself how he'd let things get this far.

Suddenly the door flew open spotlighting the semidark room in a searing shaft of sunlight. Alex squinted at the familiar silhouette standing in the door. Aw, shit.

28

Squinting into the near-dark room, Brett stared at Alex. What she saw slowly registered: Alex nude ready to take the blonde to bed. *Run,* her brain screamed, but her legs had become giant redwood stumps, rooted in the ground for centuries. Her heart refused to believe what her eyes told her. Not Alex. But it was Alex.

The bile rose in her throat, almost choking her. Don't be sick. She clamped her hand over her mouth, to stifle a low cry. The sound snapped her to attention. She spun around, then charged down the path, stumbling in her high heels, conscious of people staring. Not giving a damn. Without slowing, she bounded through the lobby, nearly knocking down the doorman.

Miraculously, her bags were still on the curb and the driver who'd taken her partway to the airport—before she'd changed her mind—was still there. "The airport." She jumped into the taxi.

Why? she asked herself. Why? Alex claimed to love her. Ha! She seethed, rage replacing anguish and mounting with each breath. He'd told her so much about himself, things he'd kept hidden, lulling her into believing she was special. Damn all!

She should have known better. Everyone from her fa-

ther to Eula Mae warned her that he was a womanizer.
She'd witnessed it herself that night at Annabel's. Now that
she thought about it, he'd behaved the same way exactly.
The model had flirted with him just as Devon had. And she
—Brett Lamont—had been left on the sidelines. Watching.

Yet she'd fallen for him. For lies.

Her bags stowed in the trunk, the taxi lurched forward
jostling Brett. She hardly noticed for hating herself. She'd
returned to Alex—nearly going back on her word to her
son. Why? Because she'd foolishly believed he loved her,
believed she was special, believed she could be happy with
him.

But she should have listened to her sixth sense. It had
kept her from saying she loved him. Subconsciously, she
must have realized something was wrong. She'd gotten exactly what she deserved. Exactly.

The fog on the mirror in his London condo blurred Alex's
reflection, making it hard to shave. He swiped at the mirror
with his towel, then stared at his half-shaved face. Dammit,
dammit all the way to hell. Usually cursing made him feel
better. Not this time. Not the thousand other times he'd
cussed since that afternoon in L.A. weeks ago. Unfuck-
ingbelievable. His luck had soured. Another minute and
Devon would have been gone.

Would Brett believe him? Possibly. If she'd cooled down.
How well he remembered the way she'd shut him out after
the mess at Annabel's. It had taken forever to crack her wall
of silence.

This time, it had been over three weeks since he'd chased
her to the entrance of the Beverly Hills Hotel only to see
her taxi speed down the hill. His first impulse had been to
follow her. But being in swim trunks with no money stopped
him. By the time he went back to his room, he'd formulated
a plan.

"Give her time to cool off. Then tell her the truth."

But she refused to take his calls. He doubted she'd even listened to the messages he left on her answering machine.

He'd flown to Hong Kong and arranged for several of Choy Tsung's craftsmen—relatives, of course—to move to London after the first of the year to work at Belage. From there he'd gone to Bucharest, then rented a deathtrap Citroën made almost fifty years ago and driven hundreds of miles over unpaved roads to Lise on the border with the Ukraine. Tenklov had met Alex and had given him a very large packet of colored diamonds.

The Russian had tried to persuade Alex to continue selling stones for his mysterious employer, but Alex refused. This was the last shipment Vic had agreed to sell; Alex would never renege on a deal, but this was it. Why play Russian roulette? One day his luck would run out. The way it had with Brett.

When he finally returned to Bucharest, he'd been so anxious to see Brett that he'd taken a red-eye flight to London. He'd planned to go directly to Brett's, but one look in the men's room mirror frightened him. He had a stubble beard that might be sexy on movie stars but made him look like a serial killer. His mismatched clothes, including shoes that were both black but not the same style, let him blend in with the Czechs. In London, though, he'd gotten nothing but suspicious stares. He'd gone home to shave, shower, and change clothes before seeing Brett.

"Aw, hell, why are you so nervous?" he asked his reflection. "C'mon, if Brett loves you, she'll understand." Love. That was what her forgiveness hinged on. And he didn't know if she loved him.

An hour later he rang Brett's doorbell and listened for the pounding of Timmy's feet as he raced to answer the door. Silence. He waited and rang again. Nothing.

He trudged down the path to the gate, thinking he'd roam around Chelsea and come back later. Behind him he heard the door open. He spun around, his heart ten pounds lighter than it had been a second ago. A jolt of fear he'd never experienced before—even with the cartel—hit him. She *had* to believe him. She *had* to understand. She *had* to love him as much as he loved her.

"Yes?" said the man standing in Brett's door. Fiftyish, pale gray hair that had receded above light blue eyes. He looked familiar, but Alex couldn't quite place him for a moment.

Couldn't be.

Aw, hell. Owen Northcote. Back from the dead.

"You rang?" Owen asked, a note of impatience in his voice now.

"Alex Savich," he finally said.

Owen smiled and motioned for him to come in. "I say, I've been anxious to meet you."

"You have?" Why? He went inside, struggling for the words that would get him the hell out of there.

"You're surprised to see me?" Owen asked, sitting on the sofa. "Didn't you read the papers?"

Alex shook his head. Owen wagged a copy of *The Times* in Alex's face. In typeset usually reserved for events like the sinking of the *Titanic:* NORTHCOTE ALIVE!

"Hugh MacLeod got me out," Owen explained. "He spearheaded the Amnesty International investigation. I guess I can thank that Nip, Alberto Fujimori, too. His becoming president of Peru changed things for political prisoners."

Of all the scenarios he'd envisioned—and there were hundreds—honest to God, he'd never imagined this. Saint Owen back from the grave. If Alex had had a prayer with Brett, it had vanished.

"I say, Brett was shocked to find out I was alive."

Trust me, she isn't the only one.

"Almost as surprised as I was to discover I had a son."

"You knew she was pregnant." The words came out smooth and sure, not betraying how heartsick Alex felt.

"She mentioned it, but I never thought—" He laughed, har-har-har. "Timmy's a great kid, isn't he?"

"One in a million."

"Good genes." Owen smiled proudly.

"He's exactly like his mother."

Owen didn't notice the edge in Alex's voice. "Isn't she something? Who would have thought she was waiting for me all this time? For me."

"Hard to imagine." Alex's brain had short-circuited when he saw Owen, but miracle of miracles, it was functioning properly now even though the very core of his soul felt as hard as a diamond. Brett hadn't told Owen about him. Well, she had waited *almost* the entire time. Close enough for government work. What had Brett told Owen? Obviously not the truth.

Owen leaned forward, his elbows on his knees. He was gaunt and definitely had a jailhouse pallor. Alex couldn't help feeling sorry for the guy. All those years in prison.

"I want to thank you for all you've done. Brett's salary means a lot. I won't have to work while I'm finishing the book about my ordeal. It's set for publication at the middle of January."

"Less than two months from now? Is that possible?"

"I wrote it in prison. All the book needs is editorial revisions. I have to turn the manuscript in right before Christmas." He laughed. Har. Har. Har. "It'll make a terrific movie. A great action-adventure."

Alex rose to leave; his knees felt weak. He didn't bother telling himself it was from lack of sleep. "I've got to run."

"Did you want me to give Brett a message?"

Tell her I love her. That I'm always going to love her. "No. I just wanted to see how things were going at Belage. I'll talk to her Monday."

"She won't be in. The three of us are going up to Hugh MacLeod's home on the Isle of Skye for two weeks while I write." Owen slapped his leg. "I say, you don't know, do you? We're getting married tomorrow."

* * *

Eula Mae sat beside Lev and Amy, who were next to Alex, in the small chapel in St. John's Wood. The only other guests at the small service were Ellis and Daphne Payne, Hugh MacLeod, and Ruth Payne. Eula Mae glanced at Alex. "Oh, Vic," she said under her breath. "It's not supposed to be this way." But who could have foreseen Owen's return?

She wondered how Alex felt about it, but couldn't tell. He appeared normal—handsome in his navy wool suit. His face was a study in self-control. Had he been a professional card shark, he could have held the winning or the losing hand. And no one could have guessed which.

He had to be upset, Eula Mae decided. Although neither of them mentioned it, she was positive Brett and Alex had been having an affair. She hadn't been surprised; Vic had predicted it. And she'd prayed for it.

What was going to happen now? Eula Mae asked herself. Brett seemed to be overjoyed about Owen, and yet she couldn't help recalling how upset she'd been when she returned from Los Angeles. Then the call had come from Hugh saying Owen Northcote was flying home.

The papers had been filled with the poor man's horrible experience. He'd been thrown in prison by government troops and left to rot. His name had never appeared on a single prison roster. Luckily, Hugh—she smiled at him— kept asking questions.

Owen Northcote waited at the altar, thin and wan but smiling expectantly down the aisle. Not a handsome man, Eula Mae conceded, but a good man. A hero, really. Oh, what that man had suffered. She glanced again at Alex, saddened for what might have been. They would have been a perfect match.

Alex rose as taped music filled the small chapel, telling himself the finality of seeing Brett marry would help him get over her. Timmy marched down the aisle, dressed in a suit and carrying a pillow with two gold wedding bands on it, his young face dead serious as he tried to keep pace with the music.

He reached the altar and stopped behind his father. Owen touched the top of Timmy's head, gently ruffling the boy's hair. Timmy looked up beaming, the adoring smile Alex had come to expect. For himself.

Until that moment he hadn't realized he thought of himself as Timmy's father.

He quickly looked away, focusing on the back of the church. Through the archway walked Brett guided by Jock Payne. She wore a simple dress with a sweetheart neckline in heather green, a shade that always deepened the green of her eyes, turning them Dresden green and every bit as intense as that famous diamond. On special occasions she usually wore her hair up, revealing the cute mole at the base of her neck, but today her hair fell in glorious waves to her shoulders. Had Owen asked her to leave her hair down? Did he find her sexier that way?

Alex sure as hell did. Even without closing his eyes, he saw her head on a pillow, the irises of those vibrant eyes reduced to thin hoops of green from passion. A waterfall of burnished gold hair caressing bare shoulders. And high, full breasts begging him to kiss them.

Like a nail in a coffin, the finality stunned him. He'd never see her like that again.

Brett glanced at her father, and they both smiled. She might look exactly like her mother, he thought, but she has Jock's infectious smile. A smile that made you want to cry. A smile that showed Alex that she was completely happy. She had what she wanted: the love of her life, her son's father.

"What had Brett told him the night of Ellis's wedding?" he muttered under his breath.

He remembered every word and the sincerity in her voice. *When you find the person you love, you fall over the edge of life's cliff. Without that person you'll be out of bounds —that means nowhere—forever.*

Brett swept by, smiling, but not meeting his gaze. Alex watched, cataloging every movement. Each one achingly familiar. They reached the altar and Timmy grinned at his mother. Naturally, she smiled.

Something twisted in Alex's gut, the truth hitting home with brutal force. No denying it, he was over the edge.

29

Alex took a swig of champagne. Jee-sus, how had he made it through that service? In his mind, he could still see Owen kissing the bride, a long open-mouthed kiss that turned Alex's stomach and left everyone else breathless.

"I worried. You were gone a long time," Lev told Alex as he stood beside Amy in the parlor of the Paynes' Belgravia town house for the reception. "I thought the cartel had killed you."

No such luck. "Na-aah. Just bad weather."

"Do you have a message from Lev's mother?" Amy asked, touching Lev's arm, her gesture so affectionate that Alex looked away.

Alex thumped his forehead with the heel of his palm. How in hell had he forgotten? "Your mother is thrilled with that red coat, but I understand she hasn't been feeling well. She's gone to a doctor. He says it's nothing to worry about."

Amy gazed at Lev, but didn't question him about why there was no letter from his mother, only a message relayed by the Gypsies. Lev had told her, Alex decided. After all these years, Lev had confided in a woman. Part

of him was happy for Lev, the other part was—aw, hell—he
was a little jealous.

"We're hoping there won't be a war with Hussein," Amy
told Alex, obviously changing the subject. "Did you get any
feeling about what might happen when you were in America?"

"There have been some antiwar protests, but my guess is
they'll fight if necessary." Alex trained his eyes on Amy and
Lev, but beyond them he watched Brett. Owen had his arm
around her shoulders, a casual gesture. A proprietary gesture. Alex forced himself to concentrate; he needed to persuade Lev not to leave for Israel unless it was absolutely
necessary. "Washington is putting pressure on Israel to stay
out of the mess."

Lev shook his head. "They will not listen."

"I don't think you should go back unless Israel declares
war." He didn't want Lev risking his life. And he needed
Lev right now, not just for Belage, but for himself. The next
months promised to be hell. Spending time with Lev
wouldn't eliminate the loneliness, but it would help.

Lev regarded Amy for a moment, his expression loving.
"I will not return until they declare war."

It shouldn't have come as any surprise, but somehow it
did. While he'd been so involved with Brett, Alex had
missed how deeply in love his friend had fallen. He had to
admit, Amy's pleas to stay had probably influenced Lev
more than his. Now, he doubted he'd see much of Lev in the
next months; with war imminent, he'd want to spend all his
time with Amy.

Alex hadn't felt this alone since he was a kid living with
his grandmother. Before Vic.

Before Brett.

A servant wheeled out a wedding cake that pushy-pretentious Ruth Payne informed them had been especially made
by Péchon Pâtisserie Française. Who cared? Alex saw
Timmy watching him from across the room. He winked.
Timmy quickly looked down at his new shoes and edged

closer to his mother. The heaviness in Alex's chest increased. So that's how it was. Timmy had been instructed not to talk to him.

Okay, he could see Brett's point. It would be hard to explain Timmy's knowing him—too well. That was a hell of a burden to put on a kid. She'd better hope he didn't slip.

A man walked up to Alex. "I'm Hugh MacLeod."

Alex nodded; he knew about MacLeod. Saint Owen's savior. And he'd noticed Jock Payne avoided Hugh; Alex guessed he didn't like him. That was good enough for Alex, who trusted Jock's judgment. Okay, he'd muffed it once by marrying Ruthless. Shit happened. Boy, did it.

Ruthless motioned for them to gather around as Brett and Owen cut the cake. Alex decided in a previous life he must have been in the Gestapo to deserve this torture.

"When this is over, let's go for a drink," Hugh said to Alex.

Alex didn't want to go anywhere with him. Yeah, it was childish as hell, but he couldn't help blaming Hugh for rescuing Owen. Not that he wanted to see Owen in prison. After all, he'd spent his youth in a cell without walls, his grandmother a tough warden. Not that his experience had been as bad as Owen's. But he didn't want to spend the evening hearing about Owen Northcote.

Owen and Brett held a long silver knife, set to slice into a lacy confection of white floral icing with tiny lavender rosebuds. The wedding cake. Finally. This would be over soon.

"I want to thank you all for joining us on this blessed day," Owen began, tears in his eyes. "We're only sorry that dear Constance couldn't be with us."

Now, Jock's eyes misted over. Ruthless looked totally pissed. Happy campers everywhere.

Owen hugged Brett. "God sent me to Peru so I could tell the world about the Communists, the *senderos,* and their reign of terror. God sent me to prison and kept me there for a reason. The Almighty wants me to share my experiences with the world."

Owen droned on about God's plan. Lord have mercy. This was shaping up to be a second Sermon on the Mount.

"God blessed me with Brett. Upon my word, she kept the faith, waiting all this time for me."

Get real. Brett had stopped smiling, her eyes on the cake. Owen kissed Brett. Aw, hell, not another French kiss. In public. Had they no shame? Mercifully, they finally cut the cake and everyone offered congratulations. Alex knocked back his third glass of champagne. Or was it the fourth?

Beside him Hugh again asked, "What do you say about having that drink? I want to talk to you about Brett."

Alex started to say no, but changed his mind. Sure, he was torturing himself, but he wanted to talk about her.

Jock reminded Owen that they had a train to catch and everyone began saying good-bye. And kissing the bride. Alex stood between Hugh and Lev, his eyes on Brett. The couple came to their group last. Lev shook Owen's hand, then kissed Brett Russian style, first kissing each cheek, then bear-hugging her and smacking her on the lips.

Alex shook Owen's hand and muttered congratulations, then Owen left to get their coats. Dependable as a St. Bernard in a blizzard, Lev distracted Ruth and Jock, who were standing nearby. Hugh also disappeared, leaving Alex and Brett alone.

Their gazes locked, they stood transfixed, the silence charged, her eyes holding him captive. His thoughts raced with a dozen things he wanted to tell her, wanted to share with her. Things she didn't want to hear.

"Fate takes care of us, doesn't it?" Brett asked, her voice low even though no one was near them. The tip of her tongue glided over her quivering lower lip. "Things work out for the best."

Not always. Definitely not for him. "Be happy," he said, sincerely meaning it. She deserved the best of everything.

Brett offered him her cheek. Hell. This was the last time he'd ever kiss her. He'd be damned if he'd settle for a cheek. His lips pressed against hers as he reeled her into his arms. He inhaled, his breath catching as her familiar scent brought back too many memories. Her arm circled his neck; for a split second hope rocketed through him.

No doubt she'd done it for appearances. Still, her lips were warm and sweet, just parted. He kissed her harder than he intended, his arms tightening another degree, flattening the soft fullness of her breasts against his chest. He edged his tongue between her lips, just touching the tip of her tongue.

Oh, Lord, how could he let her go? How could he let her leave him for a life with another man? She belonged with him, cradled in his arms like this. Always. His tongue brushed hers for the last time and he felt all the fire and vitality that was Brett.

His Brett. But deep inside he knew no matter how passionately he kissed her, how long he held her, how tightly he hugged her—he'd lost her. Forever.

This was the final time he'd be able to kiss her. And it made this last kiss even more precious. He wanted to silently tell her how very much he loved her, truly loved her. He'd always love her. And if she ever needed him, he'd be waiting.

She tried to move away, but he couldn't let her go. He just kept kissing her. He refused to open his eyes and face reality: She belonged to someone else. He felt Lev's hand on his arm, insistently tugging.

Letting Brett go was the hardest damn thing he'd ever had to do. He'd spend the rest of his life searching for her special touch, the feel of her lips—knowing he'd never find it again. Because there was only one Brett and he'd lost her.

"Try MacCallum. It's a single malt scotch," Hugh said as they sat in the Grenadier pub tucked away in a cobbled mews near Hyde Park Corner. Once the unofficial messroom for the Duke of Wellington's guards, the walls were covered with paintings of the duke and his grenadiers.

Alex shook his head. "Stolichnaya."

"Maybe you'd prefer an island malt. There are basically two kinds of single malts, you know. The island malts that have a peaty flavor and the highland malts that are smooth."

"Vodka," he told the waiter. "No ice." Screw it. He didn't want to experiment with liquor, not tonight. Not after that kiss. The last kiss.

Hugh rambled on about his family's distillery on the Isle of Skye. MacLeod Scotch. He was that MacLeod? Must be Mac-loaded.

The waiter delivered their drinks, then Hugh said, "I met Brett's mother, Constance Lamont, when I was about your age. This was before I joined Amnesty International. I was working to contain nuclear arms. She was with a troop of housewives out to protest your government's nuclear facility north of London."

Alex listened, Hugh's tone soothing him, making Alex like him. Maybe Jock was wrong. Hugh seemed okay.

"Constance had charisma, charm, a warmth to her smile." Something in Alex's chest tightened. "I confess I fell in love with her the moment I met her."

Oh, Jee-sus. This story had a too familiar ring.

"She was married to Jock and they had a young daughter. But Constance wanted to be more than just a mother. This meant a lot of fights with Jock, who believed a woman belonged at home."

Well, that explained Ruthless, who was content to stay at home and spend Jock's money. Some men got off on the lord-of-the-manor routine.

"I kept after Constance, and finally wore her down. We had one of those 'unforgettable' affairs while Jock was away. When he returned, Constance made the mistake of confessing. Jock went into orbit. He threw her out of the house and divorced her."

"You were willing to marry her," Alex guessed.

Hugh nodded. "She didn't want me. She was as stubborn

as Brett. She'd made up her mind Jock was the love of her life."

Yeah, exactly the way Owen is the love of Brett's life.

"I have money, you know. I would have given Constance everything, but she wanted Jock. Only Jock."

Alex's stomach flipped—backward. Had his life paralleled this man's? Damn straight.

"Constance never stopped hoping Jock would forgive her. I begged, I pleaded—but she never wavered. Other men tried, too, but no one swayed her. She never stopped loving Jock."

There was something so candid in this, so touching, that Alex's heart went out to Hugh MacLeod. All the money in the world hadn't bought him what he wanted the most. Love.

"Brett told me about you, and I realized you two were having an affair. I was happy for her. I couldn't stand seeing her wait, hoping for Owen to return when I knew he wouldn't. I prayed your experience with Brett would be different than mine had been with Constance, and you'd make Brett fall in love with you."

No way. Brett hadn't even come close to uttering "I love you." Not even once.

"Then I found Owen." Hugh clutched his glass of single malt. "Believe me, no one was more surprised than I to find him. I'm still checking into what happened to his friend, Eekelen Willem, but I'm stunned Owen Northcote is alive."

Alex tossed back the remainder of his vodka and signaled for another. Why me? This sucks.

"I've seen it a lot at Amnesty International. Prison is hell. It's like a crucible, it changes you forever."

Alex nodded his agreement, remembering the crucible of his youth. Not as bad as Owen's experience, but it had changed him.

"Brett's dealing with a man she doesn't know, but she's his strength right now. Like her mother, she's stubborn. She'll stick with Owen Northcote no matter what happens.

Even if she has any thoughts about leaving him, Timmy will anchor her to Owen's side—forever."

"Why are you telling me this?"

"I see a bit of myself in you." Hugh sighed. "Don't waste your life waiting for a woman who'll never love you."

Alex knew Hugh was right, but he'd never stop loving Brett. He wasn't just over the edge. He was out of bounds.

IV
OUT OF BOUNDS

30

Holding Timmy's hand, Brett led him down the path between boulders shaped long ago by glaciers, then gnarled by the wind to the Isle of Skye's northwestern shore. The wide, pebbled crescent of sand was overhung by rocky crags that thrust outward like the prow of a ship. Garlands of black seaweed marked the high-tide line. Bright sunshine gilded the gently undulating sea; the sky above was vibrant blue, Skye blue. The ocean sucked and swirled among the rocks, and Brett selected a large flat boulder for them to sit and enjoy a picnic lunch.

"My, you're getting heavy." She boosted him onto the rock.

He pointed to the water. "Look, Mommy, sharks!"

"No, they're otters." He'd heard about *Jaws* at school and was fascinated with sharks. "The mother is teaching the pup to fish." She shrugged out of her backpack, then spread their sandwiches on the rock.

"What's the mother otter doing now?"

Brett looked at the mother otter nudging the pup onto a rock. "He didn't catch anything, so she's telling him to watch her."

How well she remembered coming to this very cove with Hugh MacLeod to see the otters when she'd been about Timmy's age. Like Owen, her mother had remained behind working.

Timmy clapped his hands. "You're right, Mommy." The mother otter had returned with a large glossy black cod.

Brett gave Timmy half of his sandwich and unscrewed the thermos of hot chocolate. Timmy munched noisily, his eyes on the otters. This was the first time she'd taken him on a trek. They'd walked before, of course, but Skye's windswept moors and rocky terrain required hiking boots. Timmy's first pair were slick with mud and lichen, but he loved the trek. He was enthralled as she'd been when she'd first come to Hugh's home on Skye as a child.

She handed him his chocolate, his mittened hands circling the cup. "Mommy, when is Daddy going to play with me like Alex?"

"As soon as he finishes his book, then he'll have time for us."

"I like Alex, Mom. He's a real nutter."

A nutter. His friends at school had a profound influence on Timmy. The world, it seemed, was divided into nerds or nutters. Well, *nutter* did describe Alex Savich. What on earth had he been trying to prove with that kiss? Really, she didn't understand him. It didn't matter now; it was over. "I thought we agreed not to talk about Alex anymore."

"In front of Daddy."

There it was again, that nit-picking he used to get around her. She'd mentioned it to her father; Jock had laughed and said she'd done the same thing. She regretted, now more than ever, not telling Owen the truth about Alex. Obviously, it was affecting Timmy, but at the time she'd told Owen the lie, she'd done it feeling she didn't have any other choice.

She sat on the rock, gazing out to sea. Remembering. Remembering the day Hugh called to say Owen had been released and was returning on the next plane from Lima. She'd hung up the telephone, then collapsed into her chair, poleaxed.

She hardly remembered the ride to the airport with

Hugh, but she vividly recalled the phalanx of reporters. Many of them recognized her from the C.U.M. controversy. Their questions were endless, but Hugh knew nothing more than that Owen had been confused with another man who had been killed. Finally a security guard told them that Owen Northcote would be the next person to come through the customs door.

"Please," she said, raising her voice to get the reporters' attention. "Could we have a few minutes alone?" She walked up to the door clutching Timmy's hand, Hugh at her side.

She waited, holding her breath. The moment she'd dreamed about for years was finally here. Owen would step out and kiss her and tell her just seeing her and Timmy meant the world to him.

The door swung open and a man Brett hardly recognized emerged. Owen's hair was completely gray, lines furrowed his face, his lithe frame was emaciated. What did she expect? Prison caused physical changes. She'd better expect emotional scars as well.

Behind her she heard the whir of autowind cameras and saw the blue-white light of scores of flashbulbs exploding at once. The reporters weren't close enough to hear anything she might say, but she knew they were recording the event.

She stepped forward, dropping Timmy's hand, opening her arms to Owen. Instantly, the easygoing smile she loved lit his face.

"C-Constance," he said, his voice low, choking out the word. He almost collapsed into her arms, hugging her, clutching at her like a lifeline. "Thank God for you. Constance, you don't—"

Hugh put a hand on Owen's frail shoulder. "It's Brett."

Owen's smile faltered, then returned brighter than before. "Brett, of course. You look so much like your mother." He clung to her, his body trembling, racked by silent sobs.

She cradled him in her arms, Timmy clinging to her skirt, Hugh's eyes on her, conscious of the reporters edging closer. How can I help him? she wondered when Owen kept his head buried in the crook of her neck, mumbling he thought he'd never see her again. Telling her how much he needed her.

"I'm Hugh MacLeod from Amnesty International," Hugh told Owen, the reporters moving in, jockeying for position.

"I don't know how to thank you," Owen said. "Your queries—"

"Mommeeee." Timmy tugged at her skirt.

Owen gasped, looking down for the first time, puzzled.

She took Timmy's hand, swallowing hard. "This is your son."

Owen clutched Hugh's arm, his eyes wide. "*My* son?"

"Don't you remember?" she asked gently, seeing his confusion, not wanting to discuss this in front of the reporters. The horde had edged forward, now hearing every word, video cameras whirring, pencils furiously scrawling notes. "I told you—"

Owen dropped to his knees, staring into Timmy's eyes, shaking his head. "My son?"

Didn't he remember her telling him she was pregnant? "This is Timmy. He'll be four next week."

Owen hugged Timmy, clasping him tightly. "He looks just like Constance." Owen sobbed, tears coursing down his cheeks. The reporters couldn't get enough of it, zooming in closer, cameras trained on the father and son.

"It's all right, Daddy," Timmy said, patting his back.

Tears filled Brett's eyes: it was obvious Owen was on the verge of emotional collapse. How could she help him?

Hugh touched her arm, whispering in her ear, "He's had a rough time of it. What he needs now is your love and your support. Don't upset him. Believe me, I've seen this dozens of times. Being disoriented is perfectly normal. He's been through hell."

Owen shakily rose, Timmy's hand in his. He kissed Brett, and she tasted the salt of his tears, but she was too blinded by the flashbulbs to savor the moment she'd dreamed about for so long.

"I thought you would have married." Owen pulled her to his side. "You waited all this time for me, didn't you?"

She stared into his eyes; they were slightly unfocused. The gaggle of cameras—and microphones—made her pause. Now was not the time to confess her horrible mistake with Alex Savich. She dipped down and picked up Timmy. "We both waited for you."

The next days had been dicey; Owen alternated between euphoria and tears. Each time he talked, he kept emphasizing how she'd loyally—until she hated that word—waited for him. She wanted to confess, but Owen had been tossed about in a stormy sea. She was his anchor. She didn't have the heart to disillusion him.

Hugh arranged for Owen to have several sessions with the Amnesty International psychiatrist who specialized in freed prisoners. Owen regained his strength and with it came a sense of purpose the psychiatrist told Brett she must nurture. Owen had written a book while he was in prison, and Hugh arranged for a top literary agent to represent him. She kept postponing telling Owen; the right moment had never seemed to come.

Timmy jerked on her anorak, returning her to the present. "Look, Mommy. The clouds have dragon tails."

She gazed at the horizon; banks of sullen clouds blocked the sun. The otters had disappeared. The peaceful cove was suddenly a cauldron of spume-capped waves.

"Clouds like that mean a storm's coming." She shoved their things into her pack. "They blow in quickly here. We'll have to hurry." She hoisted him to her hip, knowing she'd make better time going up the steep embankment if she carried him.

"Mommy, don't be mad at me."

"I'm not angry." She climbed the zigzag path slippery with spongy moss and stones girdled with lichen.

"You are so. You won't talk to me."

She looked into her son's accusing eyes; she loved him so much it actually hurt. "Mommy is angry with herself, not you. If you want to talk to me about Alex, I don't mind. But let's not bother your father with him, all right?"

She reached the top of the rise where the machair began. The wild grassland was dressed in its December cloak of olive green, cropped low by sheep, who'd left nothing but islands of thistle. She remembered the summers here when the moor was filled with yellow sweet broom and violet mallow blossoms that swayed in the breeze. She put Timmy down but held his hand. "Hurry."

Over her shoulder, she saw the clouds had almost overtaken them. She'd been here enough times to know not to underestimate a storm. Usually it rained, but off the Minch channel blew squalls that brought blizzards from the Arctic this time of year.

"Faster," she said as they trotted along the path usually traveled by island women gathering peat. If it snowed hard, the trail would be covered in a matter of minutes.

The breeze kicked up, becoming a restless wind, a harbinger of a serious gale. Skye's ever-present sheep still munched, but now their rumps faced the wind. She groaned, anticipating keeping Timmy quiet enough for Owen to work during a snowstorm.

A lone snowflake landed on her nose as she saw the harled stone chimney and slate roof of Hugh's house. "Let's race the snow. The winner gets an extra oatcake."

She pretended to run as fast as she could, but kept beside Timmy. They jogged around several of the countless waterfalls that spilled from the rocks to seep across the machair to the sea. The trail twisted, dropping down into the glen where the house stood. More flakes appeared as they passed through the stone fence into the kailyard. The garden was barren except for the wood stacked in a corner. She huffed and let Timmy pass her.

He barreled into the door, hitting it with a thump and shrieking, "I won. I won."

"Good for you. Good for you," she yelled just as the snow began. She glanced up at the stone archway above the door where the MacLeod motto had been chiseled centuries ago when this had been the clan's hunting lodge: HOLD FAST.

"Two oatcakes for me," Timmy bellowed as she opened the door. He laughed, a warm, totally uninhibited laugh. Could anything be more joyous than the happiness of children before they knew how much the world could hurt them?

Owen yelled, "I need quiet to write. Is that too much to ask?"

Timmy drew back; Brett helped him out of his anorak and hung both of them on the hooks. The hiking boots with laces up the ankle took longer. Timmy didn't say a word.

After dinner, she sent Timmy off to take his bath before going to bed. She turned to Owen. "Why don't you read him a few pages from Sir Walter Scott's *Lord of the Isles*? He's really enjoying learning about Skye."

"All right. Could you proofread the chapter I just revised?"

She made certain Timmy brushed his teeth, then waited while he climbed into bed. Owen had insisted Timmy leave his beloved fire engine at home, but Sneaky By had traveled to Skye in his carrier and was curled up at the foot of the bed, a city cat exhausted by a day of mousing in the country.

The chapter was neatly stacked on the kitchen table beside the unwashed dishes. She began to read it, but before she'd finished the second page, Owen returned.

He never spent enough time with Timmy. She had to remember Owen was feeling pressed; his priority was finishing his book.

"Did you get very far in *Lord of the Isles*?" she asked.

"Timmy wanted me to tell him some story about Stalin and the doctors." Owen dropped into a chair, facing her. "I had no idea what he was talking about, so I told him the *Three Little Bears*."

Timmy had advanced beyond those bears, but Brett refrained from telling Owen this. He was trying to be a good father.

"Stalin." Owen shook his head. "What was he talking about?"

Why had Timmy asked his father for one of Alex's stories? She needed to tell Owen, before he accidentally found out about Alex and misunderstood her reasons for keeping quiet.

"Stalin hated the Jews. He imprisoned the best Jewish doctors. But on his deathbed, he summoned one of them from prison to save him. The man valiantly tried, but it was too late."

"What kind of a school teaches him those stories? I think that school is frightfully expensive. It isn't worth—"

"It's the best school in London. That story is a lesson in values, don't you see? Stalin persecuted that doctor, but the doctor stood by the Hippocratic oath and treated him."

"I liked *Goldilocks.*" Owen shook his head. "I guess I was in prison too long. I don't understand these new teaching techniques." He reached across the table and clasped her hand. "There's a lot I don't understand." His eyes filled with tears. "I never imagined you'd wait for me. I love you so much."

Brett stared guiltily at the chapter. Tell him about Alex, she thought. But she knew now was not the time; Owen wasn't ready to hear this yet. Not with those tears in his eyes.

"How do you like the chapter?" he asked.

"I've just started. Is Willem in this chapter?" They'd discussed Eekelen Willem, the Dutch worker who'd been with Owen when he was captured. Willem hadn't survived.

"I'm going to cover that at the end."

"Why? Eekelen died in the cell next to you the first year you were in prison. Isn't this the point in the story?"

"Yes." Owen covered his face with his hands. "I can't bear to write about his death . . . yet."

Her heart went out to him, thinking how he felt losing his

only friend. She couldn't imagine writing about Amy's death. "I understand."

He looked up, his eyes loving, and pleasure swelled her heart. This was love: a bond of understanding and trust. Life was so much more than a night in bed.

"Do you think you should call Eekelen's wife? I understand she's been told of his death, but I'm certain she'd like to hear the details from you."

He looked away, tears welling in his eyes. "Someday, I'll talk to her, but right now I can't."

Brett returned to Belage just before Christmas. A brunette who introduced herself as Stella sat in Eula Mae's chair. Brett paused in the reception area, a suffocating sensation tightening her throat. She'd pushed Alex to the back of her mind. She'd forgotten Belage was being partitioned to accommodate the Israeli jeweler and new staff. She'd be sharing her office with Alex.

The apprehension she'd experienced since she'd risen that morning increased. She couldn't allow her brief affair with Alex to interfere with her career. She was well on her way to proving herself a talented designer worthy of acclaim. Though Alex Savich technically owned Belage, she felt it was her company too. Her future was riding on its success.

Hold fast, she thought. The MacLeod motto seemed to fit her situation. *Hold fast.*

"Brett." Eula Mae hugged her. "How was the honeymoon?"

"You've heard of a working vacation? It was a working honeymoon, but Owen did finish the revisions the editor asked for on his book. They're furiously printing it as we speak. It'll be out in mid-January."

"My stars, I can't wait to read it." Eula Mae steered her into her new office and showed her the new computer she was using to keep track of Belage's sales. Then she introduced Brett to the new clerks and Avram Ben-Itzik, the Israeli dealer, who now occupied Alex's old office.

"The pit has a sprout," Eula Mae proudly told her when they came back to Eula Mae's office.

"Super," Brett said, reminded of Terai. She hadn't checked on him in weeks. She needed to call Nepal soon.

Finally she could no longer postpone going to her office. She walked in quietly; Alex had commandeered the side with the panther. He was on the telephone, his back to her. Something caught in her chest, but she ignored the sensation. She had a job to do; not only did her career depend on how well she performed, but so did her family's future. After all, she was the sole breadwinner.

She sat at her drawing table, making certain she didn't disturb Alex. He swiveled around in his chair, still talking, and nodded to her, a half smile on his lips. She exhaled sharply, telling herself to calm down.

Alex plopped the receiver into its cradle, then turned to her and handed her a sheet of paper. "Orders are coming in faster than we can fill them."

He sounded totally unperturbed by sharing an office with her. Then what had been the meaning of that kiss?

"Who's ordering?" she asked before she could stop herself.

Alex's back was to her now. "Lots of stores." He picked up the telephone and called Antwerp.

A part of her she refused to acknowledge longed to reach out and touch his strong shoulder and say: I'm your partner. Tell me. They were beyond that now, she realized. She'd given Alex her body, but in reality she'd given him much, much more. Before they made love, she'd risen above the level of designer, but now things had changed. She was just the designer.

Change jobs, she prodded herself. But that wasn't a viable possibility. No matter how she felt about Alex, he had put himself at risk to promote her. Leaving Belage was emotionally tempting, but it wasn't honorable.

He chuckled, a low masculine sound, triggering memories she thought she'd banished. What she felt hadn't been love. No. It had been lust, not pure elemental love like her love for Owen. Some part of her must have known this. That was why she'd never said she loved him. Those words had come so easily with Owen, but not with Alex. Deep down, she must have known the truth.

She forced herself to look at the order form Alex had given her. So many items. She picked up her pencil. She should never have taken the two weeks in Skye. Owen would have been better off alone; they'd been snowed in most of the time, and she'd spent the days struggling to keep Timmy quiet.

She picked up a charcoal pencil set to sketch a design. She stared at the blank sheet of paper. Nothing. Think of Skye, she told herself. The Cuillins, Skye's mountains, appeared on the paper with the snow-skirted cone of Gharsbheinn glowering down on Loch Scavaig. She'd promised Timmy to take him trekking in the Cuillins next summer, she thought with a smile.

But those peaks wouldn't make good earrings or pins or necklaces. What would? She sketched a freewheeling gull she'd seen above the cove. He was too much like something she'd already done. Her drawings of Skye's flowers, lacy blossoms of cow parsley, lamb's-quarters, and heather, were uninspired.

Had her creative muse deserted her?

She glanced over at Alex, who was studying figures on his computer screen. Could she do any designing with him so close?

Hold fast, she thought. *Hold fast and forget the past.*

31

Amy lay with her head against Lev's sturdy chest watching television. "I can't believe Hussein didn't pull out of Kuwait." Tanks rolled across the screen, rooster tails of sand in their wake. "Look, those are England's Desert Rats," she said with pride. The elite force had learned desert warfare the hard way—fighting Rommel in North Africa. Tobruk. El Alamein. "We've always kept units ready to fight in the desert again."

"Now the Israelis will declare war," Lev insisted.

She silently cursed Hussein. Things with Lev were going so well. They'd forged a strong bond, a love she'd only imagined possible. If he went back to Israel, he might be killed, but she knew enough not to argue with him about it. While she'd enjoyed manipulating Ellis, Amy appreciated Lev more for his strong beliefs, his sense of integrity.

Israel might declare war any second, judging from the number of diamond dealers who'd fled to London in the last few days. Lev told her many had also gone to Antwerp and New York. Only a very few crafty dealers like Avram Ben-Itzik had taken precautions and arrived earlier, establishing themselves while new arrivals vied for office space and business.

"Milochka," Lev said, his brown eyes somber, "if something happens to me, will you send my mother money? She has no one."

"Don't worry. I promise you"—she felt the hot sting of tears behind her eyes—"I'll take care of your mother."

They silently watched CNN reporters interviewing residents in Baghdad, then Tel Aviv. Amy forced herself not to think of Lev's leaving, so she thought about Brett. Had things improved since she saw her last week when Brett told her that she was experiencing difficulty designing? "How are Brett's designs for the new collections?"

"Trouble is small office. We are in each other's laps."

"I think the problem is Alex, not the size of the office. After that mess in Los Angeles—" She stopped to study Lev, who was running his hand across her bare shoulder. "You're sure Alex has never talked to you about it?"

"No." Lev's warm hand covered her breast.

"Typical men. You're friends but you don't talk." Naturally, Brett had told Amy about the incident and she'd told Lev. "I think Alex loves Brett. That was a very passionate kiss at the reception. I'm going to watch him carefully tomorrow night."

Brett stood with Amy at the back of Leighton's Books. "You don't mind seeing Ellis again?" she asked Amy. Across the room Owen was autographing a book for Ellis and Daphne.

"No. I'm over him. I honestly have no idea what I saw in him. Does it bother you to see Alex?"

"I see him every day," Brett hedged, watching Alex. "What bothers me is how few people came tonight."

"Everyone's glued to the telly, fascinated by the Gulf War."

"Yes, and it didn't help when the papers postponed reviewing Owen's book so they could give more space to war coverage. I'm praying the book's a success," Brett said, noticing Alex give Owen a stack of books to autograph. What was he going to do with all of them? "You have no idea how much Owen is counting on it."

"Is everything all right with you two?"

"Yes. Owen's short with Timmy at times, but he's trying."

"Has Timmy stopped talking about Alex?" Brett shook her head. "And you still haven't told Owen?"

"Read his book and you'll see why. I'm the epitome of loyalty—the most wonderful woman since the Virgin Mary."

"Why did you let him? I thought you proofread the entire book."

"I did, but changes were made at the publishers. They were in such a rush. I never saw the book again until it was too late."

Alex walked toward them, carrying his books, and Brett tried to smile. Whenever she was around him, it was a battle to control her tongue. She was always tempted to make a snide remark. Why? Things *had* worked out. She and Owen were happy. It wasn't that heady feeling she'd had with Alex, but it was solid, more lasting.

"What are you going to do with all those books?"

"Give them to friends in the Diamond Club," he answered Amy but his eyes were on Brett.

"Owen appreciates your support," Brett said as Owen came over.

"I certainly do. I want the world to find out what it's like in Peru, so the government will be pressured to make changes. I don't want anything for myself—just for the people. They've suffered so much with the guerrillas and a senseless civil war."

Brett put her arm around him. "Don't worry, darling."

"Gotta run," Alex said. "I don't want to miss one minute of the Living Room War in the Gulf."

Alex stifled a yawn; he'd been up most of the night reading Owen's book. He had to admit the guy had been through hell. Saint Owen. No wonder Brett loved him so much. He was the type of man she'd go for, a man who had a higher calling. He glanced across the office to where Brett sat. As usual, her head was bent forward and her hair had fallen across her shoulders revealing the graceful curve of her neck and the tiny mole. He wanted to ask her what was wrong; during the last six weeks she hadn't produced a single new design. But he didn't say anything; they shared an office, but spoke only when necessary.

The intercom on his desk buzzed and he picked up the telephone. Latrice Laveaux was on the line. He almost didn't take the call, then Brett shifted in her seat and a dangerous surge of longing hit him. Hugh was right. She was a lost cause. He had to get on with his life; he hadn't been with a woman since the disaster in L.A., an all-time record. He took the call, making certain to keep his voice low to avoid disturbing Brett.

"Alex, darling." Latrice's voice was breathy, her tone as phony as her spidery lashes. "I have tickets for—"

"Sure. What time?" He almost choked on the words. Mind over matter, he told himself.

He hung up and stared down at the columns of figures on the paper before him. They swam like a desert mirage. He tossed his pencil aside and walked down the hall to Avram's office, reminding himself that he had pressing problems. The last shipment of fancies had been twice the size of the others. Even with Belage's growing list of customers, it would take a year or more to get rid of them. Dash Boynton had been ominously quiet, but Alex doubted he could stall him for an entire year.

Avram's door was open. "Got a minute?" Alex asked.

"Sure." Avram smiled and Alex closed the door.

He didn't like telling anyone else about the fancies, but what the hell? He'd already told Avram a little when he sold him the blue diamond. He could trust him. After all, Avram had helped Lev, taking him in when Lev left the Israeli army. He'd had one of his men teach Lev how to cut and set diamonds. Most important, he'd been one of Vic's closest friends.

"What do you think, is it going to be '72 all over again?" Alex asked, sitting down. The only disaster in the cartel's history had occurred then; speculators had driven the price of diamonds into the stratosphere, forcing dealers to pay too much for their stones. The cartel tried to level off the price, but the inflation skyrocketed. Vic and Alex spent almost a year on Yugoslavia's sunny Dalmatian coast waiting it out. As they predicted, the market had crashed, bankrupting many dealers.

"I'm not seeing too much speculation—yet." Avram's concern showed in his voice. "There are more diamonds on the market now than there ever have been. Israelis selling, selling, selling."

"What do you expect?" Alex asked. "Every Israeli dealer left Tel Aviv the second the Gulf War began. They can't stand on street corners with diamonds in their pockets."

Diamond dealers never used banks. Personally, he thought it was stupid not to trust banks in Western countries, but dealers had a deep-seated mistrust of banks. Centuries ago that might have been justified, but no longer. Still, he didn't know a dealer anywhere who kept his stones in a bank.

"Not everyone has been as lucky as I have to arrange with a friend to share space," Avram said.

"Let's not kid ourselves; there's a lot of anti-Semitism still around. Some are hoping this will weaken the Israeli diamond market if their dealers are forced to sell entire inventories."

"True, and the cartel would love to see the Israelis take a fall—if the glut doesn't drive the prices too low."

"I hear the cartel's buying just to see it doesn't happen, but it's confusing as hell, even for them. Some Israelis have been hoarding stones for years. Diamonds the cartel didn't even know were out there have appeared. Now is a good time to sell."

"The market's soft. Why sell?" Avram asked.

"I need to get rid of some more fancies without alerting Intelco. I figured you'd know some Israeli who's holed up in Bombay waiting out the war. He could sell them for me."

"Bombay? Why Bombay?"

"The action's here and in Antwerp, right? Intelco is monitoring diamond sales in Europe, struggling to keep the market firm during the war. They aren't watching Bombay so closely. There's so much melee in Bombay that even if the cartel hears some fancies hit the market, they'll figure it's crap."

"Clever—but risky." Avram scratched his head. "I think my wife's cousin went to Bombay. He'll be just the man you need."

"Actually, I need two men. I want to sell a few of the less valuable fancies in Bombay. Then I want someone to pretend to sell me some fancies. I want to be seen in Antwerp buying the stones, but I'll really be getting my own diamonds back."

"You want the cartel to know you purchased the fancies. They'll think they came from Israel and won't check the source."

"Right. If I can pull this off, I'll have stones Intelco thinks are legit. I'll be out from under their thumb with a little cash from the Bombay deal to play with."

"It's a brilliant idea, but it's a monumental risk," Avram said. "Something totally unexpected can happen."

Damn straight. Like Saint Owen returning from the dead.

Alex marched into Intelco's lobby as though he owned the joint and asked the receptionist to tell Dash he had arrived. The woman ushered him into an office with enough heads of endangered species to have sent the animal rights people into orbit. He could see his head on the wall, too, eyes open, frozen in time. An example of those who crossed the cartel. It gave him a perverse sense of pleasure to know at this very moment some shirttail relative of Avram's was selling Alex's fancies in Bombay. Talk about living on the edge.

Screw it. Now that he'd lost Brett he didn't give a damn about himself. All the cartel could do was kill him.

"Hey, Dash, how's it goin'?"

Dash bared his teeth—a vampire's smile. "Market's soft. We've stabilized the prices, but if that Arab, Hussein, doesn't surrender soon, it'll be hard to keep the market from dropping."

True. The Israelis, bless 'em, were unloading diamonds, flooding a market at a time when the world teetered on the brink of a war that threatened everyone. Jewelry sales were at a standstill. Except at Belage. They were still getting orders.

"I wanted to talk to you about the enhancer." Alex gave him a hangdog look supposed to convey sadness. "My results aren't good. There isn't much of a market for brown diamonds."

Dash studied him, his eyes as lifeless as the lion on the wall. "We still would like to purchase the enhancer."

Aw, hell. He wasn't buying this. "I don't want to sell." He lowered his voice. "Look, I'm not giving up, but I can't afford to keep experimenting. Lamont's hot right now. I can't stay up with the orders if I ruin too many diamonds."

Boynton nodded. "I'm certain we could lend you—"

"No way. If I couldn't fix the enhancer, I'd owe you money it would take a lifetime to repay. Forget it."

"Hmmm." Dash toyed with the solid gold Dupont pen on his desk; Alex wasn't certain he was going for this. "I assume you have the enhancer in a safe place."

"Don't worry. No one will ever find it." For sure. He and Lev had dismantled the damn thing and had thrown it away —one piece at a time—all over London.

Dash rose, signaling the visit was over. Alex almost breathed a sigh of relief. He'd counted on Dash's being the proper British gentleman. Intelco cherished their damn reputation as "gentlemen" avoiding direct confrontations where possible. When they got heavy-handed it was on the QT.

"Dash it all, I'm sorry it turned out this way."

Trust me, I'm not. "There's one more thing, Dash. Do you know where I can buy fancies? I've got a lot of orders to fill."

32

The train chugged along, bound for Kent, and Brett sighed, grateful to be spending a beautiful May weekend at her father's estate. She was thankful Belage's move into larger offices was finished.

"My new office is terrific," Brett told Owen, who was seated opposite her. He'd been away so much these past months, touring, lecturing, and trying unsuccessfully to put together a movie deal based on his book, that she'd hardly seen him. "I think the mental block I've had about designing will go away."

"Good," Owen said, but she could tell his mind was elsewhere.

He wasn't as interested in her or Timmy as she'd expected, but she reminded herself of what the Amnesty International psychiatrist had told her. Prisoners were often consumed by their own lives, desperate to make up for the years they'd lost.

While Owen tried to find himself, she continued supporting them. She was counting on the new office—one she didn't have to share with Alex—to bring back her creative muse. She had no idea where Alex had gotten the money, but in the last few months, he'd leased new offices with a state-of-the-art security system to protect the diamonds and the designs.

The enhancer had disappeared. Alex had informed Brett that their fancies were now legitimate. Brett would have loved to know the inside story, but she refused to ask. Apparently Alex was out of danger now, and she was glad. Her anger with Alex had subsided, becoming no more than a dull ache. Miracle of miracles, she'd managed to work with him and behave professionally.

"Mommy." Timmy stood beside her; he'd been playing in the aisle with his fire engine. "Are we almost there yet?"

"No. It'll be a little while before we're at Grampa's."

"Daddy, are you going to watch me ride Felix this time?"

"Sure. I brought my camera to take pictures."

They'd spent Christmas and Boxing Day at Hayvenhurst. That had been the first time she'd come back since she stormed out years ago, refusing to go to Oxford, insisting she wanted to join her mother. She'd been dreading spending time with Ruth, but her stepmother kept her distance. The house was jammed with guests, so it hadn't been hard to avoid Ruthless.

The weather last Christmas had been bitterly cold, she remembered, looking out the window at Kent's rolling countryside, known as the Weald. Spring clouds pranced across the sky, white brushstrokes against cerulean blue. Waterfalls of pink tea roses cascaded over hedges that served as fences between pastures. Peeking out of the meadows of clover were swaying buttercups and whisks of horsetail rye. Back at Christmas, unseasonably heavy snows had fallen. But Timmy had wanted to ride his pony. While the others huddled by the fire, she and her father had gone with him to the stables.

"Did you see the invitation to Alex Savich's open house?" Owen asked. "Why is he having a party?"

"I guess he wants to show his friends his new penthouse." Since the war ended, Alex had purchased a Porsche and a penthouse. Belage must be making a lot of money; he'd given them all raises. She'd like to know more about the company's finances. Wasn't it expanding a little too rapidly?

"Do you know who's going to be at his party?" Owen's blue eyes studied her with more interest than usual. Although she wasn't comfortable with this subject, she was grateful he wasn't discussing his book. It had received critical raves, but sales had been poor. Even when the Gulf War ended, book sales remained sluggish, depressing Owen, who'd banked on a best seller.

"I imagine everyone from Belage will be there. The new craftsmen from Hong Kong speak excellent English. You'll like them. And Alex's friends in the Diamond Club."

"Maybe one of the diamond dealers would be interested in backing a movie about my book."

Please, God, don't let him ask Alex.

"Is Alex still seeing Latrice Laveaux?"

"I don't know." The tabloid press couldn't get enough of the actress. They'd printed numerous photographs of her with Alex, heralding him as a diamond magnate—whatever that meant.

"I wish I'd seen her on stage. I love the theater." He was teary-eyed again, the way he often became when they discussed something that he'd missed while he'd been in prison.

Now wasn't the time to remind him he should call Eekelen Willem's wife. Owen had been home almost six months. Just when he seemed to have the strength to do it, he'd put it off again.

"Timmy is a great kid," Ellis told Brett as he sat beside her at the dinner table that evening.

"He exhausts me," she confessed. They'd spent the day riding horses, Timmy anxious to learn what his grandfather loved teaching him. Owen came along, but slipped into one of his moods and didn't join them in the afternoon when Jock led them on a trek across the Weald. Timmy was surprisingly adept at hiking, his short legs supported by the sturdy hiking boots she'd bought him for the trip to Skye.

"Do you always read him a bedtime story?" Ellis asked.

"Sometimes Owen does." She wondered about Ellis's curiosity. He'd stayed with her when she'd put Timmy to bed before the adults had a late dinner. "Why the interest?"

He looked across the table at Daphne, who sighed, her very adoring eyes on Ellis. He picked up his fork and tapped it on the crystal wine goblet. Ruth and Owen stopped talking, and Jock looked up from his soup. "I'd like you all to know Daphne and I are expecting a baby."

In the flurry of congratulations, Brett caught Owen's eye; she desperately wanted another baby. But he thought they needed a bigger house first. He'd been counting on selling his book to the movies to do this. He was right, she thought; the house was too small. Still, it might be years before they could afford to move. She was making good money, but on her salary alone they couldn't send Timmy to school and move into a bigger house in a nice neighborhood.

While the others were discussing what Ruthless called "the blessed event," Ellis whispered, "How's Amy?"

"She's happy." Euphoric described her better. When the Gulf War ended without Israel's having entered it, Amy and Lev had become closer than ever. She rarely saw her anymore. As much as she dreaded Alex's upcoming party, at least it would be a chance to spend time with Amy and Lev.

Things had worked out for the best, she decided, recalling how hurt Amy had been when Ellis married Daphne. It turned into a blessing, just as Owen had saved her from brooding over Alex.

Ellis smiled, his ratings booster smile. "I guess I have the last laugh, not you."

"What are you talking about?"

"Remember telling me you'd have the last laugh because I'd married a woman I didn't love? I'm the one laughing now."

"You don't think"—she checked to be certain no one was listening—"I love Owen? Of course I do."

"He's way too old for you."

"Age has nothing to do with love."

"Well, you don't act happy. Can't say that I blame you. He's a colossal bore, always talking about his book."

"He doesn't—" But he was.

"You don't understand, Daphne," Owen was saying. "Alberto Fujimori was democratically elected as Peru's president."

"I read an interesting article in the *Observer*," Jock said. "It suggested Fujimori's not having experience in politics might hurt his efforts to reform Peru." Daphne frowned, obviously puzzled, and Jock added, "He used to be a college professor."

"You see" —Owen directed his comment to Daphne, although Brett was positive Daphne had never read the book and was only being polite by appearing interested—"the Maoist guerrillas called the *Sendero Luminoso*—that's 'Shining Path'—are led by a demagogue, Abimael Guzmán. The *senderos* are the worst terrorists on earth. A handful of them have brought Peru to its knees."

"If there are only a handful, then why can't the government deal with them?" Ruth asked. Clearly, she hadn't read the book; Brett doubted anyone at the table had except her father.

"Guzmán makes a lot of money from drug trafficking to bribe officials and terrorize the peasants. Anyone who informs on him is killed. The government can't protect every tiny village."

"The *senderos* had you sent to prison?" Daphne asked.

"Yes. They'd promised me an interview with Guzmán. I wanted to convince him to let us ship relief supplies into remote villages. He agreed to meet with me, then he changed his mind and had me thrown in jail. He's a real nut."

"Any luck with a movie deal?"

Brett could have kicked Ellis for asking. Owen was obsessed with the movie. If they dwelt on it too long, he'd become depressed again.

"A producer is interested but hasn't the backing." Owen waited while the servants cleared the first course and brought out the spring lamb done Kent style with a shell of ground rosemary. "I was wondering if you'd like to invest."

"I'm making decent money, but not enough to finance a movie."

"Jock," Owen said, "this would be a good investment for you."

There was an awkward silence. Brett seethed; Owen had never mentioned asking her father. She would have refused to let him.

"I'd be ruddy daft to invest in a business I know nothing about," Jock said, his tone light.

"The producer knows all there is to know. You'd just be putting up the money."

"I've been burned once too often, letting others run the show."

Ellis smiled, his good-natured weatherman's smile. "I went through a few businesses before I found my calling. Jock's patience is a bit thin because of me, I'm afraid."

"Now, darling," Ruth said, "you could have been a success at anything, but you just weren't motivated."

"Belage is a success," Owen pointed out.

"Due to Brett's talent," Jock insisted and Ruth frowned.

Brett glanced at her stepmother and saw what she'd intuitively known as a child: She was jealous of her because she was more intelligent than Ellis.

Ruth beamed at Owen. "Your book would make a thrilling movie."

She went on, but Brett hardly listened, positive the book had been too intellectual for Ruthless to have read. Again, Brett had a vision of Owen's asking Alex for the money. Maybe she should pretend she was ill and not attend Alex's open house. Maybe she should tell Owen the truth about

Alex; then he'd never ask him for money. No, she'd destroy his image of her and damage his fragile self-esteem. He wasn't ready to hear about Alex yet.

"Why don't you and Brett finance the movie?" Ruth asked.

"We would if we had the money," Owen assured her.

Ruth looked directly at Brett. "What about those earrings?"

"What earrings?" Owen demanded.

"Brett inherited diamonds from her mother worth millions."

"You never told me about them." A hostile note underscored Owen's words, and her father frowned.

"I'd forgotten about them. I don't really feel they're mine. Some man gave them to Mother."

She hazarded a sidelong glance at her father. As a child there had been a rule: never mention Constance Lamont's name. It had been hard—almost impossible—and that was why she'd relented and let Timmy talk to her about Alex.

"Mother left a note, saying she was returning them, but she was killed. If I knew who'd given them to her I'd give them back."

"What did the note say?" Daphne wanted to know.

She would ask, Brett thought. Daphne, who rarely spoke, would choose this question. "I don't remember exactly." Brett saw no reason to reveal the highly personal note.

"Your mother died five years ago," Ruth commented. "Surely if the man expected them back, he would have asked by now."

All but Jock murmured their agreement.

"My mother wasn't a material person," Brett said, her eyes on Ruthless. "She had few possessions. Other than her photographs, I have nothing to remember her by. Nothing."

"Your mother would approve of making a movie that would expose the *senderos*," Owen said. "She hated the way they'd ruined Peru. We discussed it many times."

"True," she conceded. "But even if I sold the earrings, it

wouldn't be enough to finance the movie. You'd still need—"

"I don't want you to sell them." Jock's adamant tone took everyone by surprise. "I might as well tell everyone the truth right now. I'm having a little financial difficulty. I may not be leaving you children the money you're expecting."

"Daddy, don't talk about dying." Brett couldn't face losing him after their reconciliation.

"Those earrings are your mother's legacy. If you find the man who gave them to her, then do what's right. Otherwise, I insist you keep them to finance Timmy's education. I'd like to go to my grave knowing my grandson went to Oxford. And believe me, that boy is Oxford material."

"You're angry with me," she said to Owen much later when they were alone in their room in bed.

"No. I'm merely surprised you didn't mention the earrings."

His wounded tone made her feel even more guilty. The discussion had ruined her dinner. She felt justified in not selling the earrings and her father's argument made sense. If anything, she should give her father the money. She'd taken him aside and suggested it, but he'd assured her he had his financial situation under control. Still, she wanted to make Owen happy. He'd suffered so much. "You think I'm being selfish?"

Owen shrugged. "I didn't say that."

You were thinking it. And she was ashamed of herself for not wanting to give him the earrings. "I love you. You know that."

"Yes," he said, but he didn't pull her into his arms as he usually did.

Brett turned on her side, thankful he didn't want to make love. Too often Owen became maudlin afterward, and told her how he'd thought of her every night when he'd been in prison. If he'd done that tonight, she'd have agreed to sell the earrings. And would have hated herself later.

33

The door to Alex's penthouse swung open. Brett saw that Latrice Laveaux wore a gold dress of silk gauze that she could see through except where it was artfully draped concealing selected parts of her impressive anatomy. Latrice was the type of woman who made Brett want to go through life with a bag over her head.

Owen introduced them, adding, "I'm a great admirer of yours."

Latrice lowered whisk-broom lashes, accepting the compliment. Expecting it. Brett left them talking and walked over to a table where she saw a group of housewarming presents. She'd selected a bottle of expensive wine for Alex, and attached a card that read:

Congratulations! Now you have it all.
A successful business, a Porsche, a
penthouse. Enjoy.

She should have added—the woman of your dreams. Latrice must be the woman of his dreams. They had been dating for months.

Brett glanced back at Owen, who was clearly enthralled by Latrice. He was the man of her dreams.

Timmy's father. Except the dream wasn't nearly as bright as it had been. Ever since she'd refused to sell the earrings, a shadow hovered over them. Owen never referred to the earrings, but they were there, a tangible barrier to their happiness, making her feel guilty and selfish. Still, she couldn't bring herself to sell them.

"How do you like the place?"

Alex's voice surprised her; she turned to face him. He wore a nubby-tweed sport coat in charcoal that made his blue eyes appear even bluer. His pale gray shirt was unbuttoned at the collar and she saw the gold chain. The gold cross, she knew, was hidden behind the shirt, nestled in a fan of dark chest hair.

"This is certainly stunning." She surveyed the penthouse for the first time. It was starkly modern: chrome, glass, black leather furniture. Arctic-white carpeting. She couldn't imagine Alex living here. He'd claimed to like the coziness of her home with its warm woods and English chintz.

"Are things better for Timmy at school?"

"Yes," she answered, puzzled at the personal question. They'd shared an office for months, but he'd never mentioned anything except business. "He's a hero now. His classmates think the gorillas—as in apes—sent his father to prison."

Alex chuckled, a disturbingly familiar sound. They stood looking at each other, silent islands in a sea of party chatter. Mercifully, Latrice and Owen walked up.

"Isn't this place smashing?" Latrice linked her arm in Alex's.

"I was just telling Latrice that this is exactly the type of decorating I like," Owen commented.

Since when, Brett wondered. They'd discussed a "family home" with room for children. She could just imagine the fingerprints on the chrome and glass. The spills on the carpet.

"Let me show you around," Alex said to Owen, but Brett could feel his eyes on her.

She dutifully followed him as Alex showed them a stark-white kitchen with the latest in appliances, currently a hive of activity with a catering crew preparing food. Then they went up a freestanding staircase of gleaming chrome to a bedroom that was bigger than Brett's house. Alex told them about the special stereo system, but Brett noted the enormous bed.

"That's a fabulous waterbed." The way Latrice said it left no question she'd been in it many times.

"What do you think?" Alex flicked the light on in the bathroom, revealing a sunken tub the size of the pond at Hayvenhurst.

"Great view." Owen gestured to the lights along the river.

Brett sensed Alex watching her, and looked up to see Latrice looking at her, too. *Say something.* "Timmy would love it."

Around the perimeter of the tub were votives with candles; she remembered the tub in the Beverly Hills Hotel. And making love in it by candlelight.

She moved closer to Owen. "Are Lev and Amy here yet?"

"I saw them out on the balcony earlier," Latrice said.

"Let's go find them." She tugged on Owen's arm.

"Fabulous place," Owen said as they walked off. Halfway down the stairs, he whispered, "Weren't you a bit rude? I'm not certain Alex was finished showing us around."

"Oh, I'm positive he was." She pointed to the balcony off the dining area. "There's Amy. I want to talk to her."

"I'll join you in a minute. I need a drink."

Amy turned and saw Brett, stunning in a black cocktail dress, but looking tired, her usual smile missing.

"Terrific view, isn't it?" Amy said, standing on the balcony.

"Mmmm. Where's Lev?"

"Getting a vodka," she answered, and Brett mumbled something about Owen being at the bar, too.

"So what do you think of Latrice?" Amy asked, her voice low.

"Obviously, she never goes to the bathroom or she'd be carrying a pair of scissors to cut herself out of that dress."

Amy giggled; sometimes glimmers of the old Brett appeared, but these last months had been difficult for her. "Latrice needs reassurance right now. That's why she dresses so flamboyantly. She just lost another part in a West End production."

Brett didn't answer, gazing out at the city lights.

"Is something wrong?" Amy asked.

Brett glanced over her shoulder; Amy saw Owen standing in a corner talking with Latrice. "Let me tell you what happened last weekend." After she'd finished, Brett asked, "Be honest. Am I being selfish by not selling those earrings?"

"You're being wise. Forget the earrings were your mother's. Forget feeling they don't really belong to you. Face the financial realities. Making money from a movie is a long shot—at best. You might never see a pence from your investment."

"I tried explaining that to Owen." Brett sighed.

"There may be a subtext to what your father was saying. Owen didn't make much from the book, correct?"

"He'll be lucky to earn out his advance."

"He's been offered a position as a teacher, hasn't he?" Amy asked, and Brett nodded. "Eventually, he'll have to work. He won't make much money. You'll earn more as a designer, but it won't be enough to buy a house and have another child."

"But if Belage is tremendously successful—"

"You can't count on it. We're in a recession. Jewelry sales are slow. Don't sell your nest egg."

"I guess you're right. Belage is expanding rapidly, but the opening of the shop in Beverly Hills has been postponed until July because of construction problems. We may not do well there. I hadn't thought about it, but you're right. I may need the money for my family."

Amy was positive she was right. Owen was an intellectual, a bit of a dreamer.

"Thanks for the advice." Brett hugged her. "Enough about me. What's new with you? How are things with Lev?"

"Last night, we decided to get married."

"Am-eeee! Fantastic!" Brett smiled, her familiar smile. "Have you told your father? What did he say?"

"I don't know and couldn't care less. I'm sending him an invitation and he can come if he wishes. It's too bad Lev's mother can't be here. We're trying to get word to her that we're getting married, but Lev hasn't heard from her."

"Maybe Alex can help. He has connections in Eastern Europe."

"He's trying. We just hope she isn't ill again."

"There's Lev now," Brett said, nodding toward the bar area where he stood talking with Bing Yu Tsung, the crafts-man from Hong Kong whom Alex had hired. "Who's the woman with them?"

The brunette had a cascade of hair that fell to her waist, ruler-straight, shining like mahogany silk. Her almond eyes were emphasized by black liner that made them exotic. Amy was debating whether to tell Brett when she nudged her.

"Omigod, Alex just walked over to Owen and Latrice. I can't let Owen ask Alex to invest in a movie." Brett walked away before Amy could warn her about the Tsung girl.

"I'm sorry you aren't feeling well," Owen said as they emerged from Alex's building and hailed a taxi. "The flu, you think?"

No, stress, Brett said to herself, climbing into the cab. "I hope not."

Owen slipped his arm around her, more tender than he'd been since their fight. "I've got great news. Latrice is inter-ested in *Return from Hell*. Really interested. She hasn't read it, but Alex had given her a copy. She's going to read it tonight, and we're going to meet tomorrow to discuss adapt-ing it for the stage." He hugged her. "Isn't that exciting?"

"Yes, but don't get your hopes up. She hasn't even read—"

"I told her the whole story. But the best news is Latrice has backers. All she needs is—what did she call it?—a vehicle."

He kissed her, wrapping his arms around her and squeezing tight. She couldn't concentrate on the kiss; all she could think about was how depressed he'd be if this fell through.

"Latrice invited me to meet her at her club, Groucho's, no less, for drinks tomorrow night to discuss it."

"What about your agent? Is Murray going to be there?"

"No. She wants to work this out with me first. 'Great minds working together,' she said. Then we'll bring in our agents."

Brett didn't like the idea of Owen's meeting with the gorgeous actress. A tendril of jealousy coiled in her chest, but she suppressed it. She trusted Owen. They loved each other.

"I want you to come," Owen said, validating her faith. "You have very creative ideas. You can help me."

"I'll be glad to help." She took a deep breath, praying that this time Owen wouldn't be disappointed. He'd suffered so much; he deserved to be successful. Then a question struck her. "This is a man's story with a minor part for a woman and walk-on for your friend, Eekelen Willem. Why would Latrice be interested?"

"She'll play you, of course. It'll be a bigger part than it was in the book."

34

Alex sat with Latrice in the bar of the Groucho Club. As usual, the actress was scanning the room, trolling for someone she could enlist to revive her career. He wasn't insulted. He couldn't care less. He kept seeing Latrice because she made no demands on him—except in bed.

And she was totally different from Brett.

He saw Brett and Owen arrive. Owen looked around, obviously impressed. Groucho's wasn't as ritzy as Annabel's, but it was much more exclusive. Money couldn't buy a membership; you had to be among the who's who of London's creative braintrust—authors, artists, poets, actors, and directors—to join. Brett, though, looked less than thrilled to be here.

And pissed when she spotted him.

Would she ever forgive him? Alex doubted it. Even though Brett had married Owen and seemed totally in love with him, she had erected an impenetrable barrier between them. Last night, he'd tried to be friendly, showing her around his place. No dice. She never even gave him half a smile.

"Owen." Latrice smiled. "Brett. Lovely of you to join us."

Alex muttered something as Brett and Owen sat. Brett

selected a chair that was as far away from him as she could get.

Owen asked Latrice, "How did you like *Return from Hell*?"

"I was up all night reading it." Latrice leaned over and ran her fingertips across Owen's hand. "I'm in awe. Total awe."

Total bullshit. The only thing that awed Latrice was her reflection in a mirror. But Owen lapped it up with a flavor straw, laughing. Har. Har. Har.

"It has tremendous possibilities." Latrice paused; for a moment Alex thought she'd spotted a photographer and was about to say "Sex" so her most photogenic smile would be plastered across some tacky tabloid. Luckily, Groucho's had a no-camera rule. "But it lacks drama for the female lead."

Owen pondered this while the waiter took drink orders. "Do you have any suggestions, Brett?"

"No. It's your story. All I did was wait."

Alex detected a note of tightness in her voice someone else might have missed. Did he make her nervous? He'd come tonight, deliberately torturing himself, because he seldom saw her. Belage's larger offices kept them apart. He'd hoped removing himself from their office would spur her creativity, but she was still rehashing old designs.

"You waited for Owen. Admirable." Latrice sighed; a little too dramatically, Alex thought. "I wish I could see this story as a play."

She sipped her drink and let Owen dangle. Alex gave Latrice credit. She was one hell of an actress. Anyone would think she had *no* idea how to fix this. Alex didn't know what Latrice planned, but she had a scheme. She always did.

"Without a strong woman, I can't see this as a play."

"True," Owen agreed. "It needs a strong woman."

"Doesn't it take a strong woman to wait *loyally*?" Alex emphasized the word for Brett's benefit.

"An inner strength, of course," Latrice said, "but it's not

the dramatic role audiences want to see. I remember Constance Lamont. She was so charismatic—so interesting. She would have gone back to Peru and never given up the search."

"You're right," Owen agreed. "She was one in a million."

"I did return to Peru," Brett said, her green eyes flashing in a familiar display of impatience, "but I was pregnant. I couldn't stay because of the cholera epidemic."

"Didn't the authorities insist Owen was dead?" Alex asked, defending her even though he knew she'd resent his help.

"Yes, but I went to Hugh, praying Owen was still alive. I thought Hugh had the best chance of finding Owen through his Amnesty International connections."

Owen put his hand on her arm. "You did your best."

What a sanctimonious son of a bitch. Owen's tone implied Constance Lamont would have found him herself. Alex knew Brett despised being compared to her mother.

"Constance was a martyr," Latrice said, oblivious to Brett's tight expression. "The epitome of the twentieth-century woman."

"But she wasn't a particularly good mother," Alex insisted. "She went months without seeing her own child. She also lacked staying power. She went from project to project. I—"

"Who told you that?" Owen snapped.

"Hugh MacLeod." That shut up Owen. Alex almost smiled. After all, Hugh had rescued him. Har. Har. Har.

"My mother never stayed with a project because she knew the truth." Brett's voice was barely under control. "She could help only up to a point. No one should ever starve. Most people starve because their own governments block relief supplies, or rebels won't allow supplies to pass through their lines."

"True," Owen admitted. "Remember Frederick Forsyth in Biafra. He was a reporter back then, but the BBC squashed his story of how the Nigerian government was starving out their political enemies, the Biafrans."

"Why would they do that?" Latrice asked, her interest sparked at the name of the famous author.

"The BBC is subsidized by the government, and the authorities here sided with the Nigerians," Owen said, clearly trying to impress Latrice. "He had to finance his own investigation, successfully bringing the Biafrans to the world's attention. When he returned home, his BBC job was gone. But he had the last laugh. Forsyth went on to become a multimillionaire writing spy novels."

"Mmmm." Latrice blessed Owen with a photo-op smile. Clearly, the politics of starvation held little interest for her. "Tell me how you two met."

Christ. This sucks the big one. Alex kicked back his vodka and signaled the waiter for another.

Owen again put his hand on Brett's arm, and Alex told himself he did not like Saint Owen. He hadn't from the moment they'd met. And it wasn't jealousy. Okay, he conceded, a lot of jealousy with a dash of sixth sense. The guy was no saint.

"Brett and I met in Lima," Owen said, his eyes on Latrice, who appeared mesmerized. "I don't recall where exactly."

Alex thought: The dining room at the Metropole, you ass.

Owen turned to Brett. "Was it at Daiquiri Dick's bar or the lobby of the Imperial where relief workers hung out?"

Brett tried to look past Alex, but he shifted in his seat and their eyes met. She quickly looked away, saying. "You were having dinner with my mother at the Metropole."

"That's right. I remember now. I was telling Constance about my upcoming interview with Guzmán, the *sendero* leader. Constance and I were friends. We'd met in Costa Rica, and became close. We spent most of our free time together. Naturally, when Brett arrived, she came along with us. I didn't notice her at first."

Gimme a break. How could you miss her? She had the damnedest smile.

"We were a threesome. And then one day, I found myself alone with Brett." Owen smiled at Brett, who did not smile back; then Owen directed his attention to Latrice.

Alex sipped his fresh drink, his eyes on Brett. Her naturally animated expression had vanished. Owen's book left no doubt he was intelligent, but he didn't know a damn thing about his wife or he'd realize this wasn't how she saw their first meeting. And she was pissed—big-time—at Owen's discussing this.

"One thing led to another and . . ."

"You fell in love," Latrice prompted Owen.

"Yes, after a time." Owen squeezed Brett's arm.

"You planned to marry and have a child?" Latrice asked, and Alex could almost hear her little mind whirring, envisioning a play with a sexy opening, a melodramatic pledge of love worthy of any soap opera, and a dramatic parting à la *Madama Butterfly*.

"No. I was like Constance. I had a higher calling. Wandering the world doing relief work didn't make me marriage material."

Latrice clapped her hands, and Brett flinched. "Perfect. An unwanted pregnancy just like in *Miss Saigon.*"

Brett stared into her glass, sloshing her drink around as if she were panning for gold. An interesting version of the story, Alex told himself. Owen's book had glossed over this part, concentrating on politics and his imprisonment.

"I don't think we should be discussing this," Brett said, her voice barely under control. "*Return from Hell* is the story of Peru's struggle against the guerrillas, not our story."

"Nonsense." Latrice directed her comment to Owen. "Every story has a personal angle. That's what makes them interesting. You don't mind telling me about yourself, do you?"

Don't do this, Alex silently warned Saint Owen.

"Of course not," Owen said without so much as a glance at Brett, who was now frowning intently.

Latrice lavished her most intimate smile at Owen. "So you didn't plan on having a child?"

"I don't know what happened. I used protection but—" Owen laughed. Har. Har. Har.

"Can't trust those suckers as far as you can throw them," Alex said, striving for a teasing tone, not believing this jerk was actually talking about something so personal, so private.

"I should have used two condoms, but I was short of cash."

"Two?" Latrice asked. "Why?"

While Owen explained the principle of double bagging, Alex gazed at Brett. She hadn't looked up from her drink. Honest to God, this was news to her, and she was furious. Owen was too intent on impressing Latrice to notice. Alex extended his leg and nudged Brett's foot with his shoe. She looked up, and he tried to telegraph his support. She seared him with a look that could have fried bacon.

"It worked out for the best," Owen concluded, proof positive that intelligence and common sense were not carried in the same gene. You'd think the guy would have the smarts to polish this a bit—for Brett's sake. "I have a terrific son and a wonderful marriage." He turned to Brett, grinning. "We're deeply in love, aren't we?"

She dredged up a tight smile. Trust me, Alex told himself, this is not a marriage made in heaven. That realization didn't make him happy; it made him even sadder. Hugh MacLeod was right: Brett was too stubborn to let her marriage fail. He wanted her to be happy, and until tonight he had assumed she was.

"When you were waiting for Owen, you didn't even date?" Latrice asked Brett.

"I had a few dates this year, but only *after* Hugh assured me Owen was dead."

"I was hoping," Latrice said to Owen, "for a grand passion. I'm famous for my love scenes, you know. Brett would be tempted by another man, but then you'd return and she'd fling him aside."

"Brett was never tempted," Owen assured Latrice.

Alex looked at Brett, but she didn't meet his gaze. Son of a bitch. She never told him. He'd suspected she hadn't from Owen's warm greeting at the party, but Alex thought that might have been for Latrice's benefit. How long could Brett keep Timmy quiet?

Latrice sighed, one of those breathy sounds meant to be sexy, her eyes on Owen. "I was hoping for a secret affair."

"Owen is the only man I've ever loved."

Alex kept his face expressionless, but it was hard. He knew her words, though directed to Latrice, were meant for him. The heaviness centered in his chest seemed worse than ever. What did he expect? She'd never said she loved him.

"I think you could make this an interesting play if you wrote it having another man as a love interest while you were away."

"Me?" Owen said, beaming at Latrice's idea. "Write a play?"

Latrice wagged her phony lashes. "Who better?"

Owen chuckled. Har. Har. Har. "I see your point."

"You wouldn't be telling your story," Alex said, nudging Brett with his foot again. If she didn't squash this now she'd have trouble later. "It would ruin the moral integrity of the book."

"I agree," Brett added. "It wouldn't be your story."

Under the table, Latrice kicked Alex, asking him, "Don't you think a lover would add the interest this story needs?"

"No. Same old soap opera crap. Sounds like a major snoozer to me."

"I don't think you should even discuss this without consulting your agent," Brett added.

"We're just tossing ideas around," Latrice assured her.

Alex decided the only thing going around was Owen.

Around Latrice's finger. It didn't take a rocket scientist to see what was happening here.

"You'd be so perfect to write this play, but I'd need some dramatic moments. I was hoping for a lover."

"Brett did have a difficult time with her family," Owen said, helpfully. "Her father disowned her for not aborting Timmy."

"Really?" A big smile at this grim tidbit.

"My father didn't exactly disown me," Brett said, raising her voice, then quickly lowering it. Alex didn't blame her for being upset; this was too personal to be included in a play. It would hurt Jock—and Timmy. "My father was so upset over my mother's death that he was almost comatose. My stepmother insisted I should have an abortion, but my father only halfheartedly agreed. I was furious with him, so I left. He didn't disown me. But now I understand he was only trying to give me my options. Now, we all have a warm, loving relationship."

Latrice ignored Brett. "We could emphasize the disagreement for dramatic effect. It would give me a key scene I need since I won't have a love scene for the middle act."

Owen beamed. "Good idea. I—"

"Your book was about Peru and the hammerlock the Communist *senderos* have on it. You'll be disappointing your readers and ruining future sales," Brett reminded Owen.

"Brett's right," Alex said. "A play with such a personal slant would ruin the integrity of your story. Forget it."

"Darling." Latrice smiled at Alex, but he could tell she was pissed at his continued sabotage. "Owen is a writer, a creative genius. He would rewrite this story and still maintain its integrity."

Brett stood, putting her glass down. "We've got to run. The woman staying with our son has to be home."

The surprised look on Owen's face said this was news to him. But he finally got the message that Brett was not a happy camper and rose.

Alex caught up with Brett at the entrance, Latrice and Owen lagging way behind still talking. Alex stepped outside with Brett. "Why didn't you tell him about us?"

Brett gazed up at him, her deep green eyes making his heart ache. "I didn't mean to mislead him. I—I'll tell him tonight."

Alex nodded, putting his hand on her arm. If Owen was jealous and made her quit, he'd never see her again. He'd assumed he was over this hurdle, but now he was damn worried. "Don't tell him it was me. I—"

Latrice and Owen walked out, cutting him off.

"Let's talk again," Latrice said to Owen. "Promise me you'll think about some changes."

Owen kissed her on the cheek. "Cross my heart."

Alex waited for him to hope to die. No such luck.

Brett mumbled a good night to Alex, then walked away without looking at him.

"Pretty good for openers," Latrice said once they were out of earshot. "I intend to play Brett's part with a few modifications, of course. I'll make her more like Constance Lamont, give her a torrid love affair, and a bitter fight with her family."

"Brett won't let you do it. She's a lot tougher than her mother. A lot."

35

"Are you upset about something?" Owen asked when they were home in their bedroom.

How could he not know what had upset her? she asked herself.

Brett hung up her dress, telling herself she wasn't calm enough to discuss this yet. On the ride home, she'd sat silently while Owen prattled on about making his book into a play. She'd concentrated on her father's warning: *Never say or do anything in anger.* His words echoed down through her childhood memories. Time after time, she'd been too impulsive to heed his advice.

Anger had mushroomed inside her, growing until it took all her willpower to control it. She could still feel the tips of her ears burning, Alex's eyes on her. He was the last person she'd wanted to witness her humiliation.

The perfect love. Meeting Owen had been a magical time—for her. Obviously, he hadn't shared the same experience. How could she have misinterpreted everything? The pulsing knot in her chest that had formed when she listened to Owen had grown larger with each word, hardening into anger.

She should be hurt, she thought, upset that Owen hadn't planned to marry her, that he'd assumed she wouldn't have Timmy. But she wasn't. She was as mad as hell. At herself. She'd nurtured a one-sided, romantic version of their affair. For years now she'd been living a lie.

She also blamed Owen. All these months and he hadn't told her that he'd never planned to marry her. And why did he have to drop the bombshell in front of Alex?

"I say, don't shut me out, love. Talk to me."

She stepped away from him and forced her voice to have an even keel. "What do you think I'm upset about?"

Owen brushed his hand over the crown of his head where his gray hair was thinnest. "The play. You think I'm lowering my standards to consider altering the story line."

They'd spent months together, talking, but he didn't understand her. *Never say or do anything in anger.* She tried to be rational, telling herself they'd spent most of their discussions on his problems, striving to help him adjust to his new life.

"I was shocked to learn you had no intention of marrying me." There. She'd said it calmly—without anger.

"I never asked you to marry me, did I?"

"No. But when I told you about Timmy—"

"I thought you knew I would help you through an abortion."

His honesty disarmed her. True, he'd never asked her to marry him—exactly. She'd assumed. Tonight she'd discovered how little she'd meant to him. All these years she'd lived a pipe dream, waiting for a man who hadn't loved her.

"You know I love you, Brett." Owen folded her into his arms. "You had the sense to see what I should have known then. And thank God, you had Timmy. I don't know what I'd do without you."

He loved her; that was what counted. She couldn't blame him for her misinterpretations. He could have deceived her —the way Alex had—but Owen was unfailingly honest. She had to be honest, too.

"I'm glad you're honest. There's something I should have

told you months ago." She took a deep, steadying breath. "You're the only man I've ever loved, but I did have a brief affair after I thought you were dead. It ended before you returned home."

He stepped back, his eyes narrowing. "But you said—"

"Remember, you asked me in front of a group of reporters. That wasn't the place to tell you. I should have told you long ago, but there never seemed to be the right moment."

"You did?" His voice trailed off. He was on the verge of tears. He hadn't broken down for over a month. "Who was he?"

Alex's warning not to mention his name flashed across her mind. There was nothing between them anymore, so why worry Owen that they worked together every day? "It doesn't matter. As I said, it was over before you returned."

"I guess I should look on the bright side. I can write the play and include an affair." He smiled at her; the veil of tears had vanished. "Latrice had a great idea. Instead of the affair being over, I'll write it as if you dropped him for me."

Stunned, she wondered if he even cared that there had been another man. A man she could easily have loved. What concerned Owen more was the effect this would have on his darn play. "You wanted to help the people of Peru. Latrice plans a melodramatic soap opera about sex."

"It'll earn the money we need to move out of this hole."

Hole? She liked it here. Granted, it was a bit small, but it had happy memories of Timmy's childhood. A sense of alarm gripped her. The play was going to be about her life, warping it to suit Latrice Laveaux. This had occurred to her at the club, but she'd been so distracted she'd shunted it aside.

"You weren't planning on portraying me as my mother, were you?"

"No, I'd just strengthen your character a little."

"There's nothing wrong with my character. If this play's going to focus on me, I insist you tell the truth," she said, and he nodded agreeably, but she had the sneaking suspicion Latrice's wishes would be more important than hers.

She slipped into her nightgown and got into bed, a weight she hadn't experienced since learning her mother had died settling over her. Her life had veered from the course she'd charted, and she had no idea what to do. At work, she couldn't bluff much longer; she wasn't producing anything creative. Now her past would become public—distorted to suit Latrice.

"I don't want you to cast my father as a villain."

"He did ask you to get an abortion."

"But he's Timmy's grandfather. He'll be hurt by this, and so will Timmy." At this Owen's expression became concerned, and she took heart. "When Lady Bewley created that mess, Timmy was in a serious fight. He was confused and upset. It will happen again if it becomes known my father wanted me to have an abortion."

"Was he really in a fight? Why didn't you tell me?"

She hadn't told him because she hadn't wanted to discuss Alex. "Timmy had no idea what *bastard* meant until the boys began teasing him. Do you think he knows what *abortion* means?"

Owen climbed into bed and switched off the light. Puzzled by his silence, she rolled over and tried to sleep, but couldn't. Beside her Owen tossed, not sleeping either.

"What are you thinking?" she asked.

After a few seconds, he replied, "I don't know how to please you. You're not willing to give on anything."

She sat up and turned on the light. "What do you mean?"

"This play will be our story, but you want it written to fit your version of reality. You did have an affair. Your father did advise you to have an abortion. But you don't want those things in the play." Owen sat up, glaring at her now. "You know what I think? You don't want me to succeed."

She stared wordlessly at him, filled with utter disbelief and the horrifying realization she didn't know this man at all. "How can you say that?"

"You wouldn't sell the earrings."

Somehow she'd known it would come down to the earrings. He'd harbored a deep resentment that had spread, growing silently like a cancer. Threatening to destroy their marriage.

Don't say or do anything in anger.

"You want everything on your terms. You're nothing like your mother. You're selfish."

Blindsided by his words, she gasped. An ache, raw and primitive, surged through her. And with it a rising tide of anger. For years she'd kept his memory alive, prodding Hugh to search for him. Since Owen's return, she'd devoted herself to him, curtailing her social life, spending less time with her son than she would have liked. She'd helped him in every way she knew how.

Except selling the earrings. He should have understood why she couldn't, but he didn't. He saw the world in terms of himself.

Eula Mae spritzed the last fern in the reception area, then looked up, startled to see Brett arriving so early.

Brett passed through the security door. "I'm glad you're here. I need to talk to you."

Eula Mae had been set to fill Brett in before Alex called the staff meeting that morning. Brett looked exhausted and worried. She seldom smiled these days. After this morning's meeting she'd be smiling even less. They walked into Eula Mae's office and closed the door. "Were you up all night again getting out another Badger Preservation Society newsletter?"

"No. I couldn't sleep." Brett dropped into a chair. "I've had a terrible row with Owen."

Eula Mae tried to appear surprised, but she wasn't. Brett had been despondent for months. She suspected the root of the problem was Alex, but lately had begun to consider that Owen might also be part of the trouble. Eula Mae listened to Brett's story. Halfway through she silently asked Vic for guidance.

"Am I being selfish?" Brett asked.

Eula Mae studied the glorious pit that Brett had brought her. Beside it stood the silver loving cup that was the Chelsea Garden Show's highest honor. No, Brett wasn't selfish. She'd befriended a lonely old woman. And she'd done more than her share for a number of causes.

"No, but I think you have to consider Owen's point of view. He's older; he hasn't many years to get what he wants. If he's willing to let his story become your story, he's desperate."

"I'm afraid he may hurt those I love in his desire to see this play on the stage."

"Like Alex?" The way Brett had acted around Belage assured Eula Mae that Brett wasn't as much in love with Owen as she thought—or she'd forgive Alex.

"Alex? What are you talking about?"

Normally, Eula Mae hated nosy Parkers, but Brett had come to her. "I know you two were having an affair, and somehow it ended with hard feelings—on your part."

Brett expelled a breath, blowing upward and ruffling her hair. "You're right."

Eula Mae listened intently while Brett told her about the problem in Los Angeles. "I can't say that I'm surprised. Vic was always concerned that Alex had never known a woman's love and couldn't make a commitment." She didn't add that Vic firmly believed Brett could change Alex. What would be the point now? Brett was loyal to a fault; she wasn't leaving Owen.

"Eula Mae, you take care of the books. Is Belage doing as well as it seems?"

"Why do you ask?" She was reluctant to give away confidential information, but she was concerned. Alex insisted on pressing, striving to make Belage an overnight success.

"Everything is happening so fast."

"Belage is fine as long as things go as planned. Now,

about Alex. From what you've told me, Latrice will make him into an arch-villain, a foil for Owen the hero."

"No one will know who the lover is."

"Except Alex."

V
HOLD FAST

36

Brett walked into Alex's staff meeting thinking Eula Mae was right. The play would hurt Alex. He might not have loved her the way she'd hoped, but he nurtured her career, putting himself at risk to give her a chance. And, more important, he'd helped Timmy when she hadn't known how.

"Good morning," Bing Yu Tsung said.

Brett returned the greeting, careful not to look directly at Alex, but seeing him at his desk. Next to him stood the attractive Oriental girl Brett had noticed at his party.

Lev entered, saying hello to everyone, looking happier than she'd ever seen him. Why not? He and Amy planned to marry soon.

"I've called you here," Alex began, "to tell you how well Belage is doing. Bing is helping with the goldsmithing and polishing. Lev, the quickest cutter on the planet, will be cutting for a new mass market line I've just sold to the Harrell Department Stores in America. If he doesn't finish by his wedding day, he's not going to Israel on his honeymoon."

Everyone laughed, and Brett listened to the pep talk, silently conceding Alex had tried to help her out last night. He had never loved her, but he was her friend. He couldn't help himself, she thought, watching the young lady beside him gaze at him with adoring eyes. Was that how she'd looked? Love struck.

That was then; this is now. She might have been attracted to Alex once, but no longer. Her life was set; a marriage took work and she was determined to keep hers together. Did it make sense to continue her hostility toward Alex? She was acting like a bitch. She'd apologize as soon as the meeting ended.

"This is Yai Tsung," Alex introduced the awestruck girl standing next to his desk. "She's helped her uncle"—he nodded toward Bing—"with designing in Hong Kong."

The word *designing* hit Brett full force. Her replacement? Omigod, she was losing everything—at once. Owen and her job.

"Yai will design, not with the custom lines, but the mass-market items we'll sell in the States this fall."

Brett practiced the deep breathing she'd learned to prepare for Timmy's birth. She couldn't look at Alex, but she felt his eyes on her and kept her smile paralyzed in place, convinced Yai was being groomed to take her place. Could she blame Alex? No. Her creative output had been less than zero since Christmas.

"Hello," Brett greeted the new designer. "I'm Brett—"

"I know who you are," the girl responded, her tone low. Cold. "I've seen your designs."

Yai certainly didn't sound as if she had a drop of professional admiration for Brett's work.

"I'd like to see your designs," Brett said, ignoring the girl's superior attitude.

"Alex said no one should see my work except him."

Brett stifled a gasp. Was Yai insinuating Brett intended to steal her designs?

"I'd like a word with you," Alex said as everyone left. "Brett, nothing has changed. You still have your own imprint: Brett Lamont for Belage. But I need to get some low-end designs in production. Expensive jewelry isn't selling like it used to."

Brett nodded, not trusting her voice.

"Yai is going to do those designs. I want you to concentrate on one-of-a-kind designs for the Belage store in Beverly Hills."

"I understand the opening has been postponed again," she said, justifiably proud of her level tone.

"Bunster's had some problems, but it's set to open in August." He hesitated, measuring her. "You understand why I hired Yai?"

"Yes," she lied, preserving what scrap of pride remained. Things weren't all right at home. Or at work. She wondered if they ever would be again.

"I honestly don't care that Father refused to attend my wedding." Amy let Brett help her button the traveling dress she'd wear on the flight to Tel Aviv, where she and Lev would honeymoon. "But I am concerned that Lev still hasn't heard from his mother."

"I'm sure he will soon. Send her the pictures. You were a stunning bride. I cried through the whole service."

"I'm concerned about you. Is everything all right?"

"I'm a little stressed at work. I designed a few new pieces for the shop in Beverly Hills, but they weren't my best. Meanwhile, Yai churns out one innovative design after another. Alex insists her designs are put in the safe each night, so the copycat jewelers can't get them and produce them in rhinestones."

"He shouldn't worry about the reproduction artists. Lev says Belage's security is top-drawer." Amy opened the door for them to rejoin the wedding reception. "I'm proud of Lev. He cut all those diamonds for the Harrell Department Stores so quickly."

"He is amazing. Now all he has to do is to come back from his honeymoon and set them. And Yai will be famous."

"Don't feel threatened. She's not designing at your level."

"I can't help myself. Yai uses every excuse she can to trot into Alex's office to show him a smashing new design. It's clear she intends to become Belage's top designer."

"It's not just work that's bothering you, is it?"

"No." Unspoken pain fired Brett's eyes. "My marriage is at a crossroads. I made a compromise that I'm not happy about."

Amy listened while Brett explained the changes Owen wanted to make so *Return from Hell* could become a play. Amy felt sorry for Owen, but she'd never really liked him.

"I told Owen to write the play however it suited him," Brett concluded. "I had to agree or my marriage would suffer."

"You two need to get away and talk this out. Why don't you go to your father's for a few days?"

"I can't. Hayvenhurst is being painted while my father's in Kenya on a safari."

"Have you read Owen's play yet?"

"No. I trust him to do what's right."

The only thing Amy trusted Owen to do was to kowtow to Latrice Laveaux, but she didn't want to discourage Brett.

They walked into the salon and Amy noticed Alex glance in their direction before quickly looking away. All afternoon, he'd been stealing looks at Brett. But her friend didn't notice; she was watching Owen. Of course, Owen was hanging on Latrice, who'd come with Alex.

Brett rushed to answer the bell before it woke Timmy. The wedding had exhausted him; he'd been cranky when she'd finally gotten him into bed. Owen had left to spend yet another evening with his cronies at Groucho's discussing his play. Brett opened the door and a messenger handed her a cable.

"Please, don't let anything have happened to Daddy." She ripped open the envelope, thinking Jock Payne had waited his whole life to go on safari, but had chosen this time, when his business was pressed, to go. He claimed he was going because he'd put it off too long. She read the cable, relief and sadness surging through her. It wasn't her father; it was Terai.

Another knock on the door startled her. She quickly opened it and found Hugh MacLeod.

"Brett, what's wrong?" he asked, and she realized tears had filled her eyes, blurring her vision.

"An old man I met in Nepal died," she explained as he put his arm around her and guided her into the parlor. She envisioned herself in that gorge below Annapurna, carving Owen's name into a rock for the *mani* wall. Who would carve Terai's name? No one.

"Mercifully, Terai died in his sleep. He lived for his life as a *sherpa,* you see. But he was too old and I got him a job as a runner for the reforestation project. It's sad he died without anyone to love him."

"You're so much like your mother."

"Don't say that." She clamped her mouth shut, stunned that she'd lashed out at Hugh. What was happening to her? "I'm sorry. I—"

"Don't apologize. I know you weren't expecting me. You look exhausted. I dropped by hoping to see Owen."

"He's not here, but I have coffee ready. I've missed seeing you. Where've you been?"

He followed her into the kitchen. "I just returned from Moscow. They're releasing political prisoners from the *gulags* constantly, which is great for as long as it lasts."

Brett handed him a cup, then took her own and sat at the small table. "Is there a problem?"

"I heard rumors about a coup to oust Gorbachev. It's an unstable country. The hardliners could take over. Their biggest enemy, though, is an economic freefall. Who knows what will happen in the next ten years?"

Russia reminded Brett of Lev. "Could you check on Lev's mother in Kiev? He hasn't heard from her."

"I'll check his exit papers to get her exact address and have one of our people go there. I'm surprised he's having trouble. One of the benefits of *perestroika* is the ability to communicate with people behind the Iron Curtain."

He sipped his coffee, then asked, "How's Alex?"

"Great." She tried for an upbeat tone; Hugh was a master of insight into people. "Belage has expanded phenomenally."

"I was afraid of that."

"What do you mean?" Brett asked, although she'd been concerned about this herself.

"Whenever I'm in town I spend time with Alex," he said, surprising Brett, who'd thought they were barely acquainted. "He's a true wild card. That's what we call children who grow up in relief camps or internment camps. Remember that song, 'Bobby McGee'? It said something about freedom being just another word for nothing left to lose. Those children grow up with a sense of desperation because they're powerless to control their world."

She thought of Alex and his relationship with his grandmother. Not as bad a situation as an internment camp, but similar.

"One reaction we've noticed in adults who make it out of those camps is a recklessness, a tendency to court disaster."

"Why? When they have everything?"

"Because they hear a silent message programmed into their brains as children: nothing you do matters; you can't change anything. They have the highest thresholds of fear imaginable."

She recalled Alex challenging Intelco. Nerves of steel.

"Psychoanalyze a terrorist and you'll often find a wild card—a child of desperation—willing to take enormous risks because he doesn't really think he can influence the outcome."

She decided to check Belage's books, the first chance she had. "Can they be helped?"

Hugh studied her, his eyes narrowing. "Only when they believe they have something to lose, something to protect."

She had the odd feeling he was trying to tell her something, but wasn't sure what. "I think Alex is putting down roots. He says he isn't moving back to L.A. That will help, won't it?"

"Yes." He stirred his coffee. "What about you? Are you putting down roots?"

"Yes," she responded brightly. Too brightly. She couldn't lie to Hugh, who was like an uncle. Some of her fondest childhood memories centered around him and his love for Skye, which he shared with her. Hugh had given her the copy of Sir Walter Scott's *Lord of the Isles* that she had just read to Timmy. "Things could be going better."

She told Hugh about her conflict with Owen over the play. He listened, never giving her his opinion, but encouraging her to share her thoughts. It was easy to understand his success in verifying complaints of abuse registered with Amnesty International. Hugh had a manner that encouraged a person to talk, confident he wouldn't judge—or reveal what he learned.

"I thought giving in on the play was the solution to our problems," Brett concluded, "but it just drove Owen further away from me. I feel as if I'm sinking in emotional quicksand. Everything I do only makes things worse."

"Have you two considered counseling?"

"I suggested it, but Owen refuses to go."

"I have a theory about the crucible," Hugh said. "That's what we call any traumatic experience a victim undergoes. It can be extremely short. Remember the Amnesty International mailing you did for us about women being taken to police stations?"

"Yes. In many countries women who are taken to a station are raped—usually gang raped. It's routine."

"Often these women aren't ever charged with a crime, but the police feel justified in assaulting them. The experience may be over in a matter of minutes, but it changes them forever. Owen was in prison for years. Not the worst crucible I've ever seen as prisons go. He wasn't tortured. They simply forgot him."

"You're saying he's changed; he's not the man I met."

"I don't know. Is he?"

"He's not the man I remember, but I'm not certain the mistake isn't mine," she answered with total honesty.

"I suggest a heart-to-heart talk with him. There's a bank holiday this weekend so you'll have three days off. Why don't you go to my place in Skye and straighten out your differences?"

"Great idea," Brett answered, encouraged for the first time in weeks. "The three of us can go hiking in the Cuillins. Can you come, or are you heading off on another mission?"

"Back to Peru, I'm afraid. I'm trying to get Eekelen Willem's body out before it's too late."

"Too late?"

"Fujimori is the first democratically elected president in decades, but he can't control his relatives. His in-laws have been culling through the clothing sent for the relief camps and selling the best goods in the *mercado*. When a man can't control his own family, it doesn't bode well for the country."

"I'm sorry to hear that. I packed some clothes myself at United Front headquarters this March. I remember how shabbily many natives were forced to dress."

"For Peru's sake, let's hope Fujimori improves." Hugh rose. "I must be off, but do me a favor. Enjoy yourself in Skye, and while you're talking to Owen, try to persuade him to call Eekelen Willem's widow. She has some questions—"

"He spoke with her some time ago. He—"

"Are you sure? I talked with her this afternoon and told her I was going to Lima. She said she hadn't heard from Owen."

37

It was after two in the morning when she heard Owen unlock the front door. She hadn't gone to bed because sleep was out of the question. Instead, she'd stayed up typing letters to organizations, imploring their members not to buy goods with *Made in China* labels. The Chinese used prison labor—slave labor because most of them had never been charged with a crime—to manufacture cheap goods that workers in Britain couldn't compete with.

There was so much evil in the world she was overwhelmed. How had her mother done it? Brett told herself to focus on her own problems, and she wouldn't feel so powerless.

Why had Owen lied to her? He was unfailingly honest —even when it hurt, she thought, remembering his version of how they'd met. But there was no denying he'd lied about calling Eekelen Willem's widow. After postponing the call for months, he'd told her only last week that he'd called Inge Willem.

Did she know this man? The same question kept haunting her. She'd given in on the play, letting him rewrite his story to suit Latrice Laveaux, but it hadn't helped their relationship. He spent less time than ever at home and no time with Timmy. This certainly wasn't the happy family she'd envisioned.

"I say, you're up late." He walked into their room. "Great news. Nigel Brill agreed to direct my play. I'm going to Greece with him tomorrow to spend two weeks on his yacht working on the script before taking it to the backers."

Her shoulders sagged; that let out Skye; she'd been counting on going to Hugh's place and spending time talking things over with Owen. He rambled on, not including her in his plans. She turned and watched Owen put his toe to his heel and pull off his loafers. "Hugh dropped by this evening. He's returning to Peru. I guess he has an opportunity to bring back Eekelen Willem's body."

"Is that right?" Owen responded, his tone guarded.

"Do you think Inge will be happy?"

Owen turned away, hanging his trousers in the closet. "I'm sure she will. She told me she was praying for it."

Brett took a deep head-clearing breath. Unbelievable. He *was* lying. "Have you spoken to her lately?"

"I just talked to her the one time. It's too sad."

"Hugh spoke with Inge, and she claims you never called her."

Owen kept his back to her, taking a long time to put on his pajamas. He finally turned to her. "I lied. You kept badgering me, so I was forced to lie. It's impossible for me to call Inge. When Eekelen died, I wanted to die. I was all alone."

She honestly didn't know what to say. She really didn't think she'd badgered him that much. A thought had niggled at her since the night she heard Owen describe their first meeting. The man she'd fallen in love with had never really existed. Except in her mind.

"Old Man Storr." Timmy pointed to the black obelisk-shaped mountain towering against Skye's horizon. "Why do they call it that? It's a silly goose name."

"The wind and rain have worn away the other mountains,

so he's an old man among mountains standing alone." Brett patted the tarp for him to sit. "What's different about this area?"

Timmy plopped down. "No trees. No heather. Funny rocks."

"Right." Timmy was quick, too quick sometimes. He'd asked her dozens of questions about why his father had left for Greece without them. "This area looks like the moon."

Timmy's eyes grew wide as he reached for a sandwich.

"Remember the book we have with the pictures the astronauts took of the moon? It looked very much like these rocks."

"Can the man in the moon see Old Man Storr?"

She smiled; he was so bright. "I guess he can."

Timmy gazed at the lunar landscape unique to the northern tip of the island, captivated, then a few minutes later, he said, "I wanna build a dam there." He pointed to the stream, hardly more than a trickle, running through the rocks.

"I'll watch." On the way here, they'd passed the hydroelectric station at Loch Leathan. She'd explained how damming the water provided the island with electricity.

She watched Timmy industriously hauling rocks to the stream for his dam, certain he couldn't get in any trouble, and closed her eyes for a moment. Even Skye's scenic beauty couldn't dispel the deep ache lodged in her chest. Once the star, she'd become a minor character in her own life. She'd lost control of the situation at work and at home. Work could take a backstage role in her life, but her problems with Owen had to be resolved.

Since his confession two nights ago, she'd besieged herself with questions about their relationship. He claimed to love her, but did he? When he returned, he needed her, depending on her for financial and emotional support, but as he grew stronger, he'd distanced himself. He refused counseling and wouldn't talk to her about their problems.

He accused her of being selfish, but she believed he was

being selfish himself. He expected her to agree to anything he said. If she didn't, he resorted to manipulating her emotionally. With tears. With guilty reminders she'd been free while he'd been in prison. With subtle hints she wasn't as good as her mother.

She couldn't go on like this. She hated to admit it, but she'd made a mistake by marrying Owen so quickly. True, he was Timmy's father, but was that a good enough reason to stay married?

"Mommeeee!"

Brett sat up, startled.

"Rain." Timmy pointed to the mountains behind them. Old Man Storr was now skirted by ominous clouds with leaden underbellies.

"Hurry." She stowed their things, cursing herself for hiking so far. They had taken the car and driven miles from Hugh's cottage. Could they make it to the car without getting soaked? They dashed down the trail, well worn by summer trekkers, past the flocks of black-faced sheep scavenging among the barren rocks. Timmy sprinted ahead to their car.

She hustled him inside; the instant she closed the door the rain pelted the top of Hugh's Austin mini. She drove down the narrow dirt road beside Loch Leathan, determined to get to Hugh's before the brunt of the storm hit.

"Where are we?" Timmy asked.

"We're just passing Loch Leathan." Later they passed Loch Fada, and the rain kicked up, pummeling the windshield so fast the wipers could barely keep it clear long enough for her to see the road. She eased up on the accelerator, remembering that treacherous ravines flanked the road.

Minutes went by, then Timmy asked, "Are we close?"

"Just a little farther." Had they passed the small cottage at the bottom of Loch Fada? She hadn't seen it, but visibility was almost nil. She could have missed its stone fence.

She jogged to the right following a crook in the narrow

road, and remembered the bend. No. They hadn't passed the cottage yet. They were still a long way from town. Suddenly a large shape loomed ahead, blurred by the rain. A car. She swept to the side, giving it a wide berth, but it kept charging directly at them, not giving an inch.

"He doesn't see us." She was stunned he could miss her car when they were so close. She jammed down on the horn. The car didn't alter its course, leaving her no choice but to jerk the wheel hard left to avoid a head-on collision.

"Mommeeee! Look out!"

She jammed on the brakes, a reflex action that did no good. The car was already airborne, plunging over the embankment.

"Oh, my God!" The car seemed suspended in midair for minutes, then it landed with a bone-jarring crash. The side window shattered, glass pitting her face. She pitched forward, banging her forehead against the steering wheel. A pinwheel of blinding light flashed before her, then darkness.

The rat-a-tat tattoo of rain on the roof woke her. She tried to open her eyes, but her lids were too heavy. She forced her eyes open, recalling the accident.

"Timmy?" His seat belt held him in place, and he appeared to be asleep. He wasn't cut; the blood trickling into her eyes was her own. She shook him, but he didn't respond, his head lolling to one side. With fingers covered with her own blood, she checked for his pulse. And found it, thank God.

He was unconscious, but she saw no sign of serious injury. With trembling hands she unfastened her seat belt, determined to get help quickly. Through the broken window the cold rain dashed against her face and she saw the rocky side of the embankment.

"We're down here," she screamed over and over, positive the driver of the other car had stopped. The only answer was the drumbeat of the rain on the mini's battered roof.

Don't leave Timmy. But even if she could carry him, which was impossible considering the steep terrain, she shouldn't move him. That could make his injury worse; it might kill him.

Don't leave him. What if he comes to and you're gone? She rested her head on the steering wheel to stave off a juggernaut of debilitating panic. Formulate a plan. But she felt light-headed and shaky the way she had when she'd worked with her mother in relief camps and had gone for days without food.

She swiped at the blood dripping into her eyes from a gash at her hairline. "It's not serious," she assured herself. *Go for help. It's your only choice. It can't be far to that cottage.*

She covered Timmy with her sweater and the tarp she'd used for the picnic. "Timmy?" She tried one last time to rouse him but he didn't move. She prayed she'd made the right decision. What if he awoke and she wasn't there?

Hurry up! She vaulted out of the car. Spurred by panic and adrenaline, she scaled the steep wall, gripping the rocks with her bare hands and hoisting herself up. "Help! Down here!" she screamed in case the driver of the other car was still nearby.

The wind whipped the slashing rain, driving her sodden hair into her face. She slipped on the spongy lichen that grew between the sharp rocks and gashed her knee. Sliding backward, she grabbed frantically at the rocks, tearing the skin off the palms of her hands, snapping fingernails to the quick.

She broke her fall at an outcropping of stone. The rain pummeled her, falling harder now. She ignored the searing pain in her knee and her bloody palms and scrambled upward, crawling on all fours.

Head down to combat the blinding rain, she was halfway across the muddy flat before it dawned on her she'd reached the road. She leapt to her feet, squinting to get her bearings. How would she ever lead anyone back to this spot? Her red blouse. Perfect. She stripped it off and weighted it down with several rocks, positioning the blouse where she could easily spot it.

She streaked down the road, arms pumping, feet flying. The cottage couldn't be too far, could it? She charged along, then stumbled in a pothole and hit the ground. "Dammit to hell."

She vaulted to her feet again, barely conscious of the mud on her bra and chest, reminding herself Timmy's life depended on her. Charging down the road, she kept looking for the stone fence that bordered the cottage. Where was it? Surely, it wasn't this far. If she'd miscalculated and had already driven past the cottage, it was miles to the nearest village.

Through the torrent of rain, she glimpsed the wall. She leapt over it, angling toward the gray stone cottage emerging from the obscuring rain, wooden shutters battened against the storm. She pounded on the front door, praying someone was home.

Eula Mae adjusted the magnifying glass to study the two kiwi pits. The pinhead-size seeds were tricky little devils. Identifying a male and a female pit was dicey, but she thought she was about to accomplish what had eluded most members of the Rare Plant and Pit Society—mating a kiwi. At last.

With a sterilized needle she edged the two seeds closer and closer. The telephone rang, a shrill sound in the silence.

"My stars," she cursed, then answered with a terse hello.

"Eula Mae?" She dropped the magnifying glass into the petri dish, crushing one kiwi seed, recognizing Brett's voice and knowing something terrible had happened.

She listened to a nearly hysterical explanation of the accident. Skye's crack rescue team, accustomed to saving hikers in the mountains, had brought Timmy to the hospital. But he was still unconscious, undergoing tests.

"I need you to locate Murray Hampton-Carswell, Owen's agent. He'll know how to contact the yacht Owen is on."

"I'll handle it," Eula Mae assured her. "Don't worry."

Brett was sobbing now. "I don't know what I'll do if Timmy—"

Eula Mae tried to reassure her, but Brett was frighteningly distraught. After they rang off, Eula Mae felt Brett's despair. She was as close to a child as Eula Mae would ever have.

"I would have been a terrific mother, Vic," Eula Mae said, talking out loud to Vic as she often did. "She needs someone strong right now, doesn't she, Vic? Owen can't possibly make it back from Greece for a day or two. I can be there"—she checked her watch—"by midnight."

As usual, Vic listened, and discussed the situation with her.

38

Brett stared into the mirror in the hospital's washroom. A bandage on her forehead covered several stitches. She'd washed the blood out of her hair, but it hung in damp hanks around her face, which was leached of all color and covered by small scratches from the shattered window. Her hands were wrapped in gauze up to her wrists.

Please, let Timmy be all right. He'd been in surgery for over an hour. Her stomach roiled spasmodically. She couldn't seem to get a grip on herself. *What if he doesn't make it?*

The question echoed again and again and again as it had for hours, leaving her weak, trembling, so terrified she wanted to scream. But if she did, she knew she wouldn't be able to stop.

Go back to the waiting room, she told herself. *The doctor will never be able to find you in here.*

She nudged the door open with her hip, holding her bandaged hands high. The hall was as quiet as a pharaoh's tomb. And almost as dark. The Portree Hospital had been built in the last century, a cavernous relic with dark meandering corridors.

It was almost one o'clock in the morning, more than

twelve hours since the accident, and the hospital was deserted except for the one station where the night shift monitored patients. And the operating room on the second floor.

Her little boy was up there. He'd looked so small, so lifeless as they'd wheeled him away on the gurney. *Please, God, don't take him from me. I love him so much.*

At the end of the long hall, she saw a shadowy silhouette. Recognition triggered deep inside her. Her heart lurched, skipping a beat before regaining its normal stride. She limped toward Alex, startled by the anguished look on his face.

For a heartbeat, they stood still, almost touching, and in that moment the distrust and suspicion vanished, past and present merging, unspoken feeling eddying between them. He gazed into her eyes with the kind of compassion she'd never known existed.

Her eyes flickered down for a moment to her bandaged hands. He'd come all this way. Then she surrendered to the overwhelming urge and leaned into his arms, her head coming to rest against his sturdy shoulder.

Security. His arms. Nonsense, she told herself, but her heart didn't listen. He offered the measure of strength she needed. They pressed together for a time, holding fast like two people after an absence too long to be bridged by mere words, silently confessing nothing made them appreciate life like facing death. The only emotion that had any significance was the warmth of the other person, the sharing, the comfort.

"Are you all right, Brett?" He touched her cheek gently.

She nodded, unformed words on her lips, a constricting knot tightening her throat. Silence. Soothing, comforting silence filled the hall, broken only by the steady sound of Alex's breathing. She wasn't alone anymore.

"What's the situation with Timmy?" Alex asked and she realized she had been clinging to him for minutes now, gathering his strength. He held her close, stroking the back of her neck the way he had so many times.

She allowed him to guide her to the waiting room, supported by his arm. "In the crash his seat belt cut into his torso and ruptured his spleen. He's in surgery having it removed right now." She closed her eyes, wincing at the thought of Timmy being sliced open. "I thought the seat belt protected him, but he's at that in-between age. He's too small for the adult-size seat belts. This wouldn't have happened to an older child." She met his concerned gaze. "What is it?"

"Nothing."

"You always say that." She heard the hysterical edge to her voice, but couldn't mute it. "You never say what you're thinking. Don't do that to me now."

He studied her for a minute, his arm still circling her, tightening his grip. "I don't want to worry you, but the facilities here aren't very modern."

"There wasn't time to fly him to Glasgow." She fought a wave of dizziness and despair. "The doctor says it isn't a difficult operation. They've sent his test results to Glasgow for evaluation by a specialist to see if they missed anything. They'll have a second opinion by morning."

He held her chin lightly, his eyes more serious than she'd ever seen them. "What about you?"

"Nothing serious." She showed him her bandaged hands wrapped like a mummy's. "Just hold me, Alex. Hold me tight. I'm terrified something will happen to Timmy."

"Do you need any help getting undressed?" Alex asked when he'd managed to get Brett back to Hugh's cottage. Her hands were completely wrapped in thick gauze.

"I shouldn't have left Timmy."

He'd come through the surgery without any problem. They'd visited him in the recovery room, then the doctor insisted Alex take Brett home. "The doctor will call us if there's any change. When he wakes up, Timmy'll be a pistol, hopping around, asking questions. He'll need you. And you won't be worth a damn if you don't get some rest. Now, do you need help?"

She smiled, a tentative half smile, not her melt-your-heart grin, but his heart lifted anyway. It was the first genuine smile she'd given him since Los Angeles. "I'll manage."

"Call me if you need me."

In the guest room he stripped to his shorts and flopped across the bed. When Eula Mae had called, he'd experienced a panic he'd never known before—fear and an overwhelming feeling of powerlessness. He loved Brett and Timmy more than he could ever express. He'd flown to Skye, determined to do what he could.

What now? Saint Owen would return. The best Alex could hope for was that he and Brett could be friends. Sure as hell, he missed her. Running Belage wasn't any fun without her input. Belage. He rolled over, his neck suddenly clammy as he recalled his conversation earlier that day with Bunster Creeley.

"I'd'a' never believed it. Din't think it could happen. I'm belly-up," Bunster had informed him.

Flat broke. And everything Alex had invested to open a Belage store on Rodeo Drive was gone. He'd moped around, cursing his bad luck, feeling sorry for himself. Until Eula Mae called. Then he would have given everything he had—or hoped to have—to be certain Brett and Timmy were all right.

"There is a God," he told himself, thinking how lucky he was that they had survived the crash.

His thoughts drifted, superimposed by Timmy's happy laughter and Brett's captivating smile. Then he began to wonder about Bunster's financial debacle again. Alex had the sneaking suspicion Intelco was responsible. Dash had been ominously silent since their meeting months ago. Alex had expected some reaction to his purchase of the fancies in Antwerp. The phony transaction had never—as far as Alex knew, anyway—been investigated by the cartel.

"Count your blessings," he whispered to himself. Losing the money with Bunster had been a blow, but not a crippling one. As soon as the jewelry Yai had designed for the Harrell Department Stores was delivered, Belage would be flush again. Lev would be home next week and begin setting the collection. No problem.

Maybe he did have a problem. Intelco. His sixth sense still nagged at him, insisting he'd fooled them—too easily. He rose and went into the parlor, hoping to find something to read until he fell asleep. Ahead he saw Brett's silhouette at the bay window facing Portree harbor.

"Why aren't you in bed? It's only a few hours before it'll be time to go back to the hospital."

"Oh, Alex." She turned to him, diamondlike drops beaded on her lashes, her cheeks damp. "I can't sleep. I keep thinking I shouldn't have swerved to avoid that car."

"What car?" Eula Mae hadn't mentioned another vehicle. He listened with bone-chilling apprehension as she described what had happened. An accident? God, he hoped that was all it was. "Did the police take a report?"

"They're looking for the driver. It was probably a tourist, but I blame myself."

"Stop." He put his hands on her shoulders and drew her toward him. "It was an accident. It couldn't be helped."

She edged closer, gingerly putting her bandaged hands around his waist. "But if Timmy had been killed, I don't know what I would have done. Life wouldn't have been worth living."

Boy, did he know that feeling. "Timmy is going to be fine."

"Thank God," she said. "I've never felt so alone. I didn't know what to do." She rested her head against his shoulder, tumbled waves of hair fanning across his bare skin.

This was a side of Brett he hadn't seen, a side he hadn't dealt with before now. He'd never known a mother's love, never experienced its depth or strength. But he instinctively knew what she felt went deeper than tears. Nothing was more powerful than a mother's love.

"It's all right," he said, his arms circling her as they had so many times in the past, as they'd ached to do so many times these lonely months. He stroked the back of her neck, his thumb caressing the mole at the top of her spine.

He held her for a few minutes, loving having her back in his arms, even though she belonged to another man. Her loss had been a lingering pain with images of her intruding at odd, unexpected moments. A parade of women had marched through his life, but there had never been anyone like her. Not before—not again.

"Oh, Alex." Something in her eyes caught him off guard. "I've never felt like this."

Her mouth was so close to his that he could almost feel the throb of her pulse beneath his lips. Gone was her tone-less impersonal voice and the impenetrable barrier she'd kept between them all these months. He was astonished at the sense of fulfillment he experienced at her response to him. She clutched him almost possessively, the way she would someone she trusted. And loved.

"Let's get you back to bed. The doctor insisted you need to sleep." He tucked her against his side and steered her to her room, then eased her down on the bed, taking care not to hurt her bandaged hands or sore knee.

In the shadowy darkness, her eyes seemed unusually large, her pupils dilated. Her intense expression shocked him; it was the same look she'd had a few moments ago. He had the uneasy feeling she was trying to tell him something, and he wasn't getting the message.

"Stay with me." Her voice was a shade lower than a whisper; it took a full second before her meaning registered. "Hold me."

He was struck by the raw emotion in her voice. She needed him in a way no one had ever needed him. But he acknowledged, deep inside, that this might be all he'd ever have with Brett. Owen would have her the rest of his life. He had only tonight.

He slipped between the sheets and gently pulled her into his arms. She snuggled against his chest, her bandaged hands resting on his ribs. He didn't say anything, savoring the texture of her skin beneath his fingertips, the fullness of her breast, the soft rush of her breath across his chest, warming the gold cross he always wore.

Good luck. Years ago, Vic had given him the cross and promised it would bring Alex luck. Had it? Well, maybe. It had certainly given him hope, which was what he had now. Hope that Brett had changed her attitude toward him. Hope that they could work together again. Hope—

"Thanks for coming." Desire flickered in her eyes. Very briefly. But he couldn't have imagined it.

He smoothed his hand over the back of her head, stopping at the nape of her neck. "You can always count on me. You know that, don't you, Brett?"

A few seconds passed before she moved her head against his chest, but he couldn't tell what she meant. Maybe she was thinking of Los Angeles, maybe not. He refused to risk what progress he'd made by discussing that incident.

He studied the starry reflection of the moonlight on the bay visible from the window. Brett was quiet, breathing evenly, and he thought she might have fallen asleep at last. Then she shifted positions, bringing her head up on the pillow beside his.

"Alex?" The caress in her voice alerted him. What the hell was she thinking? That intimate look again. Achingly familiar. Straight out of his too-frequent dreams.

They were so close their noses almost touched, her breath fluttering softly against his cheek. She edged forward, angling her head slightly and touched her lips to his, a fleeting brush of her mouth. She'd kissed him, actually kissed him.

He held himself rigid, his arm still circling her, trying to decide how to respond. He didn't want to make a wrong move. Not after all these months, not after he'd made some progress with her. Not when he loved her so much.

"Make love to me, Alex. I need your strength."

Strength? Make love? Convoluted logic, but then, he'd never understood women. Hell, this was a double-edged sword, that much he knew. She might need him now, and in some crazy way equate what she saw as strength with him. But would she hate him later?

"Please."

The pleading tone in her voice rattled him, an aftershock of her kiss. This was a risk—big-time—but he liked risks. Anyway, what did he have to lose? Before today Brett hated him; it couldn't get much worse.

He kissed her, his lips settling over hers, his arms around her. His tongue probed the moist heat of her mouth with soft yearning kisses, kisses that said much more than he ever could. She moved against him, pressing her hips against his, easing her bandaged knee between his thighs. Her actions were elemental, demanding. He stroked her back, his hands drifting down to her bottom, then he brushed the nightgown upward and cupped her, pressing her hard against his groin.

"Hurry." She fumbled with his shorts.

"No. You'll hurt your hands." He shimmied out of his shorts, and nestled his shaft between her thighs. Her legs were soft and smooth against his hardness. With a sigh that ripped right through him, she eased back and forth, her thighs gripping him. He smiled inwardly; he knew exactly what Brett liked. She rode him in a way that was familiar but more erotic than he'd remembered, gliding back and forth, squeezing with her thighs.

His tongue matched her pace while his hands stroked her bare bottom, exploring the cleft, delighting in the moistness of her skin. She wiggled to a stop, the way she always did, and drew back. He knew exactly what she wanted next. He eased her onto her back and nudged her thighs apart, then entered her with a sleek thrust.

"Please, stop."

Aw, hell, not now. How could she change her mind now? There were a thousand reasons why she should, but why hadn't she thought of them earlier? He froze, even though it took more willpower than he ever dreamed he possessed, propping himself up on his elbows, gazing into her eyes which were almost totally dilated. He eased backward, reluctant to end their embrace.

"Don't move." Her command came from between clenched teeth. She tried to touch his hair, but her fingers were bandaged. "Whenever you're first inside me, I have a flash of pleasure so basic"—she sighed—"I guess you'd call it a miniorgasm."

He held himself in place, hot and achingly hard, but determined to give her what she wanted. Unbuttoning her gown, he bent low and trailed kisses down her neck and across her breasts. As he sculpted one nipple with his tongue, she twisted beneath him, thrusting upward, enticing him to move again.

He did; using unrestrained thrusts, burying his face in the curve of her neck. For him making love to her tonight had nothing to do with sex. Desire, yes, but not sexual desire. He loved her and wanted to be a part of her, a physical union that would lead to an emotional bond. A desire to love and be loved.

He sensed the moment she was going to climax and hugged her tightly. A satisfied moan rewarded him, then he let himself go, his release nothing compared to the aching pang of tenderness he felt for her. Still inside her, he eased her onto her side, holding her close. There were so many things he needed to say, but he was afraid to break the spell. Their bodies still joined, she snuggled against him, her unspoken trust heart wrenching.

He tightened his arm around her. They were one, as close as two people could be. The rapid thud of her heart beneath his hand was the most blissful sound he'd ever heard. He didn't want his body to relax; he was unable to accept giving up his bond with her.

"I love you so much, Brett." He'd never meant the words more, or been less assured of them being accepted.

She didn't answer. Her rapid pulse still throbbed in her throat, but she'd fallen asleep. She was beyond exhaustion, on the verge of emotional collapse. Still, he was disappointed they couldn't talk, admitting that this would be the last time they were so close not just physically, but psychologically.

No matter what the future held, something special had happened tonight. They'd shared anxious hours, seeking comfort in each other, while Timmy had been in surgery.

Tonight. He'd had tonight. And no one could ever take this night away from him.

Brett's breathing returned to normal and their bodies separated, but Alex still held her close. He gazed out the window as the pearl-gray dawn claimed the night. What did this mean? He would have sworn she would never have made love to another man while married. Honest to God, he would never have instigated it. This had been her idea. True, her guard was down, but there had to be more to it than that.

Her marriage was in trouble. She said how alone she felt, but it wasn't just this situation. He'd bet his life it went deeper than that. He sensed she'd been alone for months, emotionally supporting Owen, but not receiving the love she deserved.

And where was Saint Owen right now? Off with Latrice. It didn't take a genius to know Latrice would screw him—literally and figuratively. She'd do anything she could to get Owen to agree to stage the play her way.

How would all this affect Brett? He doubted she'd leave Owen. His hold over her was too powerful. Trust me, she's not leaving Timmy's father.

When she'd married, he had no idea how much he'd miss her, how his love would grow to unimagined heights. Countless nights he'd lain awake, tortured by thoughts of what might have been.

They were perfect together. But not now. Not with Saint Owen hovering. No matter, you still love her. You always will.

39

Brett woke, confused, groggy. Where was she? The half-light of dawn revealed the room. She sat bolt upright in bed, remembering. The car careening down the embankment. Timmy. The ordeal at the hospital. Making love to Alex Savich.

Omigod! Why had she? The answer immediately followed: because she needed him. She had no right to feel this way about him, but she did. Why? She sank back against the pillow, searching for an explanation, but couldn't find one.

As she burrowed against the pillow, she detected the woodsy scent of Alex's after-shave. It triggered a bittersweet current of desire. Desire she had no right to feel.

A blinding rush of passion. She'd waited for it with Owen. Prayed for it. But what she'd experienced with Alex never came. And now she had to face the truth: it never would.

What about Alex, she asked herself. Where did he fit into this? He'd changed somehow during these months they'd been apart. Something was different in his kiss, his touch. Tenderness. Yes, that was there now, but had been missing before. Last night, he'd treated her as if she were a priceless treasure, more precious than a flawless—

"Brett, darling." Suddenly, Alex was gently touching her shoulder. "They need you at the hospital right away."

"Something's happened to Timmy."

"The specialists in Glasgow called about his test results."

His voice was too level, too devoid of emotion. She knew he wasn't telling her everything. "What is it? Tell me."

"It appears Timmy also has a head injury."

"No!" The mind-numbing fear Alex helped her hold at bay for a few hours swept through her, gathering force like a hurricane.

She hardly remembered Alex's helping her dress or his driving her to the hospital as the sun's halo appeared over the Cuillins, or the blue mist that clung to the heather early in the morning, disappearing as the sun warmed the valley. She prayed constantly, asking that her son be spared.

Alex's steady arm around her, they entered the hospital. "I want you to listen to the doctor, then let's review our options. We may decide to move Timmy. While I was waiting for the plane in London, I made some calls. The Great Ormond Street Children's Hospital in London has the best pediatric care in the country. We could Med-Vac him there, if necessary."

Brett managed a nod. It seemed inconceivable that this was happening. But moments later the grim look on the doctor's face assured her this was no dream.

"Your son has a head injury." She heard herself groan, a primitive animallike sound. Alex tightened his grip on her and the doctor went on. "He needs surgery immediately."

"Is there time to fly him to London?" Alex asked.

"Yes, if you can afford it."

She turned to Alex. "The earrings—"

"I have whatever money it takes," Alex cut in.

The orderly wheeled Timmy into his room in the Great Ormond Street Children's Hospital where Alex and Brett had waited while the surgeon, Dr. Ramsey, reviewed the case. Alex studied Brett as they transferred Timmy from the gurney to the bed. Her face was even paler now than it had been on the Med-Vac flight from Skye. She reached out and smoothed her hand across Timmy's head where his hair had been shaved off. The skin was bluish white. Still sedated, he looked angelic; there seemed to be a bit more pink to his cheeks. Or maybe it was just Alex's wishful thinking.

Timmy's eyelids fluttered. "Mommy."

"I'm right here, Timmy." Brett's voice cracked.

Alex whispered, "Act upbeat. Don't frighten him. I'll get the doctor." He rushed down the corridor to the nurses' station and found the doctor. "Timmy's awake, talking to his mother."

"I was just coming to discuss the operation with her." The doctor motioned to a nurse standing nearby. "We'll have to sedate Timmy again and get him into surgery immediately."

Alex turned, hearing Dr. Ramsey whisper to the nurse, "Give the mother a minute. It may be the last time she talks with her son."

The frisson of alarm haunting Alex since the phone call exploded, sending out a shock wave so powerful it brought unexpected tears to his eyes. Oh, God, don't take Timmy. As clearly as if it were happening right now, he saw Timmy sitting on his lap as they rode home after he'd been called a bastard and gotten into a fight. Alex had tried to comfort him by telling him about his own troubled youth.

"Al-wex, I'm sorry they were mean to you." Then Timmy had kissed him on the cheek.

A one-in-a-million kid. He couldn't feel worse if Timmy were his own son. How the hell could he help Brett when his own emotions were spiraling dangerously out of control? He forced the grim expression off his face and marched into Timmy's room.

"Alex." Timmy beamed, a bald gnome, but a happy one. How could he be in critical condition? "You came to see me."

"Yeah, I had to see for myself you were getting better."

Timmy's smile crumpled. "Mommy says they're going to cut me." He touched his head. "It's scary."

Alex squeezed his shoulder. "There's nothing to be afraid of."

Tears sprang into Timmy's eyes. "I'm 'fraid of the dark."

"When Timmy was coming to, he could hear people talking, but he couldn't see them," Brett explained.

"I can fix that," Alex said with false joviality, still not hazarding a glance at Brett. He took off his cross and dangled it in front of Timmy. "My uncle gave me this for luck when I wasn't much older than you are. There's no need to be frightened when you're wearing it because nothing can happen to you." He eased the gold chain around Timmy's neck and fastened the clasp.

Timmy held the cross up, smiling. "I told Mommy you still loved me."

"Why would you think I didn't?"

"You never come to see me anymore."

Alex bent and kissed Timmy's cheek. What right did adults have to do this to children? He remembered how terrified he'd been every time Vic left. Alex had lain awake at night wondering if Vic would ever return. But Timmy had known where Alex was and had known he could have visited him, which must have hurt more.

"Of course, I love you." Alex faced Brett. "I love you both."

A nurse entered carrying a syringe; Timmy's eyes widened.

"Hold on to the cross," Alex directed as the nurse told Brett they were ready for Timmy in surgery. "Be brave."

Timmy clutched the cross, wincing when the needle went in, but he didn't cry out.

"There you go, ducky," the nurse said. "You'll be sleepy in just a minute."

Already Timmy's lids were at half-mast. Alex wished he could say something to make him laugh. He'd like to re-

member him—laughing, smiling. Happy. But Timmy looked
very worried.

"Mom-meeee." He grabbed Brett's hand. With his other
hand, he grasped Alex's wrist. "Don't leave me."

"We won't," Brett assured him.

Timmy's lids fluttered closed. "It's dark."

"Don't worry," Alex said, his voice shot up an octave.
"You have the cross. You don't have to worry about the
dark."

"Alex, promise you'll be here when-n"—his words drifted
off and Alex thought he'd lost consciousness—"when I
wake up."

"He'll be here," Brett answered for Alex.

The moment of silence lengthened. Brett and Alex
looked at each other, unsure what to say.

"I love you, Mommy."

Tears welled up in Brett's eyes. She bent over and kissed
her son's forehead. "I love you, precious. You're the most
important thing in the world to me."

Alex kissed Timmy's cheek, cursing himself for not having
kissed him more when he'd had the chance. Now he might
never have the opportunity again. He was just close enough
to hear Timmy whisper, "Love you, Alex."

He put his lips close to Timmy's ear. "I love you, too."

He waited, but Timmy didn't utter another word. Brett
stroked her son's cheek as the orderlies rolled in the gurney.
They lifted his small body onto the cart, taking care to keep
his head flat, then wheeled him out the door.

"We'll be right here when you come back," Brett called.

She clutched Alex's arm, her concern mirrored in her
eyes. Her expression telegraphed despair, setting off a chain
reaction of anguish in him. What the hell was he going to do
if Timmy did not come back?

Eula Mae knew the Great Ormond Street Children's Hospital had been founded in the mid-1800s but had grown over
the years to become one of the most respected pediatric-

care facilities in the world. Early on, funds to expand the hospital had been given a boost when the author of *Peter Pan*, J. M. Barrie, had donated all the rights to his play to the hospital. Wards were named for various characters in the children's classic. Eula Mae was directed to the Wendy wing, which specialized in head trauma.

Eula Mae paused outside the waiting room, watching Brett and Alex huddled together on the sofa. She'd done the right thing by inventing a back problem and sending Alex. Vic said they belonged together—especially now.

Eula Mae walked forward. "How is Timmy?"

Brett looked up; a lethal calmness masked her usually animated expression. Her face was bruised and scratched, and her hair hung in tangled hanks. Eula Mae longed to hug her, but Alex's sturdy arm was around Brett.

"He's in surgery," Brett said, her voice a monotone.

"The surgeon is trying a new laser technique," Alex said.

My stars! Eula Mae sank into a chair, her mind riveted on the pencil-size laser Lev used. Searing hot. Blue-white light that sliced a finer line than a razor. And five times as sharp.

"He's been in surgery for a little more than an hour," Alex added. "He should be out in another hour or so."

Eula Mae didn't need to ask to know the prognosis was grim. Brett didn't deserve this. She'd been through so much. She was such a good friend. Life wasn't fair. That's what Vic had always said. But couldn't it be fair just this once? Couldn't an innocent child be saved?

She waited beside Brett, her hand on Brett's until she knew she had to leave. "I must meet Amy's flight. We'll be back in a little over an hour."

"You brought Amy and Lev back from their honeymoon?"

"I called them as well as your father," she answered Brett. "I finally reached Owen. His flight arrives late tonight."

"There's nothing Amy can do. I didn't want to ruin—"

"She planned to return anyway. Lev had to go home."

"What?" Alex vaulted to his feet.

"Lev's mother is ill. She's not expected to live." The expression on Alex's face alarmed her. What was wrong now?

"Let me walk you out." Alex hustled her out of the waiting room. "What's this about Lev going to the Ukraine?"

"All I know is what I told you. Amy will know more." Alex looked as if he'd just hit the mat after a knockout punch. She kept Belage's books and knew things were tight. "I know you're anxious for Lev to set the Harrell Collection, but Amy said he'd be back soon."

"I don't give a damn about the collection. It's dangerous for Lev to go to the Ukraine."

"My stars, I thought *perestroika*—"

"There's more to it than that. Tell Amy I don't want her worrying Brett about Lev. Tell her to act as if nothing is unusual about his trip."

"What's wrong?" Eula Mae demanded.

"Let's just say Lev has enemies in the Ukraine who'd like nothing better than to see him dead."

Alex didn't like it—not one damn bit. Too many coincidences. Bunster went belly-up. Brett's car was forced off the road. Now Lev suddenly got word about his mother. Alex's sixth sense told him that Intelco was behind this. Some of it, anyway.

He'd been arrogant to think he could deceive Dash Boynton. Intelco was out to ruin Belage. Aw hell, maybe he was imagining things. But what if he were right and he was responsible for the death of someone he loved? Brett. Timmy. Lev.

"You worthless son of a bitch," he muttered to himself. "You were in such a damn hurry to make money that you never considered who would pay the price."

Intelco didn't target women and children, he reminded himself. If they wanted to ruin Belage, all they had to do was post a notice in the Diamond Clubs. But they wouldn't do that without proof. After all, they cherished their reputations as gentlemen. And they had to retain the goodwill of the diamond trade worldwide.

Maybe he was overreacting. They'd left Skye in such a hurry that he hadn't spoken to the constable investigating the case. It might have been just a tourist who'd caused the accident.

Brett gazed blankly into space, not noticing him as he returned to the waiting room. She was at a point now beyond fear, a point where her emotions had almost shut down. He needed to get her to talk, to share her feelings.

"What was Timmy like as a baby?" he asked.

"You know, there were times that I regretted having Timmy. He was a colicky baby. I spent every night rocking him to sleep."

His heart went out to her, a single mother, raising a child alone. But she'd done a fantastic job.

"I was in labor nine hours." She shook her head. "You can't imagine the pain. With each contraction, I cursed myself for getting pregnant. But now"—her eyes filled with tears—"I'd gladly go through it all again if only . . . if only—"

He put a finger to her lips. "Don't do this to yourself. Think of the good times, the times Timmy was happy."

She took a deep breath. "He talked long before he walked."

"Why am I not surprised?"

"Because I talk so much you think it's genetic." She managed something resembling a smile. "Timmy toddled a few steps on his first birthday, then fell down. He clapped his hands and laughed. He was so proud of himself."

Alex listened while Brett recounted the highlights of Timmy's early years. He covertly checked his watch and discovered the operation was taking much longer than expected. Not a good sign.

Finally a nurse ducked in. "Dr. Ramsey is on his way."

Brett tensed and he put his arm around her, knowing he couldn't protect her if the doctor had bad news. She clasped her bandaged hands together, wringing them. Drops of blood appeared on the gauze; she'd broken the scabs forming over her palms.

Alex eased his hand between hers. She grasped his hand tightly, her fingers struggling to interlace with his. Blood pooled on her bandages, warm and sticky against his fingers. They heard footsteps coming toward the waiting room. Alex pressed a kiss to her temple. For luck.

Dr. Ramsey strode in, his greens spattered with blood. Please, God, let this be good news. Alex could hear Timmy saying, *I love you*. He kept his eyes open wide to hold back the tears.

Dr. Ramsey sank into the chair opposite them, then put his elbows on his knees and leaned toward them. Like a diamond dealer, his expression revealed nothing. "It took longer than I anticipated. I worked slowly, carefully."

"He's going to be all right?" Her voice had an hysterical pitch. "Isn't he?"

"I hope so, but we'll know more when he's conscious, and we can run some tests."

40

Amy followed Eula Mae into the Wendy wing and found Alex in the waiting room. Despite several days' growth of beard, he looked happier than she'd ever seen him. She let out a sigh of relief.

"Timmy survived the operation," Alex explained.

"Is Brett with him?" Eula Mae asked.

"Yes. She'll be back here in a minute. Why don't you wait for her while Amy and I get everyone coffee?"

He ushered Amy into the hall. "What's the story with Lev?"

"Oh, Alex," she said, the anxiety she'd suppressed blossoming as she detected the concern in Alex's voice.

"How'd he find out about his mother?"

"He met an old friend from Kiev in a café. Sasha had just immigrated from the Ukraine, so he'd recently seen Lev's mother and knew she'd been ill." She tried to decipher his expression; there was more to his question than curiosity. "What's wrong?"

Alex hesitated, then said, "I was wondering if it might be a setup. You know, someone trying to lure Lev back to Russia."

"I'm sure not. Lev's known Sasha since they were children. They both hate the Communists. Lev thinks he can slip into Kiev and out again using a counterfeit passport he bought in Tel Aviv. Tell me the truth. What do you think?"

"It's risky. Just last week the Russian Academy of Sciences—the intellectuals of Russia—met to elect new members. They blackballed Jews even though some were world experts in their fields. That tells me *Pamyat*, the anti-Semitic Russian nationalists, are as strong as ever. If one bigot spots Lev—"

Fear nearly overwhelmed her. "I tried to talk, to persuade him not to go. I'm pregnant."

He shook his head. "How could he take a chance like this?"

"Lev tried to explain it to me." Even now she could see Lev's loving gaze as she told Alex about their conversation.

"You think West has monopoly on troubled children?" Lev had asked. "I was a terrible son. For years my mother worry and worry about me. Then I am accused of murder."

"Lev. Your mother wouldn't want you to risk your life."

He'd put his hand on her tummy. "I must see her and tell her about you, about baby. We will name our children after my parents. This I wish her to know. *Milochka*, please understand. I must see her one last time. I cannot let my mother go to her grave without telling her how much I love her."

"That's Lev," Alex commented, his expression still grim. "With luck, he'll be back here soon. Please don't worry Brett with this. She has too many problems right now."

By that evening Jock had returned from Africa and Brett had enough family and friends to give her support, so Alex volunteered to pick up Owen at Heathrow. He waited outside the customs area, hanging back in the crowd, knowing Owen wasn't expecting him, not sure what he was going to say. He spotted Owen walking arm in arm with Latrice. Smiling.

Alex stepped from the crowd. "Northcote, over here."

Owen dropped Latrice's arm. "How's Timmy?"

"Better. The tests indicate he'll recover completely."

"Thank God," Latrice whispered, eking out a photogenic tear, scanning the area for reporters, primed to give them a photo op for tomorrow's tabloids. No one even seemed to recognize her.

"How is Brett?" Owen added.

"She was badly shaken. Stitches. Lots of cuts and bruises." He could have told Owen a lot more. Screw it, let someone else give him the details. They jammed into the Porsche, Latrice half sitting on Owen's lap, her thigh making it impossible for Alex to shift without brushing against her.

"How've you been?" Latrice asked Alex, holding her head at a dramatic angle so her red hair partly covered one eye and shimmered down her cheek to her bare shoulders.

"How do I look?"

"My, so cranky." She winked at Owen who laughed, har, har, har. "You'll be glad to hear we finished the play."

Why the hell would he be glad? The play could only hurt Brett.

"I'll sign the deal soon," Northcote said with pride.

"The story of your life is now Brett's story, right?"

"I say, don't be ridiculous." Owen bristled but managed a terse har, har, har for Latrice's benefit. "Do I look stupid?"

Alex was damn tempted to give him an honest answer.

Owen's arm was around Latrice's waist, his hand idly stroking the back of her bare arm. A casual gesture, yet one that signaled intimacy. Not that Alex was under any illusion about their relationship. Latrice knew what she wanted and how to get it. Leading Northcote around by his cock. Hey, he'd be willing to make a trade. Owen was welcome to Latrice. He'd take Brett.

She'd tapped a wellspring of tenderness, a need to protect at all costs, a depth of emotion he never suspected existed. But he doubted she would leave Saint Owen. After all, he was Timmy's father. In a moment of weakness, she'd turned to Alex and made love to him. But he'd bet his life that was as far as he'd get.

During the drive into London, Alex listened while they talked about the play. No more questions about Timmy or Brett. He didn't have a clue how close she'd been to a breakdown. Or how much support she still needed. With Owen it was the play, the play, the play. Har, har, har.

Alex double-parked in front of the hospital. "Wait here," he told Latrice. "I'll be right back." He walked Owen to the entrance, then stopped. "Brett needs you right now. She has no idea you were screwing Latrice—"

"I was not. How dare you?"

"Don't bullshit me. I know—"

"I don't have to listen to this." Owen turned away.

Alex grabbed Owen and slammed him against the wall. "Look, you bastard, Brett needs you. If she even suspects what went on with Latrice, I'll beat the shit out of you." Alex let him go and rushed back to the car.

"Darling." Latrice reached for him, but he turned his head and she smacked him on the cheek. "Don't pout. You know I would rather have been with you, but this was business."

Alex floored the Porsche and it rocketed down the street.

"This part will be fabulous for me," Latrice said, but he didn't respond. "The message about the kid saved me. Gawd, was I bored. I almost had to spend another week with Owen."

"Glad the accident fit into your plans."

His sarcasm kept her quiet until they passed Harrods, then she asked, "How seriously injured was the kid?"

"His name is Timmy. The doctor told Brett there was every possibility they'd lose him on the operating table."

"Really? He almost died?"

"It was touch and go. We almost lost him." The minute he said "we" he regretted his choice of words.

Latrice was gazing at him with a knowing smile on her face. "You were with Brett the whole time?"

"No." Not a lie exactly, but he didn't want Latrice tattling. "You're happy with the play," he said, to change the subject.

"I wasn't quite satisfied with the final scene, but this is just what I'm after. The valiant mother, threatened with the death of her beloved son."

Alex slammed on the brakes, nearly getting rear ended. He stormed out of the car and yanked open her door. "Get out."

"I know you're angry because I slept with Owen." Honest to God, she had shit for brains. He was afraid if he touched her, he'd deck her. "Get out."

She climbed out of the low-slung car, her famous pout in place. "I think you're jealous of Owen. He's famous, a hero. And he's made love to me. You've been stuck nursemaiding his wife."

"True. Right now, I wish I were in his shoes."

By the end of the week, Timmy was much better. Alex checked in at the hospital every day, so Timmy knew he cared, but he never stayed too long. He was determined not to make Owen suspicious about his relationship with Brett. He never had a chance to be alone with her, which was just as well; he didn't want to tell her about the situation at Belage.

Without Lev, he'd been forced to have Tsung set the Harrell Collection. Since Tsung was a novice with a laser, it would probably be Christmas before he had a quarter of the collection set. If they didn't deliver on time, Belage would be even shorter of cash. Alex stared out his office window, wondering if Intelco was behind his problems.

Eula Mae peeked into his office. "There is a Constable MacIntosh on the line."

With money so short, he'd been forced to let employees go. Eula Mae functioned as secretary, receptionist, and bookkeeper. He answered the telephone, wondering what the policeman in Skye assigned to Brett's case had discovered.

"We haven't located the driver that ran Mrs. Northcote off the road. We're convinced it was a tourist who'd sampled a bit more scotch at the MacLeod distillery than he should have."

Alex hung up, positive the cartel was behind Brett's accident. They would never have allowed their man to be found. So, he wasn't being paranoid. Intelco had targeted Belage. *Maskirova*, hell. He'd been an arrogant jerk to believe the cartel would let him get away with selling those fancies.

Granted, they couldn't have proof or they would have posted notices in the Diamond Clubs worldwide, but they were convinced he'd sold their fancies. Since they couldn't ruin Alex through official channels, they were out to destroy Belage.

Eula Mae rushed in. "There's a call from Russia on line two."

Grabbing the receiver, Alex grinned. "Lev?"

"No." A hollow echo followed. "Boris Tenklov."

Alex's shoulders sagged. Where the hell was Lev? "Yeah?"

"Your friend is being held by the Red Army."

"Aw, shit."

"What would you do to get him out?" Out echoed ominously.

"You're pissing into the wind if you think a Jew is going to get a 'not guilty' verdict from the Soviet brass."

The military was more corrupt than *apparatchiks*, party bureaucrats. Like the core of a rotten apple. Bribing them to free a Jew—no way. Red Army officers were rabid Jew-haters.

"I said nothing about a trial. It may be possible to get Rodynskov out before his court-martial."

Fat chance. The Soviet military was bloated with soldiers; most of them were posted as guards. The only way would be to bribe hundreds of men. "How much?"

"No money. Come to Kiev—now." Tenklov hung up.

Alex slumped back, the receiver still in his hand. This had to be what it felt like to be buried alive. So much had gone wrong lately. If he left Belage now, chances were he'd lose it. But if he didn't give it up, he'd lose everyone he loved.

Amy saw Alex walking into THE FIND and knew something had happened to Lev. She put her hand on her tummy and sucked in her breath, braced for the worst. "Lev's in trouble, isn't he?"

Alex put a steadying hand on her shoulder, and she realized she'd begun to shake. "He's in prison, but I think I can get him out." Her lips formed the word how, but nothing came out. "Boris Tenklov is going to help."

"Tenklov? I never trusted him," she muttered. "Do you need money? All I have is a small trust fund, but I'll sell everything. I'll even go to my father—"

"I don't need money. If I do, I've left a power of attorney with Eula Mae authorizing the sale of Belage's diamonds."

"How can I help?" she asked, stunned that Alex was willing to sacrifice Belage to save Lev. The men shared a bond that she'd never understood, and had sometimes resented, but now she sensed only Alex had the power to help Lev. She felt a rush of affection toward Alex, a man she'd often considered to be distant, even cold.

"I don't want Brett worrying about Lev. Don't tell her he's in jail." He pulled a piece of paper out of his pocket. "I need you to pick up a few things for me, so I can leave as quickly as possible."

"Who was at the door?" Brett asked Ellis as she stood in her kitchen watching Ruth prepare tea. Since Timmy had been released yesterday, she'd needed help because her hands hadn't healed. Huge scabs had formed on her palms, but she had to be careful not to flex her hands or the bleeding would begin again.

As usual Owen was out working on the play, but she had

Jock and Ruth to help her as well as Daphne and Ellis. She had to admit her entire family—even Ruthless—had been amazingly supportive.

"That was Alex Savich at the door," Ellis answered. "He had a present for Timmy, so I sent him straight up." He handed her a colorful bouquet. "He brought these forget-me-nots for you."

Brett took them, aware of Ruth's scrutinizing stare. Timmy missed Alex. She missed him more. By the time Owen had arrived at the hospital, the crisis was over. He'd been attentive, but she didn't feel nearly as close to him as she did to Alex.

She hurried upstairs and met Jock on his way down. "Alex brought Timmy a globe. They're marking places you've been."

She went up alone, pausing on the landing, hearing Timmy's laughter, a bright happy sound she once thought she'd never hear again. Alex was great with Timmy. Owen had tried; she couldn't fault him, but he didn't have time for him. No. There was more to it than that. Owen was more obsessed with his own interests than with spending time with his son.

"You're not afraid of the dark anymore, are you?" she heard Alex ask Timmy.

"Naw. I have your cross."

"Good. I have to go away on business. I want you to take care of your mother while I'm gone."

"I will." Timmy sounded as sad as Brett felt.

She started into the room and saw Alex's reflection in the mirror as he kissed Timmy. Did any man have the right to possess so much masculine vitality?

"Don't forget me," Alex said, a strange unevenness to his voice.

Brett stepped into the room. "Thanks for the flowers."

He nodded, a casual gesture, yet one filled with virile appeal. She fought the urge to hurl herself into his arms.

"I have to run," he said, "I have a plane to catch."

"I'll walk you out." Brett waited by the door while Alex kissed Timmy good-bye again. She headed down the stairs, looking over her shoulder at Alex. "Going on a trip?"

"Yeah. I've left Eula Mae instructions about Belage."

She opened the door, welcoming the blazing August sunshine and the planters full of multihued impatiens shielded from the sun by the wide canopy of the plane tree. Since she'd nearly lost Timmy, she appreciated life more now. Little things she'd hardly noticed like the graceful branches of the tree planted in Cromwell's time had new meaning for her now.

She halted halfway to the street. "I don't know how to thank you—" She paused for a thought-clearing breath. She didn't know how to express herself because she hadn't come to terms with the way she felt about Alex. Gratitude or something deeper? Something forbidden. And it was difficult to align this new Alex with the elusive man she'd thought she knew. "I'm selling my mother's earrings so I can repay you—"

"Don't. Keep them. We'll work out something later."

"All right." She touched his arm, recalling how compassionate he'd been. "I don't know what to say. You've been wonderful."

He looked at her a moment, his deep blue eyes searching her face. "Don't say anything, just listen. I meant what I said at the hospital. I love you. I love you both."

She parted her lips to cut him off. She didn't want to have this discussion. Not now. She couldn't go on with Owen; she'd decided that before the accident. But she honestly didn't know how she felt about Alex.

Totally absorbed by her son, she'd barely been aware of Owen's progress with the play. He'd sold it, that much she knew, but little else. On a personal level, she knew just as little about herself. She hadn't concentrated on anything but Timmy's recovery.

Alex touched her lips with his finger. "Listen. I know what you *think* you saw in L.A., but I never would have slept with that woman. She followed me into the bungalow and started putting her hands all over me when—"

Brett squeezed her eyes shut, against the intense sunlight and the even more intense emotional reaction his words evoked. Never forget there are two sides to Alex Savich.

"Look at me. Don't shut me out. Not now."

There it was again, the unevenness she'd detected in his voice when she overheard him telling Timmy not to forget him. She eased her eyes open. His face loomed in front of hers, his lips disturbingly close to hers.

"I swear, I was throwing her out when you walked in." He leaned even closer and she expected him to kiss her. "I've loved you from the first night I met you. Nothing's ever going to stop me from loving you."

The sincerity in his tone and his tormented expression wrenched at her heart. More than anything, she wanted to believe him.

His arms curved possessively around her, crushing her against him as his lips closed over hers, his tongue invading her mouth, seeking hers. The taste of him, the strength of his arms, the easy sweep of his hand down her back was more arousing than ever. His tongue danced against hers, gliding back and forth, mating with hers. There was a roughness, an urgency to his kiss that went beyond desire. She'd made love to him countless times, but she'd never felt he wanted her as desperately as he did now.

And she'd never wanted him more.

He drew back, his eyes shielded by thick tiers of lashes, but there was no mistaking the emotion in his voice. "No matter what happens, never doubt I love you."

He released her and rushed toward the curb where his Porsche was parked. Her hand pressed to her lips, she watched until the car disappeared around the corner. That wasn't an ordinary kiss, she realized, remembering how Alex had kissed her on her wedding day. With overwhelming anguish, with desperation. The kind of kiss meant to express what words never could.

A good-bye kiss. The thought registered, then she recalled what he'd told Timmy: "Don't forget me." And what he'd just said to her, "No matter what happens"—was something going to happen?—"never doubt I love you."

The flowers. He'd never brought her flowers before, but today he'd given her a bouquet of forget-me-nots.

VI
THE CRUCIBLE

41

"Is Lev in trouble?" Brett asked.

Amy quickly looked away. Lying to Brett wasn't going to be easy. She would never have gotten away with it this long except Brett had been too absorbed with Timmy to notice how worried Amy was about Lev's visit to his mother. "Why?"

"Alex has left on a trip, but he didn't say where." She shook her head. "I have a terrible feeling about this. I've been racking my brain, trying to think what is wrong. What could it be except Lev?"

"Are you sure you're not imagining things?" Amy hedged.

"Absolutely not." Brett gazed at her; Amy knew the only reason Brett didn't think she was lying was because they'd never—in almost twenty years of being best friends—lied to each other.

Brett dropped onto Amy's sofa and Amy eased down beside her. "Is there something you're not telling me?"

Amy couldn't resist. She spilled out the whole story, her voice a controlled monotone to keep herself from breaking down.

"So Alex smuggled Lev out once before," Brett said. "He never told me. There's so much he never mentioned."

"He's positive he can do it again. He had me get dozens of pornographic videos and fill a suitcase with Levi's and cigarettes, so he would have things for bribes."

They sat in silence, the only sound the rhythmic ticking of the grandfather clock against the far wall. Then Brett scooted closer to Amy and touched her arm with her bandaged hand.

"There has to be something we can do here. Hugh will be back from Peru soon. Perhaps he can help us. That's one thing. I'm certain we can come up with other ideas."

Amy sighed, relieved. This was the old Brett, taking charge, not the stranger who'd walked around the hospital half ghost, half robot.

"My stars," Eula Mae cursed, hovering over the magnifying glass, annoyed at the insistent pounding on her flat's door. She had a male and a female kiwi seed corralled in the petri dish, filamentlike follicles growing into each other. Mating. At last. But if she didn't spritz them with nutrients soon, they'd dry out and she'd have to start over.

She opened the door, and Brett sailed in. "I want you to be totally honest with me. How are things at Belage?"

Alex had warned Eula Mae not to worry Brett, yet he wanted her to help while he was away. How did he expect Brett not to guess the truth?

"We've had to let a lot of the staff go, but we're making it. Alex wants you to call Thomas Wiltgrin from the Harrell Department Stores. You'll have to explain to him that we'll be late delivering the collection."

"I will, but what about the expensive advertising campaign for the Harrell Collection?"

"Alex wants you to approve the final drafts. Yai Tsung was going to do it, but she hasn't come in for the last few days."

"Do you think she's found another job?"

"I don't know." Eula Mae had no use for the cold Oriental woman who'd love to take Brett's place. "I don't trust her."

"Why not?"

"I don't know. It's just a feeling."

Brett studied Eula Mae for a moment, then asked, "Alex told you about Lev and his problems, didn't he?"

Eula Mae saw no reason to deny it. "Yes."

Brett slapped one bandaged hand into the other. "Then why didn't Alex tell me?"

"He was protecting you. Can't you see how much he loves you?"

"Yes," she answered, her voice pinched with emotion. "I-I guess I knew—deep down—when he came to Skye. He behaved just exactly the way I wanted . . ." her voice trailed off.

"The way you'd hoped Owen would act."

"True. So true."

Eula Mae was tempted to encourage Brett to leave Owen, but it had to be her decision. And she wouldn't make it easily.

"I have this terrible feeling Alex isn't coming back."

Eula Mae stared at the petri dish, vaguely aware that the kiwis were drying out. But the years she'd spent trying to mate them didn't matter if she lost Alex, the son she'd never had. An overpowering need to share her concerns with Brett assailed her—even if Alex had specifically instructed her not to worry Brett.

"Before Alex left, he had the solicitor draw up papers giving you and me the power to act on his behalf. Alex wants Belage's current orders filled—then we're to liquidate its assets. He also gave you permission to liquidate his personal possessions—the Porsche, the penthouse—if necessary."

"He must have done it so we could raise money to help Lev."

"No." She stared down at the petri dish, abstractedly noting the kiwis' follicles were totally dry now, but not caring. The talk she'd had with Alex just after the telephone call from Russia had been a precious moment. Alex was nothing like Vic, who'd shared his problems with her from the first. She'd caught Alex off guard and coaxed the story out of him.

"Alex believes Intelco is behind Bunster's bankruptcy and your accident. He's not willing to risk your life. He intends to give Intelco what it wants by closing Belage."

"Does he have a shred of proof?"

Eula Mae shook her head. "Intelco has been rumored to—"

"Rumors. But has anyone ever proven anything? No. This would be attempted murder. I spoke with the authorities in Skye. A tourist left the MacLeod Distillery and was reported to be driving recklessly. They never found him. He probably hopped on the ferry to the mainland."

Eula Mae admitted it was possible. Skye was a small island with a short ferry ride to Scotland.

Brett looped a strand of hair behind her ear, gazing across the flat. "You never met Bunster Creeley, but believe me, he was one of those highfliers who could easily get into financial trouble."

"Perhaps," Eula Mae conceded. "It did sound a bit farfetched. I wondered if Alex might be feeling guilty, knowing he'd sold Intelco's diamonds."

"I think Alex is overreacting, trying to protect me from anything and everything that can possibly hurt me. I'm not going to let him give up Belage just because of some unfounded suspicions."

Brett returned home that evening after visiting Amy and Eula Mae. Naturally, Owen had gone out. She thanked Jock and Ruth for watching Timmy, being especially nice to Ruth, who was proving to be a better grandmother than Brett ever could have imagined. She mounted the stairs, worried about Belage, and concerned about her father's business, too. The economic climate in England had soured; building projects in the Docklands, which had once been the old East India docks, had faltered, threatening her father's financial security. It wasn't fair. He'd worked all his life. Alex was still young and would have time to recover.

Even so, Alex deserved better. He was a silent hero. He'd protected Lev, and he'd never mentioned what he'd done to help her with Timmy. If she could save Belage for him, she'd do it.

She walked into her bedroom, weary, but not ready to sleep, and saw Owen's script on the nightstand. RETURN FROM HELL was emblazoned across the cover, looking very official. When Timmy's life had hung in the balance, she'd decided some things weren't important. Let Owen do what he wanted with the play.

But on another level, she was curious. Since Timmy's accident she'd been sleepwalking through life, allowing the world to drift by and concentrating only on Timmy. Today's events proved she couldn't trust to fate that things would work out.

It took her almost two hours to read the script, then she turned off the light and sat in the darkness. The play was nothing more than a melodrama filled with half-truths and gross exaggerations of her suffering. She could just imagine Latrice on stage pathetically wailing as Timmy lay near death.

The play never mentioned Alex's role in building her career. Instead, he was cast as an arch-villain she'd tossed aside when Owen returned. Knowing the truth about Alex crystallized her feelings, a bedrock of emotion she'd kept hidden even from herself. She loved Alex, loved him with as much intensity as she loved Timmy, but with a passion she'd struggled to deny.

Over the edge. She was so much in love with Alex that the depth of her love frightened her. And she had no doubt he loved her. But the catch in her heart remained when she recalled the incident in L.A. Had he intended to throw the blonde out as he claimed? It took mental gymnastics to imagine a man with an erection like a stick of dynamite turning away from that woman.

Did it matter? Of course not. She wasn't free to marry him—not that he'd asked. She was crazy about Alex, but to destroy her family went against everything she believed. For as long as she could remember, she'd fought to recapture the happy-childhood feeling that her parents' divorce had destroyed. She wanted that cornerstone of security and love for her son.

Was the kind of life she longed for possible with Owen? Not now. And she doubted it ever would be. What was she going to do?

She heard Owen tiptoe in. "I'm awake," she said.

He flicked on the light and saw the script she still held in her hand. "I say, isn't it a smash? It's going to make us rich." He sat down on the bed beside her. "I invested what they gave me for the story in the play. I'll get a percentage of the profits. We—" He caressed her shoulder.

He broke off, an intent look in his pale blue eyes. She imagined him making love to her, and her stomach became queasy. She'd spent so much time at the hospital there hadn't been an opportunity until now. Suddenly, a wave of disloyalty hit her full force. Only the man you loved had the right to make love to you, she thought. Alex. But the thin gold band on her finger mocked her, shining brightly even in the dim light.

"I say," Owen continued, "we could make boodles if we invested more money. They're still lining up backers."

So the lust in his eyes wasn't for her. It was a deep-seated desire for fame and fortune. Self-love, nothing more.

"If you sold those earrings—"

"No. I need the money."

"What could be more important than my play?"

Everything, anything, she wanted to scream. She'd thought about selling the earrings, deciding to wait until they knew more about Lev's situation. She'd sell the earrings in a second to save Lev. If that wasn't necessary, she'd use the funds for Belage. "I may need the money to save Belage."

"It's that bastard Savich, isn't it?"

"Don't call him that," she warned, her voice a whisper, afraid if she used a normal tone she'd lose control and scream at him.

"Savich conned you out of the money that's rightfully mine."

His words jolted her. "Rightfully yours?"

"As your husband, your property should be mine."

His logic amplified the feeling that had dogged her for months. She didn't know this man. She never had. She was nothing but a romantic fool, who'd viewed the world through a lover's eyes. She remembered—or maybe only imagined—the love her parents had shared. She'd been so determined to recapture that magic that she'd never taken a really close look at this man.

"Alex told Latrice he's jealous of me. I'm a hero, some-one special—"

"Alex is special. When I needed him, he helped me. And now I'm going to help him."

"So Alex told you. Latrice said he would."

"Told me what?" The deceptive calm to her voice was a counterpoint to her inner turmoil. Alex spent too much time protecting her. Now what?

Owen's mouth pulled into his little-boy smile. "Believe me, I never meant for it to happen, but Latrice and I—well, there was a mutual attraction neither of us could help."

"You're having an affair with her." His confession should have shocked her, but it didn't. She'd told herself he was too honorable to cheat on her and chalked up the time he spent with Latrice to his play. "Why are we married when you're having an affair with another woman and I love another man?"

"You love Savich," he bellowed. "Latrice said so. The night of his party she noticed he couldn't keep his eyes off you. I should have known better than to trust you. Your mother—"

"Get out!" The resentment she'd held at bay so many months flared into anger and resignation. She'd made a terrible mistake.

"I'll tell you one thing. There isn't a court in this country that won't give me custody of my son."

42

"What did the solicitor say?" Eula Mae asked when Brett trudged into Belage the following afternoon.

"It isn't likely that Owen will be granted custody of Timmy *unless*—that's the key word—*unless* he can prove I'm an unfit mother. Undoubtedly, he'll dig up all the old skeletons like my arrest record. It's bound to get ugly."

"My stars, you'd think he'd want to protect Timmy."

"You'd be wrong. The attorney says there's a good chance I'll have to sell the earrings and give Owen a portion of the money to appease him."

"My stars, I can't believe it."

"Come on. We can't worry about it now. We've got work to do." Brett walked into Alex's office. "Did you reach Yai?" The designer hadn't reported to work for over a week.

"Her number's been disconnected."

"Really? What does Tsung say?" Yai's uncle worked late each night, trying to set the Harrell Collection.

"He hasn't seen her. If you ask me, it's suspicious."

"Would you mind going to her flat to check on her?"

Eula Mae left, and the phone on Alex's desk rang several times before she remembered there was no receptionist to answer it.

"Give me Savich," demanded a man with a New York accent.

"Mr. Savich is away on business. This is Brett Lamont, head designer. I'm in charge until he returns."

"Thomas Wiltgrin." She recognized the name of the CEO of Harrell Department Stores. "Tell Savich I'm terminating our contract."

"Why?" she gasped.

"Every knock-off shop in New York is selling what is supposed to be the *exclusive* Harrell Collection."

"Impossible. Those designs are right here in our safe."

"Your security stinks." He slammed down the receiver.

She dropped into Alex's chair and stared out the window at the Intelco building on Charterhouse Street. This was every elite jeweler's worst nightmare, their designs copied by jewelers who set with "faux gems." Eventually most top-notch jewelers' designs were knocked off—with slight variations to keep them legal. But to have an entire collection duplicated *before* it went on the market would bring most houses to the brink of disaster. Cancellation of this contract would be the death knell for Belage.

How could this have happened? Yai's portfolio for the Harrell Collection was in the safe on top of the few designs Brett had created for Philippe Deauville. There was only one way those designs could have turned up in New York. Yai didn't need the portfolio; she had every design in her head.

Brett found Tsung in his workroom. He held the laser, its blue-white light reflected in his protective goggles.

"Turn that thing off. There's no point in setting anymore. Yai sold our designs to knock-off artists. The order has been cancelled. Belage will be forced to close."

Tsung pulled off the glasses, his black eyes alarmed.

"How could you two do that to Alex?" Brett demanded. "He gave you jobs when everyone is dying to get out of Hong Kong before the Communists take over."

"I had nothing to do with it," Tsung assured her, his

English halting, his voice quivering with emotion. "I would never do such a thing to my friend."

"But you knew Yai sold those designs, didn't you?"

"No," he said. "She said she found a better job in Antwerp that begins in September. I tell her it is not honorable to leave, but she not listen."

"She left without giving notice or asking for a reference? Didn't that make you suspicious?"

"No," Tsung said. "She is always a disgrace to my brother. She put herself before family. Now she bring shame on me."

Brett felt sorry for him. She'd had little to do with Yai, but she'd had the definite impression that the girl was obsessively ambitious, not unlike Owen. But who would give her a job without references or a track record? Something was wrong here.

"Do you know where she is?" Brett knew Eula Mae wouldn't find Yai at her flat.

The address Tsung gave her was on "Millionaires' Row," adjacent to Kensington Palace. Many of the mansions had been converted to embassies and were guarded by the Diplomatic Police, who watched her as she walked by. The deep shadows cast by the stately trees and the fickle breeze off the Thames cooled her as she punched the buzzer on the gate, ignoring the pack of snarling Rottweilers baring their fangs on the other side.

"Yes?" squawked the intercom.

"Anneke Holme from Antwerp Diamonds." She faked a Dutch accent and used the name of the jeweler who would soon employ Yai.

Two Chinese guards appeared at the door up the walk from the gate and snapped their fingers. The attack dogs retreated to the far side of the yard and sat, panting, fangs glistening.

The interior of the Regency mansion was furnished like a pagoda, and Brett was taken to wait in a chamber where the scent of incense drifted across the room from the cupped hands of the jade Buddha in the corner. Yai hurried into the room then spun around, set to run when she saw Brett. But Brett slammed the door shut and stood with her back against it, facing Yai.

"What do you want?" Yai asked, her tone belligerent.

"You've ruined Belage by selling your designs."

Yai didn't care enough to deny it.

"We're stuck with hundreds of diamonds cut specifically for your designs. We can't sell them. We can't set them."

"Sell them as *melee*." She was cool, too cool.

"*Melee*? They're top-quality stones and you know it." Brett glared at Yai, wondering if she'd ever hated anyone this much. "How could you do that to Alex? If he hadn't given you this job, you'd be stuck in Hong Kong."

Yai's almond eyes narrowed, and Brett saw a reflection of her own hate. "I thought Alex would give me a chance to become head designer, but all he wanted was a workhorse to design the mass-market jewelry. It would always be Brett Lamont—never me."

She jabbed at the air in front of Brett with her index finger. "And you—the great Brett Lamont—weren't doing anything but hacking out the same old tired designs. You're a has-been, but he loves you too much to see the truth."

For a split second, Brett closed her eyes, cursing herself for doing this to Alex. "Who did you sell the designs to? You didn't fly to New York. Someone in London paid you for those designs, and arranged for your new job. Who?"

"You have no right to question me. Move aside."

Brett crossed her arms, elbows out, and spread her legs for balance, assuming the protester's stance, the same stance her mother had taught her when she was twelve and they'd barricaded the American nuclear facility north of London, the same stance Brett had taught Vicktor Orlov when they'd protested the slaughter of elephants outside the Japanese Embassy. The same stance that had landed her in jail for protecting the badgers.

"Alex has paid a fortune in advertising. It's going to make your name famous in jewelry circles."

That brought Yai up short. "Really? He never said—"

"The space has been reserved for months; the campaign set. It's too late for Belage to get money back. Unless you tell me the name of the person you sold those designs to, I'm filling every inch of that ad space telling the world you're a thief."

Yai tossed her head, her long hair sifting over her silk blouse, but she didn't look nearly as confident as she had seconds earlier. "No one will believe you."

"Maybe not, but there'll always be a shadow on your name. You know this business is too small for that. No master jeweler will ever trust you again."

Yai turned and walked to the Buddha, then knelt before his smoking hands. "I don't know who it was. He offered me money, a fresh start in Antwerp."

"What did he look like?"

"I only spoke with him on the telephone. The money was delivered by messenger. Then the job offer came, and someone called, telling me to stay here until September."

"There must be something, anything that you can tell me. Otherwise I'm running those ads."

"The man on the telephone had a British accent."

"Super. Millions of Englishmen have British accents."

"He was born here, not in the colonies like Hong Kong. I could hear the difference. He had an Oxford accent and he kept saying 'Dash it all.' "

Dash Boynton. So Alex's instincts had been correct. The cartel was out to ruin Belage. To ruin the man she loved.

Intelco couldn't have any proof or they would have posted a notice in the Diamond Club. What they'd done was underhanded and sneaky—totally against the British sense of fair play the cartel prided itself on, but it was effective. Belage and Alex's reputations were ruined.

In a way, she was relieved to know the truth. She'd been concerned for Timmy's safety. If Intelco had been behind the accident, she didn't know how she would protect her son in the future. But now she knew the accident was just that— an accident. Intelco hadn't needed to resort to murder to ruin Belage and her career. They had Yai Tsung.

Brett was frustrated. She wasn't her mother's daughter; she wasn't the woman worthy of Alex's love if she didn't fight for what she believed in. The trouble was, she didn't know how to take on Intelco. But she'd think of something.

Brett returned home and thanked Daphne for spending the entire day with Timmy. He was asleep, his fire engine beside his bed, and the globe, map tacks glowing in the dark, on the dresser. Thank heaven she didn't have to explain to him tonight that his father wasn't coming home.

Brett climbed into bed, her mind filled with thoughts of Alex. What she'd say to Alex. How she'd save Belage. Pipe dreams—nothing more. If only she had the chance to see Alex again.

Finally she drifted off to sleep without watching Ellis give the late-night weather forecast. She clutched the pillow, dreaming about Alex. He was back again. Larger than life again. Holding her tight again.

At other moments, he was remote. Unreachable. But always she felt the power of his love. For her. For Timmy. If he'd only return, they could start over if Belage failed.

She was dreaming she was in Alex's strong arms, Timmy playing nearby, when she detected an odd noise. The telephone, she realized groggily. She picked it up.

"Brett, it's Amy. Turn on the telly."

"Television?" Brett scrambled to all fours, peering at the dial of the alarm clock. Fifteen minutes until it rang at six as the stations came on the air. Nothing short of an international crisis was on the telly this early in the morning. She clicked the remote control and the Kremlin sprang across the screen. "What's happening?"

"The Red Army is backing a coup to oust Gorbachev,"

Amy said, her voice filled with panic. "They've closed the borders. Stopped flights. No one is getting out of there."

"Maybe Lev and Alex already left," Brett suggested, knowing it was a long shot. "Or maybe this will be good for them. The army's bound to be tied up with this coup."

"Remember Tiananmen Square. The tanks mowed those people down in seconds. Then the army was stronger than ever. Crueler."

Brett couldn't deny it. She'd worked these past months on Hugh's new fax campaign to alert Amnesty International members to the government's slave-labor camps, pleading with people not to buy anything with a *Made in China* label.

"Look, they're surrounding the White House."

Brett watched as tanks circled the Russian Parliament building, thinking this couldn't be happening to Alex. But it was.

43

"The Russian people are behind Yeltsin. The army won't dare attack with the whole world watching, will they?" Brett asked Hugh MacLeod the day after the coup began.

"I'm optimistic," Hugh admitted, looking tired, having returned from Lima and come directly to visit her. "If the coup leaders had guts, they'd cut the phone lines and throw out the TV crews."

"But they haven't. Yeltsin keeps giving interviews. Pizza Hut just delivered a hundred pizzas to the men defending the White House. Now they're munching on pepperoni pizzas and sending faxes all over the world. With all that craziness going on, you'd think Alex would be able to contact us."

"Things may be different in Kiev than they are in Moscow. The crack units of the Russian army, Black Berets, are headquartered in the Ukraine. The coup leaders need the support of the military, particularly in the key provinces like the Ukraine."

Her stomach churned with anxiety, the way it had since the moment she'd kissed Alex good-bye. "What do you think will happen to Alex and Lev?"

"Nothing until the outcome of this coup is clear."

"Waiting is hard on Amy. She's due in late December, you know. She needs Lev. I'm all she has right now."

"She saw you through Timmy's birth. You can handle this."

"You're right. Amy and I can handle the baby. But I'm so worried about Alex. When he left, he said good-bye, not just an 'I'll see you later' good-bye, but a final good-bye." The thought weighed her down, making it difficult to speak. "For some reason, he doubted he'd return."

"But he took the chance. That's Alex."

"Yes. He took a chance helping Lev the first time. He gambled he could make me a star. Then he pushed Belage, taking one chance too many."

Earlier, she'd explained about Belage's difficulties, and Hugh had applauded the way she'd handled Yai. "I'm trying to keep Belage afloat for Alex. Tsung was so upset by what Yai did that he's working for nothing. Eula Mae's living off her savings. Of course, I'm not taking any money."

"Still having a creative block?"

"No. Since my hands healed, I've sketched dozens of designs. My problem is using the same shape of stones Lev cut for the Harrell Collection. I haven't a prayer of saving Belage unless I can use those diamonds."

She wasn't certain but she thought Hugh's mind was on Alex. "It's crazy, isn't it? This is the second time I've asked you to help me find a man."

"The last time, he was the love of your life."

"I was wrong." All evening she'd skated around the subject of her divorce. "It's hard for me to admit this to you—since I spent so many hours crying on your shoulder, positive I couldn't face life without Owen. I was mistaken. The only thing we have in common is Timmy. Owen's filed for a divorce."

Hugh didn't look surprised.

"And he's trying to take Timmy away from me."

"He is?" Hugh scowled. "I'm sorry to hear that."

"I don't want Timmy to grow up without me the way I

grew up without Mother. But I have to face the possibility it could happen. Remember, my father was granted sole custody of me."

He hesitated, measuring her for a moment. "Your mother never asked for custody."

"Of course she did." Then she saw the truth in his eyes. "She didn't? Omigod! Why not?"

"Never doubt that your mother loved you. But helping others appealed to her more than staying at home and raising a child."

"My father never told me." She stared at the pink scar tissue running from her palms to the tips of her fingers. What were scars when she had Timmy? She'd never give him up, but her mother hadn't felt that way. Disappointment swelled inside her and with it anger at herself. "All this time, I blamed my father. Why didn't you tell me?"

"Your mother didn't want to disillusion you, and your father loved her too much to destroy your image of her. She belonged to the world, not to one man or one child."

"I don't understand a mother giving up her child. But then, I never understood Mother. I know I disappointed her when I left relief work, but I couldn't take it any longer."

"She would have been terribly proud of you."

"Because of a few badgers? And letters to help prisoners in slave camps in China? She saved thousands of lives."

"If everyone helped a little, the world would be a better place. Constance understood that."

Brett didn't know if she believed him. She still remembered the stark look of disappointment in her mother's eyes.

"I came over tonight because I wanted to talk to you about something." The world-weary expression in his eyes intensified. "I spent these last weeks in Peru going over prison records and documents." He paused to take a deep breath. "I'd hoped to locate Eekelen Willem's body, but I didn't have any luck. I did find a journal he kept while he was in prison."

Something about his tone alarmed her. "Tell me about it."

"Owen and Eekelen were tired of relief work and wanted to make money," he began. "They told everyone they were going to see Guzmán to convince him to allow relief supplies into the mountain villages. What they'd really planned was to disappear for a few days with a group of *senderos* they'd met and put out the word they were being held by Guzmán."

Brett couldn't believe Owen would stoop to this. She didn't know this stranger. Not at all.

"Owen was counting on your mother to make a stink when she thought he'd been kidnapped and create a lot of media hype. Something went wrong. Government troops came across their camp and there was a shoot-out with the *senderos*. Owen and Eekelen were jailed as *sendero* sympathizers."

"What a stupid thing to do."

Hugh's brow furrowed and she sensed she hadn't heard the worst.

He leaned forward, elbows on his knees, and looked directly at her. "He never wanted to marry you. You see, Owen was in love with your mother."

His words blindsided her and she stared at him a moment, not quite comprehending. "You're kidding! My mother? He loved Mother?"

"They'd met in Costa Rica years earlier and had had a brief affair. Constance went on to other causes . . . to other men, but Owen still loved her."

She didn't think Owen had the power to hurt her, but he did. She'd spent years waiting for a man who'd never loved her. "When he got off the plane, he called me by my mother's name. I thought he was just confused. Now that I think about it, he constantly compared me to my mother. I always came up short.

"I guess I should have suspected he loved Mother. But

people always admired her, so it seemed natural when Owen did too."

"I loved your mother," Hugh said, his voice low but charged with emotion. "I miss her to this day. But never think she was a saint. You're a better person in many ways."

"But you think I'm a nitwit for not seeing through Owen Northcote sooner, don't you?"

"Not at all. Don't be upset when I say you're like your mother. You're full of positive energy. You want to believe the best, so you look for it—in everyone. And when you're disappointed, you're not a person who forgives easily."

"I should have known better."

"Why?" Hugh didn't try to mask his bitterness. "Your mother was taken in by Owen, too. He seems so sincere, so honest—deeply intellectual. An act, that's all."

Brett sensed the deep love Hugh still felt for her mother and wondered what had kept them apart. They were very much alike—devoted to the oppressed peoples of the world.

Hugh spent the next few minutes trying to reassure her, but she hardly heard him. How could she have so grossly misjudged Owen? She'd been a Pollyanna, looking for love, determined to find a knight in shining armor. She hadn't seen the truth because she hadn't been looking.

Hugh said good night and Brett went upstairs. Timmy and Sneaky By were waiting at the top.

"What are you doing out of bed?"

"I heard Alex."

"No, sweetie. That was Uncle Hugh."

"Oooh." The disappointment in his young voice tugged at her heart. He was so cute, standing there, his kitty at his side, his pajamas saying TYKECOON. She wanted to hug him and hug him. No matter what Owen had done, he'd given her this treasure.

Timmy had accepted the impending divorce without being upset. He was happy when Owen called or visited, but he never asked for his father. She followed Timmy into his bedroom and he scurried over to the window.

"Look at the stars, Mommy. They look like popcorn."

Brett laughed. "Celestial popcorn."

"Ces-tails?"

"No, love. Celestial. That means the heavens."

"Celestial popcorn," he repeated, climbing into bed. "Say what Alex always says," he demanded as she tucked him in.

"Good night. Sleep tight and don't let the bedbugs bite."

Timmy giggled. "Silly Alex. Beds don't have bugs."

She lifted Sneaky By onto the bed beside him. He was too little to know that in parts of the world children didn't know beds came *without* bugs.

"Mommy, can Alex see the stars where he is?"

44

At its zenith the harvest moon washed the crushed autumn leaves in the gutters along Salem Road with light while sturdier leaves skipped across the sidewalk, driven by a frigid wind blowing in from the North Sea. Her briefcase under her arm, Brett hurried toward Owen's Bayswater flat, her mind on Alex Savich. The little coup that couldn't had long been over in Russia, but she hadn't heard from Alex. There had been no word from Lev either, although Hugh had managed to find out he was still in prison.

Had something happened to Alex? The second Russian Revolution had been over for months with Gorbachev and Yeltsin now in power, but she hadn't heard anything from Alex. No one had. Hugh's efforts hadn't turned up anything either. Was she struggling to hold on to Belage for a man who might be dead?

Brett rounded the corner and saw Owen's flat, and forced herself to concentrate on the coming confrontation. She had bided her time, not mentioning Eekelen Willem's journal to Owen. She'd tried to be fair to Owen, letting her solicitor suggest a suitable arrangement for visitation rights, but Owen insisted on sole custody of Timmy.

Over her dead body.

She marched up the steps and punched the buzzer, the wind whipping her hair across her face. Owen answered the door, startled to see her. She barged past him and stood in the foyer, clutching her briefcase.

"This is a surprise. What couldn't wait until tomorrow when I come to see Timmy?"

"I don't want him to hear this. Let's agree to a fair custody arrangement. Timmy needs both his parents."

"I'm entitled to custody, considering your arrests and the fact you sleep with men while Timmy is in the house."

Obviously, he'd hired an investigator who'd learned about Alex's nocturnal visits. Damn Owen, he was dead set on taking Timmy away from her. Or was he?

"Do you really care that much about Timmy? I find it hard to believe. I think you're manipulating me into selling Mother's diamond earrings and giving you money. You're using Timmy to blackmail me. Don't you care what's best for your son?"

"I might be willing to discuss Timmy's custody if you were more accommodating about the financial settlement. Sell the earrings."

"I need the money for Belage."

He smiled, supremely confident. "Judges are granting fathers custody more often. After all, I'm a hero."

"That's what I wanted to talk to you about." She removed the transcript from her briefcase and handed it to him.

"What in hell is this?"

"A translation of Eekelen Willem's journal." Even in the dim light of the entry, she detected the mottled flush edging up his cheeks to his receding hairline.

"Where did you get it?"

"Hugh discovered it in Peru." She couldn't control her smug smile. "He sent the original to Inge Willem."

"I don't know what you expect me to do with it."

"You really must read it. Eekelen sheds a whole new light on you. I'm certain the press would love a copy."

"I don't know what you're talking about," he insisted, but she detected the quaver in his voice.

"The so-called interview with Guzmán, the *sendero* leader. A fake. You wanted media attention, so you could write a book about Peru and sell it for a lot of money. You were caught in your own trap. But you went ahead with your plan and wrote the book. Luckily, I kept Hugh searching for you, or you'd still be in Peru."

"Staging our disappearance wasn't the best idea I ever had," he conceded, the fight going out of him.

"You're pompous, hypocritical. And a liar." Her voice rose in spite of her stellar efforts to temper it. "Other than that, you're a hero."

"I say, you have no idea what I went through." Tears glistened in his eyes, but she ignored them. "Don't judge me."

"I'm sure you did suffer, but I suffered, too. Imagine, waiting all those years, praying for you to return, loving you when you loved my mother."

He shoved his hands into his pockets and hunched his shoulders forward. "I'm sorry. I never meant to hurt you."

"Then why didn't you tell me you were in love with my mother?"

"When I got out of prison"—his voice faltered—"I needed you. I really believed I would come to love you. I thought you were more like your mother."

"Rest assured I'm not my mother. I'm warning you. I intend to publish this journal so the entire world can see just what kind of a hero you really are."

"You wouldn't dare. You—"

"Oh, yes, I would. If you don't agree to a reasonable custody arrangement, I'll see that this is made public."

"You wouldn't do that to Timmy."

"Only if you force me. You're not taking my son away from me, and you're not preventing me from saving Belage." For Alex.

* * *

"I'm proud of you. I think you handled it quite well," her father said when she returned home after Owen agreed not to press for sole custody of Timmy.

"Put this confrontation with Owen behind you. You can't change the past. You did what's right. Now, concentrate on Belage. How's it going?" Jock asked as they sat on the sofa.

"Better. I have all these diamonds that are hard to use since they've been cut for other designs, but Timmy gave me a terrific idea. He said the stars looked like popcorn. I created a new collection called Celestial Popcorn. They're supposed to be the sun and moon and the stars, but with impressionistic designs that allow me to use diamonds of any size or shape. Now, if only I can sell them."

"You will. Won't Harvey Nichols and Deauville buy some?"

"Hopefully, but this was a very big order. It's more than Deauville or Harvey Nichols can absorb. I'll have to do some selling myself if Belage is to survive. That's what I want to talk with you about. I'm running out of money."

"I'll get you whatever you need, you know that."

She slipped her arm around him, touched by his offer. In order to save his own business, he'd sold the mansion in Belgravia and now lived in his country house, Hayvenhurst. She felt closer to her father than she had in years. The crisis with Timmy meant they'd spent more time together talking than ever before.

"I can't take your money. The lease is up on my place now. In January, Timmy and I are going to move in with Amy. She'll need my help with the baby. I was wondering if you could keep Timmy at Hayvenhurst with you during his Christmas holiday. I'd spend part of the time with you and take a small flat here for the days I need to be at Belage. We'll move into Amy's when school starts again in January."

"I'll be thrilled to have Timmy. Now that Daphne had Cassandra, Ruth is always there playing the doting grandmother."

"I'll bring Timmy down this weekend, but I'm coming

right back to help Amy put things in storage so we can move in."

"Poor Amy, is there no hope of freeing Lev?"

"Hope. That's all. He hasn't been court-martialed—yet."

"How did the army know he was back?"

"*Pamyat* members in his mother's building saw him when he went to visit her. They're a reactionary group bent on ethnically cleansing Russia of Jews, Gypsies, and other minorities."

She hesitated, having anticipated this discussion for weeks now. "I'd planned to sell Mother's diamond earrings to raise money to free Lev." She waited for some reaction from Jock; his expression didn't change. "But Amy went to her father and told him he'd never see his grandson unless he put up the money to free Lev. Gordon Conrift is so desperate to have an heir that he agreed. He also said he'd give whatever it took to get Alex out. We don't think it'll be necessary. He's an American and hasn't committed any crime, so why should the Soviets hold him?"

"Have the Russians asked for money?"

"No, but we're anticipating. Israel has successfully exchanged people for cash or weapons. That's how Alex got Lev out the first time. If anything's going to work, it'll be some sort of financial swap." She combed her hair back from her face with her fingertips. "If I'm going to save Belage, I'll need to sell Mother's earrings."

"Keeping Belage is that important to you?"

"Alex gave me a chance. And I told you how he helped after the accident. If he comes back, I want him to find Belage waiting."

"Will you be waiting for him, too?"

"Alex isn't the type of man to commit to a woman. He claimed to love me, then I caught him with another woman."

"You love him, but you can't forgive him."

"Yes," she conceded. "But after Owen, it should be obvious I'm a terrible judge of character. Timmy's crazy about

Alex. It'll be a serious problem if we get together and it doesn't work out."

"You've thought about this."

"Absolutely. He's been gone almost four months. I've had a lot of time to think about my life. I realize what a fiasco it was with Owen. I'm not making another mistake." She smoothed the folds of her skirt, ready to steer the subject away from her feelings about Alex. "Do you object to my selling Mother's earrings to save Belage?"

"Your mother was a very special person," he began, a look of infinite sadness masking his patrician features.

"I'm old enough for you to stop protecting me from the truth," she interrupted. "I know Mother didn't want me, but all these years you let me believe the judge had granted you custody. Why did you let me blame you?"

"I didn't want you to hate Constance. She couldn't help what she was." He expelled a long sigh that told her this confession was difficult for him. He wasn't a man who liked to admit he was wrong. They were a lot alike, she realized. One of the hardest things about her divorce was admitting she was such a bad judge of character. "And the divorce was my fault."

"I had always assumed Mother wanted the divorce."

He gazed at her steadily for a moment, his expression concerned. "Your mother did something that caused the divorce. She didn't want it. In fact, she begged me to forgive her, but I was too proud . . . too stubborn."

Like the ice sculpture of Venus that had melted so quickly at Ellis's wedding, the image of her mother that she'd treasured for so long had dissolved rapidly over the last weeks. What now?

"Things were great when I was building my business and we both were working. Then we made enough money to have a baby, which was my idea. Your mother was never happy staying home. She began joining various protest groups, dragging you along. I put my foot down, forbidding it, and that made her angry."

She couldn't remember her mother's not championing some cause. And across every childhood memory, Brett saw her father giving his time to a sassy little girl. No. She wasn't much of a judge of character, then or now. She saw what she wanted to believe. She created her own reality.

"Then I realized Constance was having an affair. I investigated and discovered Hugh MacLeod was her lover. He was her idol, a man with a cause. I confronted her; she insisted she still loved me." He closed his eyes for a second, utterly miserable. "She begged me—oh, how she begged me —not to divorce her. But I was stubborn and proud. I wouldn't listen."

She swallowed back the burgeoning lump in her throat, deep sorrow gathering force. Jock Payne had never stopped loving her mother. That was why her name was never spoken after the divorce. That was why her father had been speechless at the funeral. That was the real reason Ruthless hated Brett—the image of her rival.

"I never stopped loving her, but it took me years to forgive her. Then one day I was walking down Bond Street and realized I could buy anything, have anything, except the woman I loved. I walked into Garrards and asked for something special for a woman who wasn't like anyone else on earth."

"The earrings." It had never crossed her mind that her own father had bought them. "You should have known she'd return them. Money meant nothing to her."

"Of course I knew, but I wanted to make up for all the times she'd settled for earrings she'd bought used at a jumble sale. She'd suffered through the lean years, helping me without a complaint. I made most of my money after the divorce."

"She was never bitter about it."

"True," he conceded, the anguish in his voice bringing tears to her eyes. "But I wanted her to have something truly unique, like she was, something really top-drawer. She never had anything pretty or new the way other women did.

No nice clothes or coats. Nothing ever from a swank store."
He rolled his eyes heavenward. "It breaks my heart to know
the nicest dress she ever wore was the one we buried her
in."

Tears welled up in her eyes. "What did she say when you
gave her the earrings?"

"That's the worst part. I never saw her. I left them for her
with a note. She flew off to Peru the following day. The next
time I saw her, she was in a coffin."

Brett still remembered her father's stricken expression at
the funeral, mistaking it then for his usual show of strength.
And the grim expression on Ruth's face. Now, Brett realized her stepmother knew she'd always play second fiddle to
a dead woman.

Suddenly she remembered her father standing beside the
coffin covered in boughs of Queen Anne's lace that Brett
had ordered. Drifts of trumpet lilies, her mother's favorites,
surrounded the open grave, swaying in the gentle breeze.
She'd assumed her mother's friends had sent them, but now
she realized her father had done it, for the card had read:
Forever in My Heart.

Her father stared at Constance Lamont's photograph on
the mantel. "Papa." She touched his hand. "Let me show
you the note she wrote when she opened the earrings."

Brett rushed upstairs, careful not to awaken Timmy, and
retrieved the note. Wondering if she should leave the room
and let him be alone, she handed him the note.

You are the love of my life, and always will be. You know
I cannot accept these. One small stone alone would save a
thousand starving children. Still, I appreciate the gesture,
but knowing you love me means more than any precious
gem. Darling, I'll love you always.

He scanned it quickly, then reread it word for word, tears
in his eyes. "After all those years apart, she still loved me."

"Of course she did." She hadn't understood her mother

completely, but intuitively she knew Constance Lamont had never loved any man but Jock. And they'd found each other again when it was too late.

"Brett." Jock's eyes were bright with unshed tears. "You're like your mother in many ways, but you inherited my stubborn streak."

"Yes. A stubborn streak and a head for business," she replied lightly, trying to ease his pain.

"I'm serious. Here's some advice I wish someone had given me when you were Timmy's age. If you love Alex, forgive him. No one is perfect. It's clear to me that you two are deeply in love. The only way to love is to realize that person might suddenly be taken from you. You can't imagine how many things you'll wish you'd done differently if you find yourself standing on the edge of a grave, staring down at a coffin.

"You'll curse yourself for letting pride or stubbornness rule your heart. You'll see a lifetime of loneliness, stretching out like purgatory. Each shovelful of earth burying that coffin will remind you of something you should have said, a thought you should have shared, a hug or a kiss you'll wish the rest of your life you'd taken the time to give."

Without another word, her father kissed her and left, the note clutched in his hand. Carrying his love with him.

45

Brett opened the door to the apartment building in Maida Vale where she'd taken an attic flat. The burning smell of the radiator mingled with the odor of cabbage cooking. Brett stopped in the hall and used the public telephone to call Timmy. Having her own telephone was a waste, considering she spent part of each week at Hayvenhurst and wouldn't be here long.

She spoke with Timmy, and he excitedly told her he'd jumped a wall riding Felix. She hung up, wishing she could have been there, but grateful her father, who'd been unhappy so long, was enjoying his grandson.

It was a hike up to the attic, and as Brett walked, she envisioned the old house as it must once have appeared. Stately. Proud. Built on the fringe of Maida Vale in an era when grace and gentility had been prized, the mansion had weathered decades of changes. After the First World War, the house had settled into a comfortable middle age, her rooms filled with a large family who barely managed to maintain the house.

Then came the depression. The family was forced out, replaced by a succession of tenants. Slowly, along with her neighbors, the old mansion slipped into shoddiness unimagined by her builders. The final humiliation: the five floors carved into small flats, with Brett's attic cubby-hole, once used for storage, being the most cramped.

Sad, she thought. The house could be restored the way Spencer House had, but London had too many legacies of a bygone era to rescue them all.

She left the grand staircase and mounted the narrow flight leading to the attic. Halfway up she noticed her door was ajar. A chill rushed through her from toe to chin. She kicked open the door, then jumped back ready to run. No one was inside. But her things were tossed around the room.

"Sneaky By, Sneaky By," she called, hoping he hadn't run out and gotten lost in the strange neighborhood.

He nosed out from under the comforter covering the bed and screeched a where-the-hell-were-you meow. She scooped him up and hugged him, burying her cold face in his warm fur.

"I'll have to get a better lock," she told him as she checked to see what had been taken. Nothing. Luckily, the diamond earrings were in a deposit box. "And a golf club to ward off intruders."

She straightened the mess, asking herself if it had been a mistake to move here. No, she could take a few weeks of this. After all, Alex might be enduring worse conditions. If —and it was becoming a bigger *if* with each passing day—he returned, he'd find she'd been forced to sell his penthouse and give up his Porsche because there wasn't enough money to make the payments.

Belage was hanging on. Barely. The Celestial Popcorn series certainly hadn't proved to be a success. No one was buying. Too modern, too surreal, too trendy, they said. Even Deauville and Harvey Nichols had refused to *even try* a few pieces.

Suspicious. She'd bet the cartel was behind this. A freeze-out. Intelco was encouraging people to boycott Belage. What could she do to stop them? she wondered, straightening her things.

"Where's a good place for Timmy's picture?" she asked

Sneaky By when she found the framed photograph. "How about here?" She put it on the dilapidated dresser that came with the flat. "I wish I had a picture of Alex, too."

She flopped across the bed, its lumpy mattress sagging. "If I never see him again, all I'll have is a memory." She blinked rapidly to stem the rush of tears.

No matter what happens, remember I love you. I love you both. She gazed at Timmy's picture, anger replacing her depression. "Feeling sorry for yourself won't help a bit."

Sneaky By purred sympathetically, kneading her thigh. If only she could do something to help Alex. But once again, she was forced to rely on Hugh. He'd discovered Alex had taken an Aeroflot jet to Kiev and disappeared. Amnesty International sources had confirmed that Alex Savich had never applied for a permit to visit Lev. "Why not? What could have happened?"

She stroked Sneaky By's head. "People don't just disappear without a trace. Wrong. Hugh says Amnesty International's files are filled with people who simply vanished. Forever. It doesn't make sense. If Alex were alive, wouldn't he at least try to visit Lev?"

"Great to see you," Brett greeted Philippe Deauville, more than a little embarrassed to have him see Belage. The last time he'd visited had been during their halcyon days, and they'd still been in the new offices with a full staff. Now, they were shoehorned into the basement of a decrepit building on Hatton Garden.

"Where's Alex?" Philippe asked.

"Away." She changed the subject. "What brings you to London?"

"Intelco's Christmas luncheon is today."

The cartel's annual bash was a command performance held each year just three days before Christmas. Top-ranking members of all the Diamond Clubs worldwide were expected to attend. Never mind that most of them were Jewish, Indians, or Japanese who didn't celebrate Christmas.

Intelco snapped its fingers and the lemmings flocked to London. The highlight of the event would be a "state of the gem market" address by Ridley Swarthmore, director of Intelco, the most important man in the diamond world.

Philippe observed, "Belage seems to be experiencing some minor difficulties."

She nodded, still smarting from Deauville's refusal to carry the Celestial Popcorn series. Her sixth sense told her Intelco was behind the rejection, but she needed to be certain. "Belage is surviving." Her calculations revealed they had three months before she'd be forced to close. "You'll be excited to see our spring collection."

"Well, we're having our own troubles," Philippe hedged. "The market's soft."

"Be honest. Do you ever foresee a time when you might buy from Belage again?"

Philippe hesitated, then shook his head slowly, saddened.

"It's Intelco, isn't it? They've blacklisted Belage."

"You know I can't verify that."

"Off the record, then. I'll never say who told me, but I need to know if hanging on is hopeless. Everything I have is invested in this company. Everything."

"Dash Boynton insisted we stop doing business with Belage, but he refused to say why. This is highly irregular, you know. No notice has ever been posted against Belage in a Diamond Club. Still, no one can afford to alienate Intelco. You know that."

Brett hurried into the Intelco lobby several hours later with Alex's Diamond Club identification card in hand, her thumb strategically placed over his picture. She waved the card as she passed through the metal detector. "I'm late, but Mr. Katimori is saving me a place."

The guard stepped aside; she wasn't certain whether the card or dropping a Japanese name had gained her entry to the cartel's inner sanctum. Probably the name. The sons of Nippon with their endless supply of yen, and a yen for diamonds, were the current sweethearts of the cartel, replacing the Arabs, who had been courted in previous years.

Brett paused outside the Intelco dining room, noting the tables crammed into the room. Mostly men. But here and there she saw women. Brett tucked an unruly curl behind her ear, making certain her upsweep revealed the ivory tusk earrings she'd made for her mother. She strode across the crowded room, bound for the podium, feeling strangely calm. After all, she had nothing left to lose.

At the head table she spotted Dash Boynton and assumed the man with the bald pate dusted with pale freckles was Ridley Swarthmore. She stood behind the podium and switched on the microphone. The unexpected, loud pop made her flinch. Startled, everyone snapped to attention. She took a head-clearing breath, adjusting the microphone for her height.

"I'm Brett Lamont, designer at Belage." Out of the corner of her eye, she noted the confused looks at the head table. "I thought you might be interested to see one of my first designs." She touched the earrings. "I made these earrings years ago for my mother, Constance Lamont."

A titter swept the room at the famous name.

"These earrings are made from elephant tusks. The elephants are alive when their tusks are chain-sawed off them." She looked pointedly at the table of Japanese, whose lust for ivory fueled the slaughter. "Young elephants just sprouting tusks were hacked for the tiny tusks I used to make these earrings." She touched one earring, noticing several women pressing their napkins to their lips. "My mother wore these tusk earrings to remind people of the injustice done to helpless animals.

"In this world there will always be those who are weak, and at the mercy of the mighty. Look around this room. You are at the mercy of Intelco. They pretend to be so proper, so British—totally committed to fair play in the name of stabilizing the diamond market. But we know they can be as ruthless as a poacher chain-sawing a live elephant."

"Now, see here. That's an absurd charge." Ridley Swarthmore's voice boomed. Dash glowered, his face a livid plum color.

"It's true. Mr. Boynton paid Yai Tsung for Belage's designs, then sold them to knock-off jewelers in New York."

An audible groan filled the room. Knock-off artists were every jeweler's nightmare, threatening everyone. Would Intelco dare commit a crime all jewelry manufacturers spent millions trying to prevent?

"When that didn't destroy us, you blacklisted Belage. You knew we hadn't violated any Diamond Club rules, so you didn't dare post a notice. Instead you started a whispering campaign. I've had to sell everything I own and all of Alex Savich's possessions to try to hold on. But it's useless. Just like an elephant facing a chain saw, Belage doesn't have a chance."

Her accusation had the desired effect. The cartel prided itself on fair play. The image of the helpless elephants cast Intelco in the worst possible light since most guests knew Belage had been blacklisted. An angry murmur accompanied frowns directed at the head table.

"Ms. Lamont, you are mistaken," Swarthmore insisted, undisguised fury underscoring each syllable. He faced his guests, who were scowling more intently with every word. "Intelco works strictly through the Diamond Clubs. We would never—" He stopped, seeing the disgusted head shakes and mumbling. "I can't imagine what all the grousing is about."

If Brett hadn't known better, she might have believed him. He seemed so sincere, so convincing as he reviewed Intelco's policy for sanctioning members through the Diamond Clubs. But Brett didn't believe him, and neither did the audience, judging from their tight expressions.

Finally Swarthmore said, "Some of you still don't look convinced. If any of you has been approached by Intelco to stop doing business with Belage, please stand."

His tone made clear his anger. He was a man who was

never questioned; having a woman challenge him in front of everyone was humiliating. Brett knew no one would rise and risk the wrath of the cartel, but she'd made her point. Everyone knew the truth.

After a minute of awkward silence, the guests staring at their plates, Swarthmore beamed a smug smile at Brett. In the center of the room, Philippe Deauville came to his feet, and Brett held her breath. Color leached from Swarthmore's face. The Deauvilles were Marie Antoinette's jewelers, for God's sake. They'd risen to the ranks of nobility. Men of honor, not liars.

Purvis Keir from Harvey Nichols shocked Brett when he rose followed by two dozen others. Suddenly most of the guests were on their feet. Staring coldly at Dash Boynton.

Swarthmore pulled in a deep breath, sucking air from between clenched teeth. "Let me assure you all that this is some mistake. I would never authorize—" He turned, realizing everyone was staring at Dash Boynton. "You didn't take it upon yourself—"

Dash lumbered to his feet. "I suspected Alex Savich was selling stones from the Rostov mine in the Ukraine. He—"

"Suspected," Brett cut in, "but you had no proof or you would have posted a notice."

Dash didn't look in her direction; his attention was focused on his boss. "Then there was some funny business during the Gulf War. I'm positive Savich pulled a quick one."

"Prove it," she shouted, and the guests echoed her words.

"I-I couldn't let our authority be undermined," Dash sputtered.

"You sanctioned this without consulting me?" Clearly, Swarthmore was telling the truth. Dash was a loose cannon, threatening to undermine Intelco's good name.

Dash collapsed into his chair. "Yes."

Brett clutched the podium, the truth hitting her full force. Dash Boynton was a madman. Alex had been right; he'd tried to kill her. It was outrageous, but he'd done it because

Alex had made a fool out of him. Dash couldn't prove it, but the knowledge goaded him into action.

"Mr. Boynton will be retiring immediately," Swarthmore assured his guests, who were openly grumbling now. "He'll never—"

"Try to kill anyone the way he did me?" Brett challenged. This was a gamble and she knew it, but she couldn't rest until she knew if Dash had been responsible for the accident that had almost cost her Timmy.

The grousing died; the room becoming silent enough to hear Dash's labored breathing.

"What do you mean?" Swarthmore's tone sounded drained, his earlier bravado gone.

"Ask him," Brett pointed to Dash. "He hired someone to force my car off the road and almost killed my little boy."

"Did you do that?" Swarthmore's voice was low but held a note of menace like a revolver being cocked.

Dash nodded, the folds of his neck fanning over his starched collar. Brett had expected him to deny it. After all, the police had never located the driver. But for some strange reason, he didn't bother.

Swarthmore turned to her. "Honestly, I never authorized this man to take any action against Belage or you."

Brett recognized the sincerity in his voice, but many of the others appeared skeptical. Wary. If this could happen to her—without proof—it could happen to anyone. Granted, they all knew some members had been "taken care of" over the years. But for just cause, not unfounded suspicions. Now Intelco was out of control and it worried everyone.

"N-naturally"—Swarthmore, hidebound by two hundred years of British inbreeding, was actually stuttering now— "we'll compensate Belage for damages and—"

"Alex Savich and I don't want your blood money. We want a chance. That's all. Stop blacklisting us. Let us make a living. Give us a chance."

She listened while Swarthmore humbly apologized for "the unfortunate misunderstanding." He professed his sincerest regrets, but he didn't deceive her. He'd been thoroughly humiliated. She knew she'd won this battle. But if Belage ever stepped out of line again and they could prove it, Swarthmore would retaliate for this public disgrace by posting a notice. Then he would be on the telephone to Sicily.

46

Alex bear-hugged Lev, then kissed him on both cheeks, Russian style, as the prison guard watched suspiciously. "Are you okay?"

"Why are you here?" Lev asked, unshed tears glistening in his eyes. "You should be in London. Get ready for Christmas."

"I've been in Kiev months, Lev. They wouldn't let me see you until now. I've been under house arrest. No one knows where I am except you. Trust me, it's better this way."

Alex had arrived in Kiev on a sweltering August day three months earlier. He had gone directly to the address Tenklov had given him.

"Screw it," he'd cursed to himself when he saw the building housed the parliament. "Tenklov's a *shishki*—a party bigwig. Should've known. The expensive suit. The gold Mont Blanc pens. A man not likely to buck the Red Army." The girth of anxiety binding him cinched in another notch. "Why the hell did Tenklov drag me over here?"

He strode into the building, a cement bunker like most constructed after the revolution when the party was bent on rejecting the architectural legacy of czarist Russia.

But in Moscow the party couldn't quite bring itself to destroy its heritage, Alex thought. The domes and spires surrounding Red Square were impressive. The only impressive thing about the Ukraine's parliament building was its size. No doubt it housed *mudistika,* corrupt bureaucrats. Well, he was prepared for them; his overloaded briefcase was difficult to close.

Tenklov's office was on the top floor—the chairman's floor. Interesting. Had Tenklov been hawking the diamonds on his own, or did he have the chairman's approval? Leonid Kravchuk had been elected chairman of the parliament last year. The son of peasants, he'd advanced within the party ranks, a ruthless, powerful leader. Kravchuk had to know about Tenklov's dealings.

"Alexei Savich," he informed the woman at the desk, using the Ukrainian intonation to pronounce his name.

Chunky like most peasant women, she used *basma,* Georgian-made henna dye on her scraggly hair, giving it a blue-red glow under the twenty-watt bulb. She scanned the visitors list, and Alex waited, ready to open his briefcase and slip her a pair of Levi's if necessary. But she didn't stall him, the usual *strelka* ploy to force a bribe.

"Good news or bad?" Alex muttered after she sent him down the hall. Either he was too important to hit for a bribe, or she didn't think he had a pot to piss in.

Alex found the room and stood outside the frosted glass doors, frowning at the name painted in gold. NIKOLAI GOLUSHKO. "Aw hell. Head of the Ukrainian KGB."

Golushko had a vodka complexion with a skein of broken veins netting his loose jowls. "Tenklov is in conference with Chairman Kravchuk."

In conference? Criminy. The Rooskies had been watching way too much American television. Alex opened his briefcase, bypassing the Levi's and the cigarettes, pulling out a videotape. *Love Canal* wasn't an environmental video, but a British porn tape featuring a blowsy imitation of Dolly

Parton who referred to sex as a trip up her love canal.
"Darik," Alex said, a gift.

Golushko grinned, and Alex knew before Saturday thousands of pirated videos of this tape would be selling across Russia. Contrary to Western images of the KGB as highly trained Cold War spies most were *zveri,* black marketeers. And nothing was more lucrative in Russia than porn videos.

"I need to see Lev Rodynskov—immediately."

"Not for a few days," responded Golushko. "Gorbachev is vacationing in Crimea. *Omon* are everywhere."

Alex nodded, thinking about the Black Beret army units whose job it was to protect Soviet leaders. During the summer the elite vacationed in the Crimea, sunning their hog bodies along the shores of the Black Sea. "That's hours from here. Why would the *Omon* be in Kiev instead of Sevastopol? It's a hell of a lot closer to Gorbachev's *dacha.*"

Golushko shrugged, obviously concealing something. "We'll come for you soon and take you to your friend."

Alex had no choice except to wait, conserving his cash, and spending time in the *traktir,* the tavern. His grandmother had hated him, but he blessed her for teaching him Russian and enough of her native Ukrainian to get along. A by-product of *glasnost* was the freedom Ukrainians felt to speak their native language, not the Russian that Stalin had forced on them.

Still, they'd spoken Russian for decades and old habits died hard. Conversations in the *traktir* were a blend of both languages. During that week, Alex learned Tenklov was Kravchuk's right-hand man. He'd been a mere worm in the Communist party woodwork the year before, so now people marveled at Tenklov's rise.

No mystery, Alex decided. The diamond deal was Tenklov's ticket to the top. But what was going on now? Why insist Alex come, then avoid him? He didn't buy the *Omon* bit. So far, Kiev seemed normal. The usual lines for *khleb* with the bread running out before everyone had a loaf. No Black Berets in sight.

He considered calling Brett. Hell, what good would it do? What could he say that wouldn't worry her? Amy had promised not to tell her where he'd gone. Besides, he wanted to give Brett time to think about what he'd said.

One afternoon he went to the *traktir*; everyone was huddled around a black-and-white television at the bar. Dead silent. He wedged himself between two burly men and listened to a wimpy guy on the set saying Gorbachev was finished. The hard-liners were taking over again. Aw, shit. A conservative *putsch*.

Hold everything. They'd waited until Gorbachev left Moscow for the Ukraine where they had Kravchuk, a party man, in power. If Kravchuk knew a *putsch* was in the works, so did Goluschko. And undoubtedly Tenklov.

Damn straight. They all knew, and they were keeping him around. Waiting. For what? Alex had suspected it might have something to do with the diamonds, but now he questioned that theory. Hard-liners kiss-assed the cartel. Whatever scam Tenklov had going before would be impossible now.

So, what did they want from him? His best guess was they'd want him to smuggle someone out of the country with Lev and help him establish a new identity in the West. With the death of *perestroika*, exit permits would again be impossible to get.

"Yeltsin's coming on television," someone shouted.

Alex realized Yeltsin's immense popularity, ignored in the West, would be a key factor in this *putsch*.

"The people will fight if Yeltsin stands firm," a man added, his opinion quickly seconded by the others.

"Vera." Faith. *"Istina."* Truth, a higher plane of consciousness. Yeltsin's words brought cheers from the mob around the White House and hearty affirmations from the men in the bar, watching the scene at the parliament building.

"Svoboda! Svoboda!" Freedom, they chanted.

Alex's heart beat faster, and it wasn't the cheap vodka he'd consumed. He felt he'd been caught up in something—

a special moment in history. What would Vic have said? He'd have been with Yeltsin. Vic had blamed everything from *shivka*—rotgut vodka—to the potholes in the roads on the corrupt Communists.

"Rasstrelyat!" blared the television.

The coup leaders commanded the troops to shoot. The cheers died as surely as if they'd been cut down with the sickle on the Russian flag. Tiananmen Square wasn't far from anyone's mind. Then the army unit assigned to arrest Yeltsin did the unthinkable: They vowed to protect him.

Honest to God, Vic would have loved this.

"Svoboda!" cheered everyone, some men openly weeping. In the midst of the cries for freedom, someone shouted, *"Omon."*

The *traktir* was silent except for the television in the background as everyone turned. At the door stood a dozen Black Berets armed with Kalashnikovs.

"I knew it was too good to be true," whispered the man beside Alex. *"Svoboda*—a joke."

The Black Berets prodded men out of their way with the barrels of their submachine guns. Alex waited, expecting them to declare a curfew or to proclaim this an unlawful meeting. From the grave Stalin's boot crushing Russia again. Good thing Vic was gone. He'd had such high hopes for *perestroika* and *glasnost.*

Shoulder to shoulder, moving in sync, the *omon* strode forward. Shiny black boots. Black uniforms. Reminded Alex of Gestapo. They had the same reputation. Cruel. They hated *Yevrei*—Jews.

Coming to a boot-stomping military halt a foot from Alex, they leveled their Kalashnikovs at him. "You are an enemy of the state."

After a week as a *zek,* a prisoner, Alex had a good start on a beard when he was hauled into Kravchuk's office. From his guards he'd learned that the coup had failed. The new government was desperate for American aid. They couldn't possibly justify holding him. Not that Russian justice resembled anything Americans expected, he reminded himself.

Tenklov met Alex at the door to Chairman Kravchuk's private office, dismissing his guards. "My apologies," he said casually as if he'd kept Alex waiting in the reception room instead of a bug-infested cell with nothing more than *sukharevskaya,* old chunks of dry toast, to eat for over a week.

"You bastards have no right to keep me in jail."

"True," Tenklov conceded with a sly smile, his eyes shifting to the older man at the desk. "We were concerned you would leave the country just when we needed you."

"So you threw me in jail? That's a half-assed idea." He gulped a calming breath. Don't blow it for Lev. Kravchuk had refused to back the *putsch,* sounding the death knell for the coup. He was *the* man in the Ukraine. "I want to see Rodynskov."

Leonid Kravchuk stood. Late fifties. Stout. *Ochi chornaya,* Alex thought, amazed that after so little time he was thinking in Russian—dark eyes. Like a *vovk*—wolf. A predator's cunning eyes. Never underestimate this man.

"I knew Vicktor Orlov," Kravchuk said, but Alex didn't know whether to believe him or not. "He told me he was part Gypsy."

Alex concealed his surprise with a cough. Few people knew Vic had Gypsy blood. He certainly wouldn't have blabbed it to a party leader and risked being denied an entry visa. Gypsies were despised. And treated worse than the Jews. The Communists had never been able to stop their wandering, their trading, their inherent love of their own special brand of capitalism.

"My uncle never mentioned you."

"We took a blood oath to keep our pact secret."

Alex's stomach pitched, realizing Kravchuk might be telling the truth. Following centuries of tradition, Cossacks hunted bears, eating their meat, tanning their hides. Drinking their blood for oaths and rites of passage into manhood.

Cossacks honored blood oaths like swearing on a Bible. Vic had been three-quarters Cossack. Now that he thought about it, Kravchuk looked like an over-the-hill Cossack too out of shape to mount one of their famed stallions. And Tenklov? For sure, a contemporary Cossack in a Savile Row suit. Toting a Mont Blanc pen.

Proof positive history was being rewritten.

Kravchuk sat, gesturing for Alex to take the chair opposite his desk, while Tenklov stood behind his boss. Alex assessed Tenklov closely. Ambitious. A rising star.

"Vicktor Orlov and I pledged to free the Ukraine."

"But you're a Communist." The instant the words passed his lips, Alex regretted his outburst. Brett had rubbed off on him. Once he'd have kept his thoughts to himself.

Kravchuk's *vovk* eyes flared. "I am Ukrainian."

"My uncle always thought of himself as Ukrainian," Alex said, backpedaling quickly.

"Vicktor agreed to sell diamonds from our Rostov mine where we have discovered a new pipe of kimberlite with colored stones."

"And Moscow knows nothing about it?"

"Why tell them?" Tenklov cut in. "They suck the republics dry. Like the Balkans, the Ukraine deserves to be free."

"The Balkans were independent until Hitler tossed a bone to Stalin, but the Ukraine has always been the heart of Russia. Home of the intellectuals. The breadbasket. Hell, you've got the only sunny beaches in the Soviet Union."

"Exactly." Tenklov grinned. "What do we need Russia for? Food, minerals, brains. We have it all."

"We already have a seat at the United Nations," Kravchuk reminded him. "We are ready to rule ourselves."

"Okay," Alex conceded, wondering if Kravchuk was a dictator in the wings. Or a good guy phoenix rising from the ashes of Communism.

"I will be elected Ukrainian president as soon as we can hold elections," Kravchuk added.

"So, what do you need me for?" Alex's voice was clipped with caution, Lev on his mind.

"*Valuta,*" Tenklov responded, hard currency. Alex decided Kravchuk should watch his back. This guy had blind ambition. "The money from the diamonds you sold for us went into our Swiss account."

"I planned to buy arms," Kravchuk added. "Then when the time was right, I would break away from Moscow."

"It happened faster than we anticipated, no?" Tenklov chuckled.

"Why buy arms now," Kravchuk asked, "when we can commandeer the army units stationed in the Ukraine?"

"Trust me, don't throw your money away."

Kravchuk detected the sarcasm in Alex's tone. "It is not a joke. I intend to keep the Ukraine an independent country."

Once Alex would have argued the wisdom of this, but after the events of the past weeks, who was he to play God? The failed coup had turned the Soviet Union upside down. Kravchuk's power, though, was intact. And Kravchuk was crafty enough to appreciate his enhanced position.

"We need money," Tenklov said, and Alex recognized the royal *we*. Clearly, Tenklov saw himself as Kravchuk's heir. "We can raise money by selling our own diamonds."

"If you want Rodynskov out, you will sell our diamonds for us."

"Hold it, Kravchuk. Intelco has a contract—"

"With Moscow," Kravchuk reminded him. "We declared our independence just before the coup. We can do what we want."

"True," Alex conceded. No way was he getting involved in this. "Cut your own deal with them. You don't need me."

"It will take time to get Chairman Kravchuk elected president," Tenklov explained, "and consolidate our position. Meanwhile, we need more money."

By God, Tenklov's eyes actually flashed dollar signs. Money.

"Money is power," Kravchuk observed, "especially in a country without any money at all."

"Easy for you to say. If I do this, I'll be signing my death warrant. Intelco will be on this in a minute. Believe me, it's pure propaganda that Intelco is fair and has a paternal interest in stabilizing prices. They're very quiet about it, but they've killed men for less."

"You can do it," Tenklov insisted. "Golushko had his best men following you when you were trading for us. Intelco could never prove you did anything wrong."

Aw, hell. He'd underestimated the Commies. He'd spotted the man before at Brett's, but he hadn't given them credit for being able to track his every move without his detecting them. "Intelco knew I was selling fancies. This time they'll be watching me every second. I won't get out of this alive."

47

"It couldn't snow for Christmas, could it?" Eula Mae asked Brett. "It had to wait another two days to make London look like a Dickens Christmas card."

Brett peered out Eula Mae's greenhouse window at the swirling flakes. "I haven't seen it snow like this in years."

"Global warming has changed the climate." Eula Mae adjusted the amber hothouse light over her mating kiwis, justifiably proud of her accomplishment. Brett knew she was anxious to go to the next Rare Plant and Pit Council meeting.

"Maybe you should spend the night here," Eula Mae said.

"Thanks, but I'd better get back to the flat. Sneaky By's been alone long enough. I just hope Mrs. Merkle remembered to feed him while we were away."

"I'm certain your landlady took good care of him. Let's hope she locked up properly, so you weren't broken into again."

"I think it was one of the tenants scavenging to see what I have. When people are poor, they're desperate. It was the same way when I worked in the relief camps. Don't worry about me. I have a golf club for protection."

"You'd better run along, then, before the storm gets much worse. They've forecast a blizzard."

"May I use your telephone? I want to check on Amy." Brett dialed, wondering if Amy was all right. She'd been too uncomfortable with the baby to travel with them to Hayvenhurst for Christmas. "Amy, how are you doing?"

"I look like a kangaroo with an elephant in its pocket and I have a constant backache. Other than that I'm fine. As fine as I can be without Lev."

The catch in her friend's voice brought a lump to Brett's throat. She'd prayed for some word from Lev and Alex at Christmas. Nothing.

"You sound depressed. Do you want me to come over?"

"No. I'm fine," Amy insisted. "Actually, I had a good laugh earlier. Did you read today's *Times*?"

"No. What did it say?"

"*Return from Hell* opened in Leeds on Boxing Day."

"I knew that. West End plays always have a trial run in the provinces. How did Owen's play go?"

"It flopped." Amy chortled. "The critics hated it. They called it a silly melodrama that was nothing like the book. The backers pulled out. It's not going to open in London."

"You're kidding." She relayed the news to Eula Mae. "I can't deny this is good news. I didn't want my life featured in some tawdry soap opera."

A little after midnight, Brett trudged up the street to her flat. Like a pack of wolves the wind off the North Sea howled through the avenue of chestnuts, their branches already laden with ice. The deep snow made it difficult to walk. She'd taken the Underground from Eula Mae's, then searched for a taxi, but couldn't find one. No wonder. The roads were barely passable.

She struggled up the walk to the apartment house through drifts of snow. Inside the dark foyer she shook off the snow as best she could, then climbed the stairs to her attic flat.

"Sneaky By. Sneaky By," she called as she came in. He greeted her with a furious meow. "Look what I have for you." She pulled a tin of river trout from Harrods out of her purse. "Your favorite. Come on. Don't be upset with me." The sound of the can opener brought him to her side, rubbing against her legs. "Here you go."

Sneaky By's whiskers disappeared into the tin while Brett sat on the bed, changing into her nightgown. The attic window was whorled with frost, but around the edges it was clear enough to see the storm had worsened, blasting the window with pellets of frozen snow. Sneaky By pounced on the pillow, his throaty purr laden with the scent of fish, saying all was forgiven.

"I miss Alex so much," she told Sneaky By.

She loved Timmy deeply and would do anything for him. But she loved Alex, too. She'd never feel quite complete without him. There was a power and a depth to her love now that she'd only imagined possible with Owen. This was how her father still felt about her mother despite years of separation. And the finality of her death.

Clump-clump. The midnight silence of the old house magnified the noise outside her flat, making it ominously loud.

"What was that?" she asked and Sneaky By looked up. Comforting silence followed the noise, and the cat yawned, then burrowed into the pillow beside Brett.

Clump-clump. The same noise on the stairs, a crisp rustling sound followed by an odd thump. Brett reached for the golf club she kept beside her bed. Sneaky By crouched low, tail twitching. Silence. Brett kept her eyes trained on the door.

Clump-clump. She identified the strange sound. Someone was coming up the stairs one step at a time, taking precautions not to alert her.

She detected a dragging sound as if a coat was brushing against the wall on the stairs outside her flat. She tiptoed to the door and peered out the peephole. Only the cracked plaster wall opposite her door came into view, a veinlike web of lines that reminded her of a map of the Isle of Skye with its jagged coast and winding roads.

Tap-tap. A muffled knock. Why knock? He could easily break down the door. And wake the entire house? Of course not. It was a trick to get her to open the door.

She saw a bent head crusted with snow. The head shook off some of the snow, revealing shaggy dark hair. The head rose slightly revealing telltale worry lines, half hidden by damp hair drooping in hanks to the tops of his brows.

Silently she eased up on tiptoe for a better look. A head still angled downward. A beard growing wild. Then he tossed his head, an abrupt, impatient gesture that made her flinch. Magnified by the convex glass, his eyes met hers dead-on.

Those eyes. *His* eyes. A thousand near-forgotten memories swept over her. She jammed back the deadbolt and jerked open the door. For a second they faced each other, transfixed.

"My God, Alex. Are you all right, darling?"

"Smile," he commanded through lips that were nearly blue.

A bittersweet current of love flooded her senses as she smiled, a welcoming, captivating smile, a smile that couldn't possibly reveal all the love in her heart.

He wore a navy peacoat, threadbare at the elbows, with its frayed collar turned up, but it had been little protection against the blizzard. His beard was a thicket of hoarfrost flanked by scraggly hair glistening in frozen hanks.

She grabbed his gloved hands and pulled him into the warmth of her room. Her heart beating in double time, she looped her arms around his neck, her fingers twining through his near-frozen hair, smelling the wet wool of his coat and the faint trace of diesel fuel. Cold radiated from his clothes, chilling the air around them, penetrating her nightgown.

Beneath an umbrella of frosty whiskers, his lips formed

her name, but this time no sound came out. She grinned again, a heartfelt smile that had nothing to do with the tears in her eyes. Their breath mingled, their eyes reflecting emotions they couldn't express; they said the same thing.

"I love you."

He pulled her into his arms, hugging her as if he'd never let her go. Their lips touched, not a passionate kiss, but a soul-searching kiss, a kiss of promise and commitment. A wild yearning to always be together.

The spell was broken by a chunk of melting ice falling off his coat to the wooden floor. She realized he was trembling in her arms, chilled to the marrow. Perhaps he was even ill.

"Are you all right, darling?"

He managed a curt nod so typical of Alex.

"Where have you been?"

He said something but it came out a throaty croak. The drawn lines around his eyes masked by the beard showed he was exhausted, so tired he could hardly stand. He'd literally had to drag himself up the stairs to her flat.

"Never mind, you can tell me later."

With her help he shucked the sodden coat, dropping it into the puddle forming around his boots. The moth-eaten sweater beneath reeked of fuel and there were spots of oil on his too-short pants. A band of skin above the boots made her doubt he had on socks. He'd gone through hell to get back to her.

"Bath," he mumbled, staggering slightly.

She clutched his hand to her cheek for a moment, then helped him through the door into the bathroom to an old fashioned claw-footed tub. She turned on the taps full blast.

"A hot bath will stop your chills. Get in and I'll brew tea."

When she returned, a mug of extra strong Earl Grey in her hand, Alex was in the tub, knees jackknifed above the water, head back resting against the tub's rim. He'd scrubbed so hard his skin was pink, his hair wet and slicked back after shampooing.

"Backbrush," he said, his voice a husky baritone.

"Sure." She handed him the tea, then found the brush and lathered it, but waited for him to drain the cup and put it aside. "Lean forward. I'll get your back."

She brushed briskly; a feeling of intimacy and renewed love grew with each stroke. She mentally prayed, a prayer of thanks for bringing the man she loved home safe. To her. While she worked, she started to give him a rundown of what had happened in his absence.

Alex interrupted, "Amy told me everything that's gone on."

"Amy? You saw Amy first?"

"Sure. How was I supposed to find you?"

"Of course." She'd moved and had no telephone.

"Besides, I needed to get Lev home."

"Lev's back?" She let the brush slide into the water. She had imagined Lev couldn't possibly have been with Alex. He looked so terrible, clad in borrowed clothes. She assumed he'd barely escaped with his life. "How? Tell me everything."

"Later. First. How's my boy?"

Tears gathered in her eyes and she wondered just how long she'd thought in those terms. His boy. Timmy had been his boy from that afternoon when he'd gotten in the fight. Maybe even before then, she wasn't sure, but in her heart Timmy was their son.

"Timmy's just like his mother. He's never stopped missing you. Not a day passed that he didn't ask for you."

Alex grinned, his teeth white against his dark beard.

"How'd you get home? Was it hard?"

"Not if you love Russian tankers. But riding in the hold of that tanker was nothing compared to you challenging Intelco the way you did when you knew I had sold their diamonds."

"If they could have proven anything, they would have."

He sank back in the tub, his deep blue eyes rolling heavenward. "Do you know what they wanted me to do to get Lev out?"

"No. What?" From his tone it sounded dangerous to her.

"Kravchuk and Tenklov insisted I sell a shipment of diamonds for the Ukraine, or they wouldn't free Lev."

He rose, rivulets of water coursing down his lean body and grabbed the towel. Suddenly, her heart became a lead weight; she leaned against the wall.

"Oh, Alex. I don't want to lose you. If Intelco finds out—"

He cupped her chin with a damp palm, the towel tucked around his waist. "I've never been in a worse situation. I wanted to come back to you so damn bad, but I couldn't desert Lev." He gazed up at the cracked ceiling for a second. "Luckily somebody up there loves me. Must be Vic. He gave me the perfect solution to the mess I'd gotten myself into."

She kissed the palm of his hand, hopeful.

"It would be damn hard to find anyone more ambitious than Tenklov, so I decided to play to his ambition. I convinced Kravchuk to let me train Tenklov as a diamond broker. He could market their stones without giving me a cut. The greedy bastards went for it. I trained Tenklov and he's selling for them now."

"Intelco won't allow them to violate their contract."

"What contract?" Alex smirked. "I persuaded Kravchuk and Tenklov to wait until the Ukraine elected Kravchuk president before reminding Intelco the contract wasn't binding."

She hugged him, nuzzling his damp chest.

"Kravchuk's a crafty old Cossack wolf. Since the coup, he got himself elected president, then he launched the Commonwealth of Independent States. Intelco will find him a tough buzzard. My guess is he'll cut a deal that'll leave Intelco smarting."

"All I care about is you're home safe. Now, we can get on with our lives."

He tipped her chin back, his steady blue eyes locking with hers. "*Our* as in you and me and Timmy?"

"Yes. Owen and I—"

"Amy told me all about your divorce. Why the hell do you think I hiked clear across London in this blizzard?"

"Because you love me"—she smiled—"the way I love you."

He put both hands on her shoulders and stared into her eyes. "I fell in love with you the moment you smiled at me. I knew—deep down—you loved me, but I never expected you to prove it by taking on Intelco and saving Belage. That was damn gutsy."

"I couldn't let them ruin Belage, not after everything you've done for me—for Timmy. I love you too much to let that happen."

"Remember my birthday when you gave me a bottle of wine with a card that said 'now you have it all'? Well, I had the Porsche and the penthouse, but I didn't have the one thing that will truly make me happy. You."

"Does this mean you're going to marry me?"

"Damn straight. We're going to be a real family."

"We won't have any money, but that doesn't matter, does it?"

With gentle pressure on the small of her back, he drew her to him. He tilted his head downward and his lips met hers. He kissed her with excruciating tenderness, easing his tongue forward to flirt with hers.

"Brett, we'll have everything that really counts."

AUTHOR'S NOTE

I like to write stories that use real incidents and situations in our contemporary world. The idea for this book came to me when I heard about the mad scramble in the diamond market during the Gulf War. The trading cartel did manage to control prices, but many diamond traders were concerned about another wild inflation like the one in the early seventies that destroyed so many businesses. In researching this unusual incident, I discovered the many innovations in the diamond trade, including laser-setting techniques.

Weaving in details about contemporary life that fascinate me is always part of the creative process. For this story, I wanted to inform readers about the "Shining Path" guerrillas who have nearly destroyed Peru. It's interesting to note that since the end of the time frame in my book, December of 1991, President Alberto Fujimori ended democratic rule in Peru. Abimael Guzmán, the *sendero* leader, was captured after eluding police for over twelve years. However, his imprisonment has not stopped his zealous followers from continuing to operate.

The situation in the Ukraine that I described is based on information published in newspapers and interviews with immigrants. The savagery of the Red Army with its ritualistic—and barbaric—treatment of new recruits has been substantiated by numerous sources. It is true that each year more new recruits are lost this way than died in Afghanistan. What happened to the fictional character Lev is a commonplace occurrence for most recruits.

The rise in ethnic unrest worldwide has troubled many people for the past several years. The Communist guarantee to treat all people equally regardless of ethnic background or religion has not been kept under the old regime or the new. The plight of the Jews has been described in this book as well as the lesser-known problem of the Gypsies, but other groups face hardships as well. In Bosnia we've seen just how barbaric this can become.

History continues to be written in the old Soviet Union. Yeltsin seems to be losing power; Kravchuk has consolidated his. Unlike my fictional characters, the people there are truly trapped by a moment in time that will change their lives forever.

On a lighter note, I like to use interesting trivia to give my characters a unique personality. I was so impressed by the pit display at the Chelsea Garden Show that I used pits as Eula Mae's hobby. Yes, mating kiwis is dicey. Try it sometime.

Dell Books Proudly Announces
Kiss in the Dark by Meryl Sawyer
Coming from Dell Books in Spring 1995

The following is a preview of *Kiss in the Dark* . . .

CHAPTER ONE

The too-real nightmare that soon became Royce Anne Winston's life began very simply, very innocently. With a kiss in the dark.

A forbidden, erotic kiss.

A kiss that changed her life. Forever. It brought her love, the kind of love she'd only dreamed existed. And danger.

But the chain of events set in motion by that passionate kiss didn't become apparent to Royce for a long time. Even when the cell door clanged shut, she didn't suspect a kiss in the dark would result in her arrest for murder.

Now, looking back, she saw how naive she'd been not to realize someone she trusted had diabolically set out to deceive her. . . .

"I hope they haven't sat down to dinner," Royce said as her fiancé, Brent Farenholt, escorted her up the steps of the San Francisco mansion on the night of the fateful party.

"I'll tell my parents we couldn't keep our hands off each other."

"Oh, sure. You'll come up with some excuse, though. You always do." Royce told herself she didn't give a hoot what Brent's parents thought. Not quite true. Within the year they'd be her in-laws. Try to get along with them.

Dance music drifted out of the French doors, filling the spring air with the sounds of a dance band. One more party where the hostess tries to outdo her friends, Royce thought. She braced herself for another encounter with San Francisco's elite. Most of them called the city home but actually lived there only a few months a year. The rest of the time they spent at country estates or villas in the South of France. Royce found many of them, especially Brent's parents, to be arrogant. Insulated by their money, the real world, the world beyond their closed circle of friends, simply did not exist.

Inside, the foyer's black and white diamond patterned floor gleamed in the soft light of the chandelier overhead. They greeted Eleanor and Ward Farenholt, then Brent fed his parents some line about the traffic making them so late. Royce doubted he'd fooled his parents. Being late was merely a symptom of a much greater problem, one she'd diagnosed as terminal Royce Anne Winston. The Farenholts were never going to forgive her for stealing their only son from Miss Perfect—Caroline Rambeau of the Napa Valley winery Rambeaus, the San Francisco society Rambeaus, their best friends, the Rambeaus.

"Royce, over here."

She left Brent with his parents, and went to her friend. "Wow! Talia, you look terrific."

Beneath bangs the color of bittersweet chocolate, Talia rolled her dark eyes. "Not as good as you. If I could wear a strapless sheath like that, Brent would have proposed to me."

"You don't think it's too low cut?"

"There won't be a man tonight who won't remember you."

The midnight-blue gown accentuated Royce's blond hair and contrasted with her green eyes, making them appear even greener, but it was very revealing. She peeked at the prim cocktail dress Eleanor Farenholt wore. One more black mark against Royce. This one she might actually deserve.

What had Daddy always said? *Royce, you're a bit of a Gypsy—all those vibrant prints and bright colors.* She refused to wear black even though Eleanor Farenholt insisted it was the only color for evening. Black made Royce feel like one of the herd. And black reminded Royce of funerals—first her mother's, then her father's.

"Don't worry about your dress," Talia assured her. "Everyone adores you. They all read your column. Just be your usual witty self. To hell with the Farenholts."

"Right. To hell with them."

Talia touched the small evening bag that fit neatly into the palm of Royce's hand. The bag was a cat of glittering crystal stones except for the eyes, which were brilliant green. "Where'd you get the money for a Judith Leiber bag?"

"Brent insisted on buying it when I admired it."

"He's going to spoil you rotten."

"I'm loving every minute of it. This bag is very impractical, though. All I can get inside is a lipstick and my keys." She leaned closer and whispered, "Carrying such an expensive purse makes me feel guilty. This would have cost my father a week's salary. Will I ever get used to all Brent's money?" She shook her head, her hair fluttering across her bare shoulders, then she studied Talia, realizing her friend looked upset. "Are you all right?"

"Fine. I haven't touched a thing. I promise."

Royce slipped her arm around Talia and gave her an affectionate hug. "If you need me—anytime—day or night, call."

"You've been terrific, but don't worry about me." Talia edged her behind a lush fern. "There's good news and bad news. Which do you want to hear first?"

This was a game she'd played with Talia for years, so Royce answered the way she always did. "The good, then the bad."

"You're not sitting with Brent."

"Why on earth not?"

"This hostess throws dinner dances so her friends can meet interesting people—musicians and actors and artists—colorful types who normally wouldn't be included in these circles. Who knows? If you and Brent weren't engaged, she might have invited you anyway—for color."

Suspicious, Royce remembered the hostess was one of Eleanor Farenholt's "oldest and darlingest friends." Was that why she'd been seated elsewhere? "Where *is* Brent sitting?"

"Don't lose your temper, but he's sitting with his parents . . . and Caroline."

"Brent and I picked out a diamond today," Royce said, bridled anger underscoring each word. "The ring will be ready next week. Why's his ex-girlfriend at his table while I'm—"

"It's a last-ditch effort. Brent and Caroline were practically born in the same crib, that's how close the families are, but he didn't marry her, did he? No. He meets you and three months later you're engaged."

"True, so why does this upset me so much?"

"Because if your parents were alive, they'd disapprove of you marrying a Farenholt."

"You're right," Royce conceded. Her parents had been liberal and literary with lots of "colorful" friends, not arch-conservatives who'd never ventured beyond their clique and had voted the party line since dirt was brown. "But they would have liked Brent. He's nothing like his parents."

"Just be cool. Ignore the Farenholts' pettiness."

"Okay," she said reluctantly, "but they are beginning to get to me. I'm having second thoughts about my relationship with Brent." She sighed, struggling to convince herself the Farenholts would learn to accept her. "Don't tell me not sitting with Brent is the *good* news."

"Part of it. You're at the Dillinghams' table."

"All right!" Arnold Dillingham owned a local cable television station. Royce was one of two women vying for the hostess position on *San Francisco Affairs*. Her first trial show was next Friday night with the second scheduled the following week.

The downward sweep of Talia's lashes hid her dark eyes, and Royce knew this was really bad news. Talia always faltered before saying something upsetting. "Now for the bad news. Tonight your favorite attorney is seated beside you."

"Obviously not Brent, then someone else in the Farenholt firm."

"No. Mitchell—'I'll-defend-you-to-your-last-dollar' Durant."

"Sweet Jesus, not that bastard."

"I know how much you hate Mitch, but for once, don't be a hothead."

Every muscle in Royce's body tensed. Mitch Durant. The Farenholts detested him—at least they agreed on something —so why was he seated beside her? They had to be responsible for this fiasco.

"While you were living in Rome, Mitch Durant defended the Dillinghams' grandson on a drunk driving charge and got him off with community service. Arnold Dillingham thinks Mitchell Durant hung the moon. Don't ruin your chances of becoming the *San Francisco Affairs* hostess by attacking Mitch in front of Dillingham. Be polite even if it kills you."

"Shouldn't I say that if it hadn't been for Mitch Durant in his days as a hot shot in the district attorney's office that my father would still be alive? Shouldn't I?"

"No. Only a few of us make the connection between Mitch Durant and your father's death. If you attack Mitch the way you did at your father's funeral, your career as a television personality is *kaput—fini—over*—before it starts."

"You're right," Royce conceded, inwardly cursing Mitch, wishing him dead.

Brent came up, saying he'd see her to her table, and Royce smiled at Ward and Eleanor Farenholt as if they had handed her a ticket to paradise instead of a seat in hell. With Mitchell Durant.

The party's theme was sophisticated black and white. Didn't any of the Farenholts' friends do anything different? Royce wondered as she walked into the ballroom. Floor-length black table skirts peeked out from beneath white damask cloths set with gleaming sterling. The centerpieces were clusters of white orchids with deep plum centers arranged with a Japanese look around bent willow twigs.

"Watch out for Durant," Brent said as they approached her table. "I don't want to lose you to him."

No chance, and Brent knew it. He spoke with the nonchalance of a man whose good looks and wealth guaranteed he'd always have whatever he wanted—any woman he wanted. A harmless form of inbred arrogance, Royce acknowledged. Still, there was nothing about Brent she would change, from his blond hair and brown eyes to his face that had been stamped at birth with an engaging smile.

Brent introduced her to the guests at the table, leaving Mitchell Durant until last, acting as if this were the first time she'd met the prominent criminal defense attorney. "Royce, this is Mitchell Durant. Mitch was with me at Stanford Law School."

Mitch had risen when they'd arrived at the table, but now, as Brent spoke, there was a split second when the men's eyes met. Instantly she sensed the hostility toward Brent that Mitch concealed with a nod. Mitch turned to her, but she made certain she was looking at Brent, smiling happily.

She slid into her chair, hardly hearing Brent say he'd see her later. Why didn't Mitch like Brent? She'd assumed the animosity was one-sided. Everyone liked Brent. He had a way of putting people at ease that certainly wasn't hereditary.

She sipped her wine, covertly studying Mitch. In his late thirties, tall with dark hair, Mitch had a disturbing way of assessing people. His eyes had never left her face, but she'd lay odds he'd noted her stiletto heels and could tell a jury her bra size.

"Your column last week on divining rods was hysterical," Arnold Dillingham told Royce, nodding his gray head enthusiastically.

Mrs. Dillingham agreed with her husband, who'd made a fortune in cable television, then added, "I howled, simply howled at your column about house dust. Why, I had no idea half the dust in my home is actually dead skin. I didn't realize people shed—like dogs."

"Our skin is always flaking off." She kept her eyes on the Dillinghams but she was disturbingly aware of Mitch looking at her. Why had she worn such a low-cut dress?

"Well, the way you described it was so darn funny," added Mrs. Dillingham.

"That's what I'm counting on," Arnold informed everyond at the table. "Royce has a humorous way of looking at the world. Offbeat. Interesting."

She beamed, justifiably proud of herself. After all, how many columnists her age—thirty-four—were nationally syndicated, producing a by-line twice a week and a feature article carried in Sunday editions nationwide.

"But can you carry a television show? And use that wit in discussing important issues?" Arnold asked her.

"I believe I can," Royce said with as much confidence as she could muster. She had no television experience, but she intended to give it her best shot. She was tired of writing a humorous column. She wanted to deal with important issues, and this was her chance.

"I'm betting you can, so I personally found someone special for you to interview on your first trial program."

"Great," she said, silently cursing. She'd expected to discuss women in crisis with someone from the center. The safe houses for abused women were unique and a subject Royce knew well. Before Royce's mother had died, she'd helped develop the program. Royce had given hours of volunteer service to the group.

"This guest has a terrific new idea for helping the home-less."

The guest must be someone special, but Royce wasn't familiar with programs for the homeless. Rather than appear uninformed, she tried for a light note. "Not Governor Moonbeam. Last I heard, Jerry Brown was trying to work off his campaign debt by waiting tables in a Thai café."

Dillingham chuckled. "Our Mitch has a plan for helping—"

"Mitchell Durant?" she blurted out. She almost cursed out loud. Mercifully the band struck up a waltz and distracted everyone. Except Mitch.

The others rose to dance, but Mitch leaned close. "My name's not a four-letter word."

"You could have fooled me."

Arnold paused by her chair. "Come on, you two, dance."

She opened her mouth to make an excuse, but Mitch was already pulling her chair out while Mrs. Dillingham babbled about how lucky Royce was to have Mitch on her show. She stood, thinking Mitch was notorious for refusing interviews. So, why now? Why me? Lucky, Mrs. Dillingham had said. Okay, remember luck is a four-letter word.

Mitch swung her into his arms. She trained her eyes over the shoulder of his expensive dinner jacket, ignoring him. Across the room Caroline danced with Brent. Where was the Italian count his former girlfriend was supposed to be dating? Don't be jealous, Royce chided herself, thinking what she really resented about Caroline was how easily she fit in with the Farenholts. Except for Brent, the group was terrified of rupturing a major artery by really laughing. Instead, they made muted sounds worthy of an aspiring ventriloquist while Royce admitted she laughed a little too loud at times. Especially at a good joke.

Royce felt Mitch watching her, subjecting her to a thorough, intimate appraisal. She studied his lapels for a moment, then lifted her eyes, making eye contact for the first time. Involuntarily she flinched at the intensity of his gaze.

She'd almost forgotten how captivating his eyes were—marine blue with flecks of black and rimmed by black bands the same dark color as his hair.

His face was thoroughly masculine with an arresting expression that made it hard to look away. Its angular planes were tempered by two curious scars, small dents like oversize razor nicks. Whatever caused the scar on the rise of his cheekbone below his eye had narrowly missed blinding him. The second scar, it, too, bone-deep, had etched a hole the size of a nailhead near his hairline. No one could see the third scar, identical to the others, that she knew was hidden by his thick hair.

Mitch had a certain way of holding his head, tilting it ever so slightly to one side as if he were listening intently, eager to catch every word. Once she'd thought this particular mannerism was endearing. Now it annoyed her. She knew him for what he truly was. An ambitious jerk who'd hounded an innocent man.

"We must be in hell," he said, more than a hint of a jeer in his tone.

"What do you mean?" Good work, Royce. You sound indifferent.

"You bastard," he mimicked her voice. "I'll see you in hell before I ever have anything to do with you again."

She recalled her heated words. And a lot more. "You're right, we *are* in hell."

"If memory serves"—now Mitch was smiling, gliding across the dance floor, holding her too securely for comfort —"when I last saw you, you promised . . . now, how did you put it?"

"To hack off your balls with a rusty machete."

"Right. So ladylike."

True, it had hardly been a refined statement. She'd gone nuts when Mitch appeared at her father's funeral. The rusty machete popped into her mind as the best way to kill Mitch —a slow, painful death—the best way to avenge her father. Mitch leaned closer, his turbulent blue eyes just inches from hers. She'd love to kill him. But it wouldn't bring back her father. Nothing would. She caught Arnold Dillingham looking at them and managed to come up with a wisp of a smile.

"About my balls"—Mitch's grin bordered on a sneer—"if you touch my fly, you'll have to come home with me."

"You know, you're a real bastard."

"You're not the first to bring it to my attention. And you haven't changed either, except I hear you're engaged." He glanced at her bare left hand. "Love your engagement ring."

"I'll have it next week. A pear-shaped diamond the size of a doorknob. Nine carats."

That stopped him. But she wished she hadn't mentioned the huge diamond Brent insisted on. The size of the stone wasn't important; Brent was the catch. Even after being with him for months, she still couldn't quite get used to the idea he'd chosen her when he could have had his pick of all the eligible women in San Francisco.

"How are you getting along with the Farenholts?"

"Fine," she fibbed, "they're delightful."

Mitch stared at her, and she felt a taste of what it must be like to be on the witness stand, being cross-examined by him. "Doesn't it piss you off—big time—to have people you don't like reject you because you're not good enough for their son?"

She reined in her temper, reminding herself that Mitch specialized in tricking people into revealing things. "What makes you think they don't like me?"

He grinned—his big-bad-wolf grin—making her wish she hadn't taken the bait. "Lots of things. Let's start with your dress."

"What's wrong with it?" Royce looked down; she hadn't anticipated dancing in the strapless sheath. Her raised arms plumped her breasts upward, dangerously close to exposing the dusky rims of her nipples. She tried dropping her arms, but Mitch wouldn't let her.

His eyes, unusually blue, unusually intense, roamed

slowly over her half-exposed breasts. "I can see what you had for lunch."

She would have whacked him except the Dillinghams were dancing too close, smiling approvingly at them.

"Caroline Rambeau, Brent's old girlfriend, would never be caught dead in that dress."

"Of course not. She couldn't possibly hold it up."

Mitch chuckled, a deep, masculine laugh she'd chosen to forget. She cursed herself for making him laugh.

The Dillinghams stopped beside them. "What's so funny?"

Think of something quick, Royce told herself. A joke came to mind, but she wasn't truly comfortable with it, considering the plight of the homeless in the Bay Area. But she told it anyway, determined not to let Arnold Dillingham know what really amused Mitch. "Since Mitch wants to help the homeless, I was telling him about a woman he should date. Instead of carrying a placard saying WILL WORK FOR FOOD hers reads: WILL WORK FOR SEX."

Arnold hooted. "That's what I like about you, Royce. You can inject humor into any topic, even a serious one."

Royce didn't think it was the least bit funny. Just what did Arnold expect on the show, a tasteless comedienne? She wanted to be serious for a change and get away from the fluff pieces she'd been writing. But Arnold probably did want someone outrageous. After all, he'd made his fortune with TV stations that played nonstop infomercials that touted ways to become rich, successful, beautiful—or dice an onion in thirty seconds—with a money-back guarantee.

Had he lived, what would her father have said? *You're a born writer. Someday you'll be famous.* Well, maybe. Someday. But right now all the newspaper wanted from her was humor. They'd rejected all her serious articles. At least Arnold was giving her a chance.

"Arnie's agreed that during my appearance on the show your questions will be limited to the homeless," Mitch informed her as the dance ended. "No questions about my practice, my private life . . . my past."

She saw Brent approaching, set to rescue her, recalling Mitch usually avoided the press. "You know what I think?"

"I'm always afraid to hear what you think."

"I think you have something to hide." She left him standing alone and went to Brent.

"What were you doing with Durant?" Brent pulled her into his arms as the band began to play another waltz.

She told him about the revised plan for the show. He gave her a reassuring smile; once again she realized how startlingly handsome he was. But unaware of it. Just being with him made her happy. Despite being rich and outrageously handsome, Brent was down-to-earth with an easygoing charm that put everyone at ease. If only his parents accepted her, everything would be perfect—except for Mitch, of course. How could she conduct a brilliant interview, an interview that would annihilate the competition and win her the show, when she hated Mitch so much she could hardly talk to him in a civil tone?

"Watch out for Mitch," Brent warned. "He'll do anything to get even with me."

"Why?" She'd assumed the Farenholts disliked Mitch because of his unconventional courtroom tactics. Once, he'd successfully defended a woman accused of murdering her husband for his insurance. Mitch had convinced the jury to acquit her using the "Halcion defense," claiming his client had been paranoid from prolonged use of sleeping pills and hadn't known the knife she'd plunged into her husband's heart was actually going to kill him.

"Durant has a hair-trigger temper. He can be violent for no reason." Brent looked at his father, who was dancing nearby with Caroline; obviously the family felt duty-bound to entertain the former girlfriend. "He broke my jaw when we were at Stanford."

"Really? Why didn't you tell me?" She ventured a glance at Mitch, who was standing by the table, talking with Mrs.

Dillingham. There was more than a hint of aggressiveness to him. His stance, legs slightly apart, suggested the readiness of a fighter, creating a compelling quality some women found exciting.

"I didn't mention the fight because I was ashamed." Brent shrugged, his cute, one-shouldered shrug that had become so familiar. "I wanted to get back at Mitch for being at the top of our class, so I called him a redneck and a cracker. I'd been first in my class at Yale and thought Stanford Law would be a piece of cake, but there's always someone smarter, richer—"

"Prettier," she finished for him. "That's what I like about you, Brent, you're unfailingly honest." He smiled at her, and she couldn't help feeling he had the sincerest smile. When Mitch smiled, she always wondered what he was really thinking.

Brent glanced over at his father, Ward Farenholt, who was laughing at something Caroline had said. "My father gave me hell for not being top gun at Stanford."

She nodded sympathetically, her eyes on Ward as he twirled Caroline around the floor, still laughing, which was rare. Hidebound by generations of wealth and tradition, Ward set rigid standards for his only child. Brent had committed the ultimate violation of those standards by not marrying Caroline.

"Do you know what happens when you try to pet a junkyard dog?" Brent asked. "He goes for your throat because he's been trained to attack. Remember that when you deal with Mitchell Durant."